THE REBERTS OF LITTLESTOWN

THE REBERTS OF LITTLESTOWN

Volume 2

Dody Myers

Copyright © 2001 by Dody Myers.

Library of Congress Number: 2001-117892
ISBN #:   Softcover   1-4010-2252-9

All rights reserved. No part of this book may be reproduced or transmitted in any form or by any means, electronic or mechanical, including photocopying, recording, or by any information storage and retrieval system, without permission in writing from the copyright owner.

This is a work of fiction. Names, characters, places and incidents either are the product of the author's imagination or are used fictitiously, and any resemblance to any actual persons, living or dead, events, or locales is entirely coincidental.

This book was printed in the United States of America.

To order additional copies of this book, contact:
Xlibris Corporation
1-888-795-4274
www.Xlibris.com
Orders@Xlibris.com

INTRODUCTION

This book was written as a portrait of a family—but a portrait pieced together of facts and conjecture, against a background of America's emerging growth, of powerful men, of great events and decisions. I have traced the stories of places and people: of Christ Church, Littlestown, and Hanover, of the aftermath of the Civil War, the Woman Suffrage movement, and of my German ancestors.

The facts call for a certain explanation. Many times I have had to rely on the authority of oral history. I have taken the author's liberty of adjusting some dates to make the story flow more naturally. And finally I have changed some names and created a few fictional characters.

Let me say, then, that I have selected facts and arranged them, to make a portrait of a family. The family is mine—for the most part these people lived, loved, and fought their own personal demons.

The portrait on the cover is that of my great-grandfather and great-grandmother—Alex and Lillie Rebert.

BOOK 1

CHAPTER 1

Littlestown, Pennsylvania—1874

Alex Rebert dreaded the evening ahead. Dreaded to learn what he knew to be the truth.

He scrambled up the frozen path winding from his father's grist mill to the pasture encompassing the family stables, his thoughts as heavy as the glowering Pennsylvania weather. The last thing he wanted to do tonight was to go Christmas caroling. He'd see Belle with Jamie. His Belle! But she could never guess he called her that every time he thought of her. And that was all the time. He didn't want to see them touching, shoulder-to-shoulder as they sang, exchanging secret glances.

His breath labored as he crested the hill. Fierce winds tumbled his hair, whipping his sheepskin jacket against his chest. Moisture laden air from Codorus Creek left exposed roots encrusted with ice while overhead, gray-blue hemlocks arched to cast brooding mid-afternoon shadows. Where Alex walked, the December air was heavy and smelled of yeasty grain and impending snow.

Ahead of him, a cluster of neat outbuildings surrounded an immense bank-barn along with a less significant brick house. It was known, simply, as Rebert's Choice.

Trudging on, face down against the wind, he heard voices and looked toward the sound. He smiled as he saw two figures huddled on the paddock rail, his ten-year-old brother Charlie, and Jamie McPherson. Jamie was the son of Patrick McPherson, his father's best friend, killed at Fredericksburg during the Civil

War. Jamie had worked on the Rebert farm since childhood and it hurried Alex to remember that he was not truly a brother.

Charlie smiled a greeting as clouds of vapor escaped his chapped lips, then scrunched his narrow butt along the rail to make room for Alex, who leaned his elbows on the fence and put a boot to the bottom rail.

"You going Christmas caroling tonight?" Charlie asked.

"Guess so," Alex said with a shrug.

"Pa's over in the barn filling the big wagon with hay. There's lots'a room in it. Don't rightly know why I can't go with you," Charlie said with a sigh.

Jamie reached over and gave him a mock punch on the arm. "Tonight's for the big fellows, half-pint. Big fellows and their girls. Your time will come soon enough."

Charlie snorted and rolled his eyes. "Guess we all know who your girl is, Jamie" he teased. "It's Belle Campbell."

"Right smart you are, half-pint, an' I got a powerful hankering for that little red-head. Come spring I just might make her my wife."

Alex's breath caught and he gripped the rail, fighting not to look at Jamie, revealing nothing, keeping his face impassive as he thought of Belle. *His* Belle.

Charlie laughed. "What's wrong with you, Alex? You're lookin' mighty sour. How come you aren't sparking a steady girl? Or," he added slowly "have you got one we don't know about yet?"

Alex protested, "Oh no, not me. Jamie's the one with all the looks . . . the one all the girls flock to."

Jamie threw his head back and laughed. "Well now, I happen to know Lillie Schwartz will be along tonight. Belle says her friend is sweet on you. Time you paid attention to females besides one of Pa's horses."

Charlie snickered, fixing Alex with a crooked grin. "I saw you kiss a horse once, remember?"

"That's when I was only ten." Alex flushed. "Anyway, tonight is to treat the town folks to Christmas carols, not go frolicking with girls in the hay wagon."

Jamie grinned, his green eyes flashing with mischief. "That Lillie's mighty cute. A little romp with her might put a smile on that face of yours."

Against his will a smile tugged at Alex's lips. It was hard to get mad at Jamie, a tall manly fellow, extraordinarily handsome, with a ready smile and easy Irish charm. Alex had always been a little in awe of him. He was envious of his ability to laugh and joke with the customers at the mill; spin yarns, and woo just about any girl glancing his way. Alex didn't know why he liked Jamie so much. He wished he could be more like him, less serious, a little easier. But he could never be that free.

"Well," he replied, spreading his hands in dismissal, "I don't care beans for Lillie Schwartz, or any other girl, for that matter . . . and, if I did, I could fend just fine for myself, thank you!"

"That's your Pennsylvania Dutch stubbornness talking," Jamie said with a sparkle in his eyes.

Alex bristled, then smiled in spite of himself. "Ei, an' that's better than your Irish recklessness."

At this moment Princess Rose, one of his father's prize trotting horses, poked her nose over the rail nearly knocking him off. She forcefully nudged his pocket looking for a treat. Alex chuckled and reached out to pat the filly's glossy neck. She wickered softly, her luminous dark eyes stared at him. Princess Rose wore all the marks of a purebred, from the white blaze on the delicately proportioned head, to the long slender legs and the full, strong chest. He stroked her nose whispering an endearment in the pricked ears.

"Are you going to kiss her, Alex?" Charlie laughed, almost beside himself.

Alex cast him a disapproving glance and gritted his teeth.

* * *

Edward Rebert stood at the open door of the stable and watched the laughing boys at the paddock fence. How handsome they are, he thought. Alex was the picture of his mother, with chestnut hair, dark brown eyes and long thick eyelashes; Charlie was blond and blue-eyed like all the other Rebert children, and Jamie had red-gold curls—just like Patrick.

Edward took a deep breath. God had been good to him. He enjoyed a rich German heritage, owned a large, prosperous farm with a grist mill and a stable of trotting horses, had a wife he adored and eight living children, three daughters, four sons, and Jamie.

He smiled as Jamie reached out to touch Alex's shoulder. They were good for each other, those two. Alex tended to be a little serious while Jamie was a maverick just like his father. Edward sobered as a cloud of memory drifted across his mind. Patrick, his best friend, with his mop of red curls and quick Scots Irish wit, as different from him as Alex was of Jamie. Patrick had died on the battlefield in Edward's arms, asking him to care for his wife and two boys. But life could be cruel sometimes. Daniel, the oldest boy, was killed only days before Lee's surrender at Appomattox and Inger, their mother, died of typhoid two months later.

Edward ambled across the barn yard to join the boys at the fence, his gaze drifting to the horses racing each other across the frozen paddock. They all showed promise but Princess Rose, with her large intelligent eyes, and perfect gait was his favorite. She would certainly add to the growing reputation of Rebert Stables.

Charlie greeted him with a grin and an exaggerated shiver. "Burr . . . Papa, it's gettin' colder by the minute. Think it'll snow tonight?"

"Ach, it'll come before morning. Air's heavy and the wind has died." Edward hugged his wool jacket closer to his chest.

"You want the horses stabled tonight or are you going to leave them out?" Jamie asked.

"I think we'd better bring them in, Jamie. They'll be easier to feed if we get a heavy snow."

"I'll do it, then," Jamie offered, starting toward the barn.

"I'll help," Alex said, following behind him.

"Me too," Charlie piped up, jumping to the ground.

"When you're finished, Alex," his father said, "I could use some help in the barn. We need to load the wagon with clean hay for the caroling party. I was hoping to use the sleigh tonight," he pondered, looking northward, "but that snow is slow putting in an appearance."

The boys scampered off, Edward watching them with approval. A man couldn't have too many sons, he thought as he strode toward the barn. It was important to pass on the Rebert name in this land that had now been home to four generations of Rebert men. For awhile he had chafed at having three girls and only two boys, but two more sons had been born after he returned from the war and then Jamie had come to live with them.

* * *

Alex stabled the last horse, shivering and blowing on his fingers as he hurried toward the bank-barn. He pushed the huge double door open, the barn's warmth embracing him, perfumed as it was with sun-cured hay and the heavy, earthy smell of cattle and dung. He paused and let his gaze sweep the shadowed interior. Bovine eyes turned to watch him, tails swished, and from a dark corner, a cat meowed.

At a sound from overhead Alex mounted a ladder set in the stone foundation wall of the barn and climbed to where his father was pitching hay into a heavy wagon. The threshing floor was a favorite of his, with its lofty hay mows rising on both sides and the shadowy rafters of the barn far overhead. Pale sunlight filtered through cracks in the walls and motes of dust danced in a shaft of light from the open star-shaped brickwork high in the eves. Pigeons cooed and strutted in the cob-webbed rafters and barn swallows darted back and forth.

Edward looked up and smiled as Alex ambled across the old plank floor to grab a pitchfork.

"About finished, I see," Alex muttered, swinging a forkful of hay into the wagon.

"Ei."

They worked in silence until the wagon was full, then Alex leaned the cumbersome wooden-tine fork against the wall and watched his father climb into the bed to smooth the hay.

Edward Rebert was a tall man, broad and large, topping Alex by at least four inches. At fifty-three, he still had a thick mane of white-blond hair with barely a hint of gray, white eyebrows and eyelashes, and a deeply tanned face that harbored laugh lines around his brilliant, blue eyes.

"The mill was awfully busy this morning," Alex commented. "Jamie and Charlie helped, didn't they?"

"Yeah, and Charlie is a darn good worker, little as he is, but Jamie spends a lot of time listening to every farmer with a tale."

"Ach. Well, son, that's part of the milling business, too, you know. Customers must be wooed with sweet talk same as a woman."

Alex smiled. "He's good enough at that."

"Seems like he's calmed down since he started courting Belle," Edward said. "I do believe he has himself a handful with that girl. She's got an independence as fiery as her red hair. Jamie seems completely smitten with her; he told me he asked for her hand and plans to post their bans after the Christmas holidays."

Alex struggled to keep his face devoid of emotion. *I can't let Pa suspect*, he agonized. *No one must suspect how I feel about Jamie's intended. That I think of her day and night.* He swallowed hard.

"Guess that leaves lots of disappointed females for the rest of us—not that I give a hoot for any of 'em." He smiled but the effort behind it was apparent.

Surprised, Edward's fair brows rose. "Alex, every man needs a good woman at his side. You're twenty years old now and I think it time you started to plan your future."

"I know, Pa. I guess the right girl just hasn't come into the picture for me." He settled himself on a bale of straw and Edward jumped down from the wagon to join him. They sat side by side, just father and son, two farmers discussing crops, the weather, and farm prices. Alex felt good. His father was treating him as a man;

he was treating him as an equal. As he talked his voice deepened to match that of his father; he crossed his ankles as his father did and chewed on a piece of straw as his father did.

They spoke of plans for the future, of Rebert's Choice, of family, of women. Things that only grown men could understand. It made them close, and very much alike.

Their talk was finally interrupted by the insistent clanging of the dinner bell. Edward smiled, a deep cleft creasing his chin, his blue eyes crinkling with amusement. "We'd better get a move on, son. Sounds like supper's ready."

Together they strode across the cavernous room to push open heavy doors at the end of the threshing floor. The sickly sun was setting in a pale gray sky and Alex sighed as a small cloud of memory darkened his euphoria.

Soon it would be time to go caroling.

Alex stopped, half-way across the side yard, hugging his arms across his chest, feeling the cold air on his face. Stocky legs widespread, he let his gaze wander across the pasture, down past the farm pond, over fields dark with corn stubble, to the purple hills outlined on the horizon. He sucked in his breath and felt a tightening in his throat. He loved this land. There had never been any doubt in his mind that he would be a farmer and own even more land; farms with substantial barns, their boundaries marked by stout stone walls, filled with prime cattle and standardbred horses. That was the consuming passion of his life.

Apart from land and horses he had a passion for his German heritage. Tradition was the framework of his life. Tradition and a sense of order. If he had one fault it was that he was too rigid in assessing others and that often put him at odds with his friends.

Another of his passions, a long-hidden desire for Belle Campbell, he just refused to think about.

His thoughts stayed with him as he left the peaceful vista and hurried toward home. Rebert's Choice, sat along a dirt road two miles northeast of the village of Littlestown. Facing due west, the farm was bordered on the south by Codorus Creek, twisting and curling through an oak-studded meadow, diverting only enough water to supply power for the grist mill.

The house, erected from hand-made brick which, over the years, had faded to the finish of a ripe melon, was fronted by a deep porch and bracketed by two broad chimneys looking exactly like a pair of bookends. Stark black limbs of horse-chestnut trees bowed before the wind, chickens clucked and scratched around the well in the side yard, and dry leaves gathered under the thorny canes of his mother's roses. The house's entire appearance suggested permanence and strength, combined with a quiet solitude that bespoke the nature of the family that owned it.

A side porch led to the kitchen. Alex bounded up the steps and walked into its welcoming warmth.

Wonderful aromas assailed him—the scent of cinnamon and freshly-baked bread, of a wood fire and of his father's pipe—smells that had become so familiar he inhaled it like fresh air. But tonight other odors vied for his attention. A tantalizing stew bubbled in a copper pot on the back of a large ten-plate stove where another kettle held steaming chicken soup. On the sideboard, warm biscuits rested beside crocks of golden honey. His stomach growled.

"Hello, Mama," he said, moving to her side and kissing her with gentle affection. "Ummm, that smells good. I'm hungry as two bears in a cave."

"Fancy that! Guess I'll have to throw another potato in the pot for my growing boy," she chided fondly.

"Best make it two extra potatoes."

"Have you seen your father, or Ellen for that matter? I sent her to gather eggs over an hour ago."

"Pa's in the barn, but I haven't seen Ellen."

"Ring the dinner bell again, then. Mercy, you'd think they'd know when supper is ready. It fusses me when everyone is late."

Alex gave her a warm smile. In his estimation, Katie Rebert was the prettiest mother in Adams County. Still slim, despite bearing nine children . . . two of them in the grave . . . her soft brown eyes, long curling eyelashes, and a whisper of freckles across a pug nose enhanced her charming nature. A cheerful blue and yellow calico dress was covered with a pristine starched apron and a white-net prayer cap rested comfortably on her chestnut hair, the only outward sign of her Mennonite upbringing.

The kitchen hummed with activity. Familiar sounds: his mother shaking the fire, the clatter of a frying pan, the clinking of silverware, as two of his sisters, Annie and Emma, set the table. Jamie and Charlie laughed as they washed up for supper at the tin sink. Six-year old John was already at the table clutching his spoon in anticipation. Only Edwin, working for the winter at Uncle J.J.'s farm over near Hanover was missing. Alex pulled a chair up beside John and ruffled his blond hair. He felt better already. Maybe the evening wouldn't be bad after all. Snow was in the air, he loved to sing, and he'd give Lillie Schwartz another look.

* * *

Lillie whisked down the stairs, trailing her bonnet in one hand and gloves in the other. Maybe . . . just maybe . . . it would be snowing outside and, if she was even luckier, Alex Rebert would be among the carolers gathering at Christ Church.

"Hurry now, Lillie. You know how Papa hates to wait," Mama said, propelling her toward the front door.

Lillie sidestepped her mother's anxious hands and paused for a final look in the long mirror hanging in the spacious entry hall. She plunked the bonnet on her head and rose to her tiptoes, trying to lengthen her image in the mirror. Lively blue eyes smiled back at her and light brown hair, cascading from the wide velvet brim of the bonnet, fell around a small, heart-shaped face. She chewed the inside of her cheek and stretched even further while she tied her bonnet under her chin. Then she giggled at her image and lowered her heels to the carpet. She was short and that was that. She could hardly walk around on tiptoes all the time.

"Oh, how I wish I were tall like Belle," she said with a groan, rolling her eyes and yanking at the full skirts brushing the tops of her tiny black boots. "She's seventeen, same as I, but ever so much taller."

"And I'm sure Belle wishes she were as small and dainty as you," Mama said, pursing her lips in subtle disagreement as she smoothed the black wool cape over Lillie's shoulders with fussy fingers. Mama, always impeccably dressed even when working in the gardens, imposed the same criterion on her daughter.

Lillie jerked her shoulder impatiently. Mama continued to poke at her, straightening her lace collar and yanking at the folds of her skirt.

"Is it snowing yet?" Lillie asked for the dozenth time that evening. "It won't be half as much fun Christmas caroling without snow."

"I don't know, dear, but if you'd get past the front door you could see for yourself," scolded Mama, good naturedly.

Lillie stretched to plant a hasty peck on her cheek, bringing a thin smile to the prim mouth. Sophia Schwartz was plain, but handsome, with a flawless complexion and reddish-brown hair that she parted in the middle and pulled to a severe bun at the nape of her neck.

Lillie opened the front door to a gust of frigid air, but no snow. With a sigh of disappointment she scurried to the carriage where Papa waited and climbed up beside him.

Half an hour later her father halted the carriage in front of Christ Church where a cluster of young people were gathered around a farm wagon piled high with hay.

Her father handed her down from the carriage and kissed her on the cheek. "Have a good time, dear," he said. "I'll be back for you about ten o'clock. Just wait in the vestry if you're finished sooner."

She spotted Alex at once and her heart bumped against her chest. Sitting on the edge of the wagon, he reached out a heavily muscled arm to pull her up.

"Why, you're scarce knee-high to a bumblebee," he said with a polite grin as she sank in a heap of skirts into the warm hay beside him. "Bet our new foal weighs more than you do."

Lillie felt her face grow red and sought in vain for a witty answer. Her mind seemed to go totally blank when she was around Alex. She had known him since childhood, but Alex was twenty now, a man in size, with the strong muscles of a man and signs of a heavy beard. Now, things were different. Her tongue lay woodenly in her mouth and all she could muster was a demure smile before crawling over several chattering girls and plopping down beside her best friend, Belle.

Belle wiggled close, pressing herself against Lillie, her red head almost touching Lillie's brown one. "I notice Alex was quick to give you a hand," she said, lowering her voice to a conspiratorial whisper. "He keeps looking over, Lillie. Smile at him."

Lillie watched him out of the corner of her eye Alex couldn't be called handsome—his squarish face was resolute and somewhat stern when he wasn't laughing—but Lillie had always been drawn to his unusual eyes; large, dark orbs the color of chocolate fudge with eyelashes as long and thick as a woman's. She liked looking at him; she liked watching him talk. She loved his mouth. His full lips showed a hint of something she didn't quite understand.

Belle fluffed her skirts and looked at Lillie with a knowing smile. "You like him . . . that's plain as day, but you're far too shy around him. He's quiet enough," Belle said, sounding far more worldly than her years would allow. "Work your womanly wiles on him. Flirt a little," she added, assuming a coyness meant for Lillie to imitate.

Lillie blushed and fingered a pleat in her skirt.

Belle smiled and leaned her head closer, whispering "Leave it to me. I'll let him know you haven't a partner for the Christmas dance."

A spasm of irritation crossed Lillie's face as she thought about her solitary state. "Trouble is," she said, "I'm so small boys treat me like I'm a child. They forget I'm seventeen and almost a woman." She pressed her hands against her bosom. "And if these things of mine would just grow a little maybe they'd realize I'm not so young."

Belle, who was already amply endowed, wordlessly squeezed Lillie's hand in understanding. Lillie looked at her thoughtfully. They had been friends since childhood, although with different personalities and vastly different economic backgrounds. Lillie's parents were substantial landowners, while Belle and her widowed mother lived nearby on a small homestead. Because Lillie was an only child and Belle was left alone while her mother worked at the hotel in town, they sought each other's company and over the years a deep friendship was forged.

Jamie and Alex settled themselves next to the girls and Jamie took Belle's hand in his. Alex sat woodenly, twining a strand of straw between his blunt fingers, his eyes intent on the passing countryside. Lillie was so shy she barely looked at him, but she was aware of his mood. Frantically she searched for something to say, but words wouldn't come.

Belle began to tell Jamie a funny story and her animated face glowed in the gathering twilight, her red curls bouncing as she tossed her head while the hay wagon rattled along Hanover Street toward Littlestown's town square. Alex had turned to listen and Lillie watched him from beneath lowered lashes. He appeared to be mesmerized by Belle, unaware of Lillie or anyone else. She bit her lip, suddenly understanding.

The wagon stopped in front of the Union Hotel where everyone disembarked amid much jostling and laughter.

All the young people formed a semi-circle around their leader, Enos Hartlaub, and Lillie noticed that Belle had maneuvered them so that they stood next to Alex. Jamie's arm was around Belle and he laughed while he whispered something into her ear. Alex stood glumly by his side.

After everyone grew quiet Enos gave them their instructions and the carolers began to stroll along the silent street, stopping to sing at each home that beckoned with an oil lamp glowing from their front window. Lillie loved everything about the season: the songs, the smell of garlands of pine and holly hanging in churches, the poignant sweetness of the Christmas message. The carolers seemed deliciously happy, eager to share their joy, and their voices soared through the frosty air. She felt light, like the meringue on a lemon pie, and her lips curved in a smile.

Lillie noticed that Jamie and Belle were walking close together, shoulders touching. Belle wore an old cape of patched navy serge, but it didn't matter because she was so sensationally pretty, with a long, slender neck, flirty eyes, and curly red hair that refused containment. Her skin was like porcelain and her smile was like a wicked urchin's grin. Alex and Jamie both vied for her attention and Lillie felt a whisper of jealousy. She noticed Belle talking to Alex and saw him glance in her direction, then away with a frown. Quickly her gaze dropped to the sidewalk as a wave of loneliness washed over her. Her voice was quavering as she reached for a high note.

* * *

Alex had watched Jamie and Belle all evening, observing their secret looks, their constant touching, and now he listened with dismay as they discussed the coming Christmas dance at the Grange Hall.

Belle moved to his side and looked at him.

"I do hope you'll save me a few dances, Alex," she said.

"I may not even go to the dance. I haven't a partner," he answered quietly.

"Why don't you ask Lillie? That way we could all go together," Belle said brightly.

He glanced at Lillie. She was a sweet little thing. He had always liked her, but she seemed awfully shy and quiet compared to the vivacious Belle, who stirred his senses to the boiling point. Still, he would only be asking Lillie to the one dance. And, with a degree of guilt, he admitted to himself he would grab any opportunity to hold Belle in his arms, even if it was only to dance with her.

"Maybe I will," he said.

* * *

With a start, Lillie became aware of Alex's presence at her elbow and her heart thumped against her ribs. His deep baritone almost drowned out her soft soprano as their voices soared and dipped in harmony. The song ended and they crossed to the south side of Gettysburg Street. Icy soil cracked beneath their boots and Alex was close at her side. Lillie hunched her shoulders and shivered as a gust of wind ruffled the back of her hair.

"You're cold," Alex said, seeing her brace against the wind.

"No."

"Yes, you are. You're shivering. Here." He pulled the woolen muffler from his neck and handed it to her. "Put it on. That bonnet doesn't give you much protection." Wordlessly, she draped it around her shoulders.

"Won't you be cold now?"

"No, I'm fine. Besides it gives me a chance to be gallant," he said with a grin

"Gallant? That doesn't sound like you," Lillie said, raising her eyebrows.

"My Pa uses it. He likes words like that. Sort of old-fashioned," explained Alex with a shrug.

"Is he old-fashioned?"

Alex laughed. "He'd never admit it but he clings to a lot of the old world ways."

"You're German, aren't you?"

"One hundred percent. You?"

"German too. On both sides."

Silence descended on them. Alex was obviously uncomfortable with the need to make small talk and she was afraid to make idle conversation, afraid she'd bore him.

"It'll snow before long," he finally said with a half smile.

"Oh, I hope so."

Silence again settled around them as they crossed the street.

Lillie noticed that his gaze was centered on Jamie and Belle. She felt her face flush with indignation. Why was he apparently smitten with a girl who was obviously in love with the boy everyone thought of as his brother?

He suddenly seemed aware of her scrutiny and looked at the ground, kicking at a frozen clump of mud. "Jamie is taking Belle to the dance. Are you going?" he asked gruffly.

"Ah . . . no," she said hesitantly.

Their eyes met. "I'd be proud to escort you if you'd care to go with me."

She tilted her head back, looking up at him from beneath the brim of her bonnet. Her heart beat wildly, like hummingbirds' wings. "I'd love to, Alex," she said coyly, feeling the heat rise in her face. She was abruptly tongue-tied. She had dreamed for months of this moment. Now that it was actually happening she felt totally witless. For one terrible second she remembered his comment that Jamie and Belle were going to the dance together. Was this his reason for asking her? Was she second best? No matter, he was asking her, wasn't he? Isn't that what she had prayed for?

He slowed and touched Lillie's arm while pointing a mittened hand into the night sky.

"Look," he said, "it's snowing."

Large, wet flakes were indeed visible in the pool of light spilling from the glowing street lanterns and soon the heavy sky began dropping its silent burden of white. It fell softly on their shoulders as they strode along Frederick Street, deadening the sounds of their boots on the road as she and Alex halted before St. Paul's.

They stood side by side, ducking beneath the drooping branches of a hemlock. The church, tucked into its sheltered, wooded corner, shimmered faintly in moonlight and the driving snow bit at Lillie's face, snipping at her nose, making her eyes water. Alex was so close she could have reached out and laid a hand on his cheek. Their bodies brushed together as they walked, and Lillie felt so happy she could hardly contain it. His woolen coat smelled of wet snow, his skin was smooth and ruddy, and a lock of dark hair escaped his cap to lie across his forehead. She hugged her arms across her chest, saying nothing, savoring his masculinity, listening to the deep timbre of his voice, almost missing what he said.

" . . . next Wednesday evening."

"When . . . what . . . ?"

His hand was warm and steady as he placed it on her arm, halting her flustered reply. "We'll talk on the way home," Alex said. "Judge McSherry's house is next door and I know Enos intends us to sing there."

The carolers stopped before the impressive brick home of Littlestown's most prestigious citizen. Candles radiant in glass globes shone from every window casting a cheery light into the shadowy street as Enos raised his hand for quiet. "We'll start with 'What Child is This?' It's the Judge's favorite."

They nodded and within minutes Alexander's rich baritone took the lead. It seemed to swell above the others and Lillie stopped singing just to watch him. He was standing directly under the flickering gaslight, its yellow flame throwing his strongly cut features into sharp relief. Snow covered the shoulders of his woolen jacket and fat white flakes of snow lay for fleeting seconds on his extraordinarily long lashes. Their eyes met and his dark gaze seemed to penetrate her very soul.

She swallowed past a hollow spot deep in her chest. Don't let him stop, she prayed; don't let the song end. I want this feeling to last forever. Instinctively, she knew it would never be like this again. Not ever. Just Alex, with snow on his eyelashes, on this street corner, in this time.

In that surging, overpowering instant, she knew that she would love him always.

She stuck her chin out and her mouth tightened into a stubborn line.

Belle might be her best friend, and obviously Alex was attracted to her, but she decided then and there that she would fight for him. She would win Alex Rebert for herself.

CHAPTER 2

Edward adjusted the wick on the oil lamp and moved the Montgomery Ward catalog closer to its glowing light. An advertisement for a lightweight sulky had caught his eye. With the addition of Princess Rose to his racing stable he could use another sulky and this one looked promising. He'd show the ad to Jamie tomorrow and get his opinion.

His perusal of the catalog was interrupted when Alex moved to the fireplace and added a chunk of seasoned hickory to the blazing fire. Alex squatted and settled the log with a poker, the sudden flare flushing his face and burnishing his auburn hair with red highlights. So like his Katie, Edward thought, as he glanced at the wife sitting by his side.

Katie was slowly rocking John, who had fallen asleep in her arms as she read to him from one of Annie's old McGuffey Readers. Her gentle hands stroked John's hair, her Madonna-like face the picture of serenity and love. *I don't deserve you,* Edward thought as his gaze caressed her. *I don't deserve you.* And suddenly he was flooded with a love so tender it was almost painful.

Edward remembered the years prior to the Civil War when he despaired of her ever marrying him because of the difference in their faith—he of the traditional church, she of the Mennonite sect. At that time, the conflicts seemed insurmountable.

Aware of Edward's gaze she turned to him with a soft smile.

"I believe we'd better add a new book to John's Christmas stocking. He's showing an interest in learning to read," she said.

"Seems like we have stacks of books from when the other children were little," he answered.

"Oh, we do. But Edward, it's so nice to have a new book to open—one you know belongs only to you. A new book has such a special smell and feel, don't you agree?"

Edward nodded. What with hand-me-downs from his siblings John got few enough new things. "Get him one, then," he said, laying aside his magazine and fixing her with a smile. "Have you finished your Christmas shopping? I'm planing to ride into Gettysburg tomorrow with a load of buckwheat for the Globe Hotel. You can go with me if you want."

"Well . . . I was planning to bake several lemon sponge pies for the Grange dance."

"Mama, we girls can do that," said Annie, sitting quietly in the corner knitting a new muffler to put in the Christmas stocking of her boyfriend, George Geiselman.

"Yeah, Mama," Charlie piped up. "Don't forget you promised me a new sled if I kept the woodbox filled."

Edward looked fondly at the family gathered around the blazing fire in the cozy kitchen: Annie, petite and pretty with her mother's smile, Emma, her childhood braids now fashioned into thick braids wound around her head, but still very much a tomboy. Shy Ellen, working diligently at a piece of needlework, Charlie, blue-eyed and blond, with the trademark Rebert cleft in his chin, and chubby little John, who had not yet lost his baby fat, snuggled in his mother's arms. They were a miracle to him—this family God had provided. He would, he knew, go to any extreme to keep them safe.

He did miss Edwin, his eighteen year old son, missed his good natured laugh and easy manner. But, typical of the boy's generosity, he had offered to spend the winter running his uncle's grist mill when J.J. broke his shoulder in a fall from a threshing machine.

Jamie was also absent this evening, having taken Belle to a church sing-a-long. Edwin and Jamie were a lot alike, both in temperament and looks, but strangely enough it was Alex and Jamie who had bonded, each drawing from the other's strength.

Different as they were in almost every way, they understood each other, much as he and Patrick had done so long ago.

The next week was clear and cold, but before dawn on the eve of the Christmas dance a new front moved in from the west and leaden skies brought snow once more. All day it fell and hip-high drifts piled up, changing fence posts and bushes into shadowy mounds. Alex attempted to open a passageway to the house, but as fast as he shoveled a path it blew shut and, finally, he gave up. He struggled to the kitchen, snow frozen to his eyebrows, his face burning with cold.

The wind whistled, blowing smoke down the chimney, giving the room a sharp, woodsy smell, but it was warm and cozy and Alex quickly shucked his outer clothes and began to prepare for the big evening ahead.

"Where is everyone?" he asked, glancing around the usually busy room, empty now except for his mother.

"In the parlor putting up Christmas garland," his mother answered as she took a granite tea kettle from the stove and poured steaming water into the big wooden tub placed in the middle of the kitchen floor for everyone's weekly bath. "Jamie finished bathing and is upstairs dressing. You'd best hurry, it's past six already."

"I will, Mama." He quickly slipped his suspenders over his shoulders, removed his shirt, and dropped his pants, then hesitated before he began to unbutton his long underwear. His mother gave him a knowing smile and reached up to kiss his cheek before discreetly leaving the kitchen.

An hour later Alex paused for a final look in the small mirror hanging above his bureau. He wore neat black broadcloth trousers, a black velvet waistcoat, and a black coat with wide lapels trimmed in velvet of its own shade. Satisfied with the effect, he placed his grandfather's heavily filigreed pocket watch in his small watch pocket, letting its gold chain drape conspicuously, and adjusted a wide-brimmed hat squarely on his head.

Jamie waited for him, huddled on the seat of their sleigh, buried beneath a fur lap robe. Princess Rose pranced in her traces and whinnied a gentle greeting.

"Cold as a witch's tit," Jamie commented as he moved over to make room for Alex.

Alex laughed and took the reins. The wind had died and unmarred snow mantled the countryside. He looked at Jamie, handsome in brown trousers and a loden-green jacket, a bright red and green plaid muffler wound around his neck, golden unruly hair slicked back and tamed for the moment. He felt the familiar tug of admiration when he looked at him, yet there was a little worm of resentment too. Despite the pains Alex took with his own appearance, Jamie always managed to look far more dashing than he.

"Gee," he commanded, snapping the reins smartly.

The bright red sleigh moved across sequined snow with a soft hiss, small puffs of steam from the horse's nostrils floating in the cold air like wisps of white fog. They rode without talking, gliding across the frozen pastures of Rebert's Choice. What Alex saw was his entire world. His thoughts seldom strayed beyond its boundaries; all he wanted lay within them.

He turned Princess Rose onto Storm's Store Road and leaned back against the leather seat. His gaze swept the distant mountains, long and low and almost black.

"Look at those mountains, Jamie. Don't they give you a feeling of comfort? Like walls protecting you from the outside world."

"Guess so," Jamie answered nonchalantly. His face became pensive and he looked at Alex with troubled eyes. "I never had a hankering to travel much, until I began courting Belle. Always thought I'd stay on Rebert's Choice forever and build me a house right down there along Conewago Creek."

"Does Belle want to live somewhere else?"

"No . . . yes . . . I don't know. She's restless. Every time I see her she has a different idea. I think she would look at those same mountains and think of them as prison walls."

"And you? Surely you don't think of them that way."

"No, of course not. I love the valley same as you do. But Belle has made me think, and her dreams are contagious."

"She's still young, Jamie. Marriage and children will settle her down—she'll grow out of that foolishness."

"But it's that darn foolish independence I'm attracted to. She's so vital and intelligent every other girl pales beside her. I've never met anybody so passionate about so many things. Do you remember the time in school when she read an essay in front of the whole class that said women should not only have the right to vote, but have the same moral rights as a man?"

Alex frowned. "I remember."

"I've really taken a shine to her, Alex. She's the real thing." Jamie cleared his throat. "I . . . I'm in love with her. I want to marry her."

Alex clenched his teeth so tight his jaw hurt.

He snapped the reins and turned to face Jamie. "You've plenty of time to think of marrying. By the time you've got yourself established Belle will have learned what's really important in life."

Jamie's eyes met his and he smiled. Alex's gaze faltered and he felt his mouth turn down as he fixed his attention to the road. "I told Lillie we'd pick her up first," Alex said.

"Good."

The rest of the journey passed in silence as they sped through the night-shrouded countryside and soon Alex turned Princess Rose into the lane leading to the Schwartz farm.

Alex handed the reins to Jamie and jumped to the ground. He walked to the front porch, boots screeching on the crusted snow, and banged the door knocker.

Mrs. Schwartz opened the door with an impatient flutter of hands and motioned him inside. "We thought they might cancel the dance if the storm continued."

"Pa just came from town, the dance is still on," Alex said, hat in hand. "Besides, the snow and wind have both stopped. It's a beautiful night with a full moon." He spotted Lillie standing at the foot of the stairs, watching the door with eager eyes.

He stared. She looked like a china doll. Tiny features were framed by long brown hair gathered into a chignon at the back of her head and she wore a brown velvet gown with a high, ruffled neckline, its fitted bodice only hinting at small round breasts before tapering snugly over narrow hips.

She simply stood there, looking very shy, and very lovely.

"You look great," he said, and meant it.

Lillie gave a nervous giggle as they went out the door and Alex smiled at her, admiring her again.

"You look very grown-up," he teased, and she smiled self-consciously as he lifted her in his arms to carry her through the deep snow to the waiting sleigh.

Jamie claimed Belle at the Campbell's and they drove in high spirits through the night to the Grange Hall where happy music and loud laughter spilled into darkness. Alex halted at the doors to let Jamie and the girls out, then pulled into a field behind the hall, hitched Princess Rose and covered her with a warm blanket. Then, with a resolute set to his jaw, he strode toward the revelry inside.

A small orchestra was at one end of the room, playing the lilting strains of "Listen to the Mocking Bird" for about fifty young people from various Littlestown churches. The room was festooned with garlands of holly and a huge, brightly decorated Christmas tree stood on the stage in all its splendor. The other end of the room held tables laden with refreshments and Alex headed in that direction where Lillie waited for him.

"You girls did a great job decorating this dreary old hall," Alex said looking around the room normally used for staid Grange meetings.

"Our Sunday School class made the paper cut-outs for the tree and we worked all day yesterday stringing it with red berries and attaching the tiny candles," Lillie said proudly. She drew a deep breath and sighed. "Don't you just love the smell of pine and beeswax."

"I like the eats best," he said with a grin as he lifted a handful of ginger cookies from a nearby tray and handed her one. He looked down at her thoughtfully. She was really quite sweet, relaxed this evening, animated and talkative.

Lillie felt his gaze on her and blushed. "You sound just like my Papa. We can't keep him out of the kitchen when we start the holiday baking. Especially when Mama is making her fruit cakes."

"I hate fruit cake," he said, turning up his nose.

Lillie laughed and turned her attention to the swirling dancers. "Everyone is so joyful and happy tonight. I think Christmas is my favorite time of the year. What's yours, Alex?"

He hesitated. "Spring, I guess. Plowing and planting, the arrival of lambs and foals."

"That sounds like you. Really, Christmas and Spring aren't much different, both celebrate new life." She tilted her head to look up at him. "We're much alike, I believe." She looked quickly away as though ashamed of her boldness.

The orchestra swung into a lively jig and Jamie and Belle twirled by, their faces flushed and laughing. Alex stood motionless, a cookie midway to his mouth, his eyes following the dancers.

"Alex . . . ?"

He looked down at Lillie with a start, and without waiting for her to finish, took her by the elbow and led her to the dance floor.

It was mid-evening before Alex, heart in his throat, could claim Belle for a dance.

"You waltz well," she commented with a dimpled smile.

"I seldom dance. I'm afraid I'm unfamiliar with most of the steps."

"Ah, but you're far too modest."

She looked ravishing in a gown of amethyst velvet, a perfect complement to her glowing hair. The low neckline of the dress bared her shoulders and more of her splendid breasts than Alex wished to see. He labored to keep his eyes from them and stepped on her foot. Belle seemed quite unaware of his discomfort. She smelled alluringly of a scent he couldn't identify, and he found conversation impossible, his mind numb, his hands sweating, as he guided her around the floor.

The dance ended all too soon and after returning Belle to Jamie, Alex rejoined Lillie with a mixture of guilt and misery.

The hall, with its hundreds of candles and overheated dancers, had become unpleasantly hot and Lillie passed a small fan back and forth before her flushed face. She sat quietly, a pensive look in her eyes.

Alex looked at her in the flickering candlelight. Whereas he had been dazzled by Belle's beauty, he had to admit Lillie was lovely—just lovely in an altogether different way. She presented a fragile femininity quite unlike the sensual allure of Belle.

He reached out and took her hand. The smallness of it startled him as it nestled in his large, calloused palm. He gave it a gentle squeeze, saying, "And now, Miss Schwartz, I believe the next dance is ours."

The orchestra began to play "Lorena," a haunting love song, popular during the Civil War. Alex sighed and pulled Lillie close to him, aware of a deep stirring need. She looked up at him. There was something nurturing . . . something soft and comforting in her expression and he felt a melting sensation in his chest, a strange tug of protectiveness and affection for this shy creature.

He was almost oblivious to the other dancers and the swirling presence of Jamie and Belle. Almost.

* * *

After a full evening of dancing they began the long trek home. Most of the party-goers followed the Gettysburg Pike toward Two Taverns, but Alex and Lillie and Jamie and Belle followed an old, scenic, logging trail that hugged a wooded ridge and a deep ravine before joining the Pike near Whitehall.

Moonlight flushed the pristine snow as Princess Rose pranced along, tail high and harness bells jingling merrily. The girls snuggled beneath buffalo robes with their feet on hot soapstones, plumes of frost from their breath hovering above their heads as Belle led them in a rollicking song to the accompaniment of the sleigh bells.

Jamie was in the back seat, telling a funny story that had both girls laughing, when Alex caught sight of movement off to his left. Slinking along the edge of the nearby ridge was a large mountain lion, its lean silhouette etched in shadow. Alex raised his hand for quiet and pointed towards the ridge.

He reined the horse and they sat perfectly still, watching.

The lion appeared to be stalking a deer, visible further along the ridge in the mellow glow of the moon. It raised its small round head to test the air and then, apparently catching the human scent, turned towards them and dropped to a crouch, its tail twitching, yellow eyes fastened on the horse and sleigh.

Alex pulled his Kentucky rifle from beneath the seat and sighted, waiting for the animal to act.

The mountain lion returned its attention to the deer and crept forward. It drew closer and closer to its prey. The deer, head lowered and unaware of danger, was intent on pawing the deep snow in search of food. Alex held his breath as the primal scene played out against the white snow.

The deer raised its head in sudden alarm and the lion sprang—lithe, supple and muscular in motion—its tawny body a good eight feet long. With a flick of its tail, the deer leapt down the ridge, the mountain lion in close pursuit. It headed straight for the sleigh.

Princess Rose reared, terrified, clawing the empty air.

"Come on, come on," Alex whispered as he curled his finger around the trigger. Effortlessly, as if the act of raising his gun and killing an animal were second nature, Alex fired and watched as the mountain lion took the bullet.

The shot further panicked Princess Rose. Dropping his rifle, Alex strained to pull back on the reins each time she raised her front legs. The sleigh started to move sideways, the runner creeping dangerously close to the edge of the road and the steep ravine. With every backwards jerk the sleigh slithered further to the right. The runner on the passenger side slipped off the road, driving Lillie back into the seat and pitching her to one side. In numbed horror, Alex watched her fall from the open sleigh, hit the icy ground, and slide toward the yawning ravine.

With a terrified scream Lillie rolled down the heavily vegetated embankment and disappeared from sight.

Both men hit the ground at the same instant and ran towards the area of distressed snow and mud, Belle close behind.

Alex skidded to a stop and peered over the edge of the steep ravine. "Oh God, what a drop."

"Lillie, Lillie," Belle yelled. "Lillie, answer me!"

Silence: poignant and terrible.

Belle began to pull at Jamie's arm, inching toward the steep embankment, her intention evident in her jutting jaw and clenched lips.

"No, Belle." Jamie pulled her backwards, his emotion-filled voice cracking with authority. "The horse is greatly agitated, she smells lion and blood. Stay with her. Please! We'll need the sleigh to get Lillie to a doctor if she's injured."

Without waiting for an answer and crying Lillie's name, Alex and Jamie plunged down the snow-covered ravine, slipping and sliding over slopes brutalized by exposed boulders and tree stumps. Uprooted weeds and scuffed snow marked the trail of her descent, but only deep, profound silence greeted their call.

Jamie finally spotted her, close to the bottom of the ravine. She lay in a heap against the trunk of a massive hemlock that had blocked her downward tumble. She was not moving.

Alex reached her first. He lifted her in his arms and put his hand to her chest. Praise God, her heart was still beating.

"She's unconscious, Jamie, but alive. We can't risk leaving her here to fetch a doctor. The climb back to the road will be tough, but I'll carry her for awhile, then you can take her."

"Right."

The terrain was downright hostile, the ground a tangled blanket of frozen undergrowth interspersed with jutting rocks. The sky was now pitch black, the moon obscured behind clouds as it began to snow again.

Using vines and boulders as a handgrip, Alex pulled himself up with one arm, cradling Lillie's still form with the other. The muscles of his arms and back began to burn with the effort and his lungs were on fire.

"Give her to me for awhile," Jamie urged. "I see the top now."

Gasping with relief and exhaustion, Alex placed her in Jamie's arms. They continued their upward climb, passing her back and forth like a sack of flour, until they finally reached the crest of the embankment.

An ashen-faced Belle stretched out her hand to pull Jamie and his inert burden onto the road.

"Oh, God, Jamie! Is she dead?"

"No. She's out, though. Probably hit her head on that tree that stopped her fall. Help us get her into the sleigh."

Alex climbed into the front seat and reached down to lift the limp girl onto the sleigh. As he laid Lillie down and covered her with a thick fur robe, she began to moan and cry out in little yelps of pain.

Alex was sick with worry; despite the freezing snow pelting his face, sweat broke out on his forehead and trickled down his chest. "Let's head into Hanover. They have a hospital there."

Lillie began to regain consciousness and struggled to sit up. She screamed with pain as she tried to right herself and fainted once more. Alex bit his lip and took the whip to the horse.

They got to Hanover in good time and drove straight to the hospital. Alex carried her inside and Belle ran in search of a doctor.

Alex sank down on a bench in the tiny waiting room, cradling the unconscious girl in his arms. Was the accident my fault, he wondered? Would the horse have panicked if I had not fired? He pushed the wet hair from Lillie's forehead with a gentle hand. No, he assured himself, the lion might have turned on us. I had no choice. And yet. . . .

His lips moved in silent prayer: Dear God, forgive my sin. I was wrong in asking Lillie to the dance when I only wanted to be near Belle. I'm the one who was wrong. Lillie is the innocent one. Please, please God, let her be all right.

CHAPTER 3

Lillie spent three weeks in the hospital, missing Christmas altogether. She had sustained a broken pelvic bone and a fractured leg. Full recovery would take months, and although she dreaded the thought of her mother poking and fussing over her, she was secretly tickled at Alex's concern. He insisted on taking responsibility for the accident and came to call once a week, bringing sweets from Bittinger's Confectionery in Littlestown or homemade cookies from his mother's kitchen.

It was early afternoon at the very beginning of February, a magic winter day of bitter cold and frost with pale, cloudless skies, when Lillie heard heavy footsteps in the hallway. She flushed with anticipation.

Her mother tapped on the bedroom door and pushed it open. "Alex is here."

"Bring him in," she urged brightly, making no attempt to keep the happiness from her voice.

Lillie smoothed the coverlet across her chest inching herself forward on the pillows. Muslin bags filled with sand were packed firmly along her sides from waist to knees keeping her immobile while the pelvic bone healed. Her mother pulled a chair to the side of the bed. "Sit down, Alex," she said, gesturing to the slender Sheraton arm chair. Without another word, she retreated to a rocker in the far corner of the room, and reached into a basket for her knitting.

Lillie smiled at Alex perched anxiously on the edge of the chair, his hands twisting a fur cap in his blunt fingers. After exchanging a few pleasantries the conversation sagged and silence, broken only by the clicking of her mother's knitting needles, settled like fog over the room. Flustered she glanced toward her bedside window where sleet rattled and scratched against the glass.

"Have you been able to work your horses in this foul weather?" she asked.

"Jamie tends the horses. I work mostly in the grist mill now that Edwin is helping my uncle over in Hanover."

"That's good, isn't it? I mean . . . it keeps you indoors, out of this foul weather."

"I guess." Alex's face grew pensive. "I help out in the stables when I have the time. I don't care to race like Jamie, but I love being around the horses just the same."

"Rebert Stables has made quite a name for itself, though. You should be proud."

"Justice ran 2:40 on the mile track at Hanover yesterday," he said, brightening.

"Is that a record?"

"No, but it's excellent time. Brandy, Pa's colt, ran 2:25 when he won in '60."

"Your father won the Lockman Trophy, didn't he?"

"Twice. In '59 and '60. He would have run Brandy at Baltimore in '61 if the war hadn't interfered."

The room was warm and Alex removed his jacket and placed it over the back of the chair. Lillie looked at his strong hands, at his rugged profile and the quietness of his expression. He had lost weight. There was a tension about him, it showed in his face, in the taut muscles along his jaw, in his brooding eyes.

Her mother put her knitting aside and approached the bed. "Would you care for tea, dear?" she asked her daughter, fussing with the coverlet.

"Yes, please, Mama."

"Alex?"

"No, thank you, Mrs. Schwartz."

"Coffee, then?"

"If it's no trouble."

Her mother left and soon returned with a tray laden with tea, coffee, and a plate of the soft molasses cookies Alex's mother had sent over. She placed the tray across Lillie's lap, handed a cup of coffee to Alex, stirred sugar into Lillie's tea, then retreated once more to her rocker.

Alex munched his cookie and Lillie took a sip of tea.

"I really don't know much about you, Alex," she finally said.

"Well, let's see, I'm fourth generation Pennsylvania Dutch. My great grandfather emigrated from Germany in the late 1750's and farmed 300 acres over near Jefferson."

Lillie toyed with the spoon beside her cup. "I mean personal things; things you like and don't like, not just your family."

"Family is very important. Family and tradition," Alex said with a humorless smile. "One is defined by one's family." He dropped his eyes, his hands worrying his cap. "My father didn't fight in the Civil War—a fact I've always had trouble accepting. Pa made my mother a solemn vow before they married that he would honor her Mennonite faith and never take up arms. But that was before the north went to war with the south." Alex stirred his coffee in slow swirls. "Pa served in the Christian Commission instead."

"Well, I think that very commendable. He honored both his wife and God," Lillie said seriously.

"Maybe, but I think it detracted from the family honor. I intend to make the Rebert name a force in Adams County. Someday I hope to be the largest land owner in the valley."

He turned to pluck another cookie from the plate and Lillie observed his broad face, rigid and unsmiling. She suspected Alex would not be an easy man to live with. Yet, during his other visits she had seen a softer side of him that he tried hard to hide.

Her mother chose that moment to pick up the empty cups and remove the tray. "I believe Lillie needs to rest," she said with a firm nod toward the door. "You may call again."

Alex retrieved his jacket and hesitated, darting an anxious look between Lillie and her mother. Then, with a nervous cough he approached the bed, leaned down, and kissed Lillie on the cheek. As he solemnly marched out of her bedroom, Lillie let out a deep sigh. If she didn't still have pain and an occasional nightmare, the kiss would have made the encounter with the lion almost worthwhile.

* * *

Lillie and Belle cupped steaming mugs of coffee in their hands and settled into rocking chairs before the warmth of the hearth in the Schwartz kitchen. The Saturday morning baking cooled on the doughtray and the aroma of kitchen spices mingled with chicory and wood smoke, while outside snow fell in heavy, floating flakes to pile up on the window-sills. Loud barks emanated from the front yard where Charlie and John romped with the farm dogs and overhead Mama's footsteps could be heard on the creaking floorboards.

Lillie's cane rested close by her side. She had been out of bed for a week but walked with a slight limp.

Belle unfolded the February 26th edition of the Hanover Sun and spread it across her lap, holding the front page at an angle to catch the flickering light of the fire. She gasped as a news item in the lower right hand column caught her attention and she brought the paper close to her face. Her foot began a rapid tap—tap—tap and she sucked her lower lip in disbelief, rereading it a second, then a third time.

"Listen to this, Lillie," she said, stilling the rocker, the paper trembling in her hand: "A Missouri couple, Francis and Virginia Minor, believing that the Constitution grants citizenship to all persons born in the United States, and that no state can abridge his—or her—right to vote, has sued a St. Louis registrar for refusing Mrs. Minor voting privileges. Supreme Court Justice Waite handed down a decision decreeing that states could indeed legally withhold voting rights from certain citizens, such as criminals, the insane—and women!" Belle threw the paper on the floor. "The gall of that man! Of all men for that matter!"

Lillie smiled at the fury in her friend's voice. Belle did tend to take politics a little too seriously, she thought.

"Surely you're not going to turn into one of these women suffragettes with their dour faces and loud voices?" she replied.

Belle stared into the flames, the coffee mug clutched in her fingers. "You may as well know that for the past few months I've thought of joining the National Woman Suffrage Association. This settles it. Jamie will probably have apoplexy when I tell him. Men are so unbelievably arrogant and bullheaded. Can't they see that women are responsible for the gentler side of life, that they would most certainly humanize politics if given a chance?"

"But, Belle, women do represent the gentler side of life. Men want their wives to be feminine, to be homemakers and mothers. They don't want them involved in political issues."

Belle flapped her hand. "Pshaw. It's time they changed their minds." She grew pensive, staring into the flames. "You know, dear, I have never believed that poppy-cock about women being the weaker sex."

"It infuriates me that the only conception men have of women is that they can be intimidated to the point of unquestioning obedience. And that is not true and never has been. There have been strong women in the bible, strong women behind the throne and throughout history. I only want to live up to my potential." She sighed. "You're hopelessly old-fashioned, Lillie. Things have changed in this country since the Civil War when women were forced to take a man's place on the farm and in factories. I just want a place in the scheme of things, an escape from mediocrity, a dream to build on. It's no different from what everyone wants."

Lillie gave her a scorching look. "I think your dream is different from mine. Not all women want the same thing!"

"You want nothing more than a brood of children hanging on your skirts."

"And what's better than that, may I ask; in fact, the more the better. And you would do well to want the same thing," Lillie said assertively.

"Never. Housework and babies? Much as I love Jamie I really don't want to get married. I want to do something worthwhile. Teach or go down south to work with the Freedman's Bureau." Her gray eyes grew dark. "That's what I'd really like to do, go south and help educate the poor Negro."

Lillie looked at her in confusion. "You mean be a teacher to colored children?"

"Yes. The Bureau's most important job, Lillie, is in building schools and providing teachers—to give the Negroes the education they've been denied under slavery."

"But you have no training to be a teacher."

"Well, if not teach, then at least work with the Bureau. They do a great deal of work no one else can do. They have handed out millions of free meals to the colored folk and to white refugees, built hospitals and helped Negro freedmen find jobs. And it is helping to bring thousands of Southerners—the darkies and the whites—back onto farms where they can make a living."

Lillie's hands fluttered and she fixed Belle with a level stare. "From what I hear, the Southerners resent our interference in their affairs. The war is over and they look at Reconstruction as a miserable failure. They're worried that Negroes are no longer being kept in their place."

Belle shook her head and plunked her empty mug on the grate. She stood with a swish of her full skirts. "Well, I for one, think the South is still at war—at war with itself. They're carrying on the Civil War under another name . . . the Ku Klux Klan . . . fighting the Negroes who only want to learn how to be free."

A log settled on the grate, sending up a shower of sparks and Lillie watched her friend. Even in anger, Belle's face was full of vibrancy and daring. It was the face of a rebel, unpredictable, perhaps self-indulgent, but always brave. Yet, despite her admiration for Belle's spirit, Lillie felt sorry for her. A sixth sense told her that Belle would always be discontented, a woman ahead of her time.

"And where do a home and family fit into all of this?"

Belle sighed. "I don't know if I'll ever be content to be little more than a farm-wife."

"Little more? You call that little more?" Lillie gripped the edges of the rocker, trying to suppress a wave of anger. Whatever had gotten into her friend? "I don't understand you. Jamie is a wonderful, handsome, funny, man." Her lips curved into a soft smile at the thought of Jamie, then tightened as she remembered Alex and the rivalry she suspected between the two brothers for Belle's favor. "I think," she said, "you should count your blessings and forget all this nonsense about woman suffrage and helping the poor Negro. Littlestown is your home and Jamie will make you a fine husband."

Belle grabbed her woolen cloak from a peg by the door and glared at Lillie. "Don't confuse your notion of the idyllic life with mine. I'll fill my platter with the morsels I favor." With a flourish, she draped the cloak about her shoulders and stormed into the gray mid-winter afternoon.

* * *

A leaden afternoon sky darkened under the threat of more snow and Alex was lounging before a cozy fire examining the latest issue of Farm Journal when Katie's quiet voice broke the silence.

"Alex, would you mind going to Stonesifer's Dry Goods for me? The ladies will be coming to quilt tomorrow and I'm almost out of white thread."

"Not at all, Mama. I've been meaning to look for a new cap, anyway."

"It'll do you good to get some fresh air. You've been looking peaked lately. Is anything wrong, son?"

"No." His mother's eyes looked directly into his. He faltered and dropped his gaze. "The long winter weather weighs on me. I can't wait to get out into the fields."

"I thought maybe there was a problem between you and Lillie. You've been very attentive to her since the accident. Your father and I have been hoping that you would continue to court her. She's a lovely girl, Alex. Perfect for you."

Without answering he rose to go. Katie reached out her hand to take his. "I love you son. And I understand far more than you might think. Please come to me if I can help you sort out your feelings."

For some reason Alex felt tears gather in his eyes. His mother, as always, was compassionate and loving and he knew she would give him good advice, but he doubted she really knew the agony of his conflict.

"I will, Mama. Now I'd better get going before the weather turns bad."

After collecting some change from a sugar bowl in the kitchen cabinet, Alex pulled his sheepskin jacket and woolen muffler from a peg by the door and stepped outside into the wind. Sparrows were picking at a handful of crumbs Mama had thrown out earlier and they complained loudly at his presence before scattering to the trees.

It was only a mile to Littlestown, but the promised snow soon covered his little carriage, a bright blue phaeton, and the frigid air cut like a razor. Farmhouse roofs wore a thick coating of white, and smoke hung in lazy veils above tall chimneys. He drew his jacket tighter and spurred Princess Rose into a trot.

Alex saw her the minute she entered the store: Belle dressed in bright green, her shining red hair only partially hidden under a square of brown wool. He kept his back toward her while he tried on several fur caps, studying his reflection in a small glass from which he could watch her turning over bolts of brightly colored fabrics.

She made her selection quickly and brought the material to the counter to be measured and cut, then she looked up and saw him watching her.

"Alex! I didn't see you."

"I've been trying on caps. John's puppy shredded my old one and I've always hankered for one of these made of beaver fur." He smiled, inviting her admiration for the furry creation resting on his head.

"Handsome! Just like the fellow wearing it," she said, giving him an impish grin.

Alex could feel warm blood move up his neck. Was she flirting with him? Jamie had been curiously silent about marriage plans and their bans had not been posted. He looked at the oval face, the elegant nose, the wide gray eyes. Eyes the color of fog. A fog he could get lost in if he didn't keep his wits. His hands fumbled in his pockets as he nonchalantly swayed closer to her. "I don't see your carriage outside. Did you walk?"

"Yes. I wanted some fresh air."

"It's starting to snow again. Let me give you a ride home."

"It isn't necessary," she said. "And it's out of your way."

"But I want to."

He picked up her parcel and tucked it under his arm. "You shouldn't be walking in deep snow with those thin boots."

"It's only a mile, Alex. I can cope with that."

"Don't argue."

She dimpled. "All right, then." She took his arm and looked at him, a soft smile curving her full lips. She was as tall as he was and their shoulders brushed. He felt her breath upon his cheek like perfumed air.

Belle settled beside him on the narrow seat of the phaeton and he tucked a lap robe around them. He could feel the heat of her thigh against his and with each bump in the rutted road his arm brushed her breast. His loins stirred.

With a bravado he didn't know he possessed, he reached out and took her hand in his.

A deep furrow appeared between Belle's brows and she turned to look at him through squinted eyes. "Alex . . . ?"

"I . . . ah . . . your hands are blue. Where are your mittens?" he said, quickly dropping her hand.

"I left them at Lillie's. We were having a rather spirited conversation and I left in somewhat of a huff."

"I can imagine you having a "spirited" conversation, but Lillie? She's so shy and quiet I can't imagine her returning your fire."

Belle dimpled and looked at him with a twinkle in her eyes. "You don't give my friend enough credit, Alex. She is much stronger than you think. We have different goals, but sometimes I think she is more likely to achieve hers than I am."

"And what are yours?"

"To be independent. To pursue the issues I feel passionately about, like suffrage, teaching, equality," she recited.

"A woman's place is in the home, always has been," Alex retorted, exasperated.

"Only if that place is equal, only if she is free to think and read, and express her opinions through the vote, same as a man." She frowned. "I believe your idea of 'place' is quite different from mine."

Alex shifted on the narrow seat, opening some space between himself and Belle. I don't really know this girl, he thought ruefully. What is the attraction I feel for her? He knew if he were honest with himself he would admit it was purely physical. His fantasies of pure everlasting love were all mixed up with the unbidden urges of his own body. He knew, with his traditional nature, Belle's opinions would drive him crazy. Yet his impulses were stronger than his intellect.

"How does Jamie feel about your ideas?" he asked.

Belle smiled, a faraway expression on her face. "I think he is completely bewildered. As is everyone else. No one understands my need to do something worthwhile."

"Don't you think raising a family worthwhile?"

"Of course, but Jamie and I are really too young to marry. In the meantime, I need to seek employment of some type to help my mother."

"But, you are serious about each other?"

"Yes, and . . . and, no."

"I don't understand."

Belle gave a wry laugh. "Neither do I. It's very complicated Alex, I'm not at all sure what lies ahead for Jamie and me."

"Jamie is a dreamer," he said ruefully.

"You mustn't fault him, Alex. You and he are just different. Jamie will never be a compulsive worker like you; he isn't interested in farming, in accumulating land. He loves working with the horses and the thrill of racing." Her emotions flashed across her face like the sweep of sun-rent clouds over a quiet landscape. "He's very special to me. I love the lightheartedness in him that you complain about." She was blushing now. "Enough about me. How do you feel about Lillie? She's the perfect girl for you, you know, sweet and quiet, and she does adore you."

He grinned sheepishly. "She doesn't give me the tingles."

Belle threw back her head and laughed. "Why, Alex Rebert, I believe you have a sense of humor after all!"

They reached the gate of her house and she jumped nimbly to the ground. Snow swirled about her like ghostly dervishes and a gust of wind flung her red hair into such wanton disarray that her scarf couldn't manage to hold it in place. "You needn't get out," she said. Thanks for the ride and for listening. You're a good friend."

"Yes. But . . . " Alex hesitated. I want to be more than a friend, fought to be spoken, an admission he could not make. She has just spoken of her love for the friend I consider a brother. Why do I insist on tempting myself like this. It's like picking at a scab. He felt the fingers of his right hand dig into his palm and he forced a smile to his lips.

"But what, Alex?"

"Nothing . . . it wasn't important."

With a wave of her hand she was gone. Alex clicked to Princess Rose and they were on their way. Friends, his mind screamed. Not by a long shot! There was trouble between Belle and Jamie. He could sense it.

There was still hope.

But from somewhere deep in his sub-conscience a small voice whispered, "Be careful what you wish for."

CHAPTER 4

April rolled around, that fickle time of the year, when one day brings snow and the next spring's sunny warmth. Katie always thought of it as "the golden month," the time when every fence was covered with lemon honeysuckle. The time when dandelion sprouted with abandon while golden daffodils and forsythia decorated her lawn and flower garden.

"I'd like to go to the race meeting with you and Jamie next Saturday," she announced one evening as she ladled potato soup from a large tureen into bowls and passed them down the table.

Edward looked up in surprise.

"I know, I know" Katie hastened to explain, "I don't generally attend unless they are part of the county fair. But this is Princess Rose's maiden race and I'd really like to be present when she wins."

Alex raised his eyebrows and grinned. "You're pretty confident that she's gonna win, Mama."

"She will," Jamie declared between mouthfuls of soup. "Believe me that little filly is ready to win."

"I think we should all go," Ellen said softly.

"Me too . . . me too," John piped up, his blue eyes sparkling with excitement.

Katie smiled. Princess Rose had carved a notch for herself in all their hearts. The little filly had a personality—a fire and independence that were uniquely hers. And the race would be a nice outing for everyone after the hard winter just passed. Maybe they could stop at Hoke's Emporium in Hanover for some summer fabric. The girls all needed new frocks.

"What about the cows?" Charlie asked. "They . . . "

"I'll stay home and tend to the milking," Anna interjected. She blushed prettily. "George said he might stop by on his way home from market."

Emma laughed. "And George Geiselman is infinitely more interesting than any old horse."

Katie looked at Alex. "Edwin will be home for the weekend. Do you think the two of you could tend the mill?"

"Of course."

"It's settled then," Edward said. "With all of us rooting for her our Princess can't fail to bring home the winning purse." He gave Katie a fond smile. "We'll leave early in the morning. I imagine you would like to add some shopping to this excursion."

How like him, Katie thought. Always so considerate, always seeming to know my mind. She could see the love in his eyes. Love that mirrored her own. She returned his smile. "I do have a few things I might want to get." Her mind was already compiling the list.

* * *

Early Saturday morning, while Katie prepared a picnic hamper with fat ham sandwiches, fruit, and a tin of peanut butter cookies, Annie was putting the finishing touches to the breakfast dishes. She had already helped John polish his boots and Ellen secure a bow at the back of her hair. Katie smiled wistfully. She would sorely miss her daughter when she married and started her own home. Annie had always been the little mother to the other children, had actually helped in the delivery of two of them. She never had to be told what to do around the house, unlike Emma who seemed to have no other thought then to be in the barn or stables, or Ellen with her nose in a book.

"We're ready," Charlie yelled as he bounded into the kitchen. "Pa's waiting."

John ran ahead to the enclosure where Jamie, in the green and white colors of Rebert Stables, was adjusting the harness used to attach the sulky. Princess Rose looked around with interest, her ears pricked and her tail high.

"Son of a gun knows what's coming," Edward said with a chuckle. He reached out to stroke the filly's poll. "Our little lady is ready to strut her stuff."

"Oh, how I wish I was Jamie. Why can't I learn to drive a sulky?" Emma asked wistfully.

"You're a girl," Charlie chided. "Girls don't race sulkies."

"Belle says girls can do anything they put their minds to."

"Yeah, well Belle is full of beans and we'd better get going if we want to get a good place at the finish line."

Katie nodded and reached up to kiss Jamie on the cheek. "Good luck, son, ride safely. That's just as important as winning."

Jamie gave her a cocky grin. "We'll do both. And that's a promise."

Princess Rose had drawn the number three position in a field of six and stood quietly behind the tape. When all of the horses were stationary the tape was drawn and the race was on.

She stepped away cleanly and immediately fell into the required square gait of a trotter—a gait requiring her to stretch her left front and right rear legs forward almost simultaneously, then follow suit with her front and left rear legs.

Katie sucked in her breath. The liquid movement of gleaming horseflesh, the whirring wheels, the wind-filled colors of the drivers, the rising roar of the crowd were almost more than she could bear.

"Oh . . . no," Edward muttered, grasping the rail.

Interference by another trotter caused Princess Rose to become unsettled and for a moment her natural gait faltered. She recovered quickly, however, and by the second lap caught up with the rest of the horses in the race and settled into position one space out from the inside of the rail.

"Come on girl, come on girl," Charlie screamed.

Edward was grasping the rail with white knuckles. "Save her, Jamie," he shouted. "The pace is too fast. The leader can't keep it up."

Katie heard the bell ring, warning the drivers they were about to commence the final lap. Her throat was dry and she seemed unable to shout as the rest of her family was doing. Princess Rose was just behind the leader when Jamie headed her wide on the track to secure a clear run to the finish. It was a wise move and Katie's heart pumped wildly as the little filly moved up to challenge the leader.

John was jumping up and down, screaming at the top of his lungs and Ellen clasped Katie's hand tight enough to crush a few fingers.

"She's feeling it, Jamie. Give her a loose rein—let her run," Edward shouted as the filly drew abreast of the leader only seconds from the finish line.

As the crowd roared the lead colt seemed to slacken and Princess Rose charged ahead to the finish line.

"She's first," Emma screamed. "She won, Mama! She won!"

* * *

That evening, as the carriage bumped along the Hanover Pike in the silky comfort of springtime, Katie leaned against the solid warmth of Edward's broad shoulders. John slept on the seat beside her while the rest of the children rode behind them in a second wagon drawn by the hero of the race.

She sighed. "It was a wonderful day. Thank you dear."

"No thanks are needed. Princess Rose and Jamie deserve all the glory."

"But your dream made it all possible."

"A person must follow their dreams, Katie. I want that for all our children. Without dreams there is no life."

"I guess. I wonder sometimes what our children dream of. John, of course, is still too young to know but Charlie has always wanted to be a carpenter. Edwin, I know, wants to take over the mill, but Alex keeps his dreams within himself."

"He wants to be a farmer, Katie. No more—no less. And I believe that's enough for Alex."

"And Jamie?"

"He's a natural around the horses. He has a great future as a breeder." Edward cocked his head to look at her, a smile playing at the corner of his lips. "I notice you don't mention the girls. Don't they have dreams, too?"

"Girls dream of marriage and babies." She smiled coyly. "As I did."

"Good thing. Babies you had plenty of."

Katie laughed and said, musically, "Deed I did." They rode in comfortable silence for a moment before she added, "I look for Annie to marry her George someday. They've had eyes for no other since that church picnic three years ago."

Edward nodded. "He's spoken to me. But he wants to get established first. I'm afraid the first one to leave our care will be Jamie. He says he wants to marry Belle."

"Oh, dear! Do you think that wise? The girl is such a maverick."

"And so is Jamie, really. He's a lot like Patrick."

Katie's thoughts flew back to another time. To Patrick, and her fears of the influence he had over Edward. But that had all resolved itself and Edward proved to be his own man, loyal to his own conscience. True, Jamie had a lot of his father's characteristics, his ready laughter, his cocky strut, his cavalier approach to life's problems, yet the boy was more settled, more focused, and, fortunately, without his father's yen for whiskey.

As usual Edward read her thoughts. "Someday I plan to buy another farm and set Jamie up with a stable of his own." He laughed. "Don't tell him, though. The boy has a lot to learn and he's much to cocky as it is."

Laughter reached them from the wagon following and in the distance bullfrogs creaked their mating call. Katie looked up at the sky milky with stars.

"We are very lucky, aren't we?"

"Very," he said somberly.

* * *

May turned into June, and then it was summer and the wheat was ready to be harvested.

On a glorious morning, late in July, Alex took to the fields on his father's new McCormick reaper. The wheat was waist-high, golden and luxuriant, swaying gently in a slight breeze. It was hard, laborious work in the hot sun, and Alex was soon covered with sweat and dust. His shirt clung to his back, but he worked in a steady rhythm, savoring the demands on his body, the smell of the freshly cut grain and the shimmering heat hovering above the open field.

The welcome clang of the dinner bell came just as he felt his arms would drop from their sockets. With a sigh of relief Alex bounded to the ground and, with his brothers close behind, made a beeline for the house.

His mother and sisters had been up since dawn, baking and cooking for the extra harvest hands. The table groaned with the weight of food. Huge platters were filled with smoked sausage and roast chicken, crockery bowls held mounds of potato stuffing, raw-fried potatoes and buttered lima beans and, of course, all of the traditional Pennsylvania Dutch seven sweets and sours: spiced peaches, rice pudding, candied watermelon rind, apple sauce, fox-grape jelly, apple and raisin pie, pickled beets, chow chow, green tomato relish, horse radish, pickled cauliflower, sour beans and cabbage.

Amid full mouths and the clanking of cutlery on plates, laughter and conversation flowed as Edwin told his father about the fluffy white "patent" flour being manufactured in the cities. They discussed the scarcity of jobs, the increased number of tramps and hobos roaming the countryside, and the economic panic farmers faced once again. Edward admitted he was over-planted, no longer getting the high prices he got during the war, and now forced to compete with western farms ten times the size of his.

Alex did not contribute much to the conversation, but he listened with keen interest, taking the dinner-time conversation with him as he returned to the fields. All afternoon he mulled over what had been said and when the last bale of hay was bound he headed for the stable.

Princess Rose greeted him with a soft nicker and watched his approach with huge dark eyes full of curiosity. Alex leaned on the top of the stall's half door and dug a sugar cube from his pocket. "Edwin said some interesting things today at the table," he said as he idly stroked the horse's nose. "Much as I hate change I think maybe we should move away from planting so many grain crops and devote our energy to more perishable items—like fruit and milk."

Princess nudged his pocket and, with a grin, Alex produced another sugar cube. "I'm gonna have a talk with Pa first chance I get—urge him to increase our dairy herd, maybe take the south field out of wheat and plant it in apple trees."

Alex scratched his horse's poll one more time, drinking in her beauty, the smooth flowing lines of her, the strong chest and the sleek chestnut coat glinting fire in the fading sunlight.

"Tomorrow," he promised. "Tomorrow, I'll get up before dawn and we'll ride out together to check the boundary lines."

A week later, Jamie suggested that he and Alex go the ten miles to Gettysburg to celebrate the end of harvest season. Alex readily agreed. Gettysburg was noted for its extensive carriage trade and he was in the market for a runabout. His father had offered to finance a buggy for him on his twenty-first birthday, and that was just a few weeks away.

Gettysburg was a lively place sporting many new hotels and taverns built to accommodate the increasing number of visitors come to see the famous battlefield that had turned the tide of the Civil War a scarce ten years ago. The streets were crowded with people, many of them young students from the Theological Seminary and Pennsylvania College.

He and Jamie had money in their pockets from summer work and decided they would go to a good hotel. After a tremendous meal at the Globe, Jamie suggested they go across town to visit the carriage shop of Walter & Bros. on Chambersburg Street.

They entered the shop and were surprised to find workers applying a final coat of paint to just what Alex had been looking for, a beautiful little runabout. Introduced in the mid-'50's, the runabout quickly became the most popular carriage in America. Most were open, four-wheeled, one-seat vehicles with a body resembling a piano box, but this was an upscale model with an optional folding top and many other extras.

"It's perfect, a real beauty," Jamie said, cocking his head to admire the gleaming vehicle. "I think you should buy one just like it." He had an odd grin on his face.

Alex's heart beat faster, filled with longing. Harry Walter, the owner of the shop, approached them with a smile.

"How much is she?" Alex asked.

"Without a top—$50.00. With a top it'll run about $125.00. This little beauty is on special order, though."

Alex's thrifty nature went to war with itself. Of course, an open model would serve him well, but the gleaming blue runabout with its fawn colored top, sitting before him, pulled at his heartstrings. He desperately wanted one just like it. After all, this would be his first material possession—the first thing he had ever bought with his own earnings. Next month he was taking Lillie to a corn husking and he pictured himself picking her up in a sporty little runabout. Still . . . .

"Are you going to order one?" Jamie asked.

"I have to think on it. It's rather pricey with a top."

"Maybe you could ask Santa Claus to bring you one for Christmas," Jamie teased.

After promising Mr. Walter that he would think about it, they left the shop and strolled up Chambersburg Street toward the square.

"Let's drop into the White Horse for a scooper of beer," Jamie suggested.

Alex was not a drinking man, although he drank a little hard cider, and a few glasses of beer on occasion. As a boy, he had seen a rider, drunk as a lord, yank the bit on a bulky horse so hard it cut the poor creature's tongue off. He had never forgotten the sight or the lesson it taught him. But he hated to dampen Jamie's high spirits, so he agreed.

They passed through the noisy taproom, entered the back room and took a table. Alex went out to the bar and bought two beers and brought them back to their table. He and Jamie sat there drinking and talking.

"I'm surprised that you and Belle haven't set the date." Alex commented casually.

Jamie gave him a hang-dog look and a feeble smile. "I'm more than ready, but Belle is dragging her heels. Says she wants to teach, of all the damn things. Wants to experience 'more of life' as she puts it."

Alex felt a small glimmer of hope. Maybe she simply was not in love with Jamie . . . not enough to marry him anyway.

He was searching for the proper words of commiseration when a door at the rear of the taproom opened revealing a stairway leading to rooms overhead. At the sound, Jamie turned his head toward the door and saw a young girl—he judged her to be about twenty—step into the room. Her gaze swept the crowded room before coming to rest at their table. She gave them a friendly smile and sauntered over.

She was dressed in a dove gray gown, trimmed with lace and ribbons, pulled up in front to reveal an underskirt of red. Ash blond hair was pulled back and tied with ribbon. She was a trifle thin, which made her look fragile and very feminine, until one looked closely at her face. Her features, formed for humor and tenderness, had been scored by the marks of her profession and in the flickering light she looked haggard. Alex was well aware of what she wanted and he tried to ignore her, but Jamie gave her a big smile.

"Hi," she said. "My name's Abigail, but everyone calls me Abby. Mind if I join you?"

"Not at all," Jamie said, whipping out a chair.

"Would you care for a beer?" Alex asked out of politeness.

She wrinkled her nose. "I prefer whiskey if you don't mind."

Alex frowned. Whiskey was expensive and it was obvious that this girl was under instructions from the tavern owner. Still, he didn't want to appear cheap, so he threw caution to the wind and ordered a whiskey for Abby and a couple of beers for Jamie and himself.

Alex knew about women who frequented saloons and were friendly with men, and lately he had been having a great deal of trouble controlling his carefully banked sexual urges. Abby, wise in the ways of men, soon had him engaged in conversation. To his surprise, it wasn't at his handsome brother that she directed her flirty smiles, but at him.

She put her hand on Alex's leg, gave it a slight squeeze, and, pretending shyness, hiked her dress back from her ankles until her bare leg was exposed. Under the table, she rubbed her knee against his.

Desire crept over Alex like liquid fire. He knew what he was contemplating was unwise, yet he felt an irresistible urge—an urge common to all males, rich or poor, educated or uneducated, single or married.

Abby, sensing his arousal, took one of his hands in hers and placed her other hand on his leg, drawing it towards her thigh. Alex shuddered and held on to his glass with white-knuckled intensity.

"Would you like to go upstairs?" she whispered.

"How . . . much?"

"Only a dollar."

He reached in his pocket and fingered his pocketbook.

This was really unwise. He knew the dangers, he knew about the diseases men picked up from girls who peddled their wares in taverns, yet despite himself he was tempted to consider her carnal offer. Of course, not all prostitutes were "burnt," but some had the French pox. It could ruin a man for life.

Jamie stood and threw a quarter on the table. "I think we better get going," he said, throwing Alex a meaningful glance. He headed for the door and Alex, torn between desire and good sense, reluctantly followed.

Once out on the street Alex placed a shaky hand on Jamie's arm. "Thanks, Jamie. My good sense was about to fly the coop."

Jamie grinned in sympathy. "I know all about it . . . believe me I know all about it, old pal, but you're better off "beating the bishop," if you know what I mean, than taking a chance with that strumpet."

Alex flushed. He had been doing a lot of that lately.

Jamie seemed to sense his discomfort and said nothing further. He and Alex headed for the livery stable on Hanover Street where they had left their carriage that morning. Suddenly he halted and turned to Alex with a wink. "I know of a fine establishment in York where the girls are guaranteed clean. What do you say we pay them a visit some Saturday evening?"

Alex shook his head. "Just because the girls aren't diseased doesn't make a place like that right. A man should be able to control his urges."

"Oh, don't be so dang self-righteous, Alex. We're men and God gave us sexual appetites and women to satisfy them."

"He also gave us will power."

"Guess my will power isn't as strong as yours. Visiting a brothel is better than letting your emotions get out of hand when you're with your girl. Lately I've been pushed to the limit," Jamie said with a mock brush of sweat off his forehead.

Alex felt a surge of alarm. "You . . . you're not . . . Belle . . . ?"

"Of course not." Jamie grinned sheepishly, kicking at a small stone lying in their path.

"Come on, Alex. Let's go to York. It'll do us both good."

"No!"

"All right, all right. Be mule-headed. I shouldn't have stopped you back there at the White Horse."

"I would have stopped myself." Alex saw the disbelief on Jamie's face and laughed in spite of himself. "I'll admit she got me pretty worked up and I was tempted, but I knew better. I'd have righted myself."

Jamie sighed. "Well, if your mighty will power ever wavers, let me know."

They finished the journey in silence.

* * *

Alex ran his finger tips over the soft canvas top of his new runabout and caressed it with pride.

His father had surprised him that morning with the buggy, saying it was a gift from the entire family, a gift befitting a man of twenty-one. Alex pulled a handkerchief from his pocket and reached down to wipe a speck of mud from the gleaming blue paint. He'd never dreamed when he saw it at Walter's Carriage Works that the special order customer was Edward Rebert. No wonder Jamie had such a wicked grin on his face when they looked at it.

Charlie came running across the yard with a whoop of delight. "Can I have the first ride . . . can I?"

"I don't want to get it all dusty. I'm taking Lillie to a hoedown tonight over at Two Taverns."

"I'll help you wipe it off, after. You gotta see if everything works right."

Alex laughed and tousled his blond head. "Ei,Ei,Ei, Charlie boy. You're a real pest. Go get Princess and hitch her up . . . and mind you, wipe the manure off your boots before you climb in."

Charlie grinned back. "Sure. Can't let your special girl get her fancy skirt all full of cow shit."

The September air was chilly and Lillie snuggled closer to Alex. It had been a fun-filled evening, and Alex had been in a jolly mood, surprising her by dancing every set. For once Jamie and Belle weren't there to cause a distraction. Why? she wondered. Belle was all excited about filling in at the public school on Hanover Street for a teacher who had recently married. And Jamie didn't seem pleased about it. Lillie suspected that the road had become a little bumpy for both of them. She shivered. The thought suddenly frightened her.

The buggy clattered onto the wooden floor of a covered bridge straddling Plum Creek and Alex pulled on the reins to halt Princess Rose.

The long, dark, covered bridge had provided a secluded spot for many a romantic interlude, and Lillie caught her breath as Alex turned toward her.

"May I kiss you?" he asked tentatively.

Her stomach fluttered and slowly she leaned toward him.

His lips were warm and soft and he smelled slightly of soap. She had often worried about the placement of noses during a kiss but amazingly every thing seemed to fit. She drew back in wonder, her heart doing flip-flops against her ribs.

Alex sat back and possessively placed his arm across her shoulder. Neither spoke.

Lillie trembled, whether from the night's chill or the warmth of his thigh against hers, she wasn't sure.

"Cold?" asked Alex.

"Not next to you. You're like a warm stove."

Alex chuckled. She was beginning to look forward to his smile. "Your eyes turn a deep, deep brown when you laugh," she said fondly. "You should laugh more often."

"I'm not Jamie."

"I know." Suddenly, she felt her shyness overtake her and it was somehow hard to talk. She stared at the wooden trusses of the structure arching over their heads. "Why do you suppose they cover the bridges like they do?"

"I don't know. Probably to protect the wooden floor . . . maybe so the horses won't be afraid to cross the river." He pushed his cap back on his head and chuckled. "Or maybe so a fellow can kiss his girl."

They sat close together, not speaking. The enveloping arms of the bridge seemed to cut her off from the outside world, from all her troubling thoughts and questions. After a while they kissed again, longer this time and a little harder. It left Lillie breathless. This is perfect, she thought. He does love me. He does.

"I think we'd better move on before we get into trouble," Alex said huskily. He clicked to the horse and they moved out to the embrace of the starry night.

* * *

Alex worked all morning at the grist mill, operating the wooden pulley set high under the peak of the roof to hoist wheat and other grain delivered by wagon to the mill door. The bags were maneuvered into a wide opening on the third floor of the mill. From there the grain passed through various hoppers and conveyors, moving by gravity alone to trickle into the center of the great grinding stones on the ground floor.

Alex had just finished raising the last heavy bag of oats from the wagon of Emil Slicter when he looked up to see Belle, holding two tin cups in her hand.

"If you're looking for Jamie he's in the stables."

"I'm not looking for him."

"Oh . . . well . . . "

"I wanted to talk to you. Emma just brought over a kettle of fresh boiled coffee. Do you have a minute to join me in a cup?"

"Sure," Alex said, throwing the last bag to the top of the pile and wiping his dirty hands on his pant leg. "I'm as thirsty as a dry toad." His stomach churned as he fixed her with a frown. It was unusual for Belle to appear at the mill.

Belle settled herself on a small bench set against the wall and with a bright smile handed him a tin of steaming coffee. Alex leaned back against a pile of grain sacks and looked at her with longing. God, she was beautiful, he pined. Sun light from the open door behind her set her red hair aglow, like that of an angel. He took a gulp of hot coffee, almost scalding his throat. "Jamie and I have had a spate," she said without preamble. "I told him I wanted to participate in a march sponsored by the NWRA in Hanover next Saturday. He became very angry and possessive . . . practically forbade me to go."

"What is the NWRA?"

"The National Women's Suffrage Association."

"Well, I can see his point. It could be dangerous."

"Life is dangerous. Don't you see, Alex? I can't live my life that way. Jamie wants to get married so he can control me and I don't want that. Not yet."

Alex looked at the floor and worried a pile of flour dust with his foot. Jamie was right, of course, but did this present a chance for him to win favor with her? His thoughts darted about like bats on a dark night. Should he side with her? It might put an end to her relationship with Jamie. And open the door for himself?

He looked up to find her eyes fixed on him, gray, stormy eyes, demanding an answer.

"If you feel strongly about the march then I think you should go." His throat tightened with the lie. "I'll talk to Jamie, see what I can do, but didn't you two have plans to attend the barn dance at the Miller farm on Saturday?"

"We did. Oh, Alex, he was so angry . . . he told me to find someone else."

Alex felt blood rush to his face. This was his opportunity.

"I'd be happy to take you."

Belle looked confused, a frown puckering her brow. "Weren't you going to go with Lillie?"

"Her mother is very ill. Lillie can't go."

Belle shook her head. "Regardless, Lillie is my best friend and you have been courting her ever since the accident. I couldn't do that to her."

A heavy wave of guilt swamped Alex. What was wrong with him that he would consider hurting Lillie that way? And she would be hurt. Yet, in his heart he knew he still lusted for this beautiful girl sitting opposite him. And probably always would.

"She would understand," he said lamely.

"No, she wouldn't. She loves you, and so long as you are a couple I wouldn't dream of doing anything that would hurt her."

As long as you are a couple sang in his mind. What if . . . Belle rose and brushed flour dust from her skirt. "I wasn't after a date, Alex. I only wanted you to try to explain to Jamie that I need more time. And more freedom."

"I'll talk to him, but I doubt he'll understand."

And secretly he prayed that indeed Jamie would do no such thing.

CHAPTER 5

On a bright Friday morning a week later, a determined Belle boarded a train for Harrisburg and engaged a carriage to take her to the National Hotel where she planned to book a room for the night. She was elated. Everything was working out perfectly and she had done it all alone. Smugly she sat in the cab as it clipped smartly through the street, enthralled with the bustling city as they moved from one neighborhood to another, deep in thought about tomorrow's march and what it represented to the country.

By linking the anti-slavery campaign to the women's rights movement the U. S. had begun to move slowly towards the women's vote. As early as 1869, Wyoming and Utah had granted women's suffrage and the issue was hotly contested in Pennsylvania and numerous other states.

Victorian England had already produced a sorority of intrepid women who climbed mountains, sought the source of the Nile, and trekked through Tibet. In America, success, although slow in coming, was gaining momentum. Across the land men began to pass laws allowing married women to enter into contracts, to sue, to go into business for themselves and control their own earnings.

And yet, their call for equality still came as lone voices in the wilderness.

Belle sighed. She knew that Pennsylvania was a long way from heeding the call. That's why this march was so important.

That evening Belle dressed in her finest frock, a hunter green taffeta sporting the newest bustle in the back, placed a large plumed hat on her red curls, and took a hansom cab to Memorial Hall where Elizabeth Stanton was scheduled to speak.

As she sat listening to the rousing address Belle's breath quickened and goose bumps appeared on her arms.

"Ladies," Elizabeth Stanton intoned, her strong voice carrying to the far corners of the hall, "you have the power to do what scores of women before you have done . . . you can make a difference. Already women have broken the sacred barriers of male-dominated fields. Woman are making a name for themselves in journalism, the arts, politics, science and medicine. Think of Anne Newport Royall, the first American journalist and Jessie Fremont, whose writings encouraged thousands of pioneers to travel west. Think of Fanny Palmer, the foremost lithographer of her time, whose Currier and Ives Prints adorn most of our homes. Remember the courageous Hannah Penn, wife of William Penn, who kept your own state intact after her husband's death despite extreme pressure from the Crown to surrender Pennsylvania to England. Why, ladies, did you know that today Margaret Laforge single handedly runs Macy's Dept. Store, a position unheard of for a woman in America. And remember Sophie Germaine, founder of mathematical physics, and Lady Mary Montague who awakened the British medical establishment to the benefits of smallpox inoculation.

But ladies these are only a few brave women whose names we know about. Many must remain in the background because of male suppression of women's accomplishments. How many of you know that Catherine Greene was the co-inventor of the cotton gin, that Sarah Astore played a critical role in building her husband's fur empire, that Fanny Mendelssohn was perhaps a better composer than her brother but wrote under his name because a woman couldn't hope to be published, that Belva Lockwood who studied law and passed her final examinations was refused her degree because she was a woman? And, ladies, this will never change until we have the vote."

Belle sprang to her feet to join the chorus of women crying, "VOTE, VOTE, VOTE." Her heart was thumping, she had never felt so proud to be a woman.

Gradually Mrs. Stanton brought quiet to the assemblage. She was perspiring profusely and moped her rotund face with a handkerchief as she directed a sudden smile to the women waiting with bated breath for her next words.

"I have always liked the story of Abigail Duniway who lectured throughout the Northwest. Ironically she found it easier to win over male audiences than female. She was once challenged by a man who said, 'I have often known a hen to try to crow, but I've never known one to succeed it at it yet.' Duniway replied, 'I once saw a rooster try to set, and he made a failure, too.'"

The auditorium erupted into laughter and Mrs. Stanton moved into her closing statement. Belle closed her eyes savoring every word. Deep in her heart she made a vow to do all she could to bring equal rights to herself and all females, even if it was only by marching and adding her voice to the movement. Jamie would just have to understand.

The next morning over one hundred women massed in front of the state capitol for the largest march yet to be held in Pennsylvania by women seeking the vote. And Belle was in the front row of the marching women, her red hair glinting in the sunlight, one corner of a streaming banner reading "THE VOTE FOR WOMEN NOW" firmly in her hand.

As they marched along, a man, his face red and angry, stepped from the sidewalk and shouted an obscenity.

Belle laughed and raised her free hand in a fist. She had never felt so alive.

* * *

A week later Lillie, Belle, and Annie rested on pews in the choir loft where they met to rehearse a song for the upcoming Easter service.

"Oh, Belle, tell us once more about Harrisburg and the magnificent Capitol building," Annie implored.

"Pshaw, I've already told you so many times you'll get tired of hearing about it."

Lillie smiled sweetly. "I'm more interested in hearing about the women and the latest fashions. Did you say that the bustle is much bigger in the back than the original ones."

"Oh my yes. They are really an elaborate affair, some had a long train attached that swept the ground."

"However do they sit down," Lillie asked.

Belle threw back her head and laughed. "They don't. And that's not all, girls. You should see the new hair fashions. They have abandoned the smooth center part and all the hair is swept away from the face to the crown, fully exposing ones ears."

Both girls gasped.

"The newly exposed ears are adorned with long, pendant earrings and the hair is arranged into a cascade of curls at the back . . . false if one doesn't have curls of her own . . . and falls down their back to the shoulders. It's really quite pretty, especially if you wear a flat bonnet tilted forward towards your forehead. I bought the sweetest little thing, all decorated with flowers, feathers, ribbons and lace. I intend to fix my hair in the new fashion and wear the hat to church on Sunday."

"Everyone will die of envy," Annie said with a chuckle.

"And, Annie, I saw the most gorgeous wedding dress in one of the storefronts. It was of a soft dimity fabric, pulled in tightly at the waist with a wide pink ribbon, high at the neck with full leg-of-mutton sleeves. Simple, but elegant, and perfect for you."

Annie blushed and worried the engagement ring on her finger. "I won't be needing a dress for at least another year. George wants to build us a house so we can start married life in our own home."

"How romantic," Lillie said with a deep sigh.

Belle turned to her with a mischievous grin. "And what about you, little miss. Has Alex popped the question yet?"

Lillie dropped her gaze and began to examine a hymnal laying on the seat beside her. "No, of course not. It's way too soon." Her face furrowed with despair. "Sometimes I doubt he ever will."

"Well, I notice he hasn't been keeping company with anyone else," Annie observed. "And he's of the marrying age. I'll put a little bug in his ear, first chance I get."

"Mercy don't do that. He'll think I talked to you about it."

"Maybe you and Annie could have a double wedding," Belle commented. "Wouldn't that be something . . . brother and sister getting married on the same day."

Annie laughed. "And how about a triple wedding, Belle? When are you and Jamie going to tie the knot?"

"Not for some time. I have lots I want to accomplish. Besides he's still mad at me about taking part in the march."

"What could you want to accomplish that's more important than getting married?" Lillie asked, her brows drawing together in a frown.

"I plan to write to Susan B. Anthony, who is Chairman of the National Women's Suffrage Association, to seek a position as a delegate to the national convention in Washington."

For a few moments none of them spoke. Lillie continued to caress the cover of the hymnal. In the back of the church the Pastor spoke quietly with a parishioner and in the nave candles cast long shadows on the stained glass windows. The organ began to play.

Lillie rose, clutching the hymnal to her chest. "At least you've given up that awful idea of going down south with that bureau to teach colored children."

"I guess I have. I don't want to leave Jamie." Her eyes crinkled. "He absolutely puts his foot down on leaving Littlestown to live in the south."

Lillie began to walk toward the choir loft. "We had better go through our song one more time. Easter is only two weeks away." She did not look at Belle.

* * *

The first pink of dawn was a crimson streak on the eastern horizon. Crossing the barnyard to the stables Alex paused and watched the sunrise grow and spread. A week of rain had delayed the spring plowing and he had risen early, eager to take advantage of what looked like a promising day. He waited now for the sky to lighten and listened to activity stirring in the stable beyond the barn.

The murmur of voices, the jarring rumble of barn doors sliding open, and the nicker of horses carried in the early morning stillness. Alex turned his face from the sky and struck out across the yard toward the low, white training sheds.

Jamie was in the first shed scooping soiled straw into a wheelbarrow strategically positioned at one of the stalls humming a lively tune. He did not hear Alex's approach until a horse snorted a greeting and was answered with a soft chuckle.

"Good morning," Jamie called as he picked up a pile of manure, carefully balancing it on the fork tines, and carried it to the wheelbarrow.

"Good morning." Alex reached across the half door of one of the stalls to pat the nose of a curious horse. "Looks like it's going to be a fine day. We can start plowing if the ground isn't too wet. Pa said I should come over and ask your help. He'll finish mucking the barn."

Jamie knocked manure from the pitchfork and moved the wheelbarrow a few inches to the right.

"Sure . . . soon as I get this stall finished." The wooden tines sliced through another pile of droppings.

Alex noticed he wore a secret smile and had begun humming again.

"What's up. One doesn't normally smile and sing a tune while pitching manure."

The smile broke into a wide grin. "Belle and I have set a date. We'll be getting married next month."

Alex felt as though he had been punched in the stomach.

"I'm surprised," he finally said, fighting to control the churning in his stomach. "I had the impression Belle wanted to wait. That she wanted to teach for awhile . . . get active in the suffrage movement. That sort of thing."

"Now she's given up the idea of teaching. She came back from that march in Harrisburg full of piss-an'-vinegar. She thinks that Elizabeth Cady Stanton is some kind of saint. The thing is, Alex, Mrs. Stanton is married and has the full support of her husband. Now Belle thinks it's O.K. to get married . . . if I let her attend meetings and march with no arguments and campaign for suffrage if it ever gets on the ballot."

Alex didn't trust himself to speak; he stared at Jamie.

Jamie's lips curved in a half-hearted smile. "I know, I know. It'll be hard to hold to." He grimaced. "An' I had to make another concession before she'd agreed to the marriage."

"What kind of concession?"

"That we'd omit the word 'obey' from our vows."

"Damn. You didn't agree with her did you?"

A ghost of a smile flickered across Jamie's face and then disappeared. "Yeah, I love her so much I'd promise her most anything to get her to marry me. It's just a whim of hers, it doesn't really mean anything."

"But why get married so quickly. Doesn't she want a big wedding? Her mother will be mighty upset and so will Mama."

Jamie returned his pitchfork to the soiled straw, this time with such force they almost missed their destination. "Belle was so wound up after that march in Harrisburg, feeling all womanly an' all, we almost let things get out of hand. She stopped us from going all the way, but. . . ."

"I don't want to know the details," Alex shouted.

Jamie looked startled and clamped his mouth tightly.

For a few minutes neither of them spoke. Jamie continued to fork manure into the wheelbarrow. In a nearby stall a horse snorted and a cat scooted across the dirt floor in pursuit of a stable mouse. A pigeon cooed from the rafters.

"We love one another . . . it's as simple as that. It's getting harder and harder to wait," Jamie stated. "Someday you'll understand."

"Does Pa know yet?"

"We plan to tell the family on Sunday. Belle is invited for dinner."

* * *

Katie hurried through her morning chores, anxious to get outside to work in her garden. She felt troubled and digging in the ground, getting dirt under her fingernails, was just the tonic she needed.

Something was wrong in her family and she couldn't put a voice to it. Alex and Lillie seemed close one moment and distant the next. And something was definitely out of order between him and Belle.

When the last loaf of bread had been taken from the oven, she donned an old work apron and headed outdoors. As she walked, deep in thought, toward her vegetable garden still wet with the kiss of dew, she saw what looked like a small bundle of rubbish lying on the narrow dirt path. Gingerly she picked it up and examined it. It was a wrens nest, apparently fallen from the tree, composed of bits of twine, cedar bark strips, dead leaves, chicken feathers, and what looked like pieces of cast-off snake skin. She laughed aloud—pleased with the resourcefulness of one of God's creatures. Sometimes the wonder of His direction in the lives of all living things brought such a wave of joy she thought her heart would burst. She smiled; her troubled thoughts eased. Surely if He could perform the miracles she saw around her every day, He would guide her children toward making wise decisions in their lives.

Katie had just patted the last sprinkling of soil over her carrots when she looked up to see Alex coming down the path toward her.

"Why, hello, dear. I didn't expect to see you, I thought you and your father were plowing the north field."

"The plow blade broke. Pa has taken it to Littlestown to be welded. Ellen told me you were working in the garden and I thought you might could use some help with the spading."

Katie wiped her dirt stained fingers on her apron and gave him her hand to help her get to her feet. "That's thoughtful, but it's all done. I got the peas and onions in and a few carrots and early lettuce. Come let's sit a spell on the bench. I seldom get a chance to talk to you alone, with everyone so busy and in and out all the time."

In the shade of an old oak they settled themselves on the garden bench and for a brief time spoke of ordinary things—how good it was to have Edwin home, a neighbor's upcoming wedding, Ellen's forthcoming fifteenth birthday.

But Katie could no longer hide her real thoughts. She turned her gaze on Alex's face and looked him full in the eyes.

"Son, I wish you would tell me exactly what it is with you and Belle. I couldn't help but see the agony on your face when she and Jamie announced their wedding plans."

"There is nothing Mama." He smiled but the effort to keep his composure was apparent. "Nothing."

"But you wish there was, don't you?"

"I . . ." He swallowed. "I've always been attracted to her. Ever since we were children."

"She's all wrong for you, Alex. Jamie is free enough in his nature to cope with Belle's radical ideas, but she would destroy you. Lillie Schwartz is the girl we all hoped you would marry. She's sweet natured and wants nothing more of life than to be a wife and mother."

"But it's Belle I can't get out of my mind."

"How does she feel about that. Is she interested in you?"

"At times I thought she was."

"You are walking a thin line. A lot of people could get hurt. You realize that don't you?"

Alex clasped and unclasped his fingers, shifting his weight, and tapping his foot. "Don't worry, Mama. No one suspects how I really feel except you."

"And Lillie?"

"I guess she does. She's never really mentioned it but I see it on her face sometimes." Alex sat quietly, his face steeped in misery.

Katie fell silent. What could she say that would help? She did not doubt that Lillie loved Alex and she must be hurting terribly. She didn't want to meddle in her son's affairs, couldn't make Alex return that love if he did not feel it, but she loved both of them and had to say something to help.

She reached over and took Alex's nervous hand in her own. "What you feel for Belle is infatuation, not love. Love is being in harmony with one another and accepting each other's faults. We often fail to love with all we have and all we are, often because we do not fully understand what loving means, often because we are afraid of risking ourselves. You must look deep in your soul, Alex, in search of your answers. God's shoulders are broad. Give your troubled mind to him and ask for guidance. You will be surprised at what He has to say."

Just then lightening flashed across the sky. Startled they both looked to see dark clouds rolling in from the west. "Mercy," Katie said, "we had better run for the house if we don't want to get wet."

She took Alex's hand and they ran across the lawn, as they had done when he was a child.

CHAPTER 6

Alex stood stone-faced and miserable beside his brother on a vibrant morning early in June. For hours, family and close friends had been gathering in the Rebert parlor for Belle's marriage to Jamie McPherson.

Guests rustled and murmured among garlands of dogwood blossoms and ivy, anxious for the wedding march to begin. A sudden hush quieted the gathering as the folding doors opened, and the bridal party could be seen descending the stairs to the heavy strains of the wedding march.

The bride swept gracefully down the circular staircase on Edward's arm. Alex swallowed a lump in his throat. She was ravishing. Reddish-gold hair, fixed in an aureole of curls, was gathered into a heavy mass that lay softly on her shoulders. She wore a creamy satin gown, a crown of apple blossoms adorned her head, and delicate netting veiled her face. Jamie stood tall waiting for her, handsome and proud and smiling.

The wedding march ended as Alex's father handed her to Jamie and the young couple faced the minister. Alex was mesmerized by Belle's beauty. He felt his father watching him, a puzzled look on his face.

Edward's glance shifted from Alex to Belle and back again. Then he looked quickly away, his eyes dark with pain and understanding.

The ceremony, conducted in high German, droned on and on. *Would it never end*, Alex thought in desperation. He glanced sideways at the radiant bride. His gut hurt and he felt the pressure of his nails biting into the palms of his hands. He had to relax before someone noticed his misery—he suspected Pa already had.

He would simply have to put all the hidden hope out of his mind. Belle belonged to his brother now.

Thank heavens it was finally over. Belle and Jamie were surrounded by friends and family, laughing, kissing, and shaking hands. Alex, with downcast eyes, gave the bride a chaste kiss on the cheek and hurried outside to fasten streamers and bells to the waiting carriage. His stomach churned and his hands trembled. Please, dear God, he prayed silently, let me get through this day without making a fool of myself.

The wedding party moved to the lawn and the guests began to move along tables laden with food. Alex, himself, had shot and dressed the wild turkey which had been broiled and basted with honey. Roast venison, aged in the springhouse and marinated in onions, thyme, and cloves, revolved slowly on a spit over a pit of banked coals. Huge pots of boiled potatoes with sweet onions simmered over the fire and great bowls of red beet eggs and coleslaw sat at the end of the table. Alex filled his plate and stood looking at it with revulsion; he'd never get food past the knot in his stomach.

Suddenly, a gentle hand touched his arm and he looked down into the small upturned face of Lillie, a smile curving her mouth and dimpling her cheek.

"Belle made her own gown, isn't it gorgeous?" Lillie chattered, filling in all the details, apparently oblivious of his lack of enthusiasm. Her little hands were never still as she talked; she waved them in the air like a maestro conducting a symphony, illustrating every point, her eyes sparking with enthusiasm.

Alex felt his tension melt away at Lillie's infectious gaiety. Her nose had a slight tilt—funny he hadn't noticed that before. She tipped her head back to look at him, soft brown hair dusting her smiling face. Alex knew her laughter was good for him. There wasn't a pretentious bone in her body; she was simple and sweet, everything he should be looking for. The accident had left her with a light limp and he still felt a sense of responsibility for that. They were perfectly suited for one another; everyone told him so. And Mama was crazy about her. Time he stopped mooning over Belle and started thinking of a wife and family of his own.

He had no other choice.

Lillie looked up at him, a smile not quite reaching her china blue eyes. "My, my, Alex Rebert, you're as grim as a rain cloud in the sunshine," she teased. "Surely a little laughter is called for on such a happy occasion."

Alex dug his fork into a pile of stuffing and searched for a suitable answer. He gave Lillie a weak smile. "Guess I've been thinking about how much I'll miss Jamie."

"But they'll be living at your home, won't they? I thought he was going to continue working at the stables and race your father's trotters."

"Yeah, but things change after a fellow gets married. It won't be the same between us anymore, and we've always been close."

"Well, I think you're lucky. Look at how happy Jamie is and Belle's such a fun-loving person. She'll be good for all of you. Especially you—old sober puss!"

Alex forced a laugh and looked away quickly. He planned to talk to Pa about moving out the first chance he got. Living in the same house with the newlyweds was unthinkable.

Lillie tilted her head to look up at him. Her face softened. "It's been hard for you, hasn't it, seeing her marry Jamie?"

"Yes." Alex's voice was quiet.

A fiddle struck up a tune and children began to dance. Alex grabbed a mug of cider from the table and took Lillie's hand. "I don't want to talk about it. Let's join the festivities. You're right. I am an old sober-puss." He slipped an arm around her shoulders and pulled her close to his side. She was sweet, but something told him she had far more fire than she portrayed.

The afternoon passed in a blur of hard cider and music. Although Lillie watched him with troubled eyes she said nothing about his alcohol induced gaiety. Dusk was beginning to fall when the front door of the house burst open and Belle and Jamie hurried toward the carriage amid shrieks of laughter and a hail of rice. The bride turned with a smile, looked carefully into the crowd, and threw her bouquet high in the air.

It fell into Lillie's reaching arms.

* * *

1876 was an election year and neither of the major candidates appealed to Alex. The country stagnated in extreme economic distress, deep within the clutches of what the papers still referred to as the Panic of '73. Four parties fielded candidates in the hotly contested election—the Prohibitionist, the Greenbacks, the Republicans, and the Democrats. Alex felt sorely tempted to support the Prohibition Party, as his father was doing.

Bad as the economic situation was, however, spirits rose as July approached and everyone prepared to celebrate the one-hundredth anniversary of the Declaration of Independence. On the Fourth of July a gigantic picnic was held and downtown Littlestown was hung with swinging banners; the Littlestown Coronet Band marched to brassy renditions of "Hail Columbia"; a long winded speech was given by Judge Henry, and old men marched proudly in their 1812 uniforms followed by the younger strutting veterans of the Civil War.

In the humid dusk, Alex and Lillie strolled along Baltimore Street toward Ocker's Race Track where stands had been set up to serve ice cream and cold drinks.

There, beside the serenity of a meandering creek, Lillie spread a blanket and she and Alex settled down to wait for the fireworks. Sweeping limbs of towering oaks created a leafy canopy, adding a shady coolness to the light breeze that flirted with the loose folds of Lillie's skirt, blowing softly against the material. Fine hair fluttered against her cheeks, happiness transformed her. Her eyes danced and her mouth smiled with sweet, fragile elation. Alex felt a lump in his throat as he looked at her. Her only imperfection was the slight limp she would probably have for the rest of her life. Time and again the scene with the mountain lion replayed itself in Alex's mind. The fleeing deer, the attacking lion, the crack of the rifle, the rearing horse, and the skidding sleigh. Did he do the right thing in trying to kill the animal—did he have a choice? And did he make the right choice? He would always feel responsible for what happened and for this sweet girl who looked at him with adoration. He mustn't hurt Lillie. She deserved better than that. He must let go of his thwarted love for Belle.

Suddenly, the night exploded with a glorious display of fireworks: roman candles, illuminated pinwheels, firecrackers, and hand held sparklers. Lillie rested her head against Alex's shoulder. He felt bloated with contentment and well-being and pulled her closer. Why didn't he just propose and put an end to his indecision!

And then all of a sudden, Charlie plopped down beside him.

"Ya know, Jamie and Belle will be home from their honeymoon soon," he said with a snicker. "I can't wait to hear all about the big goings on in Philadelphia that they're seeing and doing." Alex felt his stomach lurch.

* * *

" . . . Pa, I know I promised to stay," Alex said contritely several weeks later, "but you have Edwin to run the mill. I really want to move on," he continued, "and Mr. Martin offered me a good job at the Lancaster stock yards. The pay's good and Lancaster is just bursting with activity and chances for a fellow willing to work hard."

"And what will I tell your mother? It'll break her heart if one of her children leaves home before they're married."

"Things are changing, Pa. Trains run between Lancaster and Littlestown on a regular schedule. I wouldn't be out of touch."

His father sighed. "I think I know the real reason you want to leave, son; I saw your torment at Jamie's wedding."

Alex looked at the floor. "It's for the best, Pa. I can't be happy here."

"Well, I've a better idea than you going all the way to Lancaster. I've had my eye on a nice farm belonging to the Widow Sterner over on the Hanover Pike. With business increasing here at the mill we need more acreage in wheat and rye and I've been thinking of moving the horses to another pasture for some time now. What would you think of taking over the management of that farm if I can strike a deal with Mrs. Sterner?"

"Would I be able to live there?"

Edward chuckled. "The house is far too big for a single fellow—folks refer to it as the 'Mansion House.' It has four, maybe five bedrooms. But I believe there's a small tenant house on the hill behind the main house that would be just perfect for a young bachelor. Unless, that is, you're planning to give in to the wiles of that pretty little Lillie Schwartz."

Alex felt his face grow warm. Since Jamie's wedding he had been spending all his spare time with Lillie. He took her for walks, went berrying, communed at church socials, and visited the covered bridge every chance he got. And that was getting harder and harder to handle. He was over twenty-one now—a man with a man's urges. All too often he woke in a sweat, his stomach a sticky mess.

"I guess I could do worse than Lillie," he admitted. "I'm twenty-one. Time to be thinking of raising a family. And your offer to manage the Sterner farm is mighty appealing. If I were married, the Mansion House wouldn't be too big to handle."

"That wasn't quite the response I had been hoping for, but it will do." Papa wrinkled his forehead and locked eyes with Alex. "I do hope love enters into the equation somewhere, son." Alex looked at his father and smiled, "Oh, it does, it really does."

"Then I'll see the Widow Sterner before the week is out."

* * *

August, hot and hazy, faded into September—one of the busiest months on the farm for Alex. Rowan, the most tender of all the hay, was cut and stowed away in the barn, mounds of potatoes filled the fields waiting to be picked; and apples waited their trip to the cider press. There was certainly no time left for courting and weeks passed before he was able to call on Lillie.

Finally, one soft day early in October he saddled Princess Rose for himself, and a colt named Decker for Lillie, and together they headed toward the mountains. The air was as crisp as apple wine, and the woods burned with color; a tulip tree wore a bower of pure gold, hickories had turned a rich ocher, the sour gum were crimson, and the elms lemon yellow.

They rode across fields strewn with wigwam corn shocks and mounds of orange pumpkins, the wind blowing their hair and reddening their cheeks, until they reached the edge of the South Mountain range.

There they reined in, stirrup to stirrup, silenced by the palette of color rising before them in the shadowed red of mid-afternoon.

"Oh, Alex, look ahead. It's like an artist splashed his paints across the landscape with no thought to keeping order among the colors."

Alex felt a surge of emotion and he fought to keep Lillie from seeing the weakness on his face. He always reacted to the beauty of the land and something as simple as a golden sunset could move him almost to tears. To cover his emotions he gave her a flip answer, "A drunken artist, I must say. No hue was too gaudy for him."

"Let's eat our lunch here—where we can look at the whole painting," she said.

"I see a small pond. We'll head for it."

Lillie nodded her approval and they rode toward a farm pond, sun-drenched and sparkling, both horses cantering easily. Alex was pleased that Lillie did not ride side-saddle as so many silly girls insisted on doing, but instead rode naturally, erect and easy as any man.

While Alex tethered their horses she spread a red and white checkered tablecloth beneath the lone willow tree spreading feathery branches over the edge of the water and unpacked their lunch—thick ham sandwiches on homemade potato buns, sweet pickles, and squares of spicy gingerbread.

Alex leaned his back against the tree and watched Lillie place everything neatly on the cloth. She reminded him of his mother—inwardly serene, wearing a look of sweetness, always comfortable with her role of homemaker.

They ate quietly, their eyes seldom straying from the majestic mountains looming before them. Finally, his hunger assuaged, Alex wiped his mouth and stretched out on the grass. Lillie cleaned up the wrappings and folded the cloth into a tight square. Her hair was plaited into a single thick braid that reached almost to her waist and he reached over and gave it a playful tug. "I like your hair that way," he said.

"You don't think it makes me look like a child?"

"Of course not. I'd never think of you as a child. You are very much a woman."

She smiled at him. It always fascinated Alex to see her eyes turn color with her mood; dark blue when she was angry, a softer blue when she was happy. Today they were the color of pale corabells. He studied her gravely for a moment before he spoke. "The farm has been very demanding, but I've missed you in the short time we've been apart."

"It was not a short time," she contradicted him." It was three weeks and it seemed like an eternity."

She moved toward him and he put up a hand to pull her down to his side. The afternoon passed in comfortable silence as Alex took a short nap and Lillie rested against his shoulder.

He stirred, finally, and rubbed his fist across his eyes. "Not very mannerly of me, going to sleep like that," he said with a deep yawn.

"I'm glad you did . . . glad you feel comfortable with me." She smoothed her skirt and brushed a few strands of hair back from her face. Overhead, a V-formation of wild geese honked their way south.

"The summer has gone so quickly," she said, wistfully, reaching down to brush a crumb from her skirt.

For the next hour they talked of ordinary things: the fair, mutual friends, an upcoming husking bee. Then silence, comfortable and intimate. Alex's shoulders touched hers and he took her hand and held it to his lips. He began to hum.

"Sing to me, Alex. I love your voice."

He beamed at her. Mama always said too much pride was a sin, but he was proud of his voice. Softly he began the words of a new Irish ballad, "I'll Take You Home Again, Kathleen." Lillie joined him in the chorus.

Alex felt a glow of warmth and comfort. He pondered the difference between the two girls he was attracted to. Lillie was the many shades of spring: green, pale, soft, and restful, fragile, reaching out, unfurling slowly. Belle was the wild, violent shades of the autumn-red surrounding them. Lillie was far more suited to his nature and he knew it.

"You're easy to talk to," he said. "I'm seldom comfortable sharing my thoughts and feelings. It isn't my nature to make small talk."

"I'm glad you feel free to talk with me. I was so shy with you when we first met I was afraid we'd never be able to hold a conversation."

The sky turned the blue-gray of nearing dusk and he began to feel the intimacy, the bond of familiarity, they had grown to share. Quite simply, he realized with a jolt, he had fallen in love with her.

As he and Lillie sat close together he watched the wind tug at her hair, loosening a few strands that fluttered against her soft cheek. Suddenly, he needed to feel her body against his and he fidgeted, fighting the maddening impulse.

She smiled at him. Her eyes had changed color again. The smile lightened them to a pale blue and he was unnerved by the love he saw reflected there. He faltered, and without saying another word, leaned forward and kissed her. His lips were demanding, hers like a whisper. Then gradually Lillie's lips became firmer, warmer, bolder. He could feel her heart pound against his.

"Lillie, I want you," he said huskily against her hair. "I want you to be my wife."

She drew back, startled. Her eyes searched his, questioning, unsure. Her hands fluttered, then her face flushed with happiness. "You're sure, Alex?"

"I'm sure."

CHAPTER 7

On a chilly Tuesday morning in mid-November, when the first white frost lay heavily on the fields, Lillie and Alex took their marriage vows at their beloved Christ Church.

They honeymooned in Virginia and upon their return moved into a stately stone farmhouse, known as White Hall, left to Lillie in her grandfather Weikert's will.

She was delighted with White Hall—but she suspected Alex was a trifle reluctant to accept such largess from her family and was more than a little disappointed they would not be living in the Mansion House on the Hanover Pike. But Papa Edward still hadn't struck a deal with the Widow Sterner for the purchase of the farm Alex coveted.

And so it was at White Hall that Alex and Lily began married life.

* * *

Christmas found them at Rebert's Choice for the traditional family dinner of chicken, stuffing, candied sweet potatoes, and lima beans. All of Alex's brothers and sisters were there: Emma with her beau, Charles Duttera; Edwin with his sweetheart, Sissy Martin; Ella, Charlie, John, the soon-to-be married Annie and her George Geiselman and, of course, Jamie and Belle.

Lillie tried to be festive, but she was terribly disappointed. This morning she'd again had to fasten a linen pad inside her bloomers. How she had hoped to bring the news of another grandchild to Papa Edward and Mother Katie at the dinner table. She smoothed the skirt of her new dress, a beautiful soft wool of lavender and gray, and glanced longingly at the hand-carved cradle Mother Katie kept in the corner of the dining room, awaiting the birth of Belle's baby. Lillie experienced a guilty twinge of jealousy, but only for a second. She was happy for Belle.

"Thank heavens Emma and Ella are still too young to get married. I don't think I'd survive another wedding this winter," Katie said, her rich laughter resounding around the table.

"Well, just wait 'til all the babies start to arrive. I'll probably have to go into the cradle making business," Edward said, winking at Alex.

Lillie's fingers tightened on her fork. She felt all eyes turn on her, speculating.

"Pass the stuffing, please," eight year old John said, interested only in his half-empty plate.

"I think we should start everything around again. I see a lot of empty plates," Katie said, casting Lillie an understanding glance.

Alex reached under the table and squeezed her hand.

"I heard a funny story the other day," Jamie said, with a chuckle, searching out his father's face. "You know President Grant is a great lover of horseflesh—just like you, Papa. Well, he has this pacer he calls Jeff Davis and he likes to race his carriage around Washington. Last week he was whirling along M Street, and a Negro policeman, seeing only someone going too fast, ran out into the road, grabbed the horse's bridle, and was dragged half a block before he was able to stop. He saw it was the President of the United States and he apologized all over the place, but that Ulysses S. Grant just smiled and said, 'Officer, do your duty.' So the embarrassed policeman took the President down to the station, charged him with speeding, and now we have a President with a police record."

Alex looked at his brother and laughed. "Seems to me most of the politicians in Washington should be behind bars. Look at what goes on in New York City among those Tammany Hall crooks. President Grant makes no move at all to lock them up. Seems to me the whole dang country is corrupt and immoral."

Edward made a small indentation in his mashed potatoes and filled it with a puddle of brown-butter gravy. "The truth is, Alex, as long as small businessmen look to politicians for a piece of the pie you'll never stop political corruption." After a thoughtful pause, he went on, "When we buy what they have to sell, and then try to cover the rotten stench by occasionally rising up at the polls against the politicians—not the system—then by gum the symbol of the Democratic Party is rightly that of an ass."

"Edward!" Katie admonished, struggling to hide a smile.

Jamie jumped in. "Just the other day I was reading an interesting editorial in the paper about that; it said that post-war periods are always periods of low public morals. Because we're prosperous we look the other way when we hear about corruption. Do you find that so, Papa?"

Edward nodded his head. "Well, I for one, am glad Grant will be out of office. I think he is basically a good man, with good intentions, but he seems to have a fatal inability to choose his officials. The way I see it, he lets a mistaken sense of loyalty to his friends interfere with sound judgement."

The women had been quiet during the political talk, passing plates and taking care of the children, but Belle followed the conversation avidly. Unable to keep quiet any longer she looked sharply at Edward. "Jamie told me you support the Prohibition Party. Is that true?"

"I did for awhile." He looked at Belle with an involuntary smile. "But, like most third parties, it attracted every possible sort of reformer and crank. It offered the best platform, though—it not only prohibited the making and sale of alcohol, but proposed to reduce railroad rates for the farmer. And, more importantly, the Prohibitionist's want to enforce a strict observance of Sunday, and continue the use of bibles in public schools. In the end, though, I remained true to the Republicans and voted for Hayes."

"You left out the most important part," Belle said with a chuckle and a merry gleam in her eye. "I believe the Prohibitionists were strongly in favor of women suffrage."

"Right you are, my dear. An important part of their platform I neglected to mention."

"Women will never get the vote," Jamie said with a wave of his hand.

Belle flushed. "Tell that to Victoria Woodhull. She ran for President in '72 and she surely believed that women would someday have the right to vote."

Lillie looked at her with admiration. Belle was so bold and forthright with her opinions. Despite her marriage, she refused to let her mind dwell only on babies and recipes.

Jamie frowned and quickly changed the subject. "Grant was never cut out to be a President. He was a war hero and Americans seem to like war heroes. I think President Hayes will keep his promise to end Reconstruction and withdraw Federal troops from the South. We must give the land back to the people who owned it before the Civil War. This bitterness between North and South has gone on too long."

George Geiselman shook his head in disagreement. "I still think Thaddeus Stevens has the right idea. He wants to divide the southern plantations into forty acre farms and sell 'em to the former slaves for ten dollar an acre. It would serve those arrogant southern gentlemen right if they lost all their land."

"And who'd give the slaves the ten dollars? The Government?" Jamie asked.

"That's a better idea than the one ole Seward had when he bought millions of Alaskan snow and ice from Russia for two cents an acre."

"Politicians have the damnest ideas," Alex interjected.

"But the country is at peace," his mother said emphatically. "And don't swear, Alex."

Charles Duttera, who had been silent until now, finally spoke out. "I don't know as how we're at peace. I still hear they's fightin' with the Indians out in the West." He looked at Edward. "Emma tells me you wanted to go to Texas and fight the Mexicans when you were young, Mr. Rebert. That sounds exciting. What made you change your mind?"

Edward turned his vivid blue eyes on Emma's beau. "There was a debt of friendship I chose to pay, which kept me home, and then I met my beautiful Katie and I no longer felt the need to look elsewhere for excitement." He and Katie regarded each with open fondness.

Silver clattered on plates and the platter of turkey was passed around again. Charles gave a jerky laugh and continued his topic of conversation. "Guess it was pretty awful out in Montana this past summer. The Sioux Indians surrounded a troop of over two hundred federal cavalrymen, under General George Custer, and, mind you, they scalped every last soldier. The story is that after the battle old Chief Rain-in-the-Face cut out Captain Tom Custer's heart and ate it."

John had stopped eating and was staring at Charles in open-eyed wonder, his mouth still full.

"I don't care for war tales or politics at the dinner table," Katie said firmly. "You men can discuss those things in the parlor after dinner. Now, pass the chicken one more time, and, Belle, why don't you tell us about your plans for the new house."

Lillie noticed Alex watching the animated Belle as she launched into a funny story about drawing a complete set of plans for her dream house without a stairway to the second floor. There was an odd look on Alex's face and it stirred a twinge of uneasiness. Lillie's stomach tightened as she watched him. She shook her head and looked away—she was being a silly goose. She had no reason to doubt Alex's love, and Belle was her closest friend. Soon, she was certain, she and Alex would have their first baby and be a real family. Next year they would have a little one in that cradle under the window and Alex would be as devoted a father as he was a husband.

* * *

"I will not give up my membership in the Women's Suffrage Association," Belle raged. She glared at Jamie and threw her dishrag into the sink with a vigorous slap. "Just because I've become your wife does not mean I plan to withdraw from the causes I believe in."

"You're about to become a mother and your place is in the home, not with a bunch of radical biddies," Jamie retorted, his face flushed with indignation.

"Don't you tell me what I can or cannot do!"

"You're my wife."

"So?"

"So, that gives me the right."

"Never! Never Jamie! I'm a woman, not a piece of property." Belle stuck her chin out defiantly. "Things have changed in this country, in case you haven't heard. They began to change during the war," she went on, using words she heard so often at meetings, "when women had to work to keep their families alive through years of deprivation, when they were compelled to become equals, become more self-reliant and resourceful. You can't move the clock back. I won't return to the subservient life of the fifties," she finished with a wave of her hand.

"I'm in favor of equal rights, but not woman suffrage."

"Equal rights! What about the condition of the poor women in our northern states who work in the mills twelve hours a day for paltry wages and under deplorable conditions? They can expect little, if anything, until they have the ballot," she said, nose haughtily in the air.

"New England mill workers are not your concern," Jamie answered.

"All women are my concern. And after this child is born I intend to search for a job outside of this house."

Jamie's face grew red. "This is our home."

"Your home—it is mine, not by choice, but by necessity, to share with the entire Rebert family." Jamie stared at her, a stricken look on his face. "You know," she said, contritely, "how much I want our own home. Perhaps if I found a teaching job somewhere we could build sooner."

"For heavens sake, Belle, I'm still young. I must establish myself in the mill before we can ever think of building a home. Why, most men don't even marry until they are twenty-five or twenty-six."

"Alex is only twenty-one and already he owns two farms."

"Then maybe you should have married him."

"Maybe I should have!"

The veins in Jamie's neck stood out in vivid ridges as he clenched his fist. "I don't want to hear any more on this subject."

He stalked toward the front door and slammed it closed behind him.

Belle looked after him thoughtfully. She had never seen Jamie so angry. Her mouth crimped in annoyance. Let him fume. The next meeting of her women's group was next Tuesday and she would be there.

* * *

To her dismay, Lillie's embrace of motherhood wasn't to be next year, or the year after, or the year after that.

It had never occurred to Lillie that conceiving might be a problem, and at first she didn't worry. Alex made tender jokes about the child they were surely creating with all their love making, and in spite of her distaste for the act itself, in her eagerness for a baby she never denied him. Each month she prayed not to see the tell-tale sign, but each month she hated the red stains appearing on her white bloomers.

Alex stopped making jokes and approached her with renewed vigor and a determined look on his face. And still she didn't conceive.

She often lay awake, long after their bedtime ritual, vaguely aware of a feeling of unfulfillment. She wished she enjoyed it more. Alex seemed perfectly content with their lovemaking, and Mama assured her that sex, while expected, didn't have to be enjoyed. She wondered.

To fill the emptiness Lillie cooked and cleaned. White Hall reeked of soap and lemon oil, and Alex gained five pounds. Her sewing machine sang from morning 'til night as she made curtains for the windows and colorful pillows for all the chairs. Red geraniums in clay pots adorned every windowsill.

But sometimes when she observed mother's holding their babies to their breasts she felt an unwelcome anger. Was her failure to conceive Alex's fault? She knew he still held himself responsible for the accident that had crippled her pelvic bone. The thought disturbed her. Is that why he married me, she suddenly wondered. Was it guilt and pity not just that Belle was unavailable? She bit her lip ashamed of such thoughts and attacked her housework with renewed vigor.

On a morning, early in December, she hefted a heavy crockery bowl onto the counter to mix dough for molasses cookies. She began to beat the dough with such vigor the bowl almost ricocheted off the table, her lips pursed with suppressed fury. Why had God not answered her prayers? Why was He denying her the one thing she wanted most in the world—a child to love?

Mama said she needed more faith. More faith? She had prayed until her knees were raw, and still He had not answered.

Her brows wrinkled in vexation. Belle was once more pregnant, and urged Lillie to try Lydia Pinkham's commercial potion that guaranteed a "baby in every bottle." Yes, she vowed, pausing to silently stare at the bowl in front of her, I'll go to town today for a bottle of the potion. And I'll go to the herb lady in the village and ask for a new pow-wow potion. One of them will surely work—work where prayer has failed.

After putting the cookies to cool on her dough-tray, she donned a heavy woolen cloak and headed across the farmyard toward the barn. The sky was leaden, promising snow, and a sickly sun hung low on the horizon. Still, she loved this time of the year best of all. Winter: when she and Alex could go sledding on the deep crusty snow, when birds made beautiful lacy tracks around the feeder, and cloven hoof prints marked the visit of deer to the orchard. She especially loved it when the snow came quietly in the night and she and Alex woke in their warm feather ticks to a changed world. She could tell instantly. The light in the bedroom was always different when there was snow outside.

She liked the smell of the barn in winter and the sound of the farm animals as they moved restlessly in their stalls, although her hens seemed to go on strike when the first snow fell. They didn't lay much during the winter, but she really didn't blame them for not wanting to sit on a cold nest.

She thought of the seasons ahead. Winter set the scene for spring, when her bulbs began to poke their heads through scattered patches of snow. It was like greeting old friends. Then summer, with her garden spilling over with fresh produce, and raspberries, blueberries, and thimbleberries hanging heavy on the vine, especially strawberries, freshly picked and warmed by the sun for "eating, just so." Autumn meant canning, planting fall bulbs, and listening, with a strange thrill, to the call of Canada geese as they flew overhead on their way south. But winter . . . ah, winter meant Christmas and, as she trudged along, she visualized a group of children laughing with glee as they opened their gifts—her children. A family . . . their family. Oh, if only!

Alex attacked marriage with the same seriousness and vigor that he applied to his work. He bought another farm, which he rented for the share and began to buy more farm land with every spare dollar he could scrape together. He seemed to have a passion for land and Jamie joked that before Alex reached forty he would own half of Adams County. The farms prospered, and Alex rode his stone wall boundaries with pride. He purchased additional beef cattle, a herd of Ayrshire and Guernsey milk cows, a sty of fat hogs, and three more of his beloved trotting horses.

Together he and Lillie attended every barn raising and church social, but neither denied that their lives were empty without children. And the cradle under the window in the Rebert dining room at Christmas held not their baby, but the growing family of Jamie & Belle.

Belle laughingly placed her latest baby, Elizabeth, on Lillie's bed, proclaiming that according to Dutch tradition Lillie would now "get pregnant the next time Alex hung his pants on the bedpost." She had other advice, too—an herbal tea to relax, and a powerful pow-wow: a fertility potion to wear around her neck so that it rested on her breasts. But nothing worked. Lillie was twenty-two now and her barrenness obsessed her. The approach of her period became a time of anxiety with terrible depression upon its arrival. She dreaded the social gatherings where the women discussed nothing but their quilting patterns, recipes, and babies. Always babies, babies, babies. Could they talk of nothing else?

On a bitter cold day, just before the empty Christmas she had grown to dread, she was again forced to shake her head no to an anxious Alex.

"I think I'll ride over to the grist mill and visit Edwin," he said, trying to hide the disappointment from his voice.

"Bring home an extra sack of flour. I want to bake some gingerbread men."

"Who for?" Alex asked bitterly as he slammed the kitchen door.

Half an hour later, Alex rode from the stables on Princess Rose and turned onto an old wagon road that passed over Samuel Weikert's south pasture. For a time he followed Little Conewago Creek, savoring the beauty of the land. Princess pranced and snorted in the frosty air, impatient with the slow pace. So, after fording the creek, Alex let the stallion break into a trot. Smoke curled from the center chimney of his former home, and he halted his horse beside the kitchen door, anticipating a quiet talk with Mama and Belle. But it was soon obvious the women were too engrossed in their Friday baking to pay him much mind, still he couldn't resist slathering a slab of warm bread with schmierkase and apple butter before leaving the cozy kitchen and moseying down to the grist mill.

The mill was dim and dusty, vibrating with sound as the ponderous water wheel turned, splashing water into the tail-race, turning the drive shaft and grindstones. It smelled of dried corn, moldy wood, and dust causing Alex to stifle a sneeze as he stood silently watching Papa and Edwin dump heavy sacks of corn into the hoppers to be ground into grits. Papa had equipped the mill with the best millstones available, French buhr from Alsace Lorraine, weighing more than a ton each. The grinding surfaces of the new stones were faced with a number of sloping radial grooves which became shallower as they approached the outer edge and when the top stone rotated above the stationary bottom stone, the grooves crossed in a scissor-like fashion to provide the necessary grinding action. Kernels of golden corn, dropping from the hopper through a hole in the upper stone, were cracked near the center and the floury part of the kernels were reduced to a fine powder as they were pushed to the outer edge of the burr stone. Rebert flour was known for its fine texture and their mill was one of the busiest in the valley.

In a far corner of the mill a group of farmers clustered around a glowing pot-bellied stove discussing politics and spinning yarns. Alex wasn't in the mood for either so, when he could catch Edwin's eye, he motioned that he wanted to talk.

Edwin nodded his understanding. "The gears are going dry. Soon as I get some hog fat on 'em I'll join you," he yelled, raising his voice loud enough to be heard over the creak and groan of the grindstones.

Alex jumped in to help him and, when finished, they walked to a far corner, away from the noisy belts and pulleys and creaking wooden cogs, to squat on sacks of grain.

Edwin's hair and eyebrows and eyelashes were frosted white with corn dust and he shook his head vigorously to free it of the gray dust, wiping greasy hands on stained overalls.

"Don't know why you like this job so much," Alex said with knotted brows and pursed lips. "The noise and dust get to me."

"I like working with Papa and I like the company of the farmers who come to buy. Besides, I like the smell. It's like bread baking all the time." Edwin looked at his brother thoughtfully. "Sissy and I plan to marry soon. Did Papa tell you I'm leaving after the wedding?"

Alex's mouth dropped open. "Leaving! What ever for?"

"We're going to live in Indiana. You know Sissy is Mennonite and most of her family have settled near Goshen. Her brother has offered me a full partnership in his feed mill."

"But . . . we always thought you would take over the mill here. This is your home."

Edwin shook his head. "You're the oldest. Rebert's Choice will be yours someday. With Jamie and Belle already living here I doubt the house big enough for three families."

"But Lillie and I live at White Hall."

"That may change someday. Besides, Sissy wants to go. She misses her family and she thinks Indiana offers more opportunity."

"Boy, what with you leaving and Emma and Charles getting married next month, Rebert's Choice won't be the same."

"A new generation is taking over, Alex. Charlie and John are both old enough to work in the mill once I leave. Now enough about me. What is it you wanted to talk about? Any news from Lillie yet?"

"No, an' I . . . I guess it won't be this month either." He felt the heat rise in his face, and looked away from the sympathy in his brother's eyes. "Do you think it could be my fault, Edwin? Do you think it has anything to do with the accident I caused, breaking her pelvic bone?"

"I doubt that. Maybe you're both trying too hard."

"I don't know what it is. Maybe if Lillie enjoyed our lovemaking more, it would make a difference. She's willing enough, she wants a baby bad. She doesn't complain, but I think it still hurts her. I try to be quick."

"Really, Alex, I don't think Lillie's lack of enthusiasm matters much." Edwin hesitated. "It might hurt her less if you took more time with her. Before hand, that is."

Alex felt his face flush. "Don't tell me how to make love to my wife, Edwin."

"I didn't mean to be personal, but you did ask my advice. Honestly, it's just a matter of old Mother Nature getting things together at the right time. It'll happen, Alex. I'm sure it will. Rebert men have all had big families. You will too!"

"It isn't only that I want a baby; children are necessary to farm life, Edwin. Sons are proof of one's manhood, not only to carry on the family name, but as a symbol of family strength and permanence."

"You sound more like a professor than a lover. Relax, big brother!"

Alex glowered, then a slow smile pulled at his lips. "Guess that sounded a little serious but I've spent so much time thinking about it I could write a sermon on the subject. When Lillie told me the sorry news this morning I felt so dang worthless I went storming out of the house." He sighed. "Thanks for listening, I needed a sounding board. Guess I'll just keep on praying."

"And other things," Edwin said with a wicked grin.

Alex laughed. "I feel better already. I think I'll go up to the house, see the new baby and," he added licking his lips, "sample some of those cinnamon buns the women were baking."

"Do that. Mama and Belle are always glad to see you."

* * *

February blew in with a vengeance with drifted roads and snow banks six feet high. Lillie spent a gray, dismal Wednesday carrying the final Christmas decorations up to the garret for storage until next year. She couldn't understand why she felt so tired. All she really wanted to do was curl up by the fire for a nap and that wasn't a bit like her.

The realization hit her as she wrapped the last tree ornament in soft cotton. She flew to the Almanac and looked at the date. "Oh, merciful God," she whispered. "Please be true." Beads of perspiration gathered on her upper lip as she held the almanac with a shaking hand. She was two weeks late.

That night she was glad when Alex gave her a hasty kiss and rolled over without bothering her. She was almost afraid his penetration might bring on the hated show of blood, and her dream would be over. Just for tonight she wanted to hold the idea close, like a warm puppy, turning it over and over in her mind.

Carefully she placed her hand on her flat stomach and moved it in a gentle circle. "Oh, God, let it be," she prayed. "I love Alex so much, and I know how much he wants a baby."

She awoke long before the dawn of day, and after using the cold chamber pot she checked herself again. Still no signs of blood. She remembered a test for pregnancy Belle had told her about. As soon as Alex left for the barn she would try it.

She padded over to the window and saw a thin sprinkling of snow on the sill. It was still too early to get up, so she crawled back into bed and curled up to the comfort of Alex's warm back. A wood thrush trilled in the early dawn. She lay quietly listening to its song and drawing deep breaths of the fresh cold air. Light spread across the morning sky and filtered through her window bringing a warm glow to the deep rose patches in her grandmother's quilt folded neatly on the chest at the foot of their bed. Just one more minute of this lovely peace, she thought, before I get up to what could be one of the most momentous days of my life.

The mantle clock showed seven o'clock. Gently she touched Alex's shoulder and urged him awake. He stirred sleepily, cupping his warm body to hers and drawing her close. "Burr, it's cold." "I believe it snowed last night," she answered, wiggling away to swing her bare legs over the side of the bed.

Alex rose and quickly donned heavy trousers and a woolen shirt. "The snow will make good tracking. I'll go get us a mess of rabbits for supper."

When the breakfast dishes were finally cleared and Alex left to go hunting, Lillie hurried to her root cellar beneath the kitchen. With nervous fingers she took a jar of dried dandelion petals from a dusty shelf under the steps, then carried it carefully to the upstairs bedroom. Barely able to contain her mounting excitement, she poured a fresh sample of her urine from the china chamber pot into a small bowl. Her fingers trembled as she added the dandelion, crumbling it into the urine.

    Tears sprang to her eyes as she watched the petals turn bright red and her cry of joy filled the empty room.

CHAPTER 8

The remainder of the winter sped by; the "onion" snow came and went; freshly plowed fields stood open to the April sky; cardinals whistled, and every bird on the farm flew with bits of straw and string in their tiny beaks, preparing nests for anticipated families.

Lillie woke one morning impatient to be outdoors, hungry for the taste of fresh greens. She wrapped a shawl about her shoulders, took her little tin pail and a sharp paring knife, and headed for the south pasture in search of young dandelion.

For over an hour she scurried about, digging only the youngest plants not yet in bud, shaking the rich soil from their roots and placing them in her pail.

Her back began to hurt and she stretched, placing her hand on her stomach, feeling her baby give a vigorous kick. She shivered with pleasure, then glanced heavenward at converging black clouds. It would not do to get wet. Swinging her pail by its wire bail, she hurried across the meadow toward home.

Sleep that night would not come to Lillie, and she lay listening to the night sounds outside her open window. Locust-like cicadas chirped in steady unison, filling the air with a constant vibration, their legs moving together like musical instruments issuing a melody of love. What were they saying to one another, she wondered?

Her body relaxed, and she felt herself drifting toward sleep when she became aware of a new sound, the hard spatter of drops on the tin roof. Lightning flashed and twisted in the distance, wind gusted from the east, and a rain-soaked wind buffeted her lace curtains. She rose to close the shutters, then out of the corner of her eye she spotted a nest in her window box harboring three tiny eggs.

Lillie crawled back into bed, but found herself worrying about the nest, exposed and vulnerable as a new-born baby to the driving rain. Would the nest fill with water and wash the eggs away? The little nest, with it's promise of life, tugged at maternal cords deep within her soul. Then she smiled to herself. Surely the mother bird, frightened away by Lillie's presence at the window, was once more covering the precious nest with her soft warm body. God was always present to lead his creatures, just as He had led Alex and her out of the cold, dark tunnel of childlessness.

She placed her hand on her stomach. No longer barren and empty, but now providing a warm, vital nest for the new life taking shape and growing there. She turned and snuggled against the curved back of her sleeping husband.

* * *

Spring and summer passed quickly. Lillie reveled in her pregnancy and glowed with pride at her accomplishment. After so many years of failure and disappointment she treated her body, and the baby she was carrying, with the utmost care. Nothing must happen to this unborn child.

Secretly, she wished her mother could deliver the baby, but as she approached the final days of her confinement, and the baby still hadn't turned, Alex brought Doctor Fremont to look at her. She hated having a man in attendance and was relieved that his examination was discreet, by touch, under her skirt with the additional protection of a sheet spread across her legs. He kept his eyes focused on her face and never once looked down at his task.

She didn't miss the fact that the doctor consulted with Alex after the examination, nor did she miss the fact that Alex's brown eyes, when they looked at her, were black with worry.

* * *

By the end of September apple picking was under way—the big copper apple-butter kettles brought forth, and the spicy aroma of cooking apples, cloves, and cinnamon permeated the countryside.

On a bright October morning Lillie and her Mother sat glaring at one another. "You are not going to help make apple butter," her mother said, banging a coffee cup on the kitchen table.

"I'm not your child anymore," Lillie retorted with a like amount of anger. "I feel fine and I can certainly sit in the yard and peel a few apples. I'm sick to death of lying in bed like an invalid. Women have babies everyday and work until the moment they go into labor." With that, she heaved herself out of the chair, smoothed the starched fabric of her blue calico over her large, extended stomach, and headed for the kitchen door.

"At least put a scarf on your head," her mother called, hurrying after her. "Mercy child, you mustn't catch cold."

A small knot of women scurried about the apple butter kettle suspended from a tripod in the back yard. Alex had hung the kettle yesterday and stacked enough wood to keep a fire going all day. Apples bubbled gently over the low fire and the air was fragrant with the spicy aroma of cider, cloves, and cinnamon.

Because of her difficult pregnancy, neighbors had volunteered to take over the task so that this year's fruit crop would not go to waste. Lillie grabbed a smokehouse apple from a bowl on the wooden work table and, munching contentedly on its tart sweetness, crossed the yard, limping only slightly. Dew soaked her shoes and her footsteps left telltale prints in the damp grass. She leaned heavily against the gnarled trunk of an old hickory, moving back and forth to let its rough bark massage her aching back, and placed her hand on her distended belly as she tilted her face to the sun.

"Lillie," her cousin Louisa called from the cluster of women peeling apples, "why don't you join us here. That way you can rest."

Lillie waddled toward her and took an empty chair. Louisa placed a granite dish-pan filled with plump red McIntoshs on her knees—she had no lap—and handed her a paring knife.

She was paring the last apple in her dish-pan when the first pain hit. It took her by surprise and she finished the apple before she picked up the full pan and limped over to the bubbling kettle, not quite certain what to do. Just as she reached the fire another pain hit and she gasped in shock. A stout little Dutch lady laughed knowingly. "Ach, that bobbli don't wait, yet." Mama looked at her in alarm and jumped to her feet. "Someone ring the dinner bell for Alex and tell him to fetch the doctor at once. I'll get Lillie inside."

Mrs. Yoder, a rosy cheeked, Pennsylvania Dutch mid-wife, separated herself from the group of apple butter makers and followed Lillie and her mother into the house. Together they maneuvered her upstairs and into a nightgown and bed.

Alex came bounding up the stairs, and skidded to a stop before the open bedroom door. "Doc Freemont is finishing a delivery. He'll be here soon as possible." He looked at Lillie anxiously and she gave him a week smile.

"This is no place for a man," Sophia instructed gently, but with a thread of steel in her voice. "Stay downstairs and wait for him to come. We can manage till he gets here."

Lillie screamed for the doctor, writhing and throwing her body about the bed in agony.

"He's coming, fast as he can, already," the robust midwife said soothingly, turning Lillie on her side with gentle hands. "Let's chust check and see how ready this little one is. I've helped bring out many a baby, yet."

She began massaging Lillie's distended stomach with warm oil, her knowing fingers moving quietly as she checked and rechecked.

Lillie was clutching her mother's hand between spasms of pain when all heads turned toward the window. "Carriage coming. Doc

Fremont most likely," the midwife commented, relief clearly audible in her voice.

The doctor burst into the room and pushed past both women as he rushed to Lillie's side.

Within minutes he turned to Mrs. Yoder. "The baby has not turned," he said in a low voice.

"Ja, I know," she answered.

"I'd like you to stay and help me."

Mrs. Yoder merely nodded.

The first streaks of morning sun streamed through the bedroom window when the Doctor's voice reached Lillie through a haze of pain.

"The feet have presented themselves, Lillie. When you feel my hand pressing on your belly, push with everything you've got."

"I can't," she sobbed.

"Yes, you can, dear." The doctor's hand resting on her distended belly suddenly increased its pressure. "Push, Lillie! Now!"

She felt as though everything in her body were tearing and breaking apart. Images swirled and a thick velvet fog washed over her. Was this death? she wondered frantically. The doctor was yelling at her to push, but his voice was fading farther and farther away. Then an excited voice broke through the fog and she thought she heard her mother's voice cry the word "boy." She tried to clear the dark tunnel and hear more, but she seemed to be moving through darkness, faster and faster. Then the pain was gone and the fog enveloped her.

A baby was crying somewhere. Lillie opened her eyes and saw the face of the doctor leaning over her as he gently kneaded her stomach.

"You have a fine son," he said, squeezing her hand.

Lillie's mother appeared in the gathering light carrying a small bundle and, for the first time in twenty-four hours, Lillie smiled. Mama was a mess. Fine hair had escaped its bun to lay in damp tendrils across her forehead and shoulders, and blood streaked her usually immaculate apron.

She placed the bundle in Lillie's arms and wordlessly spread the blanket to reveal the naked body of the little boy. Lillie's eyes flew over his tiny form. He was perfect. He began crying lustily, shaking his tiny fists. Lillie lifted him to her breast and felt the wonderful, hurtful pull as he instinctively took her nipple, and his waving hands grew still.

A tide of love flowed over her, blotting out all else: the pain still throbbing through her body, the wet nightgown clinging to her legs, the blood soaked bed beneath her. "Thank you, God," she whispered. "Thank you . . . thank you . . . thank you."

Mrs. Yoder changed the bed linens and helped her into a fresh gown while the doctor gathered up his instruments and prepared to leave.

Lillie settled back against the cool fresh pillow with a sigh. She felt completely exhausted and her eyelids fluttered shut. Suddenly a sharp pain tore at her stomach and she felt an odd warmth between her legs. Something was wrong—terribly wrong. She tried to raise her head to look down, but broke into a clammy sweat, and her head fell back on the pillow. She heard herself whimper as the black fog began to sweep once more around her. The last thing she saw was the worried face of the old doctor bending over her before the velvet fog wrapped her in a warm cocoon and carried her away.

* * *

Believing that Lillie was comfortably asleep, and would rest for several hours, Alex eagerly saddled Bay Hunter, a nervous, high strung chestnut and headed for Rebert's Choice. Today he felt the need for the power of a stallion and he could feel the horse quiver beneath his legs, aching to run full out. "Yes!" he yelled, giving the horse full rein, laughing into the rush of wind with the pure thrill of the ride and the joy bubbling in his chest. They flew across the frozen fields toward the grist mill. He couldn't wait to tell someone about the birth of his son. Belle, of course. She would be waiting for news and so would Mama. He chuckled and pulled himself erect in the saddle. He had a little boy. A son!

The Widow Myers, present at the apple butter making, called at the mill for her flour and informed Edward that Lillie had gone into labor. Now, with Mama Katie beside her, Belle sat on the kitchen stoop peeling apples for sauce, waiting for Alex to bring news of the birth.

"I'm truly worried about Lillie, so tiny and frail looking, not really fashioned for child bearing," Katie said, with a dry swallow. "When Alex talked to me the day before yesterday the baby still hadn't turned."

"If there were serious problems they would surely have sent for us," Belle answered, aware that her voice was edged with tension.

Katie rose and walked to the edge of the porch to gaze anxiously up the lane. "The two of you have always been such close friends haven't you?"

"I always felt I could share a confidence with Lillie. She is so sweet and understanding—willing to sit for hours listening sympathetically to my frustrations."

"And your frustrations are many, aren't they, dear?"

Belle looked at her with a shameless grin. "I know everyone considers me a maverick. If I hadn't fallen desperately in love with Jamie I'd probably be somewhere in the south working for the Freedman's Bureau." She sighed and dug vigorously at an apple core. "Or, at the very least, I'd be more active in helping with women's struggle for social justice. Jamie grudgingly allows me to attend meetings of the National Woman Suffrage Association although I know he disapproves."

Katie gave her a knowing smile. "That's the way of men, Belle. They would never admit for a moment that we are really the strong ones. You must instill in your children a feeling of independence as strong as your own—there is nothing wrong with that."

"You know, before our marriage I traveled all the way to Harrisburg to attend a lecture by Elizabeth Cady Stanton and marched on behalf of the suffrage movement. I have never felt so alive." Belle hesitated and made a great business of cutting a bad spot from her apple. "Independence can be a trial, though."

"I know, dear. And it must be a trial for you to share a home and kitchen with your mother-in-law."

Belle blinked with surprise. Did Mother Katie suspect her growing depression at Jamie's reluctance to take on the expense of building them a home of their own? There was a spot on a slight rise behind the mill overlooking Conewago creek that they had agreed would be perfect. Her mind drifted to the house plans she still kept in her bureau drawer. Jamie promised, but he was in no hurry, not plagued by an impatient nature like hers. Until Papa Edward was ready to retire, Jamie was happily content to share both his work and home with the Reberts.

"No. You have always made me feel welcome," Belle protested. "It's just that Jamie and I see things differently sometimes."

"Most married couples do. No two people are the same. Why, Edward and I had our problems, the same as you and Jamie do."

"Problems? But . . . but you seem so content with each other. So much in love. We all envy you that."

Katie sighed. "We were of different faiths. Edward was so determined to get me to marry him that he made a vow that he would always honor my Mennonite belief in non-resistance in case of war." She turned toward Belle with an impish smile. "He never really believed he would be put to the test. But when the conflict between North and South erupted into the Civil War and Jamie's father, together with his other friends, marched off in patriotic enthusiasm, Edward had a difficult time with his conscience. It was not an easy time for either of us."

Restless now, Belle put her dish-pan aside and stretched. She joined Katie at the edge of the porch and peered through the afternoon haze, searching the road beyond the barn for sight of a horse and rider.

Belle cocked her head at a sudden sound and started down the steps just as Alex appeared around the side of the house.

With a huge grin splitting his broad face Alex related all the vital information: it was a boy, his name "Harry," a breech birth, but Lillie was fine, and he was hungry as a bear.

Belle watched with amusement as Alex wolfed down a huge breakfast of scrapple and eggs, laughing and talking non-stop. He suddenly drew his watch from his pocket and looked at it with a whistle of alarm. "Wow, I'd better be getting home."

"Don't forget to stop by the mill and tell Papa he has a new grandson," his mother reminded him.

Belle reached down and kissed his cheek. "And give Lillie my love. Tell her I'll be over later today to see the baby." She laughed at the sudden flush that swept his broad face. Happiness, she guessed.

Edward enveloped him in a great bear hug. "I'm happy for you son. And Lillie, of course. Everything all right?"

"Just fine."

Jamie, with a huge grin on his face, pumped Alex's hand. "Have you named him, yet?"

"Harry Edward Rebert," Alex said beaming.

He looked at his father who suddenly seemed to be having trouble with something in his eye. "Another Rebert to carry on the family name," he said in a voice ragged with emotion. He cleared his throat. "You will find that a child brings a whole new dimension to your life, I know that it did to mine. Go now, get home to Lillie and that new son of yours."

Alex turned Bay Hunter across the field, urging the willing horse to a fast trot. He hoped the baby was awake. He couldn't wait to hold him. Him . . . Harry . . . he tested the name on his lips and smiled.

As he turned in the lane to White Hall he saw the doctor's carriage still parked by the gate. His throat drew tight with anxiety. The doctor should have been gone long ago.

CHAPTER 9

Alex jumped off Bay Hunter, flung the reins toward a post in the fence, ran up the path and dashed through the front door. Doctor Fremont, descending the stairway from the upstairs bedrooms, stopped when he saw Alex, his hand tightening on the banister.

"Alex, I'm glad you're home. Come into the parlor. I need to talk with you."

Shutters darkened the seldom used room, and Alex hastened to light a kerosene lamp to dispel the gloom while the doctor perched on the edge of a circular sofa. A sense of dread made Alex's hand tremble as he adjusted the lamp wick and turned to face the doctor. He was afraid to ask. Afraid to hear. Something had gone wrong. It was evident on the weary face watching him.

"What . . . what is it? Is it the baby?" His voice began to shake. "Or Lillie?"

"The baby is fine. Lillie, I believe, will recover." The old man removed his glasses and began to wipe them. "You'd no sooner left than Lillie began to hemorrhage. I couldn't get the bleeding stopped—I had to operate."

"You operated? Here?"

"There was no alternative, son. Your wife would have bled to death. I've made the repairs and Lillie is resting comfortably." The doctor's eyes grew sympathetic, his voice gentle. "I'm sorry to have to tell you this, Alex, but there will be no more children."

Alex sank into a nearby chair. Despite the coolness of the room a film of sweat covered his forehead. He wiped his wet palms on his pants. "Was it . . . was it her pelvic bone?"

"No. She simply hemorrhaged."

"Lillie is going to get well, then? There is no further danger?"

"She'll need our prayers. There is the risk of infection and she lost a lot of blood. She's very weak. You should get a wet nurse for the baby until she's stronger." The lamplight flickered on the doctor's face. He looked old and tired. "I'll return in the morning. Your mother-in-law and Mrs. Yoder have consented to spend the night. You can visit Lillie when she wakes, but only for a minute. Rest is what she needs now. Come for me should the need arise and ask Mrs. Yoder about a wet nurse."

"Belle McPherson, is still nursing her last baby. I imagine she will want to come."

"Get her then. Now, I must go. I have another case waiting for me."

Alex slowly climbed the stairs and entered their bed chamber. Sophia, his mother-in-law, sat in a rocking chair beside the cradle, rocking it slowly with her foot. She looked up when Alex entered the room, but said nothing. Mrs. Yoder rustled away as he approached the bed. He stood looking down at Lillie. Her long chestnut hair, loosened from its pins and still damp from her ordeal, fanned across the pillow and framed her small face, white as the pristine sheet folded across her chest. He reached down and brushed a few moist strands of hair from her forehead.

"Lillie," he whispered.

She opened her eyes and they softened as they slowly focused on his. He leaned down and kissed her cheek. She made a feeble attempt to raise her hand and he grasped it in his rough palm and squeezed it gently.

"I feel so weak, Alex. Wa . . . What happened?"

Alex bit his lip. Did she know? Know that all her dreams of filling the empty bedrooms of White Hall with laughing children were gone. That his dreams of half a dozen sons and daughters were gone. He wondered—perhaps for the hundredth time—why children were so important to him. Anger surged through him. It wasn't fair. Why had God chosen to punish them this way?

"Sh, Sh. You need your rest, dearest one. You started to bleed again. Thank God the good doctor was still here and able to fix you with a little operation. Now close your eyes and rest."

"The baby?"

"He's fine. A handsome little fellow, fast sleep in his cradle." He stood awkwardly by her bed, stroking her hair. He felt ill at ease in a sick room. And he felt Sophia's dark eyes on him.

Lillie's eyes were closed, her breathing slow and even, her tiny hand in his relaxed and still. He released it and laid it gently at her side, then adjusted the sheet around her.

The baby whimpered and Alex rose from his knees to approach the cradle.

"He'll wake soon and need to be fed," Sophia said, quietly.

"I'll ride over and ask Belle to come."

"Go then and be quick about it. The babe will wake soon."

For two days, Alex stayed by Lillie's bedside, while hushed neighbors brought food, and Belle, still nursing her last baby, stayed in the spare bedroom to feed Harry, who never seemed to stop crying.

Within days the doctor's worst fears were realized. Fever ravaged Lillie and although she fought it with a strength that surprised everyone, she hovered near death.

After another long morning spent in and out of the sick room Alex grabbed his coat from the peg by the kitchen door and with a bleak, wintery feeling of despair set out to walk to the south boundary of White Hall. Perhaps, he thought, his land could provide the comfort he so sorely needed. He followed an old stone wall, covered with moss and lichen, to a lightning scared walnut tree that marked the corner of his farm. There, he lowered himself to the leaf strewn ground leaning his broad back against the wall. Its west face was warm with the afternoon sun and he sat motionless, lost in the serenity of the fields surrounding him. Long, straight rows of corn shocks stood etched against the ice blue sky and at their base mounds of golden corn and orange pumpkins rested among the stubble. In the distance the smoky gray South Mountain range rose against the skyline and overhead wedges of Canada geese honked wildly as they began their long journey south.

He lowered his head to pray, but nothing came. He felt empty, angry, and frightened. Lillie might die—why couldn't he pray?

A large hawk circled overhead casting its dark shadow over the emptied field. Alex pursed his lips and frowned. Since Lillie's operation his days had been clouded with anger and resentment. Could it be that there was no room in his heart for prayer? A surge of shame washed over him. God had blessed him with a son and he was angry because he had been denied more? He needed to thank God for the miracle of birth, not wallow in self-pity. He needed to let go of his anger and resentment. Only then could he ask Him to let Lillie live.

He was startled from his reverie when a nut dropped on his head and rolled to the ground. He glanced upward. Fat clusters of walnuts hung heavy on strong dark branches making plunking noises as they fell to the ground. Alex picked up the nut and rolled it slowly between his fingers—outside it wore a hard protective covering, but with strength one could break it open and taste its sweetness.

His body relaxed and his mind grew quiet. He bowed his head.

That night Lillie's fever broke.

Sophia, Belle and Mrs. Yoder kept a constant vigil bathing her face with wet cloths and changing the damp sheets beneath her. By the middle of the week a smiling Doctor assured Alex that he expected a full recovery.

Alex sat beside the bed while Lillie slept peacefully, the flush of fever finally gone from her pale face. Belle sat in a rocker by the window, nursing little Harry, her red hair sparkling like fire from the shafts of bright sunlight streaming through the window. The irony of it didn't escape Alex as he watched his son suckling at Belle's full breast while his wife lay fighting to recover her strength. Once he had dreamed of his own lips on those breasts. He flushed with shame at the sinfulness of such a thought. He had thought that all buried in the past.

Alex saw Lillie watching him. She smiled uncertainly and took his hand.

"You're awake," he said, tucking a tendril of hair behind her ear. "Good, I believe I hear the doctor's carriage in the yard." The words were no sooner spoken than Doc Fremont entered the bedroom and strode to Lillie's bedside. "Alex, if you'll wait in the hall until I examine your wife, I'd like to talk to her and then both of you together."

Minutes later, Belle slipped through the bedroom door and dipped her head at Alex, indicating that he was to enter. She gave his hand a squeeze of encouragement.

"Is the doctor telling Lillie what happened?" Alex asked, with uncertainty.

"He's telling her now." She put a hand on his arm. "Alex, she's going to need your strength and your acceptance of her condition. Please, don't let her feel less a woman. Go to her. And, please dear, be gentle."

The doctor sat on the edge of the bed and, after directing Alex to a nearby chair, spoke somberly. "Lillie has been questioning me, and I felt her strong enough to hear the truth. I have told her there can be no more children." His eyes locked with Alex's. "Your wife will recover and can start nursing again, that is the important thing right now."

Lillie lay still, staring at the doctor. Her fingers brushed her mouth, but no words passed her tight lips.

Alex fought to keep his own anguish from showing. His eyes sought out Lillie's and he knew she could read the emotion on his face. He took a deep breath and tried to smile. He could only guess how devastated she must be. Children were important to a farmer, but babies were even more important to a woman, to her standing in the community, and her self-esteem.

He rose, walked over to the bed, and reached down to kiss her on the cheek. "I know you're disappointed, dear, but we do have a healthy, robust little boy, and you're well on the way to recovery."

"But . . . ."

"Sh. We must count our blessings and not question God's way."

Lillie's eyes swam with tears and still she made no comment. Her hands, usually so animated, lay still on the white counterpane. Alex walked over to the tiny cradle and picked up his sleeping son. He carried him to the bed and placed him on Lillie's chest, next to her heart.

"Harry Edward Rebert, I believe it's time you became reacquainted with your mother."

* * *

During the month of October Rebert's Choice buzzed with activity. Tom-boy Emma finally succumbed to the gentleness of love and married her Charles Duttera. Then Edwin followed suit marrying his Sissy and moving to Indiana, and Charlie celebrated his fifteenth birthday on the same day Harry was christened. Now only John, Charlie and Ellen were still at home and she was keeping company with a young minister from East Berlin. Of course Jamie and his family were still in the old house but even they were talking more often about beginning to build their own home along the beautiful little stream that bordered Rebert's Choice.

Lillie removed two-month old Harry from his cradle and laid him on the kitchen table to remove his sodden diaper. He squirmed, babbling in pure pleasure while she applied powdery cornstarch to his chubby little legs and bottom. On impulse, she nestled her face on his warm fat belly, then burst into laughter as Harry responded with a stream of urine in her face.

"Better now than in his fresh diaper," Alex commented with a chuckle as he observed his son's action.

Lillie smilingly wiped the moisture from her face and the front of her lavender house-dress. "Naughty boy," she chided as she deftly knotted clean linen around the baby and lifted him in her arms. Humming softly, she stroked the silken head nuzzling her chest and carried him to her rocking chair by the fireplace.

"I believe Harry spends far more time in his mother's arms than in his cradle," Alex observed with a wry grin.

"He's beginning to teethe—that's why he's been so fussy of late."

"You'll spoil him. You pick him up every time he whimpers."

"Look who's talking about spoiling. Who shows him off at Christ Church every Sunday as though he were the Crown Prince?"

Lillie opened the front of her dress to nurse, contentedly rocking to and fro in her comfortable old rocker. She dreaded the day the baby would grow too old for her breast—dreaded any lessening of his need for her. The pull of his tiny mouth on her nipple was a joyful affirmation of her motherhood and, although she wouldn't have admitted it to anyone, it was rather sensuous in the satisfaction it afforded her.

Such a precious little boy he was. She absolutely adored him. She began to hum and then to sing an old German lullaby.

> God's presence surrounds you,
> His angels around you,
> The light of his love falling soft
> On your face . . .
> A heaven above you,
> A family to love you,
> Sleep, child, in your cradle
> of blessing and grace

The fire glowed warmly, hissing and crackling as a large log settled into the grate. Alex's beloved face watched her intently, his broad features awash in the golden warmth. She loved these evenings of quiet closeness with her husband and child.

The baby reached up and his chubby fingers clutched the gold pocket watch pinned to the bodice of her dress. His mouth stopped sucking and his bright blue eyes, so like his Grandpa

Edward's, looked straight at her. He gurgled gleefully, blowing milky bubbles, and tugged at the locket.

"What an appealing fellow you are becoming, Harry Rebert," Lillie crooned, hugging him tightly. Her heart swelled with pride. She hadn't dreamed one could feel such love. Her child—more precious to her than life itself!

Harry began to pull on her nipple again and she leaned down to kiss the top of his head before resuming her song. When she glanced up she noticed Alex turn away and stare into the fire, an odd look of longing in his somber brown eyes.

CHAPTER 10

Lillie, her face white as a sheet, met Alex as he entered the kitchen on a blustery November afternoon.

"Belle has been arrested," she said in a quavering voice.

"What!"

"Jamie just rode by on his way to the jail in Hanover. Can you believe, she was discovered dressed as a man and trying to vote. A man, Alex! She was wearing Jamie's Sunday suit."

Alex's eyes blinked with incredulity. "Good Lord, she must have gone daft. Did Jamie know she had it in mind to try and vote?"

"Of course not, no one did. She told Mama Katie she was going into town for dress goods. She must have changed clothes somewhere after she left."

"Jamie is at the jail, now?"

"Yes."

Alex jammed his cap back on his head and bolted toward the door. "Don't wait supper for me. I'll go see what I can do."

"Let me go along."

"No!," he shouted, his stomach in a knot. "You stay here where you belong. Next thing I know you'll be trying to parrot her rebellious ideas."

Lillie wagged a finger at him. "And it's arrogance like that will eventually force women to move from their husband's shadow and take their rightful place in society. Many western states have seen fit to give women the vote and Belle is right when she says someday every state in the union will do the same."

"See what I mean? She's already gotten to you." He shook his head and slammed out the kitchen door. "Damn women!"

Alex crossed Plum Creek and cantered into Hanover just as the sun sank beyond the western horizon. The streets were busy despite the late hour. Hanover had become a major trading center, and although most residents still kept cows, horses, swine and poultry in their back yards, it was a progressive town with a burgeoning economy.

At one time the jail was located under the old Market House that sat in the center of the Center square, and Alex rode there first; forgetting in his anxiety that the Market House had been torn down to make way for a fountain. Chagrined, he rode to the edge of town and drew up in front of the new jail, now housed in an impressive red brick building. He tethered his horse and hurried up the steps. Once inside he was informed that Jamie had left to meet with the local magistrate.

"What about Mrs. McPherson? Has she been detained here?" he asked.

The jailer hooked his finger in the direction of a cell at the end of the corridor. "Thar she sits," he said, pointing down the dark corridor with a grubby finger, stained with tobacco. "And I do believe it's a she despite her get-up."

Alex licked his dry lips. "May I see her, please? I'm her brother-in-law."

With Alex in tow, the jailer inched his way past several occupied cells, reeking of urine, disinfectant, and stale tobacco. His keys jingled from a large loop on his skinny hips, and he unlocked the door of a tiny cell with a sneer. The door clanged shut and Alex squinted in the gloom at the figure perched on the edge of a shadowy bunk.

"What in tarnation . . . ."

"Don't lecture me, Alex! I've had enough of that from Jamie."

"Are you all right? Have they mistreated you?"

"Only to insult me with their contempt. According to the authorities I'm fit only to change diapers, cook and tend to my husband's comfort."

Alex moved toward her, pulling at his mustache in a characteristic gesture. "But I don't understand. What ever did you hope to accomplish?"

"To cast a vote for Belva Lockwood."

"Who is Belva Lockhaven?"

"Lockwood . . . Belva Lockwood, and she's a prominent woman lawyer running for President on the Equal Rights ticket." Her eyes blazed defiance. "Notice I said lawyer not housewife."

Alex snorted. "A vote wasted."

"And who will you vote for? Blaine, the plumed knight of the Grand Old Party, guilty of selling his influence in Washington to the highest bidder," she asked saucily, "or does your vote go to Grover Cleveland, who sired an illegitimate child, then sent it to an orphanage and it's mother to an asylum?"

Alex snorted. "The woman was not relegated to an asylum . . . she disappeared when her involvement with numerous men became public knowledge. Cleveland gave his name to the child out of compassion as any conscientious man would do." Alex bit his tongue at the look on Belle's face, and he hastened to add "there's no reason for us to argue, now. I think Cleveland to be a man of unusual honesty and he has my vote, but our immediate problem is getting you out of here."

He sat down beside her on the bunk and she turned to look at him, tears darkening her gray eyes to the color of storm clouds. They sat silently for a moment and then he asked in a soft voice, "How did they find you out? Except for your hair you have done a good job of disguising yourself."

A smile tugged the corner of Belle's lips and her eyes softened. "It was my hair that gave me away. Someone bumped into me and knocked my hat off. The pins came loose and all was lost." She chuckled. "It was almost worth getting arrested to see the look on the election clerk's face."

Alex leaned forward to take her hand and rubbed across its back with his thumb. It was soft and warm and trembled slightly at his touch. He could feel all the small bones beneath the surface and he held it cupped in his hand, caressing it gently as he turned it over and slowly moved his thumb across her palm to push open the fingers she had made into a fist. Fine red lines marked where she had dug her nails into the flesh and she stared at them with surprise then looked into his face. She slowly drew her hand away and got up chewing on her lip.

Her gaze darted to the corner of the cell and then back to him. "Do you think they'll keep me here overnight?" Her facial muscles twitched nervously, and the tears she fought so gallantly to restrain crept down her pale cheek. Alex stood, his emotions in a turmoil. She took two steps toward him and he met her with open arms. She rested her head against his shoulder and her hair smelled of lemon and herself. "Oh, Alex," she said with a sob, "Jamie is so angry at me." He smoothed his cheek against her soft hair and drew her closer. She turned her head slightly and he kissed her temple, then he groaned and drew her tighter against his body. All of the desire he had thought forever buried surged to the surface and he reached out with two fingers to lift her chin when a loud voice jarred him to his senses.

"What is the meaning of this?" Jamie snarled, glaring at them through the iron bars, his eyes narrowed with suspicion.

Belle's face turned white and Alex jerked back as though stung by a wasp. "I . . . I was only consoling her. She . . . "

"Don't give me that. First I find my wife imprisoned like a woman of the streets and then I see my so-called brother making advances to her."

"No, Jamie, no! Alex was only comforting me. He . . . "

"Comfort, my foot. I've seen him looking at you with lust for years. Now he's taking advantage of a vulnerable moment to force his deceitful attentions on you. I should throttle both of you."

Alex's stomach knotted with suppressed rage and he reached out to grab Jamie, forgetting the bars that separated them. He pulled up short, his face hot and pinched with resentment.

"And you're letting the emotion of the moment cloud your judgement," he barked. "It's admiration for her spirit and beauty, not lust you see on my face. Your thoughts would be better directed to getting your wife out of this foul place—not heap blame where it doesn't belong. She needs comfort not condemnation."

Jamie's grip on the cell door relaxed and his hands dropped to his side. He sighed. "I came to take her to the magistrate's office. He will assess a fine . . . a hefty one I imagine . . . and let her go. He has no desire to draw attention to this foolish affair by incarcerating her."

The jailer appeared out of the gloom, keys clinking, peering down his nose contemptuously. "Guess the lady gets to go home," he grunted. "For some, money talks." He turned the key in the lock and threw the door open with a flourish.

Jamie grabbed Belle and propelled her out the door. "Come on," he muttered, "before the whole town hears this sorry tale."

But the tale of a woman dressed as a man attempting to vote was not so easily hushed. Soon every newspaper in the country picked up the story and Belle became a hero to the suffragettes.

Jamie and Alex mended their fences, but Alex knew, with a deepening sense of shame, that nothing would ever be quite the same between them.

* * *

Lillie sat on a long oak bench, sixth in a group of women working on a quilting frame that filled half of Mother Katie's comfortable kitchen. Katie, Belle, Sarah Hollinger, and two of Belle's new friends from the National Womens Suffrage Association, Carrie Shaw and Lucretia Snavely, worked with flashing needles.

Tillie, short and stout, wore a transparent Mennonite cap with narrow, untied, black strings that gave her round face an aspect of saintliness. Carrie was tall and slender with a long narrow face and eyebrows like question marks. Her straight brown hair, parted in the middle, was pulled back into a stern bun. Lucretia, short and a bit overweight, talked in short jerky sentences and was constantly bobbing her head in an effort to inspect everything.

Carrie and Lucretia were deep in a serious discussion with Belle about the new chapter of the NWSA forming in Littlestown. Lillie avidly listened to each of their arguments, her eyes sparkling with interest. The women met often at one of the houses in the valley, ostensibly to work on quilts, but really to discuss the troubling politics of southeastern Pennsylvania. They talked of public education and Prohibition, but it was really the fight for a woman suffrage amendment to the United States Constitution that aroused them to fiery debate.

"In addition to your little charade as a man I heard you once marched for woman suffrage at a rally in Harrisburg," Lucretia said, her small head bobbing in Belle's direction.

"I did, and I would again. Women should take their reform policies into the street if they want the vote and the repeal of discriminatory laws." Her lips curved in an arch smile. "Suffrage calls for a degree of activism from all of us . . . and a fair amount of risk."

"Activism is not perceived as an appropriate activity for ladies," Sarah said, with a slight frown.

"Pshaw! Nonsense!" Katie retorted. "This is one issue on which I agree wholeheartedly with Belle. Key decisions are made every day by self-important politicians that dictate the way we women must live. Women can't remain silent and inactive any longer."

"But isn't there strong religious opposition to women's participation in things that do not pertain directly to the home and the rearing of children?" Lillie questioned. "My Papa always said a woman's place is in the home."

Carrie's needle stopped its up and down journey through the muslin and cotton batting and she looked directly at Lillie. "The right to vote does not take a woman out of the home. Our suffrage movement is a natural outgrowth of other social reforms, such as the abolition of slavery, temperance and the extension of education.

Surely you do not dispute the rightness of these reforms, Mrs. Rebert."

"No, and I didn't say I was unsympathetic to your cause. But what can a handful of farm wives do about it?"

Katie smiled sweetly. "One does what one can do!"

Belle gave up all pretense of quilting and turned to Carrie. "I'd like to join the NWSA march being proposed next weekend in Hanover for our new chapter. They're pushing for an amendment to our state constitution and we must win on the state level before attempting to sway Washington."

Lillie gave her a puzzled look.

Belle smiled at her. "You think that just because I'm safely married to Jamie and have a home and children I should stop all this foolishness . . . stop worrying about the injustices women suffer. Well, my dear sister-in-law, you're wrong."

Lillie nodded yes quickly. She wasn't at all sure what injustices Belle was referring to, but she had always been in awe of Belle's spirit and if Belle believed it right to get involved in this movement, then perhaps it was right to do so.

Belle's fingers resumed work quickly, her quilting a marvel of neatness, as she continued her commentary. "You're wrong, wrong, wrong. We're all women and just as worthy and intelligent as any man. When the suffragettes marched in Washington, the President sent the U.S. Cavalry to break up the parade. Can you imagine that? The mighty U.S. Cavalry against a group of marching women. The politicians don't care beans about our rights. They sit back and laugh, calling women silly females with brains only big enough to change diapers and cross stitch."

Katie turned to give Belle an approving look. "I'm continually astonished that otherwise intelligent and sensible men have such foolish ideas about women. Edward never did. He has always treated me as an equal. Yet is seems that most men want us to appear pale and helpless. They provide us with fainting couches in our bedrooms because the clothes they like us to wear are so tight we can't breathe."

"That's just today's fashion," Lillie said, with a laugh.

"And who do you think create the fashions? Lands sake, girl, all those fancy designers are men. Who do you think designed corsets intended to make women's waists look alluring and push their breasts out so they look like harlots?"

"But Mother Katie, you don't wear a corset."

"Of course not, child. Can you imagine bending over to milk a cow with a corset on? They'd have to put fainting couches in the barn," she said, voice rising. "But the wives of politicians wear them and those very politicians make the laws governing our lives."

"And it isn't only politicians who are afraid of the female vote," Lucretia protested. "The brewing and distilling industry worry that the woman's vote will help the temperance movement."

Belle nodded. "The business men say it isn't any of our business. Well if it isn't our business as wives and mothers, what is? Someday our children will have to live in this world men are corrupting. And most of the women in this valley don't seem to give a hoot what is going on in Washington except to talk about what Frances Folsom wore when she married President Cleveland."

"Or cluck over the turkish trousers Amelia Bloomer is making fashionable in New York City," Tillie said, with a hearty laugh.

Everyone chuckled and for several moments the conversation veered to Bloomer's latest fashion sensation. Sarah pursed her lips. "For the life of me I can't understand why women want to dress like men when they're fortunate enough to be women. Why lose our femininity, which is one of our greatest charms? We can gain so much more by being charming than we could by flaunting around in pants. Things half seen are so much more mysterious and delightful."

Belle laughed heartily. "I agree. I'm very fond of men. I love them dearly. But I don't want to look like one."

Several others chimed in with opinions about the outlandish bloomers before Lucretia, bobbing her head earnestly, turned the dialogue back to the subject of her only true passion, voting rights for women. The heated discussion continued until everyone picked up their needles and headed home to prepare supper.

* * *

The winter of 1881 passed quickly and Lillie spent her days caring for the large house at White Hall, its rooms devoid of the hoards of children she had once envisioned playing there.

Snow fell in February and the roads drifted shut, but inside it was warm and snug and her geraniums in the south windows bloomed with shameless abandon.

There was another fall of snow late in March, but finally April, with its blushing bloom and bird-song, was upon them.

On one especially fine spring morning Lillie noticed an unusual number of feathers floating around the barnyard on the quickening breeze. It was time for the fowl on the farm to undergo their spring plucking, a job she didn't relish any more than the unlucky birds, but she did need new pillows and Harry could use a longer feather-tick. He had grown a good two inches since last winter.

She gathered the geese and penned them up for the night so they'd be nice and dry come morning. The next day, bright and early, she gathered the unwilling birds, one by one for the annual ritual.

Harry wrapped a strong arm around a goose's neck and grasped its feet in one hand while the other hand rapidly plucked feathers from the struggling bird which he stuffed into an old pillow case. Feathers floated everywhere, up Lillie's nose and into her hair. Goslings ran frantically around Harry's bare feet as their mother honked in alarm at the indignity she was being subjected to. One startled gosling began to peck at Harry's toes and in a fit of temper he lifted his foot, stomped on it, and kicked the hapless bird aside. The goose in his arm struggled frantically and Harry tightened his grip until the poor bird began to strangle.

Lillie looked at her son in stunned silence. She had seen flashes of temper before, but this was different. This was cruel.

She bolted across the yard and pushed Harry away from the squashed gosling. "Go to the house at once and stay there," she said with a stony expression.

The yard was filled with wild honking as the indignant bird, when released, wiggled its tail in disgust and waddled out of range. A shamefaced Harry trudged into the house.

That afternoon, still plagued by disturbing thoughts of Harry's action, Lillie headed for the tranquility of her garden. The garden soothed her; tiny purple and yellow johnny jump-ups, yellow daffodils, and dainty white columbine vied for attention among the green plants not yet in bloom, the sun warm through the cloth of her dress. A cat rubbed back and forth across her shins. A cardinal whistled, insects hummed and a slight breeze carried the heavy scent of honeysuckle. But try as she might, her mind kept reviewing the disturbing behavior she had seen in her son that morning. She always excused his flashes of temper as immaturity, but this was something more.

She rose, brushing soil and leaves from her full skirt, and tilted her head to the intense blue of the April sky. Perhaps she was reading too much into the incident. She had watched Harry's face turn from anger and annoyance to guilt and regret.

After all, he was still a young boy.

* * *

On Friday, the last week in April, Alex's father mounted Bay Hunter and walked him slowly toward Codorus Creek. At the creek he dismounted and let his horse graze while he settled himself against a tree on the water's edge.

Belle was expecting again and he sensed a deep discontent in the girl. She was very much like Jamie's father. Patrick McPherson had burst with life and laughter until burdened by the responsibility of an unplanned child. Marriage had sapped the joy from Patrick and he feared it was doing the same to Patrick's daughter-in-law.

Then too, there was something amiss between Jamie and Alex since Belle's skirmish with the law. Edward grinned at the thought of Belle dressed as a man, peering through the bars of the jail cell. What a little firebrand she was. Then he sobered, once again pondering the unrest in his family, the apparent growth of a rivalry between Alex and Jamie.

Edward was no fool. Although he knew Jamie and Belle loved one another deeply, he also knew that Belle chafed over the confining role of wife and homemaker.

Perhaps if he gave Jamie the money to build his own home it would put a spark back into Belle's eyes—give her something more to look forward to than another baby.

Edward's eyes snapped open and he sat upright. That was it—why hadn't he thought of that before? He remembered the plans she had once drawn and how they had laughed over the missing staircase. Belle would be thrilled and he bet she still had those plans tucked away in her chest.

He retrieved his horse and sprung into the saddle, then sat motionless for several moments until most of the dizziness that had been plaguing him lately passed.

Bay Hunter turned his head to look at him, waiting for the command that had not been issued. He whinnied softly, then because he had carried Edward so long, and knew the way, the stallion began to walk at his own pace toward Rebert's Choice.

"Good boy," Edward said, shakily gripping the reins. Bay Hunter's sleek head switched back to look at him once more. His intelligent brown eyes seemed to ask a silent question before he picked his way smoothly through the stubble and underbrush.

Gradually Edward became aware of an odd sensation, a numbness in his left side. He could not feel the pull of the reins in his left hand. He tried to move his arm, but nothing happened.

Fear crashed in on him like a fist to the stomach. Never in his sixty-four years had he felt this kind of fear. Not even on the fringes of the roaring battlefield during his service with the Christian

Commission, or while the battle at Gettysburg raged about his home.

What he was experiencing now was different. He feared dying. Not actual death itself, his faith was too strong for that, but the thought of leaving Katie alone.

He tried to steady himself by the pressure of his knees against Bay Hunter's sides. Only his right leg moved. The earth seemed to tilt and he gripped the reins, forcing himself to stay upright in the saddle. He was completely disoriented, trusting his horse to carry him home.

Bay Hunter walked past the corner of the barn where Edward normally dismounted and moved gently toward the front porch where he stopped and whinnied loudly.

The last thing Edward saw, before he toppled to the ground, was Katie running toward him.

Katie tried not to let Edward see the tears, the agony of her despair, as she moved about the darkening bedroom. Edward lay motionless under a blue and white quilt, his breathing labored and harsh. Only his eyes followed her as she moved about the room, closing the shutters, winding the mantle clock, lighting the oil lamp.

The Doctor had compassionately warned her that Edward might not survive the night. He had suffered a massive stroke and was almost completely paralyzed.

Katie pulled her rocker close to the bed and tenderly adjusted the quilt around Edward's shoulders. He was conscious and so she began to talk. Thousands of memories cried to be spoken: their first kiss at a corn husking, the birth and death of their first born, the bond between Edward and his beloved dog Duke. She talked of Christmases past, of Patrick and the war years, and recalled the time Edward locked her and the children in the root cellar during the terrible fighting at nearby Gettysburg and she gave birth to her sixth child. His eyes softened and although he could not smile she knew he remembered too.

Then she took the bible from the bedside table and read to him from Romans 8:1-11 the great passage of scripture that assures us that our dying bodies live again after death because of the Holy Spirit living within us. She closed the bible and as her fingers caressed the worn leather cover she recited the 23rd Psalm. Edward's eyes closed, only the ticking of the clock and his labored breathing cutting the silence of their bedchamber.

Lillie sat quietly watching him, lying in the bed where they had slept all their married life, where their children had been conceived and their love for one another grown deeper with each passing year.

She rose and moved to the wooden chest that sat at the foot their bed. Raising the lid her fingers probed its depths coming to rest on a package wrapped in thin tissue paper. She peeled back the paper and withdrew her yellowed wedding nightdress. Slowly she undressed, carefully pulled the garment over her head, and loosened the pins holding her hair. She took a brush and drew it through the long, wavy hair that only Edward had ever seen unbound, a husbands gift according to her faith.

Edward's eyes never left her face.

Lillie pulled back the covers and crawled into bed beside him, taking his big hand in hers, snuggling up so he could share the warmth of her body. In the light of the flickering lamp she could see his brilliant eyes fill with love.

Silence settled over the room and gradually the hypnotic ticking of the mantle clock lulled her to sleep.

When she woke the labored breathing had stopped and the hand still clasping her's had grown cold.

They came from far and near to pay homage, and the little church Edward had loved so well was filled to overflowing. Christ Church's new pastor, Reverend F.S. Lindaman, agreed to give the eulogy in English rather than the old High German still used for most Sunday services.

As the pastor offered his message of the resurrection, Lillie looked at the still form in the coffin, banked by vases of lilacs and forsythia, at the silver-tufted mane of Edward's hair, the distinctive cleft in his chin, and the masculine contours of his face. A strong face.

He was laid to rest in a plot just behind the northeast corner of the church and after saying their farewells Alex and Lillie left the cemetery and started toward the home-place for the traditional funeral dinner.

The carriage bumped along Christ Church Road, deeply rutted by the recent rains. Harry, too sleepy to realize he was too old to be held, sagged heavily in Lillie's arms, and she and Alex were both silent, lost in memories, unable to appreciate the lovely May morning. Apple trees, a soft haze of pink, and locust trees hanging low with fragrant white blossoms, lined the country lane.

Alex sat ramrod still and Lillie dabbed at her eyes with a sodden hanky as she remembered Edward's unwavering devotion to his beloved Katie. Most men thought it unmanly to reveal themselves so openly, but she had often seen the unashamed love on his face when he gazed at his wife.

Alex slapped the reins and the mare broke into a slow canter. "Mama was so brave today," he said. "She loved him very deeply." He smiled softly. "It's funny how children regard their parents and rarely think of them as individuals or give thought to their private lives, what they might have wanted, won or lost. But then Mama's Mennonite upbringing has always been a steadying influence in her life."

"Do you think she has ever been sorry she left her church?"

"No. Although she joined Christ Church, she never really broke with her faith. We children were lucky. We had the best of both religions."

Softly Lillie placed her hand on Alex's rigid leg. She felt so sorry for him, not only because he had lost his father, whom he looked upon as invincible, but because she sensed a brooding loneliness and vulnerability. People expected so much of men. They were not allowed to show their hidden fears and weaknesses. No tears, no failure! It was a German trait for men to present themselves as strong and unemotional. Yet she felt Alex was full of self-doubt and petty jealousies—as she herself often was. Did he doubt his father's equal love of his sons? She had often suspected that he did.

"The mill certainly won't be the same without him," she said.

"No, he was never too busy to stop and listen to people's stories. Edwin has that same quality."

A flicker of hurt crossed Alex's face at some distant memory and he snapped the reins sharply.

Lillie waited. She thought he might be on the verge of revealing a part of himself he had always managed to keep hidden. Had she been right? Had he resented his younger brother, then?

"I remember," he said, "when I was about twelve Edwin and I built a tree house in that big elm behind the woodshed and we spent hours talking about the Civil war, wondering about girls, and planning our futures. Edwin always dreamed of great things, his ideas fairly soared through the branches of that old tree. But me, I could never be like that. Even at twelve I saw things as they were. I always wished I could be less serious, more fun loving, like Papa and Edwin and Jamie. People seem to love them so." He halted, affecting a look of indifference. "Of course, I think people respect my ability to run the farms. I always treat my neighbors fairly in business."

"Everyone looks up to you, Alex. You mustn't feel any less a man because of your seriousness."

"I don't really." A sudden wave of color spread across his wide face. "I was angry with Pa during the war years. I never really understood his refusal to fight. I guess I was just too young to comprehend his religious convictions . . . young and aching with patriotic fervor to run away and join the Union cause myself."

Hoover Road brought them out near the Mennonite Meeting House and they entered Hostetter Road, leading to the grist mill. Several carriages preceded them and Alex dropped back to avoid the cloud of dust from their wheels.

Lillie shifted Harry's heavy body and looked at his slumbering face, eyelashes lying like feathery shadows against his cheeks, his fist curled in sleep. She kissed the top of his head and stroked his fine hair. He was growing so fast. Then she glanced sideways at Alex, at his velvet brown eyes so incurably sad. She loved both of the men in her life so much that at times it hurt.

"Do you think Edwin and Sissy will move back from Indiana and take over the mill? Or will Jamie continue to run it?" she asked.

"Probably, Jamie. Edwin seems very happy in Indiana. But the family will have to buy Rebert's Choice at public venue. Pa didn't leave a will." He was silent for a moment, then he turned toward her with a pleading look. "You know how much I've always loved the former Sterner property . . . the Mansion House . . . on the Littlestown Pike. I want to buy it from the Estate, Lillie." Lillie's breath caught in her throat. His request didn't surprise her, but she had been dreading it. She knew Alex had coveted that property for years and wanted to move closer to Littlestown. Still, White Hall was home and family, a network of roots almost two hundred years old that spread both wide and deep. She knew every inch of the old house, the pulse of the land. She had never wanted to be anywhere else. The fabric of life in the home of her ancestors was her fortress.

"I don't want to move, Alex. Somehow I feel I've discovered my identity at White Hall. My roots are there."

"We'll rent the Mansion House out, then. Maybe someday Harry will want to live there."

"Harry will inherit White Hall."

"But not until we are gone. The Mansion House would make a beautiful home for him when he marries. It's one of the finest in Adams County."

"What about your other brothers and sisters? Have they no interest in the property?"

"Well, of course I'll talk to them, but no one has ever shown any interest in the Sterner farm. Jamie and Belle will more than likely continue to live at the house. Mama has indicated she wants to stay there with them. And Charley and John are still too young to know what they want."

Lillie lowered her head and sighed. "White Hall is home. It's where I want to live for the rest of my life, dearest." She plucked at the ribbons of her bonnet. "You have no family ties to the Mansion House. Do what you want about it, but please don't ask me to live there. I don't want to live in a larger home. I would hate it. You belong here, in this house, with me."

Harry was beginning to stir and she propped him up against her. He rubbed his eyes with a chubby fist. "Are we at Grandma's house yet?" he asked, his voice still drugged with sleep.

"Almost," Lillie answered, tucking his shirt into his trousers. A shock of hair tended to fall in a soft wave over his forehead and she gently brushed it back. "Now, you must be a very good boy. You can play with your cousins, but I want you to stay away from those older boys and their rough games. You might get hurt."

Harry puckered his mouth in protest and Alex looked at her in exasperation. "Mein Gott, Lillie. You pamper him too much. He's a little boy. Let him behave like one!"

Later that night, Alex lay beside Lillie in their soft bed listening to the night sounds coming from the open window. Tree frogs called to one another, a calf bawled, and in the distance he heard the mournful wail of a train whistle.

He took her hand and pressed it against his cheek. "I'll miss Papa," he said, his voice trembling with emotion.

"Of course, you will, my darling. Your Papa was one of the most gentle and caring men I've ever known. But you come from a large and loving family—one I've always envied. It's not easy being an only child. We must remember that."

"Easy to spoil an only child with too much love. That is something you . . . we . . . must try harder to guard against."

Alex felt her hand tighten. He realized that at times she felt inadequate and guilty that she was unable to have more children. It was evident in her eyes, in the way she refused to look at him when they were around Belle and her increasing brood of children. Lately, it seemed to him, Lillie overcompensated her inadequacies with excessive parental love.

She sighed and nestled her head against his shoulder. "I always resented being an only child. It's a lonely life. Maybe I do coddle Harry too much, but he is such an appealing little boy and he is the only child I will ever have. There can't be such a thing as too much love. Can there?"

CHAPTER 11

It was spring again, the sixth since the birth of Alex's son and the year was 1886. Grover Cleveland was President; there were now thirty-eight states in the union; in the cities the Knights of Labor were agitating for an eight-hour work day; and the Statue of Liberty was unveiled in New York City.

Alex's dreams were still rooted in his land, but as he and other farmers put more and more land under the plow, farm products exceeded public demand, and prices for staple crops dropped steadily. In order to buy necessities and pay bills, farmers had to produce more. But the spiral only wound tighter, the more farmers produced the lower prices dropped.

Alex fought the declining price of wheat and corn by turning to cattle. Beef became the mainstay of their livelihood, and he turned every dollar he could spare into buying additional pasture land. Horses were still an interesting sideline for him, but not the love they once had been. Horses didn't make him money; beef did.

And Harry was growing into a handsome, energetic young man who talked with mounting enthusiasm of having Jamie teach him to drive a sulky, a passion Alex knew Lillie tried hard to ignore.

They were all in the kitchen on a rainy June morning, and Lillie was engaged in a battle of wills with their stubborn son.

"I don't want to wear those boots! They're black and ugly."

Alex looked at him with amusement. Harry stood with his sturdy legs firmly planted in the middle of the kitchen, his small fists clenched, his eyes ablaze with anger.

"It's raining outside," Lillie said.

"I know."

"Come on, be a good boy."

Harry stared up at her a moment then pushed his lower lip out, causing the cleft in his chin to deepen. She smiled at him and shook her head as if in mock despair. He was such a defiant little man, Alex thought, a beautiful child, with a mischievous smile, quick to laugh, just as quick to go silent when crossed.

"I wanna go with you, Papa."

"Then you must put your boots on," Lillie reasoned. "Papa is going to the Mansion House to check the north paddock and it will be a quagmire of mud after all this rain."

Harry turned imploring eyes on his father. "Will we stop at Aunt Belle's so I can play with Ian and the twins?"

"I imagine so. I usually stop there for a short visit."

Harry flopped down on the floor and began tugging at his boots, his forehead wrinkled in concentration. "I like playing with the twins—they're fun. I wish we had some babies of our own." He looked at his mother out of innocent blue eyes. "Why don't we get some babies, Mama?"

"Just because. Besides, you're enough for me." Lillie reached over to give his boots a final tug and kissed the top of his head. Harry struggled to his feet and wiped his nose on his sleeve. "I don't want to play with Ian. He'll want to play mumblety-peg and he always beats me."

Lillie put her arms around him and drew him to her bosom. "But you're much smarter, dear, and soon you'll be winning all the games. The next time we go to the grocery I'll buy you a nice new knife with a longer blade."

"And some of those marbles Mr. Barker has in his case? A nice bag with cat's eyes, aggies, and boulders? Then mine will be better than his."

"Whatever you want, darling."

Harry sniffed and thought about it.

Alex looked at his wife with despair. Why did she always reward the boy's defiance with a gift?

Lillie handed him his cap and gave him a little smack on the rump. "Now hurry along." She tucked a piece of paper into the pocket of his jacket. "And give this note to Aunt Belle. She's been asking for Mrs. Stover's recipe for walnut cakes."

* * *

Belle pulled plump green beans from the tangled vines and dropped them into the folds of the heavy apron gathered in her hand to form a deep well. A quickening breeze was warm on her cheeks and she worked absently, her thoughts drifting back to the events of the morning.

She had been baking bread in the kitchen when Alex surprised her with a visit. Impulsively, she reached up to kiss him on the cheek and when her bosom, heavy from nursing, brushed his sleeve, he wrenched his arm away with a violent action as though he had been burned. She looked at him in surprise. Alex was a married man—certainly no stranger to the touch of a woman's breast against his arm. But his face was crimson and when she looked questioning into his eyes, she was aghast at the pain she saw mirrored there.

Nervously, she pushed a stray tendril of hair behind her ear and stooped to search the vines hidden from view in the steamy, moist earth. The morning's episode deeply troubled her. She had always suspected Alex's attraction to her but she thought it long past. Lillie was her best friend, a sweet trusting soul, deeply in love with Alex. Belle pulled the folds of her apron, heavy with produce, tighter and began to walk toward the house. Maybe she was reading too much into Alex's reaction. No . . . no! A woman could tell those things. She remembered the scene in the jail when she suspected he was on the verge of kissing her. She would have to be more careful of her actions, more circumspect in her demeanor toward him. Lillie must never suspect.

And certainly not Jamie!

* * *

Each morning Alex woke at daylight supremely happy with his life, hurrying to the barn to let the cows out to pasture, then pausing to see the sun rise on the horizon before returning to the kitchen to enjoy breakfast with Lillie and Harry.

This morning, it seemed, was not to be such a happy one.

"I'm going to take Harry and Ian to the training track today," he announced, avoiding Lillie's sudden frown. She began placing the breakfast dishes on the table with a loud clatter.

"I'll not have you teach Harry to drive a sulky. He's much too young. It's a dangerous sport and it'll bring him into contact with all sorts of unsavory characters."

Harry looked at her in apparent surprise. "Daddy promised. He said soon as I was six and I've been past six for a long time now." His bottom lip poked out, and he looked at her with accusing eyes.

"Hush and eat your eggs. This is between me and your father."

Alex slammed his cup on the table, his thick brows furrowed, his eyes dark with anger. "You coddle the boy. Driving will teach him discipline—teach him sportsmanship—something he sorely needs to learn."

"I don't coddle him!"

"You do. You and your mother are always fussing over him, telling him how cute he is and buying him anything he wants. It's bad for him."

"Leave my mother out of this. You've never liked her anyway."

Alex pushed himself away from the table and stood up. "Now that could lead into a real argument. Your mother isn't the subject of this discussion. Harry is. I told Belle I'd stop for Ian at ten o'clock and take both boys to the training track. Belle isn't afraid to expose her boys to a man's world."

Harry's eyes looked from her to his father and back again. He looked like he was going to cry, but he didn't say a word. "Belle, again." she spat. "Always Belle! Why do Belle's children always have to be a part of everything you do? Isn't Harry enough for you? You spend more time with her family then you do your own. Maybe that's where you belong," Lillie cried, waving her tiny hands in the air.

Harry jumped to his feet in alarm. "Mama . . . ."

"Hush. And sit down," Alex barked.

Alex strode toward the back door and grabbed his cap from a peg. "Lillie, I think we should continue this discussion some other time."

The door slammed behind him.

The scene in the kitchen played over and over in Alex's mind as he went about his work over the next few days. He had not resumed the argument with Lillie, unsure how to handle the problem.

Lillie was clearly jealous of Belle. Did he spend too much time with Belle and her children? He certainly didn't intend to, but Rebert's Choice was always teeming with life: Mama, his brothers and sisters, Belle and her five lively children, people coming and going from the mill. White Hall seemed empty by comparison. And how was he to handle what he clearly perceived as Lillie's obsessive love for their son?

He could see the harm she was doing to the boy. All the maternal attention she should have been directing toward a whole passel of little ones, funneled into one small child. He doubted Harry could handle much more love.

And the boy himself worried Alex. The boy was self-assured and bold, but his self-assurance showed signs of arrogance; his boldness, rebellion. Harry needed a strong hand if he was to combat the duality in his character.

Alex drew in a deep breath. He would simply have to make a harder effort to present Harry with a strong father figure—spend more time with him—teach him how to be a man.

With that thought in mind he went in search of Harry. He found him behind the barn, kneeling in the dirt, playing a lonely game of marbles.

"How'd you like to go down to Conewago Creek and do a little fishing?" he asked, placing a hand on the small shoulder.

Harry jumped to his feet. "Just you and me, Daddy?"

"Just the two of us. If you'll take a spade and dig us a few worms from Mama's garden I'll get our poles. Maybe Mama will pack us some cookies and fix a jug of cold milk."

With a whoop of delight Harry ran toward the tool shed and within the hour they were walking side by side on a winding rock-studded path headed for the creek. Alex kept his pace slow and Harry matched him stride for stride. Alex hooked his thumb in the corner of his Levi pocket and noticed with a melting heart that his small son, observing him, had done the same.

Once at the creek they headed upstream toward a bend where an old willow tree clung to the bank, stretching lacy limbs and shadows across the water. "This is a good spot," Alex said, carefully placing their tin can full of fat worms in the shade. "There's a deep hole just under the shadow of those branches. Should be full of crappies and sun fish this time of day."

"And bass?" Harry asked.

Alex laughed. "Always after the big ones, huh? Spoken like a true Rebert. Well, I wouldn't be surprised if there wasn't a big ole bass lurking out there somewhere."

They propped their poles against the trunk of the tree, and Alex began to thread a nightcrawler over his hook in a series of small loops. Harry was a little rougher and tore the first worm in half. Alex reached over to do it for him, then changed his mind and watched Harry attempt another one. This time he managed to keep it on the hook, although it appeared to be slightly mangled.

The lines were soon in the water, the poles braced against two forked sticks stuck in the ground. Alex leaned back against the trunk of the willow with a deep sigh and crossed his legs. Harry did the same.

Warm sunlight filtered through the tree and glinted on the water like sparklers on the 4th of July. Insects hummed and a wood thrush called softly. Alex felt drowsy and was just about to drift off when he felt Harry's little fingers on his arm.

"I'm hungry."

"One cookie. We just got here."

"I mean awful hungry."

His eyes were bright, open and beguiling. Alex relented with a sigh. "Two, then." He was as bad as Lillie.

"Did you talk to Mama, like you promised, about letting me learn to drive one of the trotters?"

"Not yet, but I will."

"Mama says it's dangerous. But I saw Emma driving the other day and she's a girl."

"Nevertheless, your Mama worries about you."

"She treats me like a baby."

"I see." Alex watched the boy for a minute and then began the slow stroking of his mustache that he did unconsciously when he was thinking. "Harry, your Mama doesn't mean to." He smiled slightly, looking directly at Harry, holding his eye. "It's just that she loves you very much and I guess she's afraid that when you grow older and start to do grown up things you won't need her as much anymore. Can you understand that, son?"

"Yeah, I guess. But Papa, I wish she'd hurry up and have more babies like Aunt Belle and Aunt Sissy. Then she'd hug and squeeze them instead of me. I keep telling her I want a brother to play with, but she never answers me," Harry said, stuffing the last of the cookie into his mouth.

Alex grimaced, feeling a knot tightening in his stomach. He cleared his throat and stared at the chuckling silver creek. He had to explain this to Harry in a way he could understand.

"When you were born the doctor had to do an operation on your mother's belly and now God can't give her any more babies to carry there. She feels very, very bad that she can't give you brothers and sisters to play with and it hurts her when you ask about it."

Harry pondered that. "Was it my fault?" he asked, milk dribbling down his chin. "I mean . . . I mean did the doctor have to operate because of me being born?"

"No, no, son, not at all. It wasn't anyone's fault. Those things just happen sometimes and we don't understand why."

"Can't God fix it? Can't he make her belly right again?" He wrinkled his brow and cocked his head to look up at Alex. "Daddy, how do babies . . . ?" He froze as the cork on his line began to bob vigorously. "I gotta bite. I gotta bite," he yelled, grabbing his pole and yanking it with all his might, all questions thankfully forgotten.

It was a nice crappie and Harry removed it gingerly from the hook, poked a length of twine through its gill and placed it back in the water. Alex had a bite too and within half an hour they had a nice string of flopping fish.

Things quieted down for awhile and Harry rested his head against the rough bark of the tree and closed his eyes. Within minutes the sulky wallow and slap of the creek at its banks had lulled him to sleep.

Suddenly, several heavy bumps hit the bait on Alex's line. It was like an electric shock running up his arm, a sensation like none other in the world. He gave a mighty yank on his pole to set the hook and far out in the creek a large fish broke the water. This was no little pan-fish.

He wanted Harry to think the fish was his, so quickly he switched poles and shouted at him. "Wake up son, you've got a big one on your line." Harry grabbed the pole, bent almost double with the weight of the fish.

"Don't let the line go slack, he'll throw the hook. Keep winding it in. That's it, that's it—faster now—you got him close."

"I see him. I see him," Harry squealed.

"Pull him closer . . . keep your line tight or he'll jump the hook. Atta boy. There . . . I think I can reach him."

Alex stretched and pulled a large writhing bass onto the bank.

Harry trembled with excitement as he freed the hook from deep within the fish's mouth.

"Can I keep it Papa? Can I?"

"I'll say you can. That fellow must be three, four pounds. Wait 'til Mama sees it. She'll be so proud of you."

Harry seemed to struggle with the thought. "Are you proud of me, Papa?" he stammered.

Alex fought to control the tears forming in his eyes as he looked at the questioning eyes of his little boy. Why had he never spoken the words of love to his son? He always left that up to Lillie, afraid to appear soft as a parent. Yet God had recognized the need of all men for validation when he spoke to his own Son, saying, You are my son, whom I love; with you I am well pleased. Alex reached out and pulled Harry close. "Always, Harry. I'll always be proud of you. And . . . and I'll always love you."

Harry nodded and smiled, his face alight with a child's pleasure. They placed the bass on the stringer and settled back against the tree. Alex reached out and placed his big hand atop the small soft fist of his little son. "You may be too young to understand this Harry, but you must always be proud of who you are. You're a gentleman, Harry. A Rebert. A product of proud German heritage and breeding."

Alex thought that he was giving his son good advice. To him, gentleman meant landowner, breeding meant a noble ancestry. He never suspected that Harry, spoiled by Lillie since birth, might put a different interpretation on his words. That to Harry gentleman might mean that he wasn't expected to work the land he owned and that breeding might mean he was better than most people.

Hens scratched in the manure pile and a calf bawled for its mother as Lillie limped from the hen house toward the kitchen, replaying the previous day's scene in her memory, fighting the coiling tightness in her stomach. Why did she seemingly resent the time Alex spent with Belle's children? She had no real cause to be jealous, but it was like an acid eating away at her. Was it his apparent joy in tumbling about with the unruly brood or was it his constant exposure to the vibrant Belle that worried her. She shook her head, appalled. Such thoughts were unchristian and she would spare no time thinking of them. Still, the gulf between Alex and herself seemed to be widening, his anger more easily provoked.

She wiped tears from her eyes, ashamed of them, yet unable to stop. The stringent scent of the farmyard vied with the intoxicating smell of honeysuckle and drying wash that fluttered on the line. She sighed. Conflict—always conflict and choices. But life needn't be sad she reminded herself as Harry went running toward the barn carrying a large fish by its gills.

Lillie was gathering zinnias for the house when she heard Harry scream and Amos, their hired hand, shout, "Missus Rebert! Missus Rebert! Come here—hurry!"

She dropped the flowers and raced across the side yard to the brick barn. Harry sat on the earthen barn floor, sobbing and clutching his hand, rocking back and forth, blood gushing from a gaping cut that spurted blood from his wrist and the palm of his hand.

"He done it guttin' that there bass," Amos sputtered.

Lillie tore the ruffle from her skirt and twisted it around a sliver of wood. "Ride for the doctor. Doc Fremont. Go directly to his house. And hurry!"

Amos ran.

"Am I gonna lose my hand?" Harry clung to her, eyeing the bloody knife and the pool of dark blood on the floor.

"No, no, child. But you must sit still, now, to keep the cut from bleeding more."

Her son lay against her, pale and sobbing. Lillie stroked his hair and held him tight.

Alex, alerted by Amos, rushed into the barn and dropped to his knees beside Harry.

Lillie held out Alex's fillet knife.

Alex took it from her, his face white. He picked Harry up in his arms and, with Lillie at his heels, carried the sobbing boy to the house.

They laid him on the couch in the parlor and within minutes Lillie had assembled clean cloths, sheets, blankets, hot water, and a collection of her garden herbs. Alex sat beside him, keeping pressure on the wound, loosening and tightening the tourniquet, trying to keep Harry calm.

Lillie sat down and opened her bible.

Harry's eyes grew wide with terror. "Am I dying? Is this dying?"

"Of course not, honey. I just want to say a little powwow." She withdrew a slip of paper, put her hand over the awful cut, and began to recite: "This is the day the wound was made. O Blood! thou shalt stop and be still until the Virgin Mary bears another son."

Alex glared at her. "You know I don't believe in your silly, superstitious powwows."

"Well, you can call it superstitious if you want, but my Papa always believed in powwowing and so do I!" With her free hand she reached up to finger the pouch of muslin she wore about her neck to ward off the cholera that was currently sweeping the region. "It isn't magic—a powwow cures through faith. Remember when you had that terrible pain in your bowels and I treated it with a potion made from the buds of balm of Gilead steeped in whiskey? It stopped your cramps, didn't it? And look, Harry's bleeding has almost stopped."

And indeed only a small amount of blood seeped from beneath the compress. It seemed like hours before she heard the familiar sound of hooves on the cobbled stable-yard announcing the arrival of the doctor.

When Harry's wound had been stitched and swathed in clean bandages Alex carried him to the bedroom while Lillie prepared a cup of tea made from wild cherry bark to lower his pulse and calm him.

When Lillie reached the bedroom with the steaming tea she found Alex sitting at the head of the bed, one arm around Harry while the other gently stroked the bandaged hand.

Harry began to cry again the minute he saw her.

"Will I . . . will my hand be ugly, now?"

"Of course not. You'll have a very interesting scar that you can show off to all your friends."

Harry stopped sobbing to consider this. "I'll have something that Ian doesn't have, won't I?"

"Yes. And you can brag about the big fish you caught and how brave you were when the doctor sewed up your hand."

"And about how Papa let me use his knife, all by myself."

Lillie's eyes sought Alex's, but he dropped his gaze to the floor and gave a small, embarrassed cough. She bent down to push the wayward wave of fair hair from Harry's forehead and kissed his cheek.

"I'm very special, aren't I, Mama?" he asked, his voice growing sleepy.

"Indeed you are, sweetheart. The most special Rebert of all."

Harry's eyes grew heavy and his head nodded against Alex's sturdy arm. Lillie lit a lamp against the gathering gloom of an approaching storm and settled in a rocker close to the bed. She watched Alex's face as he looked down at his sleeping son, love softening the harsh planes of his strong face. Father and son. Oh God, how she loved them both.

Lillie rose to stare out the window at the gray, turbulent afternoon. Dark, thick clouds were approaching from the west. A flock of Canada geese honked noisily over the farm pond, riding the erratic wind. She directed her gaze toward the awesome mountains that rose from the valley floor so close she felt she could reach out and touch them. They gave her a feeling of sadness she couldn't explain. She shivered.

She felt Alex's presence behind her, then felt the light pressure of his hand on her shoulder. "Somebody walking over your grave?" he asked.

"Something like that I guess. I don't know why but those mountains seem to speak of a coming sorrow."

She sagged against his shirt front, trembling slightly in the aftermath of the traumatic afternoon. "Laws, Alex, it's begun to rain," she said, smiling a little.

"Lillie . . . "

She turned and looked up into his beseeching, dark eyes. His shirt was unbuttoned at the top, and she could see his heart pumping in his chest. His sleeves were rolled up too, and she saw the knotted muscles in his arms. She knew he expected recriminations, but any words of anger that came to mind flattened before the force of the love she felt for this man, as flattened as the sodden leaves of the trees outside.

Alex seemed to read her message because he gathered her in his arms and they stood that way for long minutes as the wind slammed against the stone house; slammed in angry, relentless gusts, rattling the window, causing the candle to flicker, while Lillie languished in her husband's love, and her son slept peacefully beside her.

CHAPTER 12

On a humid, cloudy morning late in October Alex hurried from the barn toward the house where lazy smoke curled from the chimney. Horse chestnuts littered the ground while on the lawn a thin crust of frost lay like white gauze, and Alex drew his jacket close to his body, anticipating the snug kitchen and a hearty breakfast.

The pungent aroma of smoked sausage and boiled coffee assaulted him as soon as he opened the back door. He grabbed a chair at the table next to Harry and heaped his plate high with fried potatoes, eggs, and sausage, watching his son with amusement as he piled twice as much on his own plate. Lillie limped from stove to table, filling the empty platters, and the three of them talked of the upcoming Harvest fair at South Mountain until Harry dashed for the door, already late for school.

Alex's brows shot up in wonder as Jamie strode into the kitchen, his rifle slung over his shoulder.

"Well, this is a surprise. Anything wrong at the mill?" Alex asked.

"Nothing 'cept bad times and this darn drought. Lots of folks aren't going to have feed enough to get them through the winter. Katie says we're about out of venison so I thought I'd take the day off and see if I couldn't get us a buck. Thought maybe you'd like to go along."

"The woods are tinder dry. Make tracking hard an' I don't know as how it's safe to be firing a gun," Alex said slowly, pondering the wisdom in going.

"Up to you. I seen a big buck, at least a ten pointer, over on the ridge behind the meeting house last week."

Alex pushed his chair away from the table and with raised eyebrows shot a questioning look at Lillie.

"I'd enjoy some fresh venison stew," she said. "My canned meat is nearly all gone and so are our salted steaks."

Alex nodded to Jamie who had settled himself at the table. "Help yourself to some of those delicious sausages, while I wash up and get my rifle." He pushed away from the table and walked over to the tin sink where he pumped some water into his hands, carefully cleaned remnants of potato from his mustache, and dried his hands on the roller towel.

While Jamie busied himself at the table, Lillie made a packet of sandwiches for their lunch. Alex took his Kentucky rifle from the brackets above the door, retrieved his powder horn from a peg on the wall, and filled his pockets with percussion caps from a tin box in the cupboard.

"Let's go," he said, briskly.

Jamie shoved a final sausage into his mouth and followed him out the door.

Within an hour they were deep in the woods behind the Hostetter farm. For awhile they hunted together, jumping several doe, but with no sign of the ten-pointer Jamie was after.

"Why don't you cross over to Big Flat atop the ridge and take up a post? I'll wait for half an hour and then start driving toward you," Alex said.

"Good idea." Jamie glanced heavenward where black clouds roiled over the mountains. "Much as we need rain I hope that storm holds off awhile."

Alex watched Jamie stride away then settled himself on a fallen log and pulled a sandwich from his pocket. Two thick slices of Lebanon bologna, highly flavored and smoked hard, rested between slabs of homemade bread. He munched contentedly while his left hand caressed the intricately carved walnut stock of the Kentucky rifle lying across his knees.

The wood of the Kentucky seemed to grow softer and more lustrous with each passing year. It had been a prized possession of his great-grandfather, Johann Rebert, bought originally from Frederick Sell, a local gunsmith and one of the finest craftsmen of Kentucky rifles in all of Pennsylvania. Johann had passed it down through the generations to the oldest son. Gently Alex rubbed his fingertips over Sell's trademark on the patch box, that of a bird plucking a feather from its wing. The iron for the muzzle came from Lebanon, Pennsylvania but Johann had provided Mr. Sell with the wood for the stock from the root of a big walnut tree on his farm near Jefferson. Although called "Kentucky," the rifles had been invented by gunsmiths in Germany and everything about them was German. The rifle's range and accuracy was unsurpassed and Alex felt an intense tug of pride in his heritage as he slung it across his shoulder and rose to his feet to start across the field toward the ridge.

As he walked along he kicked out a covey of quail, who exploded in the air with a flurry of wings like popcorn over a hot fire, and far up the ridge a wild turkey yelped once. Overhead a lone golden eagle circled in the darkening sky and thunder rumbled in the distance.

Alex entered the woods and had barely covered a hundred yards before he jumped the buck, bedded down in thick brush. The buck broke no more than twenty yards away with a violent crash and Alex glimpsed his magnificent rack and flag of white tail as he disappeared like the wind.

Alex started forward, faster now, his heart racing. So intent was he on his quarry that he lost sight of the approaching storm. A booming clap of thunder and a flash of lightning stopped him in his tracks and he looked up at the ominous sky. The smell of rain hung heavy on the gusting wind and claps of thunder drew closer.

He continued forward until fat drops of rain began to pelt his shoulders and then he crawled into the nearest thicket to wait out the storm.

Alex stretched out on his stomach, his rifle beneath him to protect it from the rain, his head buried on crossed arms. "Tarnation," he grumbled, yanking his cap down over his ears. "I had that ole boy moving toward Jamie, I know I did. Now he'll bed down again and I'll never find him."

He jumped as lightning tore through the heavens, cracking like a rifle blast, and the ground trembled beneath him. That was close, he thought with a shudder. That hit something!

Crash after crash of thunder and lightning stabbed the black sky and he lay inert on the trembling earth, protecting his rifle from the torrents of rain and the fury of the storm. Gradually the storm blazed its way east, the rain slackened, and the thunder faded like the rumble of a passing train.

Alex rose to his knees brushing mud and leaves from his clothing, the back of his jacket sodden, but his rifle and powder mercifully dry.

His thick brows bunched together and he sniffed the air, turning his head this way and that, searching the sky. Was that smoke he smelled?

He slung his rifle over his shoulder and for the next half hour tramped through the underbrush in a futile attempt to kick out the bedded buck before beginning the climb toward Big Flat. The odor of scorched earth was more distinct now and ahead, a thin column of smoke rose into the clearing sky. Lightning must have hit a tree he mused. I hope Jamie is alright.

Earlier, Jamie had climbed the steep embankment covered with hardwoods and hemlock until he reached a flat at the summit of the ridge. A dead hardwood surrounded by small pines and dense underbrush stood sentry to the woods beyond and he scrambled up the tree until he reached a branch that gave him an unobstructed view of the meadow beneath.

He straddled the limb, letting his legs dangle in the air, settled his rifle on his shoulder and leaned back against the tree trunk to wait.

His thoughts drifted, but his gaze never stopped sweeping the woods fronting his tree. The sky had turned leaden and a sharp wind worried his cap. A grouse twittered in a thicket, thunder rumbled nearby. He looked up at black clouds approaching fast. Lightning was flashing in the distance. He began to make moves toward leaving the tree, but when he looked to the woods again he froze, motionless, all thought of the gathering storm forgotten.

The buck stood at the edge of the meadow just beyond the protection of the trees. He was a massive, majestic, ten-pointer and he lifted his magnificent head, testing the wind with flaring nostrils.

Jamie's breath caught in his throat, his heart bumping against his rib-cage. Slowly, he brought the butt of his rifle to rest against his shoulder and took aim.

The buck stamped one forefoot and began walking toward him. Jamie sucked in his breath. He had ten, maybe twelve, points. His carriage was that of a king and he trod as though he owned the earth.

Jamie fixed him in his sights and waited. Rain began to fall and lightning flashed close by, but Jamie's thoughts were only on the magnificent animal moving toward him.

He reached up to wipe rain from his face. I must let him get a bit closer. There. That should do. His finger trembled and he took a deep breath to steady himself.

At the instant he pulled the trigger a bolt of lightning rent the sky and the hollow tree in which he perched split in half and exploded into flames.

Jamie fell to the ground. Searing flames ran down the forked trunk, pinning him to the earth as merciful blackness claimed him.

Alex strode from the cover of the dripping forest into the open flat where he could now see the source of the smoke he had been following. A tree had indeed been struck and it, and the surrounding pines and underbrush, were burning fiercely as the wind caught the fire.

A sense of foreboding washed over Alex all thought of the hunt forgotten.

"Jamie! Jamie, where are you?" he yelled frantically.

No answer. No sound other than the hissing and crackling of burning wood. With rapid strides Alex hurried forward, his gaze desperately sweeping the area around the fire. The entire tree was ablaze, the wind whipping it into a wall of flame. He ran toward the smoke and flames, fear clutching his guts. And then he heard him. A muffled moan—coming from the direction of the downed tree.

Alex flung his rifle to the ground and ran toward the sound. The burning hardwood had pulled several small pines with it when it fell and the tangled mass was burning fiercely. He circled, trying to get closer.

Something moved near the center of the conflagration and suddenly he saw Jamie's head and upper torso protruding beneath the massive trunk of the blazing tree.

"Jamie," he screamed. "Oh, my God, Jamie."

Jamie moaned again, but his eyes remained closed.

Flames were creeping up the hollow tree, closer to Jamie's still form, and Alex crawled as close as he could get, but the wind was whipping the fire through the underbrush. In desperation he removed his jacket and began beating the flames, hands burning, the nauseous smell of burning hair filling his nostrils. His jacket caught fire and, sobbing, he fell back. He took a deep breath, his lungs screaming with pain.

He couldn't get any closer.

Jamie began to cough and thrash his head. "Help," he cried. "Someone help me."

"I'm here," Alex shouted, gagging when his lungs filled with acrid smoke. "I'm coming."

Once more he tried to penetrate the slackening flames. Fire singed his eyebrows and he wrapped his smoldering coat about his head. Then the fire flared up again with a giant whoosh as the front of the tree exploded and Alex raised his hand to shade his face from the heat. He couldn't breathe, his lips blistered and his wrist smeared with blood from a long scratch. He had to pull back.

A sob tore from his raw throat as he took in the pitiful scene. Jamie was pinned deep within the tangle of branches and brush, his legs and lower body hopelessly crushed by the weight of the tree. Even if Alex could reach him it would be impossible to free him without help and the flames were creeping inexorably closer.

Jamie was fully conscious now and aware of his plight. Flames were licking the branches close to his head and he threw his hands across his eyes.

"Shoot me, Alex," he yelled desperately. "For God's sake, don't let me burn."

As Jamie's plea ripped through the smoke filled air Alex dropped to his knees in despair. He threw his arms up in supplication, his spirit crying out in rebellion. "Oh, Lord, I can't. He's like my brother. How can I possibly do such a thing?"

"I can't, Jamie," he shouted angrily. "Don't ask me to do this."

"You must! If you love me, you must. Don't let the fire get me."

Sobbing, hardly aware of his actions, Alex retreated to where his rifle lay, picked it up, and ran back, drawing as close to Jamie as he could get. He looked through the smoke and hissing flames to Jamie's pleading eyes.

A scream tore from Jamie's lips as the fabric of his jacket caught fire and without conscious thought Alex raised his rifle and pulled the trigger.

Slowly Alex moved away from the heat of the fire and the scene he could no longer watch. He sank to the ground and bowed his head. For a long time, he knelt, mute and dazed, the prayer like a millstone in his breast, a cold heaviness that bore as much guilt as grief. Could he have done more? He wanted to pray, needed to pray . . . but he was so exhausted and depleted he could not find the strength to pray. And so he merely knelt there, letting the enormity of the tragedy wash over him, until he could bring himself to begin the long trek home.

CHAPTER 13

Lillie took Alex's cold hand in hers. "You mustn't blame yourself, dear. It was the only thing you could do." She looked into eyes haunted by inner pain and raised his hand to her lips. "You did it out of love. It . . . it called for a strength not many of us are capable of."

"Belle will . . ."

"Belle will thank you for your mercy, not condemn you for it. We must go to her at once." And to herself she whispered, "and, please Lord, let me forget my petty jealousies and reach out in Christian love to my friend in her time of need."

"Oh, Lillie. Five children left for her to rear alone; the twins are barely three," Alex sobbed.

Lillie pressed his head against her shoulder and let him cry, let him pour out the agony of the past few hours.

It took them an hour in the driving rain to reach Rebert's Choice where Charlie and John had brought Jamie's charred body. Alex pulled the carriage up to the front gate. His stomach contracted like a fist and sweat trickled down from his armpits. Lillie gathered her heavy skirts in her arm and ran to the porch while Alex pulled horse and buggy to the shelter of the wagon shed. Breathing a silent prayer he walked slowly to the porch, where Lillie stood waiting.

The front door flew open and nine-year-old Rebecca stood before them with tears streaming down her thin cheeks. From the hallway young Ian came running toward the open door and practically threw himself into Lillie's open arms. "My daddy died, Aunt Lillie," he cried, burying his face in her long skirt.

"I know, Ian," she said, hugging the small boy to her. "I've come to be with you and your mamma."

Elizabeth, standing in the shadows behind Rebecca, looked at them with quiet dignity. "Mama and Grandma Katie are in the parlor with Ellen's beau, Reverend Stauffer," the little girl said.

Such a serious, reserved child, Alex thought sadly. Elizabeth must be almost eight now. He wondered if the child had been able to cry.

"Then we will all go to the kitchen while the good Reverend is comforting them," Lillie said, taking Elizabeth's small hand and placing an arm around Ian who was still clinging to her skirt. "Maybe Ellen can make some hot chocolate for all of us."

Rebecca followed them as they walked down the hall, past the closed parlor door.

"Ellen fixed our supper," she offered.

The kitchen was warm and smelled of chicken pot pie and warm bread. The twins, Adam and Carolyn, were playing with some building blocks in front of a crackling fire and Ellen's arms were buried in a pan of soapy dish water. She looked up and smiled sadly.

"What a tragedy."

Alex nodded. Just then little Adam angrily scattered the tower of blocks he had been carefully constructing, causing Carolyn to cry. Adam looked up, his big brown eyes somber. "They took our Papa away. They wrapped him up in a big sheet and put him on a big board and he didn't even move and he didn't even say goodbye."

Lillie took the chubby little boy in her arms and hugged him tight. "Your Mama will tell you all about your Papa when she has finished talking with Reverend Stauffer."

"Mommy has been crying and crying," Carolyn said, her own lip trembling.

Alex squatted on the floor and began restacking the blocks, his thoughts racing. *What in heaven's name could he say to these children?*

Rebecca ran to him and buried her head on his chest. "Oh, Uncle Alex," she sobbed, "they couldn't even leave him here with us."

Alex rose and stood quietly for a few minutes, stroking her silken head, and then placed a finger under her chin and raised it until her eyes met his. "I know how hard it is, Rebecca, but you're old enough to understand that your father was badly burned. He needs to be taken care of by the undertaker in town; it's not a job for the women to do. You don't want your brothers and sisters to see your Papa like that, do you?" She blinked and looked down at the floor. Alex pulled her close and hugged her again.

"What happened to your eyebrows and eyelashes, Uncle Alex?" Elizabeth suddenly asked. "They're all gone."

"Uncle Alex was trying to help your Papa and I'm afraid he got burned. They'll grow back," Lillie said, taking his hand in hers.

"But Papa won't come back, will he?" Rebecca cried, the tears spilling over once more."

Alex sank to his knees and pulled the trembling child into his arms. How, oh how, could he explain the events of the past twenty-four hours to these children? A wave of doubt swept through him like sand through an hourglass. Help me God, he prayed.

"Rebecca . . . "

Lillie gently interrupted. "I think that we should go into the parlor to talk with your Mommy, dear. Ellen says that Annie and George and Emma and her husband have been sent for. They'll be here shortly to help."

Ellen, finished with the supper dishes, sat quietly watching the proceedings. "Why don't I take the children upstairs and read them a story."

"Yeah, yeah," Adam chirped.

Ellen rose and smiled at all the children. "I'll bet you'll like the one about Harry the Bootblack," she said.

"That sounds like an excellent idea," Alex said. "Lillie and I want to talk to Belle."

He smiled at the children as they trooped out the door behind Ellen, then took Lillie's arm and they walked to the family parlor where Belle sat on the edge of a tapestry covered sofa, her head bowed, her hands twisting a lace hanky.

"Lillie . . . Alex," she sobbed, rising unsteadily to her feet. "Oh Alex, I've been waiting for you. Whatever am I going to do?"

Alex reached her in three quick strides and gathered her into his arms.

"Belle . . . ach, Belle, how can I explain, how . . . "

Belle reached up to place her fingers on his lips. "Hush. No words are necessary. You did what God called upon you to do. You were your brother's keeper 'til the end and I'll be eternally grateful to you for that."

The tears started again and Alex rocked her in his arms, amazed how thin Belle's trembling shoulders felt through the fabric of her dress. Thin and vulnerable.

Lillie stood quietly and waited until the weeping slowed and Belle pulled away from Alex. She held out her arms and they embraced.

"I don't pretend to know your pain, dear," Lillie murmured, "and I don't have any idea what to say to you, except that we are here to share our love and our sorrow."

Lillie's words caused Belle to break down again and for a few minutes her body shook. Then with a mighty effort she moved away and pulled herself erect. "I must be strong," she said, dabbing her eyes with the sodden hanky. "I have five little children to try to explain this to."

"Where is Mama?" Alex asked.

"She went upstairs. She felt the need to talk with the Lord in the privacy of her own room."

Reverend J.J. Stauffer had been waiting quietly in the corner of the emotion-packed parlor. Now he moved toward Belle with outstretched hands. He was a small man, thin and slight, with pale thinning hair, a full mustache and a neatly trimmed goatee covering his chin. Wire rimmed glasses covered eyes soft with compassion. J.J. was a perfect match for the quiet Ellen and everyone expected them to post their bans before the end of the year. "I will talk with the children if you tell me what you want said," he murmured.

Belle looked at him hopefully and then her shoulders sagged. "I do appreciate that, but I must talk to them myself, each one individually in a way I feel they can accept. Perhaps Alex will help me, his presence will be reassuring to the children." She turned her anguished face to Lillie. "The children are trying very hard to be brave. They'll be a great comfort to me and Mother Katie in the days to come, as will Alex. I hope you don't feel excluded, Lillie, but Alex has been like a father to the children and we'll desperately need his help at the mill until Ian is older."

"Ian is only five," Lillie gasped, jumping up in dismay. Belle nodded. "I will run the mill until then, of course, but someday Ian will need to take over and he must learn the business as he grows."

Alex felt his jaw drop. "What do you mean you will run the mill? That's no place for a woman!"

"Don't tell me my place! I'm as strong and intelligent as any man." Her gray eyes blazed with defiance before her voice began to break and Alex moved to her side and took her hand.

"We'll talk about it later," he grumbled. "I'll help in any way I can. We're a family. God will give us the strength to get through this . . . He will tell us what to do. I believe that."

Lillie sat down beside Belle and the three sat wordlessly, each locked in their own thoughts.

Finally Alex cleared his throat and broke the pregnant silence. "Come, Lillie. We'll leave Belle to talk with the Pastor. They must make plans for the funeral."

"Oh, stay, please. Both of you," Belle cried. "I need your help. Someone must tell my Mama and, of course, get word to Edwin and Sissy."

Alex leaned back on the stiff sofa and sighed. All the earthly details of death did have to be arranged. He wondered if God in His wisdom gives us all of these little things to do, things to turn our minds from the first terrible grief.

Belle sat with red, swollen eyes, staring at the floor, her hands turning and twisting the sodden hanky. "The funeral will be at

Christ Church, of course. Jamie will be buried in the McPherson plot, next to his father."

* * *

Carriages stretched for over a mile and the little church was unable to accommodate all the mourners as Jamie was laid to rest.

Numb with grief, Alex looked away from the casket covered with a blanket of soft pine boughs and glanced at Belle standing beside the open grave, a three-year-old twin on each side holding tightly to her hand. Ian stood in front, leaning heavily against his mother's legs with Elizabeth and Rebecca beside him.

Belle stood with her head slightly bowed. The cold wind whipped the black veil from her face, stirring the mass of lustrous red hair about her face. In her wanness she reminded Alex of a Renoir painting he had once admired on the cover of a book. He flushed with guilt, immediately ashamed of his thoughts at a time like this. What in the world was wrong with him? Clenching his jaw he forced his mind away from Jamie's widow and tried to follow the minister's final prayer.

Alex threw himself into work as one possessed, falling exhausted into bed at night, his body demanding a sleep that refused to come. Night thoughts haunted him and the scene on Big Flat played over and over in his mind. The screams of terror, the fire snapping and cracking, the blast from his rifle ringing out in the bellowing smoke. Could he have done more? Had he valued his own safety more than Jamie's life? Why had God put him in the terrible position where he had to make such a terrible choice? Was it the Devil telling him to kill the friend he thought of as a brother, prodding all the dark recesses of rivalry and envy lurking in his soul?

No. He could blame no one for his decision. Neither God, nor the Devil. It had been his and his alone.

Late one afternoon, a week after Jamie's funeral, he closed the mill early and wandered up to the house to talk to Mama. He found her in the parlor, sitting alone in the gathering shadows, her hands folded quietly in her lap. Alex observed the blue veins jutting upward from the work worn hands like mountain ranges. Mama is getting old, he realized with a start, and I never really noticed.

She moved to the sofa when she saw him and patted a spot next to her. "Come sit with me, son."

Alex settled back with a deep sigh and closed his eyes. The words he desperately needed to say would not move past his lips. The assurance he so desperately craved seemed out of reach.

"Can I help?" Katie asked quietly.

"Ach, mama. It is I who should be helping you. I have lost a friend, but you have lost a boy you looked on as a son."

Katie nodded sadly. "Jamie was a son and brother to all of us."

"It's only been a year since you lost Papa."

"And I miss him every day of my life. But, Alex, I have been able to ease my sorrow through the process of grieving. I suspect that you have been so tormented with self-chastisement that you have not afforded yourself that comfort." Her eyes searched his. "Really dear, you must surrender yourself to God's healing power."

"God! Where was God when Jamie needed Him . . . when I needed Him? Where is He now when I wrestle with my conscience and my nightmares? He deserted me in my hour of greatest need."

"God's presence with you does not depend on your feelings. We cannot always feel his presence. You'll pass through this dryness, Alex, and be stronger for the experience." Katie picked up the bible lying in her lap and began to turn its tissue like pages. "Esther . . . Job . . . Psalms . . . ah, here it is . . . Psalm 139. Listen to these words, Alex, my dear:"

> O LORD, you have searched me
> and you know me.
> You know when I sit and when I rise;
> you perceived my thoughts from afar.
> You discern my going out and my lying down;
> you are familiar with all my ways.

> Before a word is on my tongue
> you know it completely, O LORD

"And then this, Alex, verses 9 and 10:"

> If I go up to heaven, you are there;
> if I make my bed in the depths, you are there.
> If I rise on the wings of the dawn,
> if I settle on the far side of the sea,
> even there, your hand will guide me,
> your right hand will hold me fast.

Alex felt the cleansing tears roll down his cheeks and his body, held taut as a bow-string since the terrible accident, bent as a willow before the wind. He sagged against his mother and she gathered him in her arms, pulling him close to her bosom like she had when he was a small child in need of comfort.

"Oh, Mama. I guess I have been searching and searching for God and He was here all along."

* * *

Belle petitioned the courts to make Alex guardian of the children and Lillie resolved to make them feel a part of her family. Mother Katie, together with Belle and her children, would continue to share the house at Rebert's Choice and one of the young apprentices was put in charge of the grist mill. Alex took over the stables and devoted the rest of his time to getting Belle's affairs in order. It seemed he spent all his time at Rebert's Choice and Lillie tried to quell her uneasiness. Belle's children were always in his lap or clinging to his hand—even Harry noticed it and was unusually demanding when Alex was home. Edward's estate still was not settled and Alex had to go to court to resolve settlement on the Mansion House since he and Jamie had been joint administrators.

In January, Adams County suffered the worst blizzard of the

century. Belle and the children were visiting at White Hall when the blizzard hit and after putting the little ones to bed the adults sat huddled before the fire watching the huge drifts of snow form outside the windows. The blazing fire seemed to dance in Belle's brilliant hair and Lillie marveled, as she had often done, at Belle's beauty. Belle noticed her look and reached over to clasp her hand. "What would I do without you during this terrible time?"

"Alex and I will continue to help all we can, but you must try to gain strength from your children, Belle. Ian, young as he is, wants desperately to be the man in the house. And Rebecca has become a regular little mother to the twins. She's old enough to understand your loss. Don't be afraid to lean on her for the companionship you so desperately need."

"I'll try, Lillie. I will try. But when I look at Ian I see Jamie. I see him in all the children, but most of all in Ian. And it's hard, awfully hard. They are, after all, still small children." Belle's eyes flared with sudden fire and her jaw grew stubborn. "I plan to take back control of the mill. I'm as capable as that young apprentice. More so."

"But you are still grieving . . . you are still wearing widow's weeds."

"I will not sit idly by, twisting my handkerchief and looking for pity." At the stricken look on Lillie's face she hastened to add, "Oh Lillie, you're the best friend I have . . . you've always understood me. You've always been so sweet and willing to share Alex with us. I appreciate that, but I must learn to stand on my own two feet."

Lillie glanced quickly away, feeling tension knot the pit of her stomach. Share Alex with a women he had once been in love with? A woman who was now a widow. She pulled at her lip with a fluttering hand, dismayed at her foolishness. Alex was a devoted husband and father. Chagrined she gave Belle a soft smile and took her hand. "And you'll always have both of us, I promise."

CHAPTER 14

The next two years flew by quickly and suddenly it was Christmas again and Harry was eight years old.

His Christmas wish list grew every day. The Sears catalogue was dog-eared with things he felt he simply had to have. The newest thing on his long list was a cumbersome looking self-propelled vehicle called a bicycle with a huge front wheel and tall seat and a smaller rubber tired rear wheel.

Alex's lips curled in disgust as he looked at Harry's long list of desired possessions. To his thinking, America was becoming a decadent society and his family was no exception.

During the years following the Civil War the country had begun to shift its focus from production to consumption in a desperate attempt to put the horrors of war behind them. Farms and industries were producing so much that most people could afford to re-orient their attitudes toward material wants. What had once been accessible only to a few suddenly became available to many; what had formerly been dreams became necessities. No trend had ever affected the lives of people in Alex's community more decisively than this one. He understood the reasons, but he could not condone it. His neighbors were rushing towards an uncharted future, losing sight of the things that brought real meaning to this country.

He threw the list aside. "What in tarnation does Harry need with a contraption like a bicycle," Alex sputtered. "He'll break his neck."

"The advertisement says it's the perfect way to travel."

"What's wrong with a horse?"

"Harry says that is old-fashioned."

"At least there's no need to feed it."

Lillie smiled and thumbed the pages with rapidly moving fingers. "A new baseball and mitt would be a nice surprise."

"Mein Gott, woman, you are eternally trying to satisfy needs and wants the child may not even be aware he has."

"Harry is a good boy, and the only child we have. We are certainly prosperous enough to give him a few Christmas presents."

"That's not the point and you know it," he said sternly.

"I know that for this past year you seem serious and restrained when it comes to showing affection for your son, but open and loving with Belle's brood."

"They don't have a father," Alex shouted, his face red.

"And you are not their father. You are Harry's father."

A scowl covered Alex's face and he stalked to the back of the kitchen where he grabbed his hat from a peg and headed for the door. "Harry is at Rebert's Choice now, sledding with Ian and Adam. I'll get them to help me cut a Christmas tree from the woodlot. I'll be back by supper," he said, slamming the door none too softly.

Alex found Belle alone in the kitchen angrily stuffing sheets of paper into the open grate of the cook stove. Her red hair floated about her face, gleaming with fire in the golden light cast by the flickering flames.

"What are you burning?" he asked, acutely uncomfortable with the feeling she still invoked in him. "You look as though you are mad at the world."

"The silly plans for our house down by the creek that I will never have. Dreams, Alex. That's what I'm burning . . . silly dreams."

Alex grimaced, still churning with his own vexation. He wasn't good with words, didn't know how to deal with Belle's anger and disappointment. "We all have dreams that must be put aside for one reason or another. The trick, Belle, is to open your heart and mind to new dreams that can take root and grow. The children will help you put your life together again if you'll give them the chance."

"But Alex, the children are daily reminders of Jamie." Her voice shook as she struggled for control. "When I look into Rebecca's eyes full of laughter and imagination, so like her father's, or push back that unruly lock of blond hair that falls onto Ian's forehead as Jamie's always did, I see him with such an intensity I sometimes cry out. It frightens the children." She bowed her head and the flaming hair fell about her unhappy face. "I'm . . . I'm consumed with loneliness and a desire to feel a man's arms about me." She spoke slowly, and her voice was barely above a whisper. "I think the worst part of being a widow is not being touched by a man's loving hands."

Alex stared at her beseeching face, at the agonized pout of her lips. The yearning in her beautiful gray eyes was more than he could stand. He couldn't swallow, couldn't breathe for the wanting of her.

Without thinking, Alex drew her into his arms. She looked at him with an intensity that was both serious and fervent, her smoky eyes round in apprehension.

Slowly he lowered his lips to hers.

He hadn't meant to kiss her, didn't remember taking the initiative, but now that he felt the tentative pressure of her lips against his he couldn't stop himself.

Years of pent up desire exploded into that kiss. Belle seemed to go liquid and she sagged against him, her full bosom pressing against his shirt front. He moved one hand into her hair, the other between her shoulder blades, pulling her closer. She seemed to melt into him, his hands dug deep into the glorious hair he had always dreamed of caressing and he buried his face in its fiery splendor. "God forgive me, I want you," he groaned. His breath came fast as he lowered his lips to hers once more—demanding and possessive. "Now, Belle. Right now."

His words seemed to awaken her and she began to push him away, her breath coming in jagged gasps.

"I . . ." Turning away, she pressed her hands against his chest. "I'm not ready for this. Not with you. I'm not sure what made me respond as I did. Everything happened too fast. I craved a man's caress. But you are married, Alex. Married to my best friend. I could never betray her trust."

Alex trembled from head to foot as desire and guilt struggled for control. He shouldn't be doing this. Not to Jamie's wife and certainly not to sweet, trusting Lillie. God would surely punish him. This was wrong, wrong, wrong!

Still he reached out and drew her resisting body to him, pushing hard against her, churning with need. He wondered if she felt his erection, wondered how she could not. He realized Belle was now fighting to twist her head away, but her long red hair streaming wild and free caused a sexual response in him that took his breath away. Guilt suddenly fled, replaced by a pent up passion he couldn't control. He wanted her . . . always had! Her struggle to get away only incensed him more.

And then, as Belle struggled, a sudden whiff of scent—lavender—assailed his sensitive nostrils. Lillie's scent. The aroma rocked him and he relaxed his hold on her. His passion, raging just a second ago, ebbed.

Belle seemed to feel the difference and pushed him away with a muffled sob.

"That must never happen again, Alex. You caught me in a moment of despair and I don't know what possessed me to respond like I did. Loneliness I guess . . . I've been so terribly lonesome. But it must never, ever happen again. It goes against everything I believe to be morally right. How can I ever face Lillie? You are my dearest, dearest friends."

Alex hung his head. Give up now? He had imagined this encounter all his life, in different places, different circumstances, but always of Belle in his arms. Once more he grew feverish with desire. "We can't go back, you know. Can't pretend it never happened. Things can never be the same between us—every time I look at you I'll remember this moment."

Belle kissed his cheek gently. "I know . . . I know."

"Lillie need never suspect. She is used to me spending time here, helping you and the children. We'll be careful."

"No . . . no! It can not be, Alex."

Unmindful of her resistance he pulled her to him. "Yes," he breathed, his voice ragged with desire, "it can be."

Suddenly, the plaintive voice of young Adam rang out from the hallway. "Mommy, where are you?" Alex thrust Belle away in a blind panic. She was flushed and she clutched the trailing ends of her shawl while he tried to smooth his clothing and brush the hair back from his forehead.

Adam came running into the kitchen, followed closely by Harry. Adam stared in surprise at his obviously distraught mother and uncle. Harry stood stock still. His eyes traveled from his father to Belle and back to his father. A knowing leer spread across his young face as his eyes ranged freely up and down his father's body.

* * *

Belle watched Alex leave the kitchen, his face flushed and angry, still tugging at his clothing.

She studied her reflection in the tiny mirror hanging beside the kitchen sink. Her long hair was disheveled; her lips looked unusually full; and her apron was untied in the back. What had gotten in to her to respond to his embrace the way she had? It was nothing more than the wanton act of a woman hungry for a man's love. She ached with an inner longing. For several unexcusable moments she had lusted for fulfillment, and her body grew warm once more with self-conscious pleasure at the memory.

But she must not give in to carnal desires. A woman must belong to herself, must follow the conscience of her heart, not her flesh.

She and Jamie had shared a deep and passionate love. Their private life was deeply satisfying to both of them and she had felt no shame in their unreserved sexual stimulation of each other. She was a sensual woman and she missed that part of her life, but she could never violate the memory of her love for Jamie . . . or of her friendship with Lillie.

Belle coaxed the boys to the table and placed a plate of cookies and glasses of cold milk before them. "What have you fellows been up to?" she asked.

"We went to the woods to get a Christmas tree. Wait till you see it, Mommy. It's huge." Adam exclaimed, his mouth full of cookie and a mustache of white milk covering his upper lip.

Harry was quiet and Belle looked at him uneasily. What had he seen when he entered the kitchen? Was he old enough to guess the significance of their guilty appearance?

"How about you, Harry? Do you have your Christmas tree up yet?"

"Pa cut it yesterday, but he didn't put it up. Mama says everyone is coming to White Hall for Christmas dinner."

"Yes, that will be fun, won't it? The children are looking forward to it. Would you care for another glass of milk?"

"No, ma'am. I must be getting home." An agonized smirk lifted the corner of Harry's mouth and his eyes narrowed. "Mama needs some wood chopped and I guess Papa wasn't home this afternoon to do it."

His chair scraping across the floor was like an animal's howl and he ran from the kitchen without a backward glance. Belle wiped Adam's face and scooted him into the yard where the other children were playing a game of Blind Man's Bluff. Wearily, she sank down onto one of the empty chairs. What a mess. She'd have to examine the details of her behavior this morning. Her affection and dependence on Alex had undoubtedly encouraged him to rekindle the attraction she had always suspected he felt. She sighed and put her hands up to smooth her rumpled hair into place. Better get control of herself before Mother Katie appeared. That wise old woman didn't miss a thing.

* * *

Alex leaned against the bottom half of the stable door, listening to the silence and thinking of Belle. He quivered, hot with shame and a self-imposed burden of guilt.

Belle was alone and vulnerable and he did not know how strongly she would continue to oppose him were he to pursue what he had started that afternoon. Of course it would have to be a clandestine affair. He desired Belle—had as long as he could remember—but he didn't mistake desire for love. Yet, he didn't want to hurt Lillie. And God only knew, he loved her. If only she enjoyed sex more, if only she had given him more than one child. Guilt flooded him. Would that have made a difference? Did he really think that? Surely not. Surely he didn't blame Lillie. But if he didn't why had he given voice to the thought? Or was it his own guilt and fear that the accident had left her crippled and unable to bear more children?

He gazed across the fields at the neatly fenced paddocks where mares and foals were silhouetted against the cheerless sky. The leaden sky promised snow by day's end, but perhaps he had time to ride over his boundary lines. It always gave him a sense of stability, a sense of where he belonged in the scheme of things.

* * *

The seldom used parlor at White Hall was festooned with Christmas greenery. Garlands of laurel were draped over the front door and across the top of the fireplace. The tree was lit with candles of carnauba wax and decorated with ornaments that had been handed down since the early 1800's: round and pear-shaped balls, teardrops, and some made of colored glass painted inside with mercury to give them a silvery appearance. Gingerbread animals, painted with white icing, hung from fragrant branches. The fire, lit and blazing, glowed restfully on polished wood, softening the green and rose flowers of the Persian carpet, and warming the framed cross-stitch mottos "God Bless our Home" and "Whiskey Is Sin" that hung above the mantle. A cat slept peacefully in an old wicker basket.

Belle paused in the open doorway that connected the steamy kitchen with the cool parlor to push a damp ringlet of hair off her forehead and smooth her apron.

Lillie's father sat with Ian and the twins playing a game of cards, Elizabeth was immersed in a new book, and Rebecca was in the kitchen helping the women prepare dinner. Harry sat at the piano picking out familiar Christmas tunes. A mischievous grin spread across his handsome face when he looked up from his music and saw Belle standing in the doorway.

"Pa, Aunt Belle is standing under the mistletoe," he called.

Alex was tacking a final garland of holly to the mantle and stood only inches from the startled Belle.

Belle tilted her head, looking up at the center of the doorframe where someone had tacked a tiny piece of greenery with white berries, then looked anxiously at Alex who seemed frozen to the spot.

Lillie was at the dinning room table spooning fruit salad into small cups and paused at the sound of Harry's voice to look at the scene before her—Belle with an uncertain smile on her lips and Alex looking as though someone had thrown ice water in his face.

Lillie froze; a wave of acid welled up from her belly, and she felt like she could not breathe. Her hand began to shake. She could feel the blood drain from her cheeks like water through a sieve.

She could deny the truth no longer. All the times Alex had shown undue interest in Belle and her children she'd not known whether she wanted proof something was going on or not. Now, it was all there, in that one paralyzing second, written indelibly on his stricken face. The ladle trembled in her hand as she watched him step toward Belle with a weak smile and plant a chaste kiss on her cheek.

"Come on, Papa. That's no way to kiss a lady pretty as Aunt Belle," Harry cried as he bounded across the room and gave his aunt a big smack on the lips while his cousins, giggling in amusement, ran up and planted various kisses on their mother's face.

Lillie felt like someone had hit her squarely in the stomach. Belle was laughing now, hugging the children and flouncing across the room. Was she unaware of Alex's feelings? Could she possibly be so naive? Or was she just an excellent actress, knowing that Lillie was nearby? But then, Lillie reminded herself, she too had been naive for a long time.

She chewed on her lip and stiffened her back. This was not going to spoil her Christmas—nor the children's. Harry had spent hours tying wax candles to the boughs of the huge spruce tree standing in the corner of the parlor. Jamie's children needed all the gaiety and love she could give them at Christmas without their father.

Belle turned back to the kitchen with a grin. "Guess I got caught under the mistletoe that time. Such a bunch of smooching!" "The children do seem to be having fun," Lillie offered as she followed Belle. "The buns should be baked if you want to take them from the oven." She carefully avoided looking at Alex who had busied himself with the drooping garland.

Harry stuck his head through the door. "How soon will dinner be ready? I'm starved and the smell of that turkey is driving me crazy."

Lillie smiled at him fondly. Let her not forget how lucky she was to have this happy, carefree boy. "The turkey's done. We're about ready to start lifting things now. It would help if you'd get the children washed up, Harry."

Within half an hour the family was seated in the dining room. The oval table, made from black walnut trees felled on the farm, had been extended with three boards, covered with Lillie's best lace tablecloth, and set with her prized Austrian china. The dishes, a wedding gift from her mother, were a soft pearly white adorned with tiny blue-gray flowers, and the fluted tureens were filled with mashed potatoes, candied sweet potatoes, baked corn, and Dutch rice pudding. Cut-glass relish trays held the traditional seven sweets and sours, there were two baskets of warm potato buns and bowls of fresh creamery butter, apple butter and schmirkase. And in the center of the table a huge turkey, browned to perfection, overflowed her largest meat platter.

Alex, seated at the head of the table, bowed his head and reached out to clasp, first the hand of his son and then the hand of his mother, seated on either side of him. One by one, around the table hands were taken and heads solemnly bowed. Katie's gray head next to Lillie, the small golden heads of the twins on either side of Belle's red tresses, towheaded Ian, and Elizabeth and Rebecca with fat pigtails tied with red ribbon. And of course, Alex's young brothers, blond Charlie and John. Lillie's mother, Sophia, sat with her chin tucked firmly on her chest, her brown hair, salted with gray, gathered into a bun so tight Lillie thought it must surely hurt. Henry Schwartz's salt and pepper head, thinning on top, but long and wavy over his ears sat with folded hands at the far end of the table.

The prayer finished, platters began to be passed. Heaping piles of turkey, candied yams, mashed potatoes, buttered lima beans, squash and generous helpings of the seven sweets and sours served at every Pennsylvania Dutch dinner overflowed every plate. Everyone seemed to be talking at once, laughter rippled like ocean waves, except for Lillie who seemed unusually quiet.

That night a weary Lillie saw the last guest to the front door and she and Alex mounted the long set of steps to their bedroom. As Lillie gained the sanctity of her soothing green bed-chamber all the tension of the evening seemed to explode in her body. She felt sick inside and hugged her arms about her middle, her throat raw with pain. Two tears ran down her cheeks, their taste wet and salty on her lips. Her mind seemed numbed by the day's shattering discovery. She clasped and unclasped her hands. She must not convey her distress; she must not spoil Christmas.

Alex was close behind her and he entered the bedroom and went directly to the wardrobe where he began to remove his vest and tie.

Lillie slipped her silk dress over her head and donned her nightdress. She stood before her looking glass, her back to Alex, tying and retying the ribbons under her chin, fighting to keep her voice from betraying her inner turmoil as she commented, "Belle seems to be recovering quite well from Jamie's death. She seemed quite gay today." The tall mirror reflected the four-poster bed, with its wedding-ring quilt and lacy bolsters. It also reflected Alex's face. Christmas or not, she couldn't keep back the question searing her brain.

"How far has it gone, Alex?"

He wouldn't look at her. Instead, he combed his fingers through his hair and sank to the side of the bed.

"I don't know what you're talking about. How far has what gone?"

Seeing the color rise in his face she knew she was right.

How far had things gone between Belle and Alex? She really didn't want to know, didn't want to give credence to the suspicion by acknowledging it. Did she want to feel the relief of knowing or the self-righteous indignation of being betrayed? But she had asked, she had to respond to his question.

"I think you know." She forced herself to meet his eyes. "But this is Christmas and I don't want to spoil it with jealous accusations. We'll talk later, after the holidays."

Lillie sat on the edge of the bed and loosened the pins to let her long hair fall about her shoulders. She grabbed the hairbrush and with hard, brisk strokes raked the bristles through her hair until her scalp tingled with pain.

Alex sat down beside her. He regarded her wistfully. "I love you, Lillie," he said, holding out his arms. "You know I do."

She did not move, staring into his unfathomable deep brown eyes, trembling with the force of her resentment. She resented Belle for being the complete woman she appeared to be, resented

Alex for wanting her. And she resented the circumstances that forced her to feel the way she did.

"And I love you. Now lets get to bed, it's been an exhausting day."

They lay side by side, barely touching and neither speaking.

Hours later Lillie lay sleepless beside her softly snoring husband. Try as she would she could not force away the memory of Alex's face when he looked at Belle. Guilt and longing had been so evident. How could she continue to love a man who so clearly yearned for another? Tears threatened to leak from beneath her lashes and she blinked them back. No, she would not resort to weak tears . . . she would not cry!

Mama had always expressed the idea that men had natural appetites which must be satisfied, and a decent woman didn't share in these hungers; therefore it was expected that a man might commit adultery, and a wife was expected to conduct herself in such a way that she was seen never to know of it. But this was different. This was her husband—this was her best friend. She might pretend to be unaware, but she knew she could never forgive the knowledge.

Was this, then, how it ended? Years of loving and caring for a man—just gone? Was she dying slowly from a hurt she did not believe she could bear?

"No, no," she whispered in the darkness. "I won't let it end like this. I could no more stop loving him than I could stop breathing."

She had always suspected that she was not as responsive a bed partner as she should be. Was this the reason for his attraction to Belle? Or was it her inability to have more children? She couldn't change that, but she could show more interest in him, fake more response to their lovemaking.

She shifted restlessly under the covers. She could no longer deny the truth, but she could live with it. She drew a deep breath into her aching throat, filled with a sudden fierce protectiveness of what was hers. Right or wrong she would fight for her husband and her marriage.

And, she thought, *I still have the love of my precious son to cling to.*

She turned on her side, drawing her knees up, and snuggled deeper into the warm feather tick, but sleep came only in snatches as she reviewed all the tell-tale signs she had ignored for years and had imaginary conversations with a contrite Alex. The dawn came furtively and morning was on its way. It was very quiet; Alex slept deeply. Cold air flowed through a small opening in the window and outside the bare branches of the maple tree embraced a gray and barren sky.

CHAPTER 15

Alex avoided direct contact with Belle as best he could, but his presence at Rebert's Choice was desperately needed and he could not stay away altogether. He sensed Mama's worried eyes watching him and he wondered if she guessed the reason for his discomfort.

Whatever had possessed him to let his long banked desire for Belle burst into flame? He had a wife and son, both of whom he loved dearly, how could he think of dishonoring them? Yet, he suspected that Belle was vulnerable now. Vulnerable and lonely. He sensed a passion in her that she tried hard to control. Of course, a permanent alliance was unthinkable. Divorce simply did not happen in his culture. But something else?

No . . . no . . . no! He would have to bury those longings deep in his sub-conscience where they had lain hidden for years. He would immerse himself in work. The farm adjacent to White Hall was for sale, he would contact the owner immediately. And when he visited Rebert's Choice he would see to it that he was never alone with Belle again.

* * *

Early in January Belle sent a message that she would pick Lillie up after lunch to travel to Carrie's house for the monthly quilting bee.

Six inches of new snow had fallen during the night and Belle arrived by sleigh, drawing as close to the house as she could get. The path Alex had shoveled didn't quite reach the sleigh so he lifted Lillie in his arms and carried her through the drifts, plunking her down on the seat beside Belle with a strained laugh.

Belle smiled a greeting then flicked the reins and they were off. Lillie glanced at her, a faint twinge of jealousy knotting her stomach, and then looked away. "Where's Mother Katie?" she asked.

"She has a cold and didn't feel up to going out today. Said she was afraid her nose would drip all over the new quilt. It's good to be alone with you, Lillie. We don't get a chance to talk like we used to."

Lillie nodded. Alex, the children, or Mother Katie were always present during their visits. She felt a sudden twinge of uneasiness at what might be coming. Just for a second she let her emotions rule, then she pushed them aside.

They sped along, sleigh runners screeching across crusted snow, bells jingling as the horse pranced under a chicory blue sky, throwing blue shadows against virgin snow.

"Alex says Ian has taken a real interest in the mill. Dogs his footsteps everywhere he goes," Lillie said.

"And he's so patient with him; with all the children. I hope you and Harry haven't felt neglected, Lillie. I'm really trying not to lean on Alex, to become more independent and resume my own life."

Lillie felt a flush of heat in her cheeks. "Since you put Christian Nunemaker in charge of the mill Alex has been home a lot more."

"Christian is doing a fine job and he's teaching me. You know how self-reliant . . . and stubborn . . . I've always been. I see no reason why I can't run the business as efficiently as any man. But I finally realized I must learn milling from the ground up and Christian is better able to teach me. Alex has his hands full with his own farms and what remains of the horses, plus handling legal matters for me . . . you know Papa Edward's estate is still not settled."

"Alex was so worried that you might not forgive him for the action he took against Jamie . . . that you would feel he could have done more to save his life. It still eats at him. I see him wrestling with his conscience."

"Ah, Lillie, there has never been anything to forgive. I'm surprised to hear that he torments himself with thoughts like that."

"Alex is unbending when it comes to forgiving what he construes as sin in others, especially in himself."

Belle sucked in her cheeks. "You know a wise man once said, 'A brittle tree snaps in a buffeting wind, but a willow sways and remains whole in the face of a storm.' We can all learn from that." Belle was silent, momentarily looking at Lillie through hooded eyes, eyes that seemed to reflect an inner struggle. "Mother Katie says we must always be willing to forgive." Her green eyes held a glint of challenge. "Believe me, we all have something to be forgiven. Love that expects perfection, with no mistakes, is foolish love. None of us passes through life without acts to be ashamed of." Her strong hand sought Lillie's beneath the lap robe and grasped it tightly. "If we can accept that, if we love not only the strengths, but also the weaknesses, then the connection between us grows stronger."

Lillie recognized the hidden meaning in Belle's words. The unspoken apology. She looked at the questioning eyes of her dear friend and with a deep sigh squeezed her hand, the pressure of her fingers speaking her understanding.

* * *

Alex extended their holdings to four farms over the years Harry was growing toward manhood. His thirteen-year-old son had become a handsome, fun-loving rebel, his entrancing charm fulfilling the promise of his childhood.

Wonderful labor saving technology—running water, the telephone and electric power—had come to the growing towns of Hanover and Gettysburg, yet life in the rural areas of Adams County remained much the same. White Hall was still heated by wood and lit by oil lamps; they had no bathroom, only basins and a tub indoors with a privy in the back yard. To Alex's satisfaction Nature still dictated life on the farm and ruled the traditional institutions of his family and church.

Although he worked from dawn 'til dusk he made time to socialize with his siblings and their families—Annie and George, Emma and Charles, and Ellen and her new husband, Rev. J.J. Stauffer. He still missed John who had gone to Ohio to join Edwin and his growing family, and he seldom saw Charlie who was busy courting a pretty Mennonite girl from Mengus Mills. And although they were friends with their neighbors, the Weikerts, Kindigs, Waughs, Eckerts, and Spanglers, he was still very much a loner.

These were also the years when his interest turned once more to harness racing and he strove to become recognized as a serious horse breeder. Mixon Farms had produced a horse named Apollo, reputed to be faster over a quarter mile than any other Standardbred in the state. Alex vowed to have such a horse himself one day, but in the meantime he was content to re-build his stable around the sons and daughters of Bay Hunter. Bay Hunter had proved himself for Edward, not only on the race track, but in recent years as a valuable breeding stallion. He was at his prime and in February Alex bred him to his champion mare, Princess Rose, and sat back to wait.

Lillie had always resisted becoming involved with the horses. They were a man's world, part of a strange masculine fraternity that she did not understand. She attended the county fairs because she always had pies and canned goods in competition and she reluctantly watched the sulky races because Harry sometimes rode.

Now all of the talk at the dinner table was about the pending birth of Princess Rose's foal.

"You've gotta come down to the stable and see her, Mama," Harry pleaded. "She's expecting her foal any day now, and she's so dang proud of herself."

"Yes, Lillie. Please come . . . it would please both of us," Alex said.

She smiled with pleasure at the invitation. When the supper dishes were finished and put away she tucked a shawl around her shoulders and accompanied them to the stable.

Proudly, Harry led her to the stall where Princess Rose was feeding from a bucket of oats fastened to the wall.

Harry ran his hand over the mare's smooth belly. The animal snuffled and took a hesitant step forward, but Harry shushed her, patting her neck and talking softly into her ears.

Harry's lips lifted in a crooked grin. "This is her first time and she's a little nervous about being a mother." He took his mother's hand in his and ran it down the contours of the mare's body to her swollen underbelly. Lillie gave a soft laugh of pleasure when she felt a swift kick of movement against her palm. "The foal is very active," Alex said, from a corner of the stall where he watched with a pleased look on his face. "Princess Rose is breeding us a winner, for certain."

"And it will be my horse," Harry stated with authority, running his hand across her muzzle.

Two nights later Alex informed Lillie that he and Harry would be spending the night in the barn. Princess Rose was showing signs that she was ready to foal.

Dawn had already streaked the sky with bands of pink and orange when Lillie appeared at the stall with a tin of warm biscuits and a pot of coffee. Harry was slumped against the wall sound asleep and Alex put his finger to his lips and gave Lillie a broad smile as he nodded toward the stall.

In the far corner a tiny colt lay on fresh straw, golden brown from a shaft of light filtering over the box stall, its forelegs folded beneath it. Lillie gave a gasp of pleasure. "Oh, Alex, it is beautiful . . . a perfect little creature."

"God's creation," Alex said, his voice choked with emotion.

"He's mine Papa," Harry said, wiping sleep from his eyes. "You promised. Wait 'til ol' Grandpa Schwartz sees him. He's better than the new foal they have, an' I thought nothing could top that."

They named him Tansy and at once he became Harry's horse, a colt with a smooth natural gait and astonishing speed; surely destined, in everyone's opinion, to become a great trotter.

CHAPTER 16

The Chicago World's Fair opened May 1, 1893 and the Hanover Sun carried excited reports of the unbelievable wonders and wickedness that could be found there.

One sultry July afternoon, Harry came careening into the yard at Rebert's Choice on his bicycle. He pulled up to the fence and while supporting himself with one hand, dismounted from the bicycle's tall seat, and rushed breathlessly into the kitchen.

"Where's Ian," he called to Aunt Belle. "I have the most wonderful thing to tell him."

"Over at the mill. What are you so excited about?"

"Tell ya later," Harry cried, racing out the door.

He found Ian unloading sacks of rye from a farm wagon. "I want to talk to you," he began. "In fact I have the most wonderful plan to tell you about. But I'll help you finish unloading if you like."

"Done," agreed Ian.

They worked side by side and when the load of rye had been stowed on the upper floor of the mill Ian said, "That's the lot. Come on—there's a spot over along the wall where we can sit and talk."

They sank down on a bale of straw, and Harry launched into a breathless tale about what he had learned that morning.

"Jeremy Wheeler is back from the fair in Chicago, and you ain't gonna believe what he saw there. They have a thing called an "Egyptian Village" with hootchy-kootchy girls."

"What in tarnation are hootchy-kootchy girls?"

"Well, the way Jeremy tells it they're luscious, corn-fed gals with dark eyes and big tits. They do a dance where only the upper part of their body moves. Imagine that, Ian . . . you know the part with the tits! They sway back and forth in such a way it'd like to drive a fellow crazy. Ian, we must talk my father into taking us to Chicago. I gotta see those girls," he finished, with a smirk.

"Yeah, but if I know your Papa, he isn't about to waste money on a trip to Chicago and even if he did he wouldn't let us go to the Egyptian Village and watch dancing girls."

"Maybe, but there's more I haven't told you. They have a new ride, a great big wheel that was built by George Washington Ferris and they call it a Ferris Wheel. Jeremy said it goes up almost two hundred feet above the Midway with about three dozen cars and each holds more than forty people. He and his Papa rode it and they were scared stiff when a wild wind off Lake Michigan started rocking their car back and forth. Everybody was screaming and they were rocking like crazy. Jeremy got sick and threw up all over his new trousers."

"Don't that beat all," Ian said. "Imagine being way up there in the sky in a bucket, lookin' down on the whole world. Think there is really a chance your Papa would take us?"

Harry pursed his lips and gave Ian a big wink. "Maybe if I went to work on Mama. She gives me just about anything I want. I'll be fourteen in September. I could tell her it's an advance on my birthday present."

Ian chuckled. "I allow, Harry Rebert, you ain't never in a fix. I'll just bet you can pull it off."

"I'm gonna run on home and do a whole mess of chores she's been after me to get done, and then I'll start working on her this evening." Harry jumped up, brushed the hair back from his forehead and grinned at Ian through narrowed eyes. "Course if that don't work we could always hop a freight to Chicago on our own. I just gotta see them "hootchy-kootchy" girls."

"Ma would have my hide," Ian replied with a worried frown.

"It'd be worth it, wouldn't it?" Harry answered, the cleft in his chin deepening as he grinned mischievously. "In fact, hopping a train sounds like a whole lot more fun than going to the fair with my old strait-laced father. Let's talk some more about that idea."

He pulled two battered cigarettes from his pocket and leaning nonchalantly against the wall handed one to Ian. "Say, do you know where old Moses keeps that flask of whiskey I always see him nipping at? We gotta make some plans."

Ian pointed to the corner. "In the bottom of that grain bucket. Bet you don't dare take a sip, though."

Harry puffed out his chest and swaggered over to the bucket hidden in deep shadows. He lifted out the dusty bottle of whiskey and pulled the cork, watching Ian from the corner of his eye. Ian was watching him in admiration.

Harry took a huge gulp before he passed it over. Ian shook his head no. Carefully Harry placed the flask back where Moses kept it hidden.

That one swallow was a mistake, though, for it seemed to call for more, and as he and Ian sat dreaming up a scheme to run away he was back to the bottle taking another, and then another sip. Harry had never felt so wonderful in his life. Visions of dancing girls swam in his head—the adventure they were planning got better and better.

Finally Ian jumped to his feet. "I better get back to work afore Moses finds me loafing and has my head."

"And I'm gonna skedaddle home and go to work on Mama. You work on yours. Papa would probably give in to Aunt Belle sooner than he would Mama."

With that parting remark Harry jumped to his feet and headed for the door. He found he had difficulty walking, for the floor seemed to shift and tilt under him. "Wow," he muttered as he clutched the wall for support.

"You're corned," Ian said, with a deep laugh.

"Yeah, but I like the feeling that booze gives me. I'll have to try that again." He moved cautiously out the door and, after several tries, was able to mount his bicycle and head home.

"No!" Alex bellowed. "Mein Gott, woman, don't you know the country is in the midst of a depression. Farm prices are the lowest they've been in a century and you want to take the entire family on a vacation to Chicago!"

"I thought the last batch of steers you sold at the Lancaster stock yards brought a good price."

"Yes, and I paid twice as much for the calves I had to buy. The answer is no! This time I put my foot down. With four farms to manage, and the cost of hired help sky-high, I need Harry's help this summer. It's time he learned to work for a living."

"There are hoboes stopping at the farm every day looking for work. Can't you hire one of them?"

"You know, full well, most hoboes have drinking problems and can't hold down a full time job. Do you want to take a chance on having that kind of character around Harry?" He cast an exasperated look at Lillie. "That isn't the real problem though, and you know it. Harry is a demanding child, demanding both love and material possessions. I've seen that since he was small. You mollycoddle him and when he does wrong, you know what happens? I lose my temper and start yelling at him. Then he sulks and runs to you."

Lillie knew Alex was right. Harry had become increasing belligerent and it was beginning to concern her. "All right," she said with a sad smile. "I'll try to explain to him the reasons we can't go. He's a good boy, he'll understand."

"I wish you would, Lillie. It isn't fair, you know, to make me the disciplining parent all the time. I love Harry, too."

The morning's harsh words had upset Lillie. It wasn't her nature to second guess her husband's decisions, but the disappointment and anger she had seen on Harry's face when she told him that his father would not consider taking him to Chicago worried her.

A vague sense of uneasiness plagued her all afternoon as she found herself opening and closing cupboard doors, rearranging things on shelves that didn't need rearranging, and finally, because she couldn't seem to settle herself down, to assemble the ingredients for several shoe fly pies.

After preparing dough and lining three pie pans she pulled Grandma Weikert's old mixing bowl from the shelf and began mixing the ingredients for the filling. Absently, she stirred the molasses, brown sugar, eggs, soda, and water for the bottom part of the pies.

As she worked she sang softly to herself. "Sweet hour of prayer, sweet hour of prayer, That calls me from a world of care. That bids me . . ."

The comforting words of the old hymn filled the quiet kitchen. She had made shoo fly pies so often over the years that she did it without conscious thought. She ladled the thick, gooey mixture into the waiting pie shells and began to prepare the crumb topping by cutting flour, brown sugar, baking powder, and lard together. Absently she sprinkled the crumbs, still humming the old hymn, and carried the pies to the stove.

Suddenly a sharp knock rattled the kitchen door.

Lillie rubbed her hands together to free them of pastry dough and hurried to open the door. A tall, heavy-set man in the dark blue garb of a policeman doffed his hat and looked at her apologetically.

"Mrs. Rebert?"

"Yes," she stammered, the uneasiness of the afternoon sharpening into fear.

"Is your Mister home?"

"No, he's out in the fields. Come in please. What . . . what's wrong?"

The policeman entered the kitchen and stood uncertainly by the door twisting his cap in beefy fingers. "I'm afraid I have some unpleasant news, Missus. Your son, Harry, was involved in a carriage mishap over in Hanover this afternoon and we're holding him at the jail until we can get the matter straightened out."

Lillie felt her knees grow weak and she sank into a nearby chair.

"Was Harry hurt?"

"No, Missus, but I'm afraid an old gentleman, a Mr. Klunk by name, suffered an acute injury when he crossed the street in front of your son's carriage."

"Oh, dear me! What ever was Harry doing in Hanover? Are you sure it was our son?"

"Yes, ma'am."

"Sit down . . . sit down. What happened?"

Ignoring her request to take a seat, the policeman drew himself erect and noisily cleared his throat. "Your son was fleeing the railroad yards where he had been routed from a box car. He was apparently preparing to run away from home on a train bound for Chicago. He'd tied his horse and rig at the rear of the station house and when the yard-man gave chase, your boy jumped in his buggy and raced off at great speed. He drove into Hanover and went careening into the center square—his horse lathered and frothing at the mouth. When the horse tried to swerve to miss the old man crossing the street, the front of the carriage caught the gentleman and he was thrown under one of the wheels."

"Oh, dear Lord. How badly was the man hurt?"

"Mr. Klunk's left leg was shattered and his hip broken. He will live, but at his age I suspect the accident may leave him crippled." The policeman looked at her sternly. "I'm afraid there is more, Mrs. Rebert. Your son was quite drunk!"

"Impossible," Lillie cried. "He couldn't have been drunk. Frightened, maybe, but not drunk. We keep no liquor in this house and he is only thirteen. Where would a boy that age get alcohol?"

The policeman looked straight at Lillie, pity plain in his face. "There is no question regarding his state of inebriation. He was drunk as a toad and reeked of whiskey. Now I must get back to the station house. There will be a hearing before the Justice of the Peace, Joseph LeFevre, at eight o'clock tomorrow morning. If you and Mr. Rebert want to see your boy this evening, you can call at the jail."

He let himself out of the kitchen and Lillie sat huddled in her chair, fear and anger finally giving way to tears.

Drunk—in jail at age thirteen—an innocent old man perhaps crippled for life. How could she tell Alex, and what would he do? And how, in Heavens name, could she protect Harry from his father's certain fury? The thoughts whirled in her mind as the tears ran down her cheeks, and the kitchen filled with the scent of baking pies.

Harry was released the next day after Alex paid a hefty fine and guaranteed payment for all of Mr. Klunk's medical bills. The old man would require extensive care and the sum estimated sent shivers down Lillie's spine. Alex would have to borrow against one of the farms and he was furious.

Harry blamed everyone but himself.

"Ian refused to go along after we had made all those plans to hop a freight to Chicago in case Papa refused to take us. I should have known Ian would be too skeered to run away with me."

"But, where did you get the whiskey?" Lillie asked.

"At the mill. Ian showed me where ole Moses keeps a bottle hid. If Ian had kept his part of the bargain I wouldn't have gotten mad and tried to hop the train by myself," he retorted, his voice, as always, a mixture of charm and impudence.

Lillie stared at Harry in disbelief. She was suddenly filled with a sense of foreboding—a terrible premonition of sorrow and despair. What lay ahead for this beautiful child of hers? And what heartbreak for her?

They drove home from the hearing in complete silence and when they alighted from the buggy Alex took Harry by the collar and marched him toward the barn.

"Where are you going . . . what are you going to do?" Lillie cried, in alarm.

"I'm going to get a switch from the backyard and beat the tar out of this impudent youngster. I'll teach him a lesson he won't soon forget. I should have done it a long time ago."

"He's sorry for what he did, Alex. He didn't mean to hurt the old gentleman. It was an accident."

Alex fixed her with a keep-your-mouth-shut look. "You don't know anything when it comes to your golden boy," he growled, poking his finger emphatically at her, his dark worried eyes shuttered and remote. "Now get in the kitchen and leave this matter to me."

* * *

As the next few years sped by Alex bought more and more land. He now had over five hundred acres under cultivation, and his farms in Mount Pleasant and Union Township were among the most prosperous in Adams County. He planted corn, wheat, barley and rye, but his main investment was in cattle which he bought as scrubs, fattened over the summer, and sold at the livestock auctions in Lancaster every fall. Tirelessly, he experimented with different farming arrangements. One year it was a tenant farmer for the half; the next year a farmer on a fee basis. Always his main consideration was frugality. Then in the spring of 1896 he bought a tract of land called the "Ore Bank Field" from James Lefevre and expanded his interests to mining. They were quite wealthy now.

August of that year was unbearably hot. At the end of each day the sun sank, a glowing red ball, in the western skies, bringing no relief from the hazy heat. Alex found himself restless and irritable, unable to sleep. Then, one afternoon when sporadic thunderstorms ripped across the black sky, he decided to pay a long overdue visit to his mother at Rebert's Choice.

First he stopped at the mill with a load of corn for Ian to grind into meal. Only it wasn't Ian who met him on this stormy day. It was Belle. She was standing in the doorway watching the dark sky and she greeted him with a hesitant smile.

His voice caught—she was still as beautiful as ever—dressed today in the newest fashion, a dress of silk that clung to her body in the damp heat.

"Alex, its so good to see you," she called. "Come inside, quick before the rain starts again."

He jumped from the wagon and made a dash for the door just as fat drops of rain wet his head and shoulders. "Whew," he said, "just made it in time!" He looked around the mill, quiet except for the creaking of leather belts and the steady splash of water turning the huge paddles of the water wheel. His eyebrows bunched as he searched the empty space. "Where is everyone?"

"The customers are few today, I guess the heat and storms are keeping them indoors."

"And . . . Ian?"

"He took the opportunity to take some broken tools to the smitty."

She was alone he realized with a start.

"Come, sit down and visit awhile till the rain stops," she said leading him to her small office at one end of the mill floor.

She settled herself behind a scared desk and Alex perched on a wooden stool, fingering his mustache, his eyes darting everywhere but at her. What the devil was the matter with him today? he wondered. For years, now, he had managed to maintain a steely rein on his emotions when he was around Belle. Was it the unexpected solitude of the empty mill, the intimate feeling evoked by the smell of yeast and warm rain that had his senses reeling. Or was it the revealing dress clinging to Belle in the damp heat?

He cleared his throat. "How are the children?"

"Fine. Except the twins both have head colds and Rebecca just got over her annual dose of poison ivy. They keep Mother Katie busy. I don't know what I'd do without her."

"I haven't seen them for awhile."

Belle smiled softly. "I know . . . and I . . . I think I know the reason why. And I understand, Alex."

Silence descended on them, broken only by the sound of rain pelting the tin roof of the mill.

Belle was the first to speak. "The mill is prospering. Ian is doing a fine job. He'll soon be able to take over."

"I'm sure the prosperity is a tribute to your management," he replied rather stiffly. "You'll miss the challenge once you turn the reins over to him."

"Then I can devote more time to the women's movement," Belle said with a twinkle in her eyes. "There is a march in Harrisburg next month protesting abuse of child labor and I plan to attend. Once Pennsylvania makes Women's Suffrage a part of their Constitution I plan to run for public office."

Belle's animated face shook him. He wholeheartedly opposed her political views but, by God, she was a woman with fire and vitality. It was enough to make a man's blood boil.

At the sound of a wagon pulling up before the doors she jumped to her feet. As she moved past him she laid a hand on his arm. "I must tend to our customers, Alex, but please don't wait so long to visit again. There is no need to, your know."

Huh, he thought, his groin stirring at her touch, little does she know!

* * *

As fall approached Alex found himself once more using every opportunity to visit Rebert's Choice. The situation could not continue. He had to talk to someone, needed to ease his conscience and come to terms with his problem, and in a moment of desperation he saddled Princess Rose and rode across stubble fields toward Christ Church. The wind stung his cheeks, the horse's hooves rose and fell in perfect rhythm. Alex rode easily, the old habit of a good seat and steady hands on the reins as natural as breathing.

He slowed the heaving horse as they approached the church, a lovely house of prayer, shrouded in quiet in the gathering twilight and he followed a dim path to the tall granite spike marking Edward's grave, rosy in the oblique light. Alex stopped and stood quietly, then knelt and placed his hand on the cold smooth surface of the monument, trying to draw into himself a feeling of Papa's presence, of quietness and peace.

He had always known that in temperament he was more like his grandfather Jonas than like his father. But his father had always tried to soften Alex's hard edges with compassion, had tried to instill in him a sense of integrity. And today it was integrity that blocked his way.

He admitted that he had not loved Lillie as much as she loved him when they first married. That he had settled for her calming, nurturing nature when denied his passion for Belle. Had she sensed it even then and preferred to look the other way? He sat back on his heels and looked across the empty field. The Mansion House and his land lay just across the road. Solid ground; black and white, no surprises there.

His thoughts churned. He tried to relive the intense moment in Belle's kitchen when he had held her compliant body in his arms, but instead Lillie kept invading his thoughts. He seemed to see Lillie's face on the granite monument, hovering there with her sweet expression—that soft smile about her eyes that was so familiar. Belle's features became clouded in his mind; there was only Lillie now, all around he saw her reflection.

Alex remembered how she had looked holding Harry against her breast, singing a sweet lullaby to the nursing infant; remembered how she looked sipping hot chocolate with him in the restful kitchen on a winter afternoon.

The entire atmosphere of their home spoke of her. Yes, restful was the word that described White Hall, it bore Lillie's heart and soul. He had never really appreciated how warm and inviting it was. When he came home, after a laborious day in the fields, every muscle in his body knotted with fatigue, walking into the kitchen was like crawling into a warm feather tick.

They had so much. Not just Harry and the farms, but years of sharing, some of it great, some of it funny, some of it sad.

But maybe, that was the true essence of marriage, not wild passion, but the simple day to day lives shared by husband and wife.

He wondered how he could have ever not recognized her fully.

Alex lowered his head and began to pray: God, I know I'm a very judgmental man, self-serving, and I suppose quite independent—the center of my own universe. With my secret longing for another woman I've violated your moral laws. I've not lived my life in a way pleasing to you. The Bible says, 'Submit to God; Resist the devil and he will flee from you.' I submit Lord. Show me the way and . . . help me, please.

In the serenity of the still cemetery a change came over Alex. A change so profound it left him limp and spent like a balloon pricked by a pin. He felt lightheaded, and filled with thoughts that arose from another source. Was God working in him? he wondered wildly, his brain spinning. Gone was the torment of unrequited desire. It no longer mattered. In its place was a feeling of awe at the magnitude of the devotion he had grown to feel for his wife. "Gott im Himmel," he muttered, "I've been in love with Lillie, only Lillie, all along, and didn't even know it." His heart soared. How was that possible? How foolishly he had wasted his years; thirty-four years agonizing for someone he thought he wanted when all the time he had Lillie, his Lillie. He jumped to his feet, eager to go, reeling with unfettered joy. Should he talk to Lillie—tell her how foolish he had been? He fairly bounded across the graveyard to the church where Princess Rose waited, her big liquid eyes looking anxiously at him. She blew loudly, and nuzzled his sleeve. Alex stroked her neck and whispered in her ear. "We'll go home now, old girl, and get you an extra ration of oats. I probably shouldn't have ridden you so hard, but, you see, I had this terrible problem. God straightened it out for me, and now I wonder if I should tell Lillie. You know how poor I am with words. It isn't like me to make declarations of love. Maybe I can just show her how I feel, let time heal the wounds."

Princess Rose pricked her ears, responding to the sound of his voice, and whinnied as if she understood. "Yes," Alex continued, "Lillie's been awfully careful to avoid further discussion about Belle. I guess it is better to follow her example and pretend nothing ever happened. I'll show her by my actions that I love her."

November, like March, is a Janus month—two faces looking in opposite directions—sometimes cold, raw and dreary, but more often a prolonged Indian summer—soft, golden days that Lillie treasured. Then suddenly it was Thanksgiving again, Lillie's personal favorite holiday of the year. With the hay in the barn and the wood in the cellar, the tension of preparing the house and barn for the long winter over, she could relax with family around the Thanksgiving table and give thanks for whatever manner of harvest had come to them during the past year.

With the sumptuous meal over, her parents, Mother Katie and all the McPhersons patted their bellies and retired to the parlor. Coals glowed in the fireplace, and the oil lamp on the sideboard cast a cheery, golden light over the room as everyone began to draw chairs into a semi-circle for an evening of singing. Lillie gritted her teeth when Alex gallantly whipped out a chair for Belle with a smile.

He stood beside the piano, one hand resting lightly on its gleaming mahogany surface, the other tucked into his vest as he prepared to sing.

Harry's fingers moved across the keyboard and Alex's rich voice picked up the notes of "Lorena." Lillie felt the tug of memory—remembering their first dance so many years ago. Did Alex remember, she wondered? A deep wave of hair fell idly across his broad forehead; his strong, square jaw was softened by song and he idly stroked the flowing mustache that adorned his upper lip. He was watching her intently.

In the soft light of the fire he looks younger, Lillie thought with a lurch of her heart, like the boy I first loved.

Funny how snatches of memories are indelibly seared in one's mind. She remembered that night so long ago when a young Alex stood on a Littlestown street corner in the golden light of flickering street lamps, the snow falling softly on his broad shoulders and crusting his eyelashes, his clear baritone voice rising in the cold night air to capture her heart.

Love comes to us in many forms during our lifetime, she thought, pensively, but first love, poignant and terrifying in its intensity, can never be felt again.

Belle sat nearby, but Alex's gaze, she saw, wasn't on Belle—he was looking straight at her. And he wasn't just looking, it was the way he was looking. Lillie's heart trembled, fear and hope mingled together in terrible anticipation. Alex was facing her and his dark eyes found and held hers as his voice trembled with emotion over the memorable words:

> We loved each other then, Lorena
> More than we ever dared to tell;
> And what we might have been, Lorena,
> Had but our loving prospered well-
> But then, 'tis past, the years are gone,
> I'll not call up their shadowy forms;
> I'll say to them, "Lost years, sleep on!
> Sleep on! nor heed life's pelting
> storms.

His voice caught, then once more became strong:

> "A hundred months have passed, Lorena
> since last I held that hand in mine
> and felt the pulse beat fast, Lorena
> Though mine beat faster than thine."

When the song had ended his gaze lingered, dark with a silent message.

She felt her lips tremble, and fought the tears. What does he want from me? What is he trying to say?

He walked toward her.

"We need to talk," he said in a low voice. "The kitchen. We'll have some privacy there."

She didn't argue. Just nodded and followed him.

They walked to the window and silently looked west over the fall hues of their land. The hills were a warm pinkish brown, deep shadows outlined bare trees and sparrows scratched busily among the fallen leaves.

I am being foolish, she thought, misinterpreting the look in his eyes. He's going to tell me he wants to leave. Her face felt hot and tight as though she were coming down with a fever. I hate endings, she thought. Like in books when you turn the last pages and the characters you have grown to love are gone. You feel deserted.

She finally forced herself to speak. "I think I know what this is all about, Alex. It's about Belle isn't it? You've always loved her and wanted her instead of me."

Alex grabbed her by the shoulders. "Don't ever say that!" His fingers trembled.

"Why not?"

"What makes you think you know what I want?"

"Of course I know. I knew it when I first met you, deep down, and I wanted you badly enough to marry you anyway. I thought I could make you love me. But you can't make a person love you. Can you?"

"Lillie, I'm sorry I've hurt you and I know I have. It's true that for years I was enchanted with Belle. There is evil lurking in all of us and for awhile I let some foolish emotions mislead me."

Gently Alex turned her to face him and in the setting sun's red glare she could once again see his eyes, dark and burning with heat.

"Lillie . . . "

Say it, her mind screamed. I can't go on pretending nothing is wrong with our marriage. Get it out in the open and get it over with.

" . . . I love you."

She pulled away and stepped back trembling. A new, futile hope quickened inside her. "But . . . "

"I know it hasn't always been this way. Maybe in the beginning your love was stronger than mine. Maybe I wasted years imagining something I didn't really want. All I know is how I feel now. I love you. I've been waiting for you to see the truth, but ever since last Christmas you've been holding me away. I've tried . . ." He stopped, took her hand in his rough calloused palm. "Oh, I know I should have taken the bull by the horns, but you know how difficult it's always been for me to verbalize things. All I know is I love you and I want to start all over again."

Lillie stared at him, her eyes moist with joy. Her Alex, never good with words, so suddenly eloquent.

"Are you sure it's me you want, not Belle?"

"You, my sweet Lillie." He pulled her into his arms. "It has always been you in my heart. Only you."

She pulled in a deep breath, kitchen smells that tasted of warmth and love and family. She felt buoyant, clean and shining. As if, just now, this very minute, her marriage had been born.

"Please, Lillie . . ."

She felt her heart leap and put a finger on his lips. "There is no need to say anything more, Alex. From now on there will be no silent accusations, no mistrust. I love you . . . and I trust you . . . completely."

His eyes were searching hers. He took her hands into his and raised them to his lips. "And I . . . Belle and I . . . we never . . ."

"Sh. That door is closed; that is past."

He reached to gather her in his arms and she moved into them.

These past few years she had harbored feelings of jealousy toward Belle, like a stubborn wound that would not heal itself. How senseless that was, she thought. How foolish that people should waste their lives on all the fleeting hurts, the supposed injustices, the imagined unfairness. Life was hard enough and so terribly, terribly short! And we walk with blinders on, she thought, pensively.

Alex held her close and touched her lips with his. She smiled up at him, her heart finally at peace, knowing she had the love of a husband, not just the love of a son. She should have trusted that all along.

"Oh, boy!" Harry cried a minute later, walking in on them. "Smooching in the kitchen!"

Lillie smiled and turned a beaming face toward him. He had it wrong though. It wasn't smooching, it was forgiveness.

BOOK 2

CHAPTER 18

October 1903

The handsome, fashionable young man whipped the lathered chestnut colt pulling his elegant brougham as it sped along the kidney-crushing plank road from York Street to the fairgrounds.

"Go, you bastard!" roared Harry Rebert. "Go!" It was a wine-crisp evening in 1903, and Harry was wildly, crazily drunk. The plank road was wide enough for only one vehicle and a second buggy raced toward him at a similar speed. The game, of course, was one of raw courage. Who would falter and use one of the pullovers strategically placed every quarter mile?

Harry cracked the whip one more time.

Both horses raced flat out as Harry's inflamed eyes calculated the distance. The approaching horse and carriage passed its last pull-over. His own was dead ahead. His heart pounded in his chest and with wild abandon he hammered the whip handle against the carriage shaft. Even drunk he would not flail his horse.

"Go, Tansy!. Don't yield! Go!"

His pull-off passed in a blur. The other horse and carriage were almost upon him.

"Go!" he screamed.

At the last second the oncoming horse veered. The rival carriage tilted like a wobbling top, spinning off the plank road. As Harry sped by he had a fleeting vision of a rearing, foaming horse and a wide eyed, pale youth.

He reined Tansy with trembling hands, laughing in exhilaration. *God, life was good!*

* * *

A week later, on a crisp October evening that promised a full Harvest moon, Harry donned a white shirt, brown suit, and a stylish polka-dot bow tie full of anticipation for the coming evening. As he carefully straightened the stiff collar of the shirt his thoughts strayed to the upcoming county fair, only weeks away, where Tansy was a sure winner for the half-mile harness race. Harry wrinkled his brow in a deep scowl. Tansy might be top notch, but his racing sulky was outdated and Pa held a tight purse string. He'd have to go to work on Mamma; Mamma bought him anything he wanted.

But tonight he couldn't be bothered with worries about such trivial matters. Tonight he had a date with Effie Riffle!

Bouncing down the staircase with the long-legged grace of a frisky colt, he rushed into the kitchen, skidding to a stop before the comb-box hung low on the wall beside the tin sink. At twenty-two, he was a good eight inches taller than his diminutive mother who had hung the comb-box, with its tiny mirror, to reflect her own face. He had to sag at the knees to see his image, and he cocked his head to one side and smiled with self-satisfaction. He thought his features rather aristocratic—a thin face with a long slender nose and arching eyebrows that emphasized deep blue eyes hooded by heavy eyelids and long curling eyelashes. He smiled, deepening the cleft in his chin. The girls he dated seemed fascinated by that small indentation, always finding excuses to run their finger tips over his chin.

Carefully, he parted his brown hair slightly left of center and combed it back. A deep wave fell forward onto his forehead. He ran the comb through it again and patted it into place, then straightened his bow tie one more time and adjusted the vest of his suit. A fellow had to look spiffy when he had a date with a beauty like Effie.

Finally satisfied with his appearance, he turned to his mother for her approval.

Lillie was in her rocker by the window, one hand turning the pages of the latest Ladies Home Journal while the other hand idly petted a loudly purring tiger cat. She wore a pale orchid dress that perfectly matched the blue eyes absorbed in her magazine. He noticed with surprise that the hair, fastened in a tight bun at the nape of her neck, was beginning to show signs of gray.

She looked up at him and smiled sweetly. "My, don't you look handsome tonight. That Riffle girl must be mighty special to get my boy all dressed up in his finest. I expect you're taking the new carriage?"

"Yep, she's hitched and ready to go. I can't wait to see the look on Effie's face when she sees it."

"Will you be late?"

"Yep, Don't wait up, Mamma. The dance is in York and won't end till well after mid-night."

"Have a good time, then. And watch you don't drive Tansy too fast."

He grinned at her with all the charm he could muster and strode out into the crisp October evening.

Bupp, their hired hand, waited beside the front gate holding the reins of the prancing horse.

Harry's father had just taken delivery of the new buggy and what a sight it was. Harry glided his hand over it's shiny finish. The body of rich, golden oak, trimmed in crimson, rode high on special springs over bright yellow wheels, and sported a hand carved dashboard, high enough to protect him from any mud that might be thrown up by the horses. The seat was finely upholstered, far more comfortable than the usual wooden affair, yet still narrow enough to put his girl comfortably close to him. Harry stepped back and grinned in appreciation. A roof of soft beige leather finished it off, and the carriage maker had installed both fancy side curtains and a flap that hung down behind the passengers to keep out the cold wind. But the carriage's crowning glory were the two gleaming brass oil lamps mounted in front to allow night driving.

Harry walked around Tansy and gently rubbed his velvety muzzle. The horse nickered softly, nuzzling Harry's shoulder, looking at him with velvet-brown eyes. Harry's heart swelled with love as he stroked the sleek reddish-brown colt, its coat gleaming like molten gold from the reflected rays of the setting sun. One could trust a horse. Far more than one could trust an adult. His nostrils contracted reflexively as he remembered his father and his Aunt Belle in the kitchen at Rebert's Choice when he was young.

"You and I are gonna give Miss Effie an evening she won't soon forget," he whispered softly while digging a sugar cube out of his pocket. "I'm trusting you to know the way home, cause I plan to be right busy with other important matters."

Tansy shook his head in reply and pranced impatiently in his traces.

Harry took the reins from Bupp and climbed nimbly to the carriage seat. He pulled an ornate buggy whip from it's holder and with a grand flourish touched the whip to the horse's flank. They were off.

It was an October evening to make the blood sing and Harry let Tansy pick his own pace, the yellow carriage wheels whispering through scarlet maple and brilliant golden sycamore leaves. The early evening fragrance of fallen leaves and drifting wood smoke evoked a melancholy quite unusual for him.

How quickly his school years had passed. With a smile he thought of his terrible crush on Miss Miller, his third grade teacher. Except for third grade he had never liked school, never been good with books, but to his mind that didn't really matter. What mattered was riding well, dressing like a gentleman and being graceful on a dance floor.

His thoughts strayed to other things: his first bicycle, first horse, first gold watch. Good years. He liked only too well the material luxuries his family's money provided.

He rode on deep in thought, the occasional twinkle of an oil lamp glimmering in the haze of near-night. His contentment wavered as he thought of his mother and the occasional worry he observed on her sweet face when she looked at him. He should be kinder to Mamma—make more of an effort to return the exorbitant love she showered on him. He knew how much she craved a large family and sensed an unspoken need in her.

Swallowing hard, he clicked to Tansy and forced a smile. It was not in his nature to be sad for long. A wonderful evening was ahead and he began to whistle, urging Tansy to a faster pace.

As Harry reached the outskirts of Littlestown he sat erect in the seat and directed the new carriage down Queen Street, through the square, to the front of the august Union Hotel owned by Effie's father.

The hotel, the largest building in Littlestown, soared beside the railroad tracks, three stories high, unadorned and durable, like a staunch Republican. Jauntily, Harry jumped to the ground and tossed Tansy's reins to a small boy gawking at the astonishing carriage. He threw his shoulders back and bounded up the front steps of the hotel.

Effie was waiting in the lobby. Never in all his twenty-two years had he dated a girl prettier, or harder to catch, than Effie Riffle. She had the natural healthy coloring of the German-Swiss, cheeks like rose petals, and a straight elegant mouth with well defined red lips. Her shining chestnut hair was marceled into soft waves that framed an oval face and she wore a shimmering silk that clung to well-rounded hips.

Tall, distant, classy, haughty: she portrayed it all.

Then too, the Riffles had standing in the community; George Riffle was a former burgess and was now owner of the town's best hotel, and Effie greeted her date with quiet self-assurance.

Proudly, Harry escorted her out of the lobby, to the waiting rig.

"Oh, Harry, it's absolutely gorgeous," she gasped, her lips curving into a smile. "I've never seen such a grand carriage."

"It's the finest money could buy," he boasted, drawing in his stomach and squaring his shoulders. He cocked his head and winked. "But then a fellow needs a fine carriage to take the most beautiful girl in Littlestown to the Harvest Ball."

Effie blushed prettily.

He helped her into the carriage and she carefully arranged her cloak and long silk dress around slender legs. He glanced over his shoulder to make sure anyone watching saw this fine spectacle, then jumped up beside her and turned the horse and carriage onto South Queen Street.

The grand ball room of the Yorktown Hotel glowed with color and light. Huge chandeliers, the first in town to be lit by electric light bulbs, threw romantic shadows on the faces of the swaying couples waltzing to the soft strains of William Dalton's orchestra.

Harry held Effie lightly in his arms, gliding in perfect step across the polished floor, thinking not for the first time what an elegant girl she was. Effie's transformation from childhood to womanhood was obvious—her full busted figure and narrow waist tantalizing in the sleek silk gown she wore.

They returned to their table after a lively foxtrot, and she flashed him a smile when he held the chair for her.

"It's been a while, Effie," he said.

"I know, but I've been busy with graduation and our high school choir sang for a lot of benefits before school ended."

His jaw tightened and warm blood rushed up his neck. Effie had turned him down as an escort to the graduation dance, saying she had promised another. It still rankled. Girls didn't usually say no to him.

"My friend, Jerome, told me that you have a beautiful voice. I've never heard you sing," Harry observed.

She assumed an elaborately casual expression. "I sing at Redeemer's every Sunday. You must come sometime."

"Well, I guess Christ Church won't miss me if I sneak off to hear my girl sing next Sunday," he said, giving her hand a possessive squeeze.

He felt her hand stiffen, but then she gave him a slow smile. "I'd like that."

"Jerome also said you won a scholarship to Hood College. Does this mean you'll be leaving Littlestown in the fall?"

"Not this year. Mother isn't well and Hood graciously agreed to give me an extra year to accept their offer. Father needs my help at the hotel until Mother is better."

"I can see I'll be spending a lot of time at the Union Hotel this summer," Harry said, cocking his head to look deep into smoky-blue eyes, thickly lashed and hooded by heavy lids that gave her a sleepy look. Did he imagine it or did the hand holding her glass of wine tremble slightly?

The music began again and he got to his feet and led her to the dance floor.

The waltz was slow and dreamy, the lights low, and he held her lightly in his arms. Intentionally, he stumbled slightly, pulling her closer so that her breasts brushed his vest. His arms tightened and he rested his cheek against her silky hair. God help him, he wanted this girl with a passion he had seldom experienced. Did he detect a knowing look in her eyes? Coyly, she backed away and dropped her gaze.

"Why, Harry Rebert, you're a regular flirt!"

"I'm worse than that," he said with a grin, drawing her close once more. "I'm a spoiled brat and I drink too much. That's why the girls find me so devilishly irresistible."

Effie threw back her head and laughed. Years of singing had fine-tuned her voice into a husky alto and her hearty laugh made several nearby couples smile. "Well, this girl prefers a little more distance between dance partners," she said, once more moving away from him, her eyes sparkling with merriment.

Against her better judgement Effie felt herself succumbing to Harry's easy charm. *You think you're a real demon, don't you, Harry Rebert,* Effie mused, as they whirled around the dance floor. The hand holding hers was firm and smooth, not callused and hard like most of the farm boys she dated. A faint prickling of pleasure crept up her arm.

Harry was a superb dancer, but then she had known he would be.

The music continued and she felt herself relax in it's seductiveness. His hand on the small of her back was warm and possessive, his lips brushed her hair, the clean scent of his skin teased her senses.

He nonchalantly swayed closer to her. "There's a dance at the Grange next Saturday night. Are you free?" he asked.

She shook her head. "I can't. Saturdays are busy at the hotel. I don't expect Daddy to let me off every weekend."

"All right, we'll compromise. Will you ask him for every other Saturday?"

"You're taking a lot for granted, aren't you?" The coolness in her voice was intended to warn him he was going too fast.

As the music stopped and they stood waiting for another number to begin, he looked at her with a touch of humor. "Will you try to make a little time for me, anyway?"

"I'll try," she replied noncommittally.

"Please. I want to date you, Effie."

It was the way he said it, Effie told herself, that caused a tingling sensation in her breast.

His voice was honey—rich, warm honey, confident and caressing.

The orchestra swung into a rendition of "A Pretty Girl Is Like A Melody." "Umn, good," he murmured as he gathered her into his arms. "I like the slow numbers, best."

Her head was level with his shoulder, causing her to tilt her face back to look at him. Was that mouth as passionate as it looked, she wondered? This close, she could see the closely shaven stubble of his beard. He was every inch a man; a man with a tantalizing cleft in his chin and a sweet way of talking.

"You only like the slow numbers because it gives you a chance to hold a girl close," she teased.

"Why else?" He gave her a lopsided grin and pulled her closer. Effie felt a shiver of passion sweep over her, totally uninvited and unexpected. Harry must have felt it because he had an immediate reaction that she felt beneath the thin silk of her dress. What would it be like to let restraint crumble, to surrender to this dashing, spirited man? Not so fast, Effie, she told herself . . . not so fast . . . .

The music stopped and she snapped back to reality. She must control the sensuous nature she knew lurked beneath the surface of the cool, controlled face she exhibited to the public. She couldn't make the mistake of being an easy conquest.

Especially if she were to capture the wealthy Harry Rebert.

CHAPTER 19

Without speaking, Harry took Effie's hand and led her off the dance floor. During the evening he was forced to relinquish her several times to other partners, but had no interest in dancing with another girl. It took a great deal of restraint to stay away from the bar, but he didn't want to spoil things by drinking too much. He would need his wits about him if he were going to seduce Effie before the night was out.

The final waltz ended and the musicians packed away their instruments. Harry collected Effie's cloak and bonnet and led her to the front door. He called for his carriage and Effie held herself like a queen when she was handed up to the seat by the costumed doorman.

The October night was clear and balmy, typical Indian summer weather, and Effie sat silently beside him as he competently handled the new rig. Tansy trotted briskly, ears alert and tail high. Harry left the motion of the rocking carriage jostle him closer to Effie's warm body and casually he put his arm around her. She tensed slightly, then he felt her relax with a small soft sigh and settle against him.

"Look at those stars, Harry. They're so close I think I could reach up and grab a few just to see what makes them sparkle so."

With a soft chuckle, Harry shook his head. "You don't need to hold them in your hands, I can see them in your eyes." He tightened his arm.

"What are your plans for the future, Harry?"

"I'll continue to work the farms and cattle with Papa. He considers me a full partner now. We buy young scrubs down in Virginia, ship them by rail to Littlestown, fatten them over the summer, then sell them at the Lancaster livestock auction in the fall. It's a good business."

"Your Papa should be happy that you work together."

"I guess he is. He doesn't say much." Harry snapped the reins and Tansy picked up his gait. Effie was a good listener and for a moment he was tempted to tell her of his true relationship with his father. The truth of it was, he was treated more like a helper than a partner. He doubted his father would ever give him control of the farms; Alex seemed to have little faith in Harry's judgement—always grumbling about his friends and drinking habits. But Harry wanted to impress this girl, so he said, "Someday I hope to enlarge the horse barns at our stable on the Hanover Pike and breed trotters full time."

"Will you continue to race, too?"

"As long as I can, until I have a trotter fast enough to run on the Grand Circuit, bred and trained at the Rebert Stables and raced by yours truly."

"You said trotting horses. Don't you like pacers?"

"I never liked the idea of hobbling a horse; the trotting gait is more natural, more fluid and beautiful." He crooked his eyebrow and gave her a lopsided grin: "just like a shapely girl on the dance floor."

Effie smiled. "Harness racing can be dangerous, can't it?"

"Dangerous and challenging." He gave her a steady look from hooded eyes. "I like challenging things."

They passed slumbering Hanover, the only sound Tansy's clopping shoes on the macadam street, the jingle of harness chains, and the soft whisper of the carriage wheels.

"The whole world seems to be asleep," Effie said drowsily, snuggling her head on his shoulder.

Harry pulled her closer.

As they approached Littlestown and breasted the last small rise on the Hanover Pike Harry slowed Tansy and glanced to the west at the shadowy outline of Christ Church. Its elegant steeple, bathed in a shroud of silvery moonlight, stirred an emotion that rippled from the depth of his being and which he did not care to analyze.

Effie's gaze followed his own. "Your grandfather Edward helped rebuild Christ Church, didn't he?" she asked.

"He did. And he's buried there. I was little when he died, but I remember him well . . . a remarkable man whose whole life was wrapped up in that little church." He smiled gently. "The church and my grandmother, Katie." Harry pulled slightly on the reins wheeling the carriage into a narrow dirt lane, opposite the church and just beyond a large brick home his folks had always referred to as the Mansion House. He hoped Effie didn't realize that Tansy seemed to know the way.

But Effie's attention was elsewhere, her eyes feasting on the Mansion House. "What a magnificent home," she murmured. "I've always wondered why you don't live there, Harry."

"Papa would like to, but Mamma doesn't want to leave White Hall; it's been the Weikert family home for generations." He laughed. "I think she loves that house more than anything in the world . . . next to me, that is."

"Will the Mansion House be yours someday?"

Harry shot her a look. For just a moment he thought he detected a look of speculation on her pretty face, a quiver of real interest in her voice.

"Someday. This farm is where I want to build the breeding barns. Right now a tenant farmer lives here."

They had reached a woodlot at the summit of the hill behind the house and Tansy entered a small glade where he stopped and dropped his head to nibble at dew-dampened grass. Harry and Effie sat in comfortable silence looking at the gentle countryside encased in moonlight. Before them sat the farm's large bank barn and the stately brick house, across the road the tiny church, and far away the purple outline of South Mountain. Effie shivered as a cold gust rustled the trees and Harry placed the lap robe around her shoulders. Gazing down at her elegant face washed with moonbeams he found himself longing for something that had never bothered him before—a desire to commit himself to a girl . . . this girl. To make her his alone.

Gently he settled his mouth on hers. She resisted at first, but gradually her lips softened and became warm. The kiss was slow and undemanding at first, but gradually it became more intense and he heard a barely audible sigh of pleasure. When he finally lifted his mouth from hers his breath was ragged and it gratified him to notice that she slumped in his arms and her breathing was faster than normal.

Once more his lips sought hers. As he slowly moved his mouth an electrical shock fired his nerves, heating his body and swelling his sex.

With a shudder, Effie pulled away from him.

"Cold?" he asked softly, although he knew better.

"No. Afraid . . . afraid of getting involved with you."

"What's so wrong with that?" he asked, his eyebrows lifting.

"I think a girl could get very hurt by you. I don't want to rush into something I'll be sorry for. We hardly know each other."

"Trust me," he said, his hand caressing her silky smooth arm. "I won't force you into anything. When you say "No," I'll stop." Harry studied her face, hidden in shadows. He suspected a hidden passion in this strangely aloof girl. She was everything he desired in a woman.

"Effie, oh Effie," he moaned, drawing her to him. Again their lips met and this time he could feel them part as her passion seemed to rise to meet his own. He was thoroughly aroused, but experience told him to go slow. This was no ordinary town girl.

Cautiously, he went into action with the deftness and subtlety of an experienced seducer, easing her gently, but firmly, down onto the upholstered carriage seat. She looked up at him, startled, and then her eyes grew wide, warned of his intent. She stiffened and tried to raise herself. Cupping the back of her head with his hand he covered her mouth with his own, pushing her back against the seat, kissing her with all his pent-up passion. He felt the wild beat of her heart against his own as she responded with surprising fervor.

And then desire began to rule and he forgot his earlier determination to take things slowly. He moved his hand to her breast. She began to struggle from beneath him and he felt her hands pressing for freedom.

"No, Harry. We must stop."

"Not yet."

"Yes!"

"I promise we won't go all the way. Just let me hold your breast in my hand. No more."

"We can't. It won't stop there." She looked him full in the eyes and reached a shaking finger to trace the deep cleft in his chin. "You are far too handsome and persuasive for a girl to resist. I don't trust myself with you, Harry."

"Then why resist? I can tell you're as attracted to me as I am to you." He reached up and untied the strings of her bonnet, which had gotten pushed back on her head, and stroked her soft hair.

They kissed again and he took her hand in his and guided it toward the bulge in his trousers. She jerked her hand away with a violence that surprised him and smacked him hard across his face.

"Stop that," she cried, shaking with anger. "This has gone far enough, Harry Rebert. I think you'd better take me home." Her face was set like flint.

Harry sighed. He could tell he wasn't going to make it tonight. The mood had been broken. Darn it, he should have known better—shouldn't have tried to make her touch him. He tried to readjust himself so he was more comfortable, then gave her a slow smile and kissed her as gently as he could. "I think I've fallen in love with you, Effie," he whispered.

She smiled, her eyes narrowing wickedly as she sat back and settled herself on the seat. "We'll see, Harry. We'll see."

* * *

Effie carefully pondered her options. Her life was not following the course she had envisioned. Winning a scholarship to Hood

College had seemed a dream come true, then her mother became ill with palsy and her brother went into the cabinetry business. Now instead of going off to college she found herself in the menial position of waitressing at the hotel. The fact that her father owned the hotel didn't help her self-image one iota, and the idea that this might be the end of the road for her was totally unacceptable. She wanted to be at the hub of Littlestown society, respected and secure. Harry Rebert could give her that security. As his wife, she would have the status she craved—fine clothes, elegant furnishings and china, the Mansion House her home.

Given time, she believed she could tame the wildness in Harry. The trick was to thwart his sexual overtures so that marriage would be the only solution to his frustration.

When Harry appeared in the hotel the next evening and pressed her for a date Effie accepted. They went to a play in Hanover and the following week to a concert at Gettysburg College. Soon they were in the midst of the Christmas holidays and there were parties, church socials, and theater performances every week. Everyone considered them a couple, and although they kissed and occasionally petted, she always stopped him before things got out of hand.

Effie had been rehearsing with the Redeemer's choir for the 1903 Christmas Cantata since Thanksgiving and, as the evening for the performance approached, she was tense with excitement. She had a solo and Harry promised to be present.

Daddy agreed to host refreshments for the choir members and selected guests in the hotel dinning room following the concert. Full of cheer, she planned the menu: cold roast beef, potato salad, rolls, champagne, and fancy cakes. Her father balked at the idea of serving expensive champagne, but Effie was adamant. Anyone who was anyone drank champagne nowadays and all of Harry's friends would be present. As her enthusiasm grew so did the guest list.

About nine o'clock on December 12th, parishioners and guests began to arrive at the hotel as carriages and phaetons left the august entrance of Redeemer Reformed Church and flowed up King Street. Among them were the Schwartz's, Sellers, Zucks, Kings, and, of course, Pastor Hamilton Smith. Harry's entire family—his grandmother Katie, his Aunt Belle and her five children, and his parents Lillie and Alexander Rebert—were all there. *All except Harry.*

Group after group of guests milled around the festively decorated dinning room, the women exchanging the latest gossip, the men gathered in clusters discussing politics. The men talked of Teddy Roosevelt their flamboyant President, a restless man, brimming with physical and mental energy—a President like none the country had ever seen. They talked of his celebrated "Big Stick" policy toward big business, his determination to build the Panama Canal, and his threats to declare war on California when San Francisco barred Japanese children from its public schools.

Effie had been standing with her mother, greeting the guests and keeping an anxious eye on the door.

Harry was nowhere in sight!

The guests were served and Effie moved from group to group trying her best not to appear anxious about Harry's absence. A friend cast her a sympathetic look. "I expected to see Harry here this evening," she commented, "but then I guess a farmer's life is never his own. Always a sick animal needing attention."

The word "farmer" took Effie by surprise. Somehow, she never thought of Harry as a farmer. Still, she felt a surge of relief at the possible reason for his absence. Once more she left her gaze search the room. Anger, hot in her throat, threatened to choke her and she felt her jaw tighten and her lips compress into a tight line.

Effie stood ramrod stiff glaring at the front door which suddenly swung open to a blast of frigid air and a grinning Harry Rebert.

His face was red and his blue eyes sparkled, not, Effie suspected, from the exhilaration of a cold December night, but something far stronger. He barged into the gaily decorated dinning room and headed straight for the refreshment table where he grabbed a glass of champagne before heading in her direction. "Effie," he called in a loud, thick voice, "my sweet little nightingale." He put his arm about her waist and planted a noisy kiss on her cheek. In disgust, Effie pulled away from his reeking breath and obvious inebriation.

With a foolish giggle he swiped at the wave of thick brown hair which had fallen forward on his forehead and raised an eyebrow as he rocked back on his heels. "My, now, aren't we the prim, proper maiden," he said in a voice loud enough to be heard by all present.

A silence, thick as heavy cream, filled the room. No one spoke. A woman coughed. Then, Harry, weaving back and forth on shaky legs, began to hum "A Hot Time in the Old Town," a smirk contorting his handsome face.

An uneven murmur of voices resumed as the guests tried to ignore Effie's apparent discomfort. "Dear God, help me," Effie whispered.

"Harry," she said, trying to quiet him, "did you have duties at the farm? Is that why you are so late to my Christmas party?"

"Late? Am I late? It's only ten o'clock." He fumbled in his waistcoat for his pocket watch, and with elaborate care peered at the time. "I guess in this little hick town it's late. Now in the cities things are just getting started." He began to drop the watch in his patch pocket, but it slithered to the floor. "Oops," he mumbled. He picked it up, polished the case on his sleeve, and cocked his head to give her a lopsided half-smile. "My revered Grandpa Edward's timepiece. Mustn't hurt that, must I, sweetie pie?"

Effie's father suddenly appeared at her side. "Effie's needed elsewhere," he said, taking her elbow in a firm grasp. "I suggest you help yourself at the refreshment table . . . at the coffee urn!"

"Coffee! I need more than coffee to slack this thirst of mine. And so, Mr. Riffle, does this beautiful daughter of yours. Waiter, fetch us a glass of champagne."

The look on Daddy's flushed face scared Effie. His normally genteel face looked like a storm cloud, and Effie couldn't tell whether he meant to hit Harry or let fly a string of well chosen curses.

He did neither. Instead, he roughly pushed Effie ahead of him and addressed Harry in a voice barely covered by the flurry of forced conversation around them. "Let my girl alone. If you must drink go to the bar and satisfy your thirst there . . . with the rest of the drunks."

Harry reached up and, with an imaginary tip of a hat, gave Mr. Riffle a foolish grin, then with a final squeeze of the hand he left Effie standing alone and headed to the bar.

For a long moment Effie stood staring with unseeing eyes at the room before her. She had grown to love the capricious, devil-may-care spirit in him, but this was different. Very, very, different. Was Harry a drunk? Would his drinking always disrupt their lives or could she change him, once they were married? With God's help, she thought she could. Harry needed a strong influence in his life and she knew her own strength. She looked deep inside herself, doing her level best to sort out whatever she was finding there. Perhaps it wasn't the smart thing to do, but she did want Harry in her life.

Her father, clearly aware of the tears swimming in her eyes, took her hand and led her toward the refreshment table. "You have guests, dear. Dry those tears and forget that unfortunate boy. He can bring you nothing but trouble. Don't let your heart rule an otherwise good head."

* * *

Harry truly felt miserable. January blew in with a vengeance: the roads drifted shut for weeks, the wind howled down the chimney, icicles hung from the eaves of the kitchen ell, and Effie steadfastly refused to see him.

On an especially nasty morning early in the month Harry hitched Tansy to the sleigh for a ride to Rebert's Choice. Maybe a talk with Ian would revive his spirits.

The sleigh moved silently across the farm covered in a heavy shroud of motionless snow. Harry followed the black line of the stream, locked in its deep, narrow channel, surrounded by bare forest stirring stiffly in the breath of the bitter wind.

The mill stood silent, the millpond covered with thick ice, the huge water wheel motionless. No one was about, so he headed for the house where a beckoning finger of smoke curled from the chimney, promising warmth and a pot of hot coffee.

He entered the kitchen with a loud hello. The smells rushed at him: corn meal mush fried in salt pork fat, freshly baked bread, and boiled coffee. In the corner of the warm room his Grandmother Katie rocked by the glowing fireplace and returned his greeting with an affectionate smile.

She wore a plain green dress, trim and neat on her frail body, and a pristine white apron that seemed to swallow her in its starched folds. A lace prayer cap perched on snow white hair, coiled into a tight bun on the back of her head, yet laying in soft waves around her smooth face. Her hands, fragile as tiny bird bones, held knitting needles from which a woolen sock was taking shape. Harry regarded her fondly. She was still lovely despite her seventy-five years, a mature beauty born of peace and strength.

"Harry," her low throaty voice called as she looked at him in surprise. "Whatever brings you out on such a foul day?"

"I was hoping to see Ian, but the pond is frozen over and the mill closed." He bent over and brushed a kiss on her soft cheek. It was like silk-tissue, firm and warm.

"You're looking well, Grandmamma," he said.

"And you grow more handsome every day. Do you know you're the picture of your grandfather as he was at your age?" Her pale blue eyes smiled at him with affection. "Sit down, son," she said, waving her hand toward an empty rocker beside her. "I haven't had time alone with you for a long while."

Harry eased himself into the chair. "Where is everyone?"

"Ian rode over to the tannery to get leather for some new belts and your Aunt Belle and Adam went with him. Carolyn is in bed with a bad cold."

Harry leaned back and let his eyes roam the warm, comfortable room. His grandmother had a passion for neatness; the table was cleared and every dish put away and a pile of freshly ironed sheets were folded neatly on a black walnut chest in the corner of the room. The wooden floor was a soft honey color from frequent washing, and red geraniums, queen of the kitchen window, cast a cheery glow to the otherwise austere room. Harry closed his eyes and gave a deep sigh. There was peace in this room, peace and serenity.

"You look unhappy, Harry."

He fidgeted, crossing and uncrossing his long legs, glancing away from her searching eyes. "I'm afraid I made a fool of myself . . . myself and Effie . . . at her Christmas party. She refuses to see me."

"Yes, you did. That was quite a performance you put on. Effie has every right to be hurt and angry. She planned that party for weeks and you completely disrupted it. I was ashamed of you."

"It was the drink."

"It's always the drink." Her voice grew strong and she pinned him with her eyes. "Some men can handle whiskey and some can't. Your grandfather Edward knew that and he risked everything to defy his father and distance himself from the family distillery. Drink ruined the life of Belle's father and it is going to ruin yours if you don't accept the fact that it's like poison to you."

Harry felt a spasm of annoyance. "I can handle it Grandmamma. Life would be pretty dull in this little hick town without some spirits to brighten the day. Why, my friends would laugh me out of town if I suddenly began to drink milk."

"But I believe it would make your girl very happy."

"If she's still my girl."

"She will be if you put your life in order. Effie Riffle is a nice young woman, intelligent and refined." Katie's mouth curved with just a trace of her old impishness. "She is certainly cut from a different cloth than most of the girls I've seen you with."

"Not as free with her favors, though."

Katie's mouth twitched and she began to laugh. "I'm glad to hear someone has the courage to resist your charms."

"She has that and more," Harry replied with a rueful smile.

His grandmother's face suddenly became serious once more and she fixed him a steady stare. "Apologize to her, Harry. Promise her . . . and me . . . that you will stop drinking. I don't mean ease off. I mean stop! It's a demon that will consume you."

Fear flared beneath his outward calm. Could he indeed stop? Sometimes he admitted to himself that he seemed to have no control over the craving. Then he shook his head. Of course, he could stop! He simply enjoyed the feeling of power it gave him.

They sat in the fire-flickering silence. The walls shimmered in the glowing light and gradually he felt peace begin to envelop him like an envelope. He gave her a smile of mute appeal. "I'll try Grandmamma. I promise, I'll try."

* * *

Harry went to see Effie the next day and they made a tenuous peace. He attended church every Sunday to hear her sing and she went skating with him at Rebert's Choice. Then toward the end of February Harry came down with the grip. For days he lay in bed with a high fever while his head throbbed and every muscle in his body ached. His mother fussed over him constantly, placing cool cloths on his forehead, making hot toddies of lemon, honey, and whiskey and feeding him hot chicken soup. He had to admit he enjoyed being babied. Effie's continued rejection of his attempts at love making still hurt.

It was mid-March before he felt well enough to resume his courtship. One evening he rode into Littlestown and went directly to the hotel dinning room where Effie was working. He took his favorite table near the bar and waited for her to approach. He could hear her hearty laugh as she joked with the customers, pretending to be unaware of his presence.

She finally reached his table and gave him a beaming smile. "I've missed you, Harry. Your cousin Ian told me you were sick. You look awfully pale—should you be out in this chilly air?" She pulled at her stiffly starched apron and two spots of color appeared on her cheeks. "I wouldn't want you to get sick again."

"I'm still a little weak, but anxious to get back in circulation. I've thought about you a lot." He furrowed his brow and tried to look hurt. "I thought you might have come to see me when I was so sick."

She blushed prettily and quickly looked at the order pad she was carrying. "I'm not sure your mother approves of me. Now, what would you like this evening?"

"You," he said with wink. "But maybe I'll save that for desert. For now, let's try the roast beef and a glass of claret."

"Well, I see you haven't lost your sense of humor . . . or your appetite."

"Can I walk you home after work?"

"I won't be finished until after seven."

"That's alright. I'll wait in the bar. I saw several of my friends there when I came in. I plan to drive Tansy in a few races and I want to check out the spring schedule. Send the bellboy for me when you're ready to leave."

By seven-thirty he had quite a buzz on. After his illness the drinks affected him much quicker than usual. Effie frowned in disapproval when he joined her in the lobby and he made a determined effort to appear sober as they walked down Baltimore Street to the Riffle home.

"Your house is all dark," he said in surprise when they mounted the front steps.

"No one is home. Mother is staying with my Aunt who's been awfully sick. Robert has a date tonight and, of course, Daddy will be at the hotel until it closes."

Harry couldn't believe his luck. It was the moment he'd been waiting for and he could hardly hide a grin. "It's been so long since we talked, Effie. Could I come in for just a little while? Maybe have a cup of coffee. I've been sick, you know."

She hesitated briefly then gave him a smile that made his heart thump. God, she was beautiful.

"I think a cup of coffee would do you good, and not just because you've been sick. As long as you promise to behave!"

"I'll be the perfect gentleman," he said, fighting to keep the glee from his face. He took the latch key from her hand and unlocked the front door.

Effie led him into the parlor and while she turned up the kerosene lamps he bent to light a fire in the grate.

"I'll make the coffee while you get the fire going," Effie said leaving for the kitchen.

Harry withdrew a small silver flask from his inside jacket pocket and snuck a quick nip before she returned.

Soon they were snuggled up on the hard horsehair sofa, watching the flickering flames, sipping mugs of hot coffee. Effie chatted about family affairs and he told her of the exciting races coming up. The room became warmer and he removed his jacket and loosened his tie. He was sweating, either from the fire, the whiskey, or the nearness of Effie; he wasn't sure which. He put his arm around her and pulled her roughly to his chest. He took her lips hungrily and they began kissing with all the pent up passion of weeks of separation. She pulled away to catch her breath and he noticed little beads of perspiration on her upper lip. Her eyes looked heavy and she was breathing deeply. This was not the aloof, controlled girl he was used to seeing. Effie had the look of a woman ready to be loved.

He eased her back on the sofa until she was almost reclining then covered her lips with his hot mouth while he slipped his hand under her skirt and began tugging at her bloomers.

Suddenly he was aware of her hands pushing him away. She tore her mouth from his and fixed him with a scorching look. "No!", she hissed. "Not until we're married."

The words startled him and he looked at her in confusion. Married? He didn't want to get married. He wasn't ready to get married, not now and not in the foreseeable future.

Effie began to cry and he took a handkerchief from his pocket and tried to wipe her tears while he took her trembling hand and pressed it against his cheek.

"I'm sorry, darling," he groaned.

"I thought you loved me," she sobbed, her lips still trembling.

"And I do, Effie. But marriage? We're both awfully young to get married. Besides, I thought you were going to college in the fall."

"I thought that's what I wanted. Now I'm not so sure. One thing I do know, though," she said, her face tight with determination. "I'm a virgin . . . and I intend to stay that way. No man will ever have me unless he is my husband."

The fire cast a golden glow on her flushed face; the flames threw flickering highlights in her tousled hair. He wanted to smooth the small frown puckering her brow and hear her deep throaty laugh. He felt protective and tender, but more than that, with every fiber of his being he wanted to possess her.

Now he knew the price of that possession.

CHAPTER 20

The crowd of party-goers leaned on the racetrack railing, yelling and urging on their favorites from among the field of seven Standardbreds streaming down the home stretch.

Harry perched precariously on the tiny seat above the singing wheels of a lightweight sulky as Tansy sped toward the finish line. Swirls of dust rose from the dirt track, his identifying red sash with the large number "four" fluttering in the warm air. He could hear Effie screaming, "Tansy, Tansy, come on Tansy," as he swept across the white line, a winner by a full length.

Harry turned his horse around, came back across the finish line, and reached out to grab the bright yellow purse that hung from the finish pole. Like the gladiators of old, he drove his sulky over to the rail and tossed the purse to his flushed and laughing girl.

Ocher's Race Track, just off "M" Street and a few blocks from George Riffle's Union Hotel, was the most popular gathering place in Littlestown. Horse racing, either flat or harness, was the community's favorite sport and most Saturdays found a few young men, anxious to test their horses before running them on the more prestigious County Fair circuit, wagering considerable amounts of money.

Harry had decided the track was the perfect place to throw a party and announce his engagement to Effie. After unhitching his sulky, and hastily washing the dust from his face, he headed across the infield to the red and green striped tent his hired hands had erected that morning. Large plank tables were heaped with fat ham sandwiches, pretzels, potato chips, baked-beans, and watermelon. Cold beer flowed freely from kegs buried in tubs of ice and a small group of musicians from the Littlestown Cornet Band played lustily.

Harry hurried toward Effie waiting at the tent entrance. She looked lovely today, standing tall and regal, her rich chestnut hair piled high on her head, her cheeks flushed with excitement, her blue eyes shinning with happiness. She was wearing a long, navy gored skirt, with a white eyelet shirtwaist, high at the neck and decorated with a large broach. Harry grabbed her about the waist and swung her around to plant a kiss on her cheek, sending her skirt in a swirl around her slender ankles.

With a broad wink and a big grin on his face he leapt onto the nearest table and waved his arms to gain the attention of his friends milling around the tent.

"As most of you know," he yelled, "I'm a winner today—not only in the race just finished—but in a most special way." He paused for effect. "Effie Riffle has consented to be my bride."

Cat calls and whistles from his male friends and giggles from Effie's girl friends greeted this announcement.

"Kiss her, kiss her," shouted one of his friends and as the band played a small drum-roll he jumped off the table and gave her a lusty kiss.

The kiss ignited with the beer he had consumed. Despite the rowdy laughter from the party-goers, he moved one hand into her hair, the other between her shoulder blades, pressing her close so that he could feel her breasts.

She pulled away, her cheeks flaming, and then her normally solemn eyes began to dance and her straight, elegant mouth broke into a smile. "Harry . . . ."

"Shhh, pretty one. We'll continue that kiss later." His laughter was bright, mischievous, and a little wild as he swaggered over to his buddies crowding about the beer keg.

Effie was soon surrounded by a circle of her closest friends. Her fingers shook as she held out her hand for their admiration and worked the large diamond around her finger.

"When will the wedding be?" asked Pauline Lott, one of her friends from the Redeemer's choir.

"We haven't set a firm date. Harry wants to wait until after the fall cattle auctions and he's committed to a race at the York Fair in October. After that I guess."

"Have your parents given their blessing yet? I notice they aren't here today," Pauline asked, looking shrewdly at Effie with raised eyebrows.

"No . . ."

"Well, you're eighteen. I guess you can do what you want."

"Daddy is the one who disapproves. He thinks we should wait. But he'll come around when he gets to know Harry better. I do want a nice church wedding and Mamma has always looked forward to having me married in her wedding gown, yards and yards of old Swiss lace with a long train and hundreds and hundreds of tiny, hand-sewn seed pearls."

"Oh, it sounds beautiful, Effie Will you have bridesmaids?" another girl asked hopefully.

"If I have a large church wedding, of course I will," Effie said, tartly. "And you will certainly be one of my bridesmaids. Maybe it will be at Christmas and the attendants will dress in red velvet and carry little white muffs."

"But first you have to get your father to agree," another girl reminded her.

Effie waved her hand impatiently. "Don't worry, he'll come around when Mother goes to work on him."

Meanwhile, Harry was having a grand time, passing out mugs of cold beer, laughing at the ribald jokes of his friends, his shirt unbuttoned at the neck, his hair hopelessly tumbled over his flushed face. Effie was without a doubt the best catch in town—both beautiful and intelligent and he loved showing her off. He knew they made a handsome couple. Harry took a big gulp of the tangy beer and licked the foam from his lips. He grabbed a handful of pretzels, lit a cigarette, and sat down on a nearby bench. A sudden breeze wafted sun, dust, horse dropping, and yeasty beer, snapped the tent roof and set the branches of a huge oak to gentle whispering. A doughnut like wisp of smoke curled about his head and he gave a happy sigh. The world was his oyster. He had the fastest horse, the finest sulky, and now the prettiest girl in town.

Still . . . Effie's father disliked him and he didn't understand why. He had always been a good patron of the hotel, careful to pay his bill on time, and except for the debacle at Christmas time never rowdy or loud. Hopefully, now that the engagement was official, Mr. Riffle would unbend and give him a chance.

He shook his head, pensively, to dispel the disturbing thoughts that still plagued him when he thought of the many ways marriage would alter his life. Pangs of guilt assailed him when he questioned his reluctance to assume responsibility for a wife and family. Was he only marrying Effie for sexual gratification? So far he'd refused to work out the answer to those feelings, and carefully he swept them under the rug of his conscience. He really didn't have any choice if he wanted to bed this elegant girl, did he?

The sound of singing roused him from his solitary thoughts. One of his buddies hailed him and he jumped to his feet, draining his glass and crushing his cigarette beneath his foot. He felt his humor return and hurried to join in the song.

Alex and Lillie sat on chairs in a far corner of the tent, watching the merriment in disapproval.

Lillie's heart was heavy. She felt the love of her son shifting away from her towards this girl who would share his heart and bed. She prayed nightly for God's help to release the shame of jealousy she felt. Surely it was a sin for a mother to feel this way. She knew she spoiled Harry, but years ago when she first suspected her husband's infidelity with Belle, she had poured all her love into her son and even when she learned her fears about Alex were groundless she was unable to quell her obsessive attachment to Harry.

Lillie drew her heavy eyebrows together until they formed a

straight line across her forehead. "Effie's pretty enough, but she struts around like royalty. Mark my words, Alex, that one will give our son a hard time."

Alex grunted.

Silently Lillie watched the bright couple laughing gaily as they made their rounds from table to table. "She's rushing him into marriage. He hasn't had a chance to make something of himself."

"Mein Gott, woman, you can't cling to him forever; he's a man grown, already. The boy'll be alright, if you untie the apron strings. He needs a woman's love now, not a mother's."

Lillie smiled sadly. "Harry has always required a lot of love. In a lot of ways he's still a little boy and I'm not at all sure Effie Riffle is capable of supplying the attention he needs." She sat quietly twisting her hands in her lap, before adding reluctantly, "I do notice he hasn't been drinking as much since they started courting."

"No, that's true. Unfortunately, he hasn't slowed down on the amount of money he's spending. You do realize who is paying for all this don't you," Alex asked sourly, looking in the direction of the free flowing beer kegs.

Lillie's eyes darkened suddenly and she reached out to clutch Alex's arm. "Look, Alex. That shiftless Jerome Sinclair has taken Harry aside and it looks like they're arguing. Ach, I don't like that man. I hope he doesn't spoil this day for Harry."

Harry placed a placating hand on Jerome's arm and lowered his voice. "I'll pay the wager next week. Be a sport, buddy. I need all my money for this affair today."

"Honoring your debts is more important than throwing a damn picnic."

"But this is my engagement—not some ordinary picnic. I've always paid before, haven't I?" A sudden idea occurred to him and he cocked his head, grinning at Jerome. "Why don't we race for the wager. Double or nothing. My Tansy against your Dolly." Jerome scowled, his face dark and cold. "Not Dolly, she's too old. My new colt—Demon Runner."

"Flat race or sulky?"

"Flat. Demon will be a good trotter someday, but he isn't fully trained yet."

"Where?"

"Here. Next Saturday morning. Nine o'clock."

Harry stuck out his hand. "Done."

Harry was careful to keep his plans from Effie. She had made it clear she didn't approve of his gambling or his friends—more specifically, of Jerome Sinclair. "Women," he muttered darkly. They just don't understand men things.

By eight o'clock Saturday morning the temperature was already hovering at eighty degrees. Despite the heat, Tansy was frisky and alert, anticipating the fun ahead. Harry vaulted into the saddle, flexed his shoulders and turned Tansy's head down Storm's Store Road for the short trip to Littlestown.

The countryside was lush and green after an unusually wet spring. The air hung heavy with sweet honeysuckle and wild roses that climbed in profusion over stone boundary walls. Horse-chestnut trees were a mass of white blossoms and he could hear the whistle of bobwhites from the fence row they were passing. At times he longed for the excitement of big cities he had visited, like Philadelphia or New York, but other times like today, trotting peacefully on Tansy, watching the interplay of light and shadow on tree-lined Whitehall Road, he couldn't envision living anywhere but here in beautiful Adams County.

Jerome was waiting at the entrance to Ocher's Track. They greeted each other with curt nods while Harry's eyes roamed over Demon Runner with undisguised admiration. What a magnificent horse! He had a large intelligent head, bright inquisitive eyes, and a coat of glistening ebony. Demon Runner—he fit his name like a glove, and Harry felt a flush of envy. He'd like to own that horse.

The two horses touched noses briefly and Tansy pranced sideways, shaking his head and mouthing the bit.

They walked the horses to the starting line. Jerome had given a young lad a quarter to act as starter and he was waiting for them at the white chalk line, whip in hand. Harry leaned over Tansy's neck, holding the reins loosely, feeling the muscles in Tansy's sleek body quiver in readiness.

The crack of the whip split the still air. Harry dug his heels into Tansy's flanks and they were off.

Demon shot forward like a cannon-ball and had gained a full length before they passed the first post. Harry urged Tansy forward, using the whip sparingly, letting the horse set his own pace. Slowly Tansy started to close the gap, his hooves drumming a steady rhythm. Harry bent low over his withers, hot air rushing through his hair, his blood feverish with the pure thrill of the race.

"Come on, boy, come on! You can do it."

Tansy stretched and reached his full speed with long, rhythmic strides as they reached the half-way post. Head to head—Tansy, burnished bronze; Demon, gleaming ebony—they rounded the turn.

Demon Runner was a fine horse with a great competitive spirit, but he was no match for the experienced Tansy. His starting pace had been too fast and he quickly used up his reserves. Coming down the stretch Tansy began to ease ahead, inch by inch, then by a full neck.

Jerome used his whip freely and Demon Runner tried to respond by giving a last desperate effort, but he could not regain the lead. Harry and Tansy flashed by the finish line ahead by a neck-and-a-half.

Harry allowed the horse to run to the turn before pulling him up and trotting back to the finish line where Jerome had already dismounted.

Harry swung out of the saddle, patted a lathered, heaving Tansy on the neck, and offered him a sugar cube, his reward for winning.

Harry turned to face Jerome whose face was ugly with displeasure.

"The wager's satisfied," Jerome said through tight lips. "But we'll race again before the year is out. Demon's young, he needs seasoning, but he'll beat Tansy the next time."

"We'll see about that."

"No, I guarantee you we'll win." Jerome said in a dangerous tone. He yanked Demon Runner's reins, causing the colt to neigh in pain as the bit cut into its soft mouth, and stalked away.

* * *

Lillie settled herself into a rocker in the warm kitchen at Rebert's Choice and ran fussy hands across her starched apron before fixing Belle with a baleful frown.

Belle sat at a small table shelling peas, the stove giving off the tart fragrance of bubbling rhubarb that Mother Katie was preparing for sauce. "I don't understand why you have doubts about Effie," Belle said. "She seems nice enough and she comes from a good family."

Lillie sighed. "I ask myself the same question. I don't know, Belle—I just feel uneasy about it. She seems cold . . . unfeeling almost. Harry is such a warm, carefree boy."

"Boy? He isn't a boy any longer, Lillie. What is he now? Twenty-two, twenty-three?"

"Twenty-three. But he isn't as mature as other boys his age. Maybe it's my fault; I know I spoil him. If we'd had more children it might be different."

"Well, personally, I think Effie Riffle is good for him. Harry needs responsibility and a strong hand, not a simpering girl who'll cave in to his good looks and the charm he spreads around like thick butter."

"And you don't think I give that to him?" Lillie blazed.

"Not the type of strength he needs if he's going to fight his appetite for strong drink and gambling. A wife and children might be just what he needs. Effie is a smart girl, she knows his problems."

"Too smart, I fear. She's far cleverer in book learning than Harry, you know. She won a scholarship to Hood College and he barely made it through school."

Belle pushed the peas aside and rested her arms on the table, fixing Lillie with a look of compassion and understanding. "I've seen the two of them together. He loves her, and mark my words, he is going to marry her. If you fight it you'll lose them both. Accept her, Lillie."

Lillie rocked slowly, her chest tight with the fear of the loss she sensed and felt unable to fight.

But if Harry's mother seemed reluctant to accept Effie; George Riffle was adamant in his refusal to give his daughter his permission to marry. He made it perfectly clear to Harry that he considered him spoiled and irresponsible and began to push Effie to break her engagement, accept her scholarship at Hood, and leave Littlestown.

Harry was furious and running out of patience. He had found a little barmaid at a tavern in Hanover, willing to satisfy his needs, but it was getting harder and harder to juggle the two girls.

Something had to be done—and soon!

Late in September Harry approached his mother for help. "Talk to Mr. and Mrs. Riffle for me, Mamma. Remind them of our standing in the community and of my ability to provide well for her."

"Humph. I'm as much against your marrying as they are. The best thing Effie could do is go off to college and let you grow up a little more."

"You just want to keep me home, at your beck and call."

"You are my life, don't you understand that? I can't just stand aside and see you throw yourself away on a conniver like . . ."

"Don't you dare speak like that about Effie!"

"And don't you dare talk back to me. Ever." Mamma stood looking up at him, eyes blazing, every inch of her tiny frame taut with indignation. "I have her measure. She's after your money. She wants to establish herself in the Mansion House and be a lady instead of waiting tables in her father's hotel."

"Don't be foolish. Effie's father is a respected tradesman and she's giving up a college education to marry me. She's a bright, beautiful girl who could have her choice of beaus." He ran his fingers through his hair. "Don't treat me like an adolescent child. I'm a grown man, mother, in case you haven't noticed."

As he watched her she seemed to grow smaller, her face crumpled, and her eyes filled with tears. Mamma took hold of his hand and clasped it tightly with both of hers. "I don't want angry words between us, Harry. You'll always be my little boy. I love you more than life itself."

Tenderly he kissed her cheek. "I know Mamma. But too much love can be as hurtful as not enough. In time you'll learn to share all that extra love with Effie. She can be the daughter you never had."

"Never . . . never! You're all I need, all I'll ever need."

CHAPTER 21

Effie gathered her shawl against the October chill and cuddled closer to Harry on the narrow carriage seat. The last cattle auction was out of the way and he flourished his wallet bulging with cash before her eyes. They were parked in their usual spot, the woodlot above the Mansion House, where he had brought her just a year ago after the Harvest Ball.

"I'm tired of waiting, Effie," he groaned, pressing her tightly against his chest. "Your father will never give his approval. Why don't we take the cattle money, catch a train to New York City, and get married? We don't need a fancy wedding."

"Oh, but Harry, I've always dreamed of something special; something to remember all my life. I've dreamed of my wedding since I was a little girl."

"We'll make it special, just different. I've lots of money. We'll stay at the finest hotel in New York . . . maybe the Waldorf . . . take in some Broadway shows, go shopping on Fifth Avenue and do it up proper."

"But doesn't some of that money belong to your father?"

She noticed a flush of heat in his cheeks, but he smiled in his most beguiling manner and tossed his head nonchalantly. "Not much of it and Mamma will make it right with him. Don't worry your pretty head about that. I have all the money we need."

"But where would we get married?"

"City Hall, maybe. I don't know. There's bound to be a Justice of the Peace somewhere in a big city like New York."

Effie shook her head. "It must be a church."

"How about St. Patrick's? That's supposed to be the biggest church anywhere."

"Silly! That's a catholic church. We're not Catholic."

"We'll find a church. One that is important and looks pretty, too." Harry took her by the shoulders, tilted her chin with his thumb, and looked deep into her eyes. "Marry me, now," he breathed. "Will you?"

Effie could only nod. Her mind raced wildly, evoking pictures of fantasy and the future.

"Does that mean yes?" he asked, his voice like velvet.

"Yes," she whispered.

He covered her trembling lips with his. He tasted of cigarette smoke and something else. Something sweet and strong. His kiss was like lightning, crashing and tumbling through her senses. Her body began to tremble, she was turning to hot liquid. Harry wrapped his arms tightly around her and she pressed against him, trying to get closer, closer, closer.

Frightened at her response she pulled away. *Not yet, Effie,* she reminded herself. *Not yet.*

Their eyes locked. Her heart was pounding like a hammer and she could feel the heat in her face. Gently, she pushed back the lock of hair that always fell onto Harry's forehead and fingered the deep cleft in his chin with trembling fingers. "New York sounds fabulous. We mustn't let on to anyone, though, especially my father."

"I'll make all the plans. We'll spare no expense."

A thrill ran up her spine. Her girlfriends would die of envy if she did something romantic like eloping to New York City, spending her honeymoon at the fabulous Waldorf Astoria. Sedate church weddings were commonplace—this was important and daring. She buried her head on his shoulder and whispered against the rough tweed of his jacket: "Whatever you want, dearest. I don't think I can wait much longer, either."

* * *

Harry clasped Effie's hand tightly in his and gazed in awe around Pennsylvania Station; its vast interior, its towering heights, took his breath away. He inhaled deeply, air laden with steam, the fragrant tang of soft coal smoke, perfumed women, tobacco smoke, hot dogs, and roasting chestnuts.

They walked through the massive doors into the teeming street. Beside him Effie shivered in excitement.

"Oh, Harry! It's marvelous. Look at those tall buildings. I've never seen anything like it."

"Didn't I tell you; just imagine living here. A man could feel truly alive."

Harry loved the grimy, throbbing city, loved its energy and staggering variety with fierce and joyous approval. With a self-confident flourish he hailed a passing hansom cab and they sped through the crowded streets toward the plush Waldorf-Astoria.

He registered as Mr. and Mrs. Harry Rebert and they were shown to the bridal suite on the sixteenth floor, facing 34th Street.

After dismissing the leering bellboy with a tip that made Effie gasp, he gathered her in his arms. "Now," he said, with a soft twitch to his lips, "we must find a church to make this all legal."

He saw Effie cast an apprehensive look at the bed and his groin throbbed with excitement. It was all he could do to restrain himself.

"Freshen up and I'll go down to the bar and make a few inquiries."

In answer to his question the barkeep, a tall, lanky man with a pale, thin face pushed a tumbler of whiskey toward him. "Know just the place for you and the young lady. Just off Fifth Avenue, at East Twenty-ninth Street. There's an Episcopal Church that'll do the job for you. New Yorker's call it "The Little Church Around The Corner."

"But we aren't Episcopalian."

"Makes no difference." The barkeep swiped the counter with his rag.

"Odd name."

"An amusing story, that. Back about twenty-five years ago an actor named Joseph Jefferson wanted to provide a funeral service for a fellow actor who had died penniless. Jefferson went to one of those fashionable churches over on Fifth Avenue to talk to a minister about arrangements and was told in no uncertain terms that they couldn't possibly hold funeral services for that sort of person." The barkeep chuckled. "Actors weren't considered to be of much worth. Anyhow, the minister went on to say there was a little church around the corner that might help him. So, Joe Jefferson, he went round the corner and the church gave his friend a Christian burial and has been marrying and burying folks ever since. Guess the name just stuck."

"Is it nice, though? My girl wants a fancy church."

"Prettiest little church you ever want'a see. Has all those tall spires and fancy statues. Your girl'll be right pleased."

And so she was. Late that afternoon, with a pale, lemony November sun filtering through the stained glass window of the Gothic Revival church, Harry took Effie by the hand and walked into a new chapter of his life. On that day life was happy and gay, full of laughter and promise.

* * *

Harry pulled his cap to a rakish angle over his tousled head and drove the carriage into the side yard of their new home where he parked beside Mamma's empty buggy.

Papa and Mamma had given them a farm with one hundred forty acres and a two story brick house in which to set up housekeeping. The home sat on a narrow lane just off Plunkert Road in Mt. Pleasant township about three miles west of Littlestown and only a mile from White Hall. A stone tenant house, a large bank barn and numerous outbuildings sat high on a hill, separated from the main house by fields and orchards.

Effie had assumed they would live in the Mansion House on the Hanover Pike and she cried with disappointment when he told her of his parent's gift. He tried to convince her the Plunkert Road farm was better, with more land and two houses, instead of only one, where they could house a tenant family. Secretly, he suspected Mamma had a hand in the decision, determined to keep him close by.

The next two years passed swiftly as Harry adjusted to married life.

Effie conceived almost immediately and they now had a bright-eyed little girl, whom they named Evelyn Anita. Anita was a pretty child, with large cornflower blue eyes and fine brown hair. She was a mirror image of Harry in every way but temperament; from the beginning Anita was a quiet, serious child who clung to her mother and seemed almost afraid of her father.

Harry worked hard and drank sparingly. All in all, life was good and he was happy.

September was unseasonably rainy that year of 1906 and one day, unable to do any work on the farm, he saddled Tansy and rode into Littlestown. He went immediately to the Union Hotel and had just settled on his favorite stool at the bar when he looked up to find Jerome Sinclair at his elbow. Jerome looked at him with a sour expression before extending his hand.

"Haven't seen you around lately. The missus got you tied to the bedpost?" he asked with a smirk.

"Hardly," Harry threw a bill on the bar. "A whiskey and soda for me, and whatever my friend here is drinking." He cocked his head and looked at Jerome with a smile. "In fact, you haven't seen me because Papa and I have been building a new broodmare stable. We plan to retire Tansy and put him to stud."

"Don't forget you promised me a rematch," Jerome said sharply.

Harry swirled the amber liquid in his glass and thought quickly.

Papa would be angry if he raced Tansy again. They had already promised the horse's service to several farmers who had mares coming into season this spring. Still, if he reneged on his promise of a rematch Jerome would have it all over the local bars. One more race couldn't hurt.

"I haven't forgotten," he answered. "Why don't you enter Demon Runner at the Hanover Agricultural Fair the end of this month. The first race is an all-out-dash. Should be a good test for both horses. What's your wager?"

"One hundred dollars, first place finish."

"Done." Harry stuck out his hand. They shook on it and he turned back to the bar. "Barkeep, I'll have another of the same. This looks like a thirsty afternoon."

Jerome, nursing his first drink, looked at Harry with a frown. "If you're building another stable it sounds like you're gonna do some serious breeding. How many mares do you plan to carry?"

"At least four."

Jerome snorted. "Mighty ambitious. From what I hear your Pa keeps a pretty tight rein on the pocketbook." He threw off the last of his drink. "But then, there's always Mamma, isn't there?" he said with a sneer.

Harry set his glass on the bar with a bang, heat rising in his neck. A muscle jerked in his jaw and he clenched his fist. "Papa and I are full partners and he wants to improve the stables as much as I do. We'll breed a few standardbreds, race them on the Pennsylvania Fair Circuit, and hope for a colt that can go on to the Grand Circuit meetings at Lexington or Goshen. Mark my words, someday the Rebert Stables will be producing quality foals, same quality as the Rebert whiskey my great-grand-daddy produced."

"First, you need a quality stallion."

"We have one—Tansy. He has an entire wall of blue ribbons from races he's won."

"Just because he won trotting races doesn't mean he'll be a winner at stud."

"Well, if he isn't, we'll get us a proven stallion. What ever it takes," Harry said heatedly.

"You're talking big money, there."

"I have faith in Tansy. If he's as good at stud as he is on the track he'll sire some real winners."

"But first he has to beat Demon Runner."

"He'll win. It's his retirement race. I'm gonna tell him about all the fun he'll have from then on making babies." Harry chuckled. "He won't be able to wait to get that race over with and get down to real business."

Jerome stared at him with eyes cold and distant. "No man has ever beaten me twice," he said, an evil smile curling his thin lips.

Harry didn't like that smile. He really didn't like Jerome very much and he certainly didn't trust him. He reminded himself to be very, very careful in that race.

Cool temperatures, more like October than September, greeted the exuberant gathering crowding the rail for the opening harness race. Fairs were a welcome relief for farmers and their families and harness racing was a favorite part of "Fair Week", which since 1884 had always been held the third week in September.

The horses, many with fancy plumes fastened to their heads, and their drivers in brightly colored silks, were waiting behind a white starting line and a hush fell over the crowd as they anticipated the starting call.

There were eight entrants in the first race, with Harry and Tansy in the number eight position. Harry sat calm and ready to go, holding the reins loosely in his right hand, the whip in his left. For just a second his eyes found and held those of Jerome in the number six slot. He hated those eyes. They were like grey flint.

Twice, horses bolted forward and had to be moved back before the race could begin. Finally everyone seemed to be in line and the starter raised his whip.

"Gentlemen, are you ready?" he shouted.

All eight drivers nodded and Harry's muscles tensed in anticipation.

The starter's whip cracked like a pistol and horse and sulky surged forward. It was a clean start and Harry barreled into the first turn looking for an opening at the rail. The number one and two horses had taken the lead and three and four were in position just behind them. He saw a hole and settled in. Harry knew the horse in the lead was a pulling horse and would run himself out quickly so he was content to ride fourth at the rail. He couldn't see Jerome and Demon Runner, but he sensed their presence just behind him.

With light hands he kept firm control of Tansy's head as he hit his stride, listening with his hands to the messages Tansy was sending him, interpreting the vibrations, talking to his horse through his hands. The wheels of the lightweight sulky sang on the hard-packed dirt, throwing out tails of dust behind them, the horse's hooves rising and falling in perfect rhythm. Tansy had been bred to compete under harness, his gait developed as a trotter rather than as a pacer. A trotter moves its left front and right rear legs forward at the same time unlike a pacer who is trained to move both legs on one side of his body forward at the same time. Tansy and Harry worked as one, confident of each other, both loving the exhilaration of the race.

Harry knew he had plenty of horse and the pace was not too rugged, but he was making decisions with lightening quickness. As they approached the three-eights pole he saw the number four horse had moved into the lead with the lead horse beginning to drop back on the rail. Harry pulled Tansy to the outside and as he did so he took a quick look over his shoulder. Demon Runner had moved into position directly behind him.

There were three horses on the outside and five stretched along the rail. Harry was riding just behind the third sulky and Jerome was behind him. It was going just the way Harry liked it. He always liked to trail a horse on the outside going into the last half of the race.

They were heading into the backstretch and now Harry had to make a decision. He knew Demon Runner would move out soon and he didn't want to take a chance of being penned in.

They were approaching the three quarter pole and he watched the horse now out in front. He was tiring, but Harry could sense Demon Runner edging out just behind him and that was who he really feared.

Harry clucked to Tansy and the horse pricked his ears and moved forward. They were at the top of the stretch and had gained the lead, Tansy's gait so smooth and rhythmical he hardly seemed to be moving, Harry perched in the tiny seat behind the spinning, flashing wheels, his silks streaming in the wind.

Suddenly the glistening ebony horse was alongside him and closing fast. The race was now between Tansy and Demon Runner. Harry went to the whip.

He knew Tansy was a horse that responded to whipping on the sulky shaft. Harry had the reins in his left hand, whip in the right, and began banging away at the shaft. Tansy didn't feel anything, but the noise of the whip against the shaft told him it was time to do his best.

Harry was suddenly aware that Jerome was crowding dangerously close.

"You're too close," he shouted angrily.

Jerome kept his eyes straight ahead and took his whip directly to his horse as he moved even closer.

Instantly Harry realized what Jerome was trying to do. Their wheels bumped lightly, then harder. Tansy never broke stride, he was giving it everything he had, the finish line dead ahead.

And then in a blinding flash it happened. On the last hard bump the axle on Harry's sulky gave way, the right wheel snapped off and the sulky collapsed on its side. Harry felt himself falling and when he hit the ground he instinctively threw his arms over his head in a desperate attempt to protect himself from the thundering hooves of the trailing horses.

It was the last sulky that got him. The driver tried vainly to pull his horse to the rail, but there simply wasn't enough room to miss his inert figure on the ground. The big outside wheel caught

Harry's left leg and blinding pain tore through his body as he heard a sickening crunch.

People began screaming when they realized what had happened and ran onto the track. Papa was the first to reach him and he dropped to his knees, sobbing as he cradled Harry's head in his lap.

"My leg . . . oh, God . . . my leg," Harry croaked as waves of nausea swept over him. He looked down. Bones pierced the skin of his right leg which was twisted into a grotesque position and he could see blood soaking his pants.

"Don't move him," Papa said to the spectators now kneeling beside them.

"The ambulance is on its way," a man said, pointing to a team of horses and wagon streaking across the infield with clanging bells.

"How is Tansy?" Harry stammered.

Papa peered down the track toward the finish line where the gallant horse still struggled along, pulling the damaged sulky behind him. "He appears to be undamaged. I don't see him limping, but the darn fool tried to finish the race without you, dragging a sulky without a wheel."

Despite his pain, Harry smiled.

A doctor jumped from the ambulance and hurried over to him. After a quick examination the doctor ordered a makeshift splint to support the shattered leg. While they were busy attaching the splint a young boy came up holding Tansy by the reins. The boy had thoughtfully disconnected the broken sulky and it lay in a heap on the dirt track.

Tansy dropped his head and nudged Harry's shoulder, nickering softly. Harry reached up and gently touched his satin nose. "Sorry, old fellow. I haven't any sugar handy. You did your best, though."

Gentle hands lifted Harry onto the stretcher and placed him in the waiting ambulance. As they rode past the finish line he glanced up at the big tote board where a large white number six had been posted. Damn that Jerome. He wouldn't forget this—not by a long shot. He'd kill that no-good sleezeball!

CHAPTER 22

After Effie recovered from her initial fright and concern over Harry's accident she became angry. Very angry. Harry simply had to stop associating with the unsavory characters that hung around race tracks. She had never liked sneaky looking Jerome Sinclair and she could easily believe the talk she had overheard between Harry and his father that the sulky might have been tampered with before the race. The wheel had come off too easily to be caused by a bump alone. Unfortunately, they couldn't prove anything. Knowing Harry's temper, she worried what revenge he might be plotting.

She sighed as she moved about the parlor, preparing it for Harry's return from the hospital. It was high time he forgot about racing and concentrated on the cattle business. Men associated with farming were respected members of the community and she wanted to be able to hold her head high.

At first the doctors were fearful that Harry might be permanently crippled. Lillie and Alex had spared no expense and brought in a bone specialist from Johns Hopkins Hospital in Baltimore to reset the fractured leg. Harry was a good patient, vain enough about his looks to fight being deformed, and he did his exercises faithfully.

Effie gave a final swipe with her dust rag to the spinet piano and looked about the parlor with satisfaction. Until Harry could handle stairs the parlor would simply have to serve as a temporary bedroom. Yesterday Harry's father had installed a comfortable cot in the corner of the spacious room and she had worked all morning washing windows and polishing furniture. The room smelled of soap and lemon oil and a large vase of yellow mums sat on the deep window sill. Friends and family would be stopping to visit Harry and she certainly didn't want the parlor to look like a sickroom.

She missed him terribly. He exasperated her at times, but she missed his carefree kidding, the way the cleft in his chin deepened and his blue eyes turned almost violet when he laughed. She missed the tender way he kissed her and she missed him at night when she crawled into the big, empty bed. Harry was a skillful lover and she had to admit that most of all she missed their lovemaking. She gave a wistful sigh. They would simply have to sleep apart a while longer—bringing the big double bed downstairs would completely ruin the look of the parlor.

That night, as cold November winds rattled the windowpanes, Effie settled herself on the edge of a narrow cot and pulled the coverlet back. Gently she started to massage Harry's damaged leg running light fingers around an angry red scar that ran from knee to ankle.

"Umm, that feels good," he said with a deep sigh. "The leg still feels like it wants to cramp."

"Let me help you flex the knee. Pull your leg up."

"That hurts."

"I know, dear, but the doctor said it was important to keep bending it so it doesn't get stiff. Later we'll try the crutches again."

"If you keep running your hands up and down my leg like that something else is going to be stiff," he said with a wicked grin. Effie gave a hearty laugh. "Is that a threat or a promise?"

"That's a promise sweetheart," he said, yanking her down on the cot.

"There isn't room for two on this narrow bed," she said, giving him a playful shove.

"There's always the floor."

"You'll hurt your leg."

"I don't make love with my leg." Harry's eyes became dark and imploring. "Please Effie. It's been so long."

She felt her body grow warm as she looked into those violet-blue eyes. She reached up to smooth the thick wave of hair back from his forehead, her breasts brushing his chest. He had an immediate reaction and she felt it. She pressed tighter against him, encircling his neck with her arms, a wave of desire making her tremble. Harry was a wonderful lover, never in a hurry, always kissing and caressing her until she would be frantic for the consummation of their love making. She wanted to feel his knowing hands exploring all the sensitive places on her body that he knew so well. She wanted to pull him to the floor and make wild unbridled love. Her response to Harry both surprised and alarmed her. She liked to be in control. Besides, it was the middle of the day. She would get all mussed, Anita might awake from her nap, and someone might come to the door.

"Friends might come calling and you know your mother is over here every day."

"Put a chair under the door knob and draw the drapes. I want you . . . woman," he said, reaching up to yank the pins from her hair.

She stopped him with shaking hands. She had just remembered something else. Since Harry's accident she had not been taking the herb potion to prevent a pregnancy, the potion Harry didn't know she had been using. Until she was certain he had his life under control she simply would not have another baby.

"Tonight, dear. I'll bring the feather tick from our bed and lay it on the floor and we'll have a nice fire in the grate." She could see the disappointment on his face. In resignation he released her. "Don't you ever let go and do something just for the hell of it?"

"Don't swear! Come on now, let me massage your leg and then I have a nice lunch ready for you. There's a time and a place for making love and broad daylight on the parlor carpet isn't one of them."

* * *

All that winter Harry's mother spent every afternoon with Harry, massaging his muscles, bending his leg, helping him walk, first with crutches and then a cane. Effie welcomed the help—Anita had started to walk and was into everything. She found it hard to object to MaMa's constant presence, she was so sweet and so full of love for her son, yet at times Effie felt a stab of jealously. There was a depth of feeling between mother and son that was unnatural.

One morning, early in March, Harry came into the kitchen as she stood at the sink mixing her potion of herbs.

"What's that vile-smelling brew you're stirring up?" he asked, eyeing the tall glass of amber liquid.

"Ah . . . something Bernice suggested for my monthly craps," she stuttered. Effie could feel the heat in her face; she wasn't in the habit of lying.

Harry looked at her with suspicion. "I guess that means there isn't a baby this month." Impatiently, he pushed his hair back from his forehead. "You wouldn't do anything to prevent another baby, would you?"

"Of course not. It just hasn't happened. Anita isn't two yet. We have plenty of time for more children."

"I want another child, Effie. You know that. A son to carry on my name. My line of Rebert's will die out if I don't produce some boys."

"We don't always get what we order."

"Then we'll just keep trying till we do."

"There should be more reason than that to have a child. And how will you treat any other girls that may come along in the meantime? Like Anita? You don't seem to have much interest in her," she said angrily.

"Anita doesn't seem to have much interest in me. She's her mother's little girl. Of course, there is more reason for having another baby than just continuing the line. I want a family. I was an only child and look at the result. Look how spoiled and demanding I am," he finished with an impish grin.

Effie sat her empty glass on the table with a resounding thunk. At times Harry seemed like a little child himself. She didn't want another baby. Not until Harry matured and grew up to his responsibilities.

He walked over to the stove and poured himself a cup of coffee, then, after hesitating a second, reached into the cupboard and lifted out a bottle of whiskey. He poured a healthy slug into his cup and returned the bottle to the shelf without looking at her.

Effie pursed her mouth, watching him from the corner of her eye, but said nothing.

"I think my leg has healed well enough for us to take a vacation," he said, turning to her and lifting the steaming mug to his lips. "What do you say we renew acquaintance with New York City? Mother will keep Anita till we get back. We can go dancing and stay at the Waldorf again."

Effie's mind raced and suddenly she was excited. This was more like it, she loved New York and all its fabulous department stores. She looked at him eagerly. "I can shop for a few dresses and a new coat. And I'd like to buy some new linens for the guest room. Oh, Harry, it sounds like a glorious idea."

"I was thinking more of a second honeymoon than a shopping trip," he said ruefully as he downed his drink.

"Of course, dear. So was I," she answered contritely.

* * *

Effie and Harry walked hand in hand bundled snugly against the cold wind blowing off the East River and the Hudson palisades. The bright sunshine and clear, cold sky made Effie feel like singing and she began to hum the strains from "The Sidewalks of New York."

Riverside Drive is a grand old street, she thought, her heart racing with excitement. With grand old homes and grand old trees, it curved and meandered alongside the park where couples strolled and starched nannies pushed prams. Littlestown seemed far away and provincial; walking here was like escaping to another time and place.

She glanced at Harry and found him looking at her with affection. They smiled at each other. Could it only be a few hours since they had made love? Effie could feel the warm blood creep up her neck and spread to her cheeks. This trip to New York was working miracles.

Last night, after making passionate love, still wrapped in each others arms, he had said sleepily, "Effie, I believe you're right . . . I'm not . . . not . . . really cut out to have a large family. I guess I'm selfish, I want you all to myself, like now, with no crying interruptions. I need to hear you laugh and sing . . . just for me."

She pushed herself away and raised herself on her elbows so she could look into his eyes. "Ah, Harry, I'll try not to let motherhood spoil our fun together. I don't mean for it to be that way, but Anita clings to me so, and . . . "

"The child seems to be afraid of me. I think my drinking distresses her, small as she is."

"It distress me too, Harry."

"I know . . . dearest . . . but if we can always make love to one another as we did tonight I promise I'll never touch another drop."

"If you mean that, then this is only a sample of things to come." And she had climbed back into his arms.

Now, as they strolled along, the thought made her smile and she was still smiling as a fashionably dressed lady passed them on the elegant avenue. She was wearing an immense yard-wide hat, laden with plumes and feathers, perched atop an elaborate hairdo fashioned into an intricate pompadour drawn high over "rats" of false hair.

"Look at that woman, Harry. Isn't she the height of fashion. It looks to me like she's wearing one of the tortuous corsets that push your bosom forward and thrust your hips back into an S line."

"Makes her look like her top is a foot ahead of the rest of her," Harry snorted.

"Oh, but I must have one of those hats before I go home". Effie narrowed her eyes, mentally framing the picture of herself sashaying into the parlor with the magnificent hat atop her head during the next monthly meeting of the Littlestown Bridge Club.

"Just as long as it isn't one of those corsets that make you look like the bow of a ship!"

Effie laughed heartily. "No, I jut out enough in the front as it is. A fancy hat, like that one, though, will make my lady-friends green with envy."

"Well, I think I'll buy myself that pair of tweed knickerbockers I saw yesterday in Bloomingdale's window. We'll go shopping tomorrow before we start home."

Effie squeezed his hand and pressed tight against his side. Despite Harry's occasional bouts with alcohol she couldn't remember ever being happier. Marriage to Harry had brought money, position, respect . . . all the things she had always longed for. Living up to one's "position" was terribly important to her and Harry, seemingly aware of this, indulged her shamelessly.

Hand in hand they walked north, past Grant's Tomb to the Claremont where Harry had made dinner reservations. Effie caught their reflection in the glass doors of the restaurant and sighed with contentment. She was wearing a black velvet cape over a high necked gown of tucked linen and lace secured with a velvet ribbon belt. Her hair was puffed out and pulled over artificial pads inserted along the front of her head and perched on top of this was a large Merry Widow hat adorned with roses. Harry looked equally handsome in a short top coat of reddish-brown cloth, striped brown trousers, a brown derby, and black shoes. She twirled her dainty linen parasol in her gloved left hand and placed her right hand possessively on Harry's arm as they entered the Claremont.

That evening, after dinner, they attended a Schubert

production at the Lyric Theater on 42nd Street and after another night of glorious lovemaking Harry treated her to a full day of shopping on her own while he bought the suit he wanted and attended the boxing matches at Madison Square Garden.

On their last night in the city Harry stood at the window of the Waldorf, looking down at the bright lights and bustling traffic on the street below them, a wistful smile on his lips. "God, what I wouldn't give to chuck everything and become a part of all this. It's a new century, Effie, and here we are stuck on a farm going nowhere. This is the life I long for, laughter and excitement, a city pulsing with excitement, but I've still no money in my own right. Papa holds the purse strings and he's not about to let go."

"You are important in Littlestown, though. I'd rather be a big fish in a small pond than a little minnow in the vast ocean."

He shook his head. "No, this is where I want to be and someday . . . who knows!"

* * *

The three years after their return from New York were happy years. True to his promise Harry stopped drinking, his leg healed, straight and true, with no trace of a limp and he worked on the farms like one possessed, determined to prove himself to his father. He desperately wanted the Mansion House property deeded to him so he could concentrate on horse breeding and build Rebert Stables into a presence to be reckoned with in Adams County. He dreamed of producing a champion trotter that would make his fortune at the track and buy his way into the world he envied.

The only sadness to touch their lives during this period was the death of Harry's grandmother Katie. She died in her sleep in 1908 at the age of eighty.

In July of 1910, when Anita was four, Effie discovered she was pregnant once more. She knew how much Harry wanted a son and he seemed to have his drinking under control so she had stopped taking her herb potion months ago. Besides, it was time Anita learned to share her toys. Being an only child, and an only grandchild, was not good for her.

On a bitter cold February morning in 1911 Effie gave birth to her second child. It was another girl and they named her Helen.

Harry perched on the edge of the chest at the foot of their bed holding his new-born. Effie watched him in silence. "I know you're disappointed, Harry," she finally said. He didn't answer, but his eyes showed it clearly. "We'll have more children. And a little girl will be a nice playmate for Anita. The baby is fat and healthy; that's all that's really important." To her it was anyway, but it was plain that to Harry it wasn't.

Harry placed Helen in her cradle and moved to the bed to give Effie that funny tilting smile that still brought a lump to her throat. "Get some sleep, dear. She's a beautiful little girl, just like her mother."

Effie reached up to push the heavy wave of hair from his forehead and smiled weakly. "As soon as I'm strong enough we'll start working on that boy."

He winked, pulled the coverlet over her shoulders, and gave her a quick peck on the lips. She listened to his footsteps as he went slowly down the stairs and pretty soon she heard the cupboard door slam. *He's after his whiskey*, she thought, a tear trickling down her cheek.

Winter faded into spring. Days of sunshine turned once pristine snow into a world of mud and along creek bottoms skunk cabbages poked through the soggy ground. Then the first crocus opened golden cups, maple buds began to swell, and cardinals whistled from the treetops. The world was born again and life on the bustling farm resumed its rhythms.

Helen was a joy to everyone and, unlike Anita, who had been a fussy, colicky infant, had a sunny disposition, laughing and gurgling at anyone who looked in her direction. Harry was completely smitten with her.

On a soft afternoon in early May, Effie carried Helen onto the back porch and laid her in her wicker carriage before settling into a rocking chair where she could keep a watchful eye on the sleeping infant. She gazed across the emerald lawn to the meadow sloping gently to a small creek where weeping willows arched their lacy boughs to the water's edge. "Sad trees" her mother had always called them, but Effie thought of them as graceful dancers bowing to the applause of their audience.

Hens and their chicks foraged across the lawn where peacocks strutted in haughty disdain and a long line of fresh laundry flapped in the wind. Her roses were pushing up dark red shoots and would bloom soon—the trellis of pink tea roses that arched over the back gate, floribundas that grew along the curving walk, beds of roses with names like Queen Elizabeth, Peace, and White Dawn. This year she planned to enter her new Peace Rose in the competition at the Hanover Fair, a certainty to earn her another blue ribbon. Her mouth twisted in a secret smile. She carefully guarded her little secrets of cultivation, spring pruning and the use of fish heads for fertilizer which she buried around the roots in late fall.

Effie pushed the carriage back and forth with the toe of her shoe and hummed a lullaby. She thought Helen resembled her; her little face was fuller than Anita's and she had a tiny nose and plump, pouting lips. Effie took a deep breath of air sweet with apple trees in blossom and let her thoughts drift as lazily as the fluffy white clouds in the blue sky above her.

What a wonderful age her children had been born into. It was an age of abundance, an age of wonder. Gleaming automobiles chugged along new macadam roads, electric lights illuminated public streets and buildings, and Hanover had a theater that showed moving pictures. Her house had the newest of inventions, a glorious enameled bath tub in a little room just off the kitchen, and a kitchen sink with an inside hand pump that wouldn't freeze up in the winter. They bought bakers bread and ready-made clothing. Women's dresses were sleek and figure flattering, the bustle all but dropped from style and Harry had just bought himself something called a safety razor to replace his old straight edge.

William Taft was President now and Effie smiled at the image that thought presented. He was, as one newspaper quoted, 'three hundred pounds of solid Republican flesh wrapped around a kindly heart and a somewhat timid brain.' But before Taft, America had bloomed under a president named Teddy Roosevelt, the like of which the country had never seen. Brimming with energy, he had bounded in and out of the White House, run off to the Rocky Mountains to shoot big horn sheep and went on long, colorful safaris in Africa. A man's man; he fairly reeked of masculinity and his infectious drive became a rallying call for every young man seeking adventure.

Not everything was peaceful, she knew. Women suffragists swarmed from state to state fighting state legislatures for the right to vote, temperance societies and evangelists were still screaming for prohibition, and in the cities workingmen fought their employers with sabotage and violence, seeking better working conditions and higher wages.

Still, the country was thriving. It seemed every week one read in the newspapers of some new millionaire. It was hard to keep one's perspective, especially in a small town like Littlestown where boys growing to maturity watched in open mouthed wonder at the fortunes being made—wondering if it could happen to them.

Harry was as eager as the rest and she knew that with each passing day he became more frustrated. His father still refused to relinquish control of the farms to him and Effie felt a knot of fear at the thought of Harry's increasing discontent.

Helen began to fret and Effie picked her up and placed her at her nipple. Tomorrow, if she got the chance, she would talk to Lillie about her concern over Harry's disquiet. She didn't want him to retreat to the bottle again. Her chin quivered. Two children or not, if Harry began to drink heavily again she would be forced to leave him—his entire personality changed when he was drunk. She would not have him humiliate her or the girls.

CHAPTER 23

1914

In the spring of 1914, the year the Imperial Germany Army began its European march through Brussels, Harry took delivery of a new Buick—a birthday gift from his mother.

The "machine", as Lillie referred to it, was long and sleek, capable of 25 miles per hour. Finished in a lustrous deep crimson, it was open on the sides and sported a light blue canvas top that could be raised or lowered, rubber tired wheels with golden oak spokes, tufted royal blue leather seats, wide fenders, running boards, and an important brass horn.

Secretly, he had wanted a sexy roadster, but Mamma had insisted on the practical two seat family car and it was hard to fault her judgement. The elegant machine spoke of money.

A man couldn't be worried about a simple thing like a little war clear across the ocean when such marvelous material things could be enjoyed here at home.

He pulled the Buick into the carriage house where the strange new odors of lacquer, gas and oil mingled with the familiar stable smells of hay, leather and horse. Tansy watched nervously as the Buick moved into the stable, the whites of his eyes showing and his foot pawing the ground.

"Don't you worry, now, old fellow," he said, as he parked it next to his older Tin Lizzie. "I'm not ready to replace you quite yet. You still have a few good miles left in those legs of yours and these new machines, while pretty to the eye, still aren't very reliable."

Pulling a handkerchief from his pocket he wiped a few flecks of dust from the fender, then strutted into the house. Privilege has its rewards, he thought. I'll have to remember to thank Mamma.

Several weeks later he gave in to Effie's demands to be taught to drive and prepared the new automobile for its all important journey. Four year old Helen stood beside him, hopping up and down and chattering non-stop.

"Please Daddy . . . please, please, please!"

Harry glared at her. "No, you can't go along. Your mother wants to learn how to drive the new Buick and having you along will make her nervous." He ran a clean cloth over the gleaming brass head-lamps, removing a tiny speck of mud. Helen stood with an angry look on her chubby face and dug her bare toe into the dirt. "Ain't fair. Anita gets to ride in the new car. Anita gets everything."

"Don't pout, Helen, and don't use ain't. You know how upset your mother gets when you speak like that. We must pick Anita up at school, that's why she will get a ride. Besides, she knows how to be quiet and act like a lady."

Tears began to run down Helen's face, making rivulets through the dirt that always seemed to smudge her cheeks. Harry's heart melted at the sight. A curious bond had developed between him and this child. She was beautiful, as pretty as Effie must have been when she was small, with an appealing smile and a deep dimple in her left cheek.

He sighed. "Suppose we take you along and drop both you and your sister off at MaMa's before we drive the Buick into Littlestown. Would you like that?"

Helen threw her arms around his legs and nodded enthusiastically, tears gone and dimple in place.

"Then run into the house like a good girl and tell Mommy we are ready to go," he said, fighting to control a grin.

Helen slammed through the front door and ran to Effie, tugging on her long skirt. Effie sighed with annoyance as she looked down into the dirty little face and firmly pried Helen's grubby hands loose from her new riding outfit.

"What do you want, child?"

"I'm to ride in the big black car. Daddy says you're picking siser up at school and he's going to take us to MaMa's." As an afterthought she added, "he's ready to go and we must hurry."

"Sister, not siser, Helen." Effie pulled a lace hanky from her pocket and wiped Helen's runny nose and tear streaked face. "Laws, child, I don't know how you get yourself so dirty. You're worse than any little boy. Anita never gets dirty."

"Siser . . sister . . . don't play, neither."

Effie threw her hands up in exasperation and hustled the barefooted child to the kitchen sink where she washed her face and dirty feet. "You're brown as a little Indian," she complained, pulling a box of powder from a shelf which she slapped on Helen's face, making her sneeze. "Come now, get your shoes, Daddy is waiting."

Helen flew out the door with a whoop. Effie stopped before the small mirror on the hall rack, gave her bonnet a final pat, and swished out the door behind her.

She wore the latest in driving vogue, a full-length linen duster with a bonnet to match. An ample dust-proof motor veil was draped over the bonnet and tied securely under her chin. Harry gave a soft whistle of appreciation when he saw her and she preened. He also wore a new duster with a slouch hat sitting rakishly on his head and driving goggles. She gave a self-satisfied smile. One must live up to one's position and, after all, this would be the first automobile from the Buick Motor Company to be seen in Littlestown. She couldn't wait to show it off.

"Sure you want to drive this machine?" Harry asked with a raised eyebrow.

"Yes, indeed. I can't wait to see the look on Bernice's face when she sees me driving up Queen Street. They still have their old Model T. By the time we get to White Hall with the children I should be able to handle it well enough to take it out on the main road." She spoke with more confidence than she felt.

"O.K. Remember, though, it's a lot different from driving farm equipment."

Harry plunked Helen on the hard back seat, then held the door for Effie to take her place behind the steering wheel. She gripped the wheel with gloved hands and took a deep breath. The new corset pinched terribly, and she had to sit straight as a board, but she knew she looked like one of the fashionable ads in the magazines.

Harry walked around to the front of the car, removed an iron bar from a sturdy leather hook and inserted it just under the grill. After giving it a few hefty cranks the engine roared to life and he ran quickly to the passenger side and jumped in beside her.

"Now, the very first thing you do is pull out on the throttle," he said, guiding her gloved hand with his own. "Good. Now, press down on the gasoline peddle and let your foot off the clutch while you operate the throttle."

The car jumped forward and stopped dead.

Helen screamed with delight and Harry looked startled. He climbed down and returned to the front where he repeated the cranking maneuver. "The trick," he said, leaping back into the passenger side, "is to get the proper amount of gasoline when you let out the clutch and pull the throttle. Try it again."

This time the car kept going and they went lurching out the driveway. With a leaping heart Effie hung on to the steering wheel with both hands, Harry grabbed his cap, and Helen clapped her hands with glee. They were on their way, and she was finally driving.

She kept to the middle of the dirt road and clouds of dust billowed around their heads as they moved along at a brisk ten miles an hour. *Please, dear God*, she prayed, *don't let us meet a horse and wagon on this narrow lane.*

Gradually she began to relax, the motor chugged smoothly, Harry grinned like a Cheshire cat and they rolled merrily along.

Anita was waiting by the front gate of her one-room schoolhouse and, after the Buick jerked to a sputtering stop, Harry leaped to the ground. Within minutes a group of admiring boys and girls were clustered around the gleaming new automobile. Anita's face flushed and her thin body trembled with pride as Harry gallantly assisted her into the back seat. She sat ramrod stiff, looking straight ahead and ignoring her bouncing, chattering sister.

Effie beamed fondly as Harry strolled slowly around the sleek Buick to point out its finest features to the open-mouthed teenage boys. He looked so handsome in his rakish cap and long duster.

"Look at the upholstery," he bragged, "It's genuine leather. And those head-lamps are pure brass."

"Blow the horn, Mr. Rebert," a young boy pleaded.

Importantly, Harry squeezed the rubber bulb, producing a resounding honk.

"Wow, how much did it cost you,?" another boy asked.

"Well now, I don't know as how I want to divulge that bit of information. Let's just say it cost more than that horse and buggy over yonder."

He jumped back into the seat and, after several jerky tries with the stubborn clutch, she had them in motion once more.

A good hour later, after delivering both girls to her mother-in-law, and driving past the grist mill where an enthusiastic Belle exclaimed over her driving abilities, she maneuvered the gleaming black machine through the tiny hamlet of Whitehall and rolled along the Littlestown Road. The land was not as flat now and the car worked harder as they approached town. They were doing a good thirteen miles an hour and cautiously she took one hand from the wheel to clutch her hat, the wind rushing through the open automobile, pulling at her veil. Soon the roofs and chimneys of the village came into view and she slowed down as they rumbled onto Queen Street.

People stopped to watch them and she swelled with pride, laughing at the commotion they were causing. Not only was this the finest car ever seen in Littlestown, but nobody had ever seen a woman driving. She put a gloved hand up to adjust her veil and stiffened her back and shoulders, not that her back wasn't already stiff. Lord, but that corset was tight!

Automobiles were still a novelty in Littlestown and Effie knew that most of the conservative German farmers hated them. Harry waved with gusto to the gaping townspeople, dogs barked furiously and children ran to the road to clap their hands in excitement at the sight of the fancy machine. A stout woman pushing a baby carriage shook her fist as her baby screamed at the noise.

"I think everyone sees us," Harry chortled.

"Oh, I don't know. There's old Mr. Singmaster and he won't even look in our direction. Let's go by the hotel. Maybe Daddy will be out front."

The Buick chugged along, through the intersection of King and Queen Streets, past her father's old hardware store, and past Crouse's grocery. Effie slowed as they neared the Union Hotel. A few patrons were lounging by the hitching posts in front of the building, but Papa was nowhere to be seen.

Harry cocked his head. "Don't see your father anywhere."

"Probably hiding from the spectacle of his daughter driving an automobile."

Harry laughed. It had a rich love-of-life sound.

Effie hung onto the steering wheel with one hand and waved gaily to the hotel patrons with the other as they bumped across the railroad track.

"I do believe it's customary to stop before a railroad crossing," Harry admonished, glancing nervously up the fortunately empty tracks.

"I was afraid if I stopped you wouldn't be able to get it started again. Besides, I didn't hear any trains coming."

"I doubt you would with all the noise this machine makes."

Just beyond the railroad the houses began to dwindle and the road started to rise sharply. She felt the automobile begin to slow as it struggled up the grade until finally it gave a tremendous shutter and stopped dead.

Harry yelled at her to pull the hand brake, but she couldn't seem to find it. Her heart pounded. The automobile began to drift backward and although an ashen faced Harry was frantically pointing to the floor on her left, Effie's mind seemed to have shut down as completely as the motor. They were gaining momentum, going backwards, and she hung onto the steering wheel as though frozen in place. With an oath Harry reached over and swung the wheel with all his might and the machine responded with a vengeance.

Through a rail fence and into a field of corn they careened backwards. She had an impression of rows of green corn parting on either side of the car until with a sickening thud the Buick's wheel dropped into a rut and it tilted on its side and jerked to a stop.

Harry's face was white as paper and his cap was knocked askew. He pushed his hair off his forehead with a trembling hand and glared at her.

The terror she had felt only moments ago gave way to a shaky laugh. "What a sight we must be, Mr. Rebert, with our brand new Buick sitting among the corn stalks."

Harry began to chuckle and soon they were both shaking with laughter. He untied her veil and gave her a hearty kiss.

A farmer, driving a team of heavy draft horses and a wagon, noticed them sitting in the cornfield and stopped out of curiosity. Harry shouted that they needed assistance and the old man seemed delighted to be in a position to use his horses to pull the heavy automobile out of its predicament.

* * *

Americans had been watching the war news emanating from Europe with increasing trepidation. The conflict had started innocently enough, as all wars do, when an Austrian archduke was shot by a Serbian citizen. The Serbs refused to apologize, and in a flush of anger Austria, went to war with them over the incident. Then neighboring Russia mobilized. The German Kaiser, fearing an alliance between Russia and France, struck suddenly at France through Belgium. An alarmed England declared war on

Germany and the entire European continent was embroiled in the madness.

President Wilson called on Americans to be 'impartial in thought as well as in action,' but American sympathies were strongly anti-German and far from impartial.

Alex strode into the kitchen on a warm evening in May with a newspaper and threw it on Harry's lap.

"Read this. We're in for it now—America can't stay out of the war in Europe much longer."

'THE UNTERSEEBOOT 20 SINKS THE LUSITANIA' screamed the black headlines. Harry raised his eyebrows and began to read aloud.

> "*Shortly after 2 P.M. on May 17, 1915, the German submarine Unterseeboot torpedoed without warning the unarmed British luxury liner Lusitania, bound from New York to Liverpool with 1,924 passengers. Among the 1,198 persons who died were 128 American citizens and 63 small children.*"

"I look for a declaration of war within the week," Harry commented quickly, scanning the rest of the article. Listen to this: "The Lusitania sinking is 'deliberate murder' and the Germans are 'savages drunk with blood.'" He put the paper aside and fixed his father with a wry smile. "Not a popular time to be German."

"Ach!"

"President Wilson promised we would stay neutral," Effie commented from her rocker where she had been listening quietly.

"But the loss of American lives is something he can't ignore," Harry commented sadly.

His father nodded slowly. "I don't think Wilson can keep us isolated when they violate freedom on the open seas. Germans are called `Huns' you know, and not in jest. The Kaiser's ugly attack on neutral Belgium at the start of the war was a good example of his unbridled militarism."

"Oh, I don't know," Harry remarked. "I secretly admire him. He's showy, has a lot of power, and can control people. He has charisma."

"The Kaiser is an arrogant, strutting peacock. Not someone you should admire," Alex exploded, his face flushed with anger. "You young people today make hero's out of the wrong people."

"And I think the world needs more men like him who can take charge of events . . . not like Wilson who is afraid to make a decision that will hurt his image," Harry retorted just as angrily.

"Wilson says there is such a thing as a nation being so right that it does not need to convince others by force."

Harry walked to the cupboard where he removed his bottle and poured himself a drink. "Nevertheless, I don't believe he can keep us isolated from what is happening in Europe. I'm thirty-four with two children. Too old probably to be called up for service if we do get involved. But if it's a long war, who knows?" He drained the glass with a single gulp.

Effie looked at him in dismay. "Harry, please. You . . . "

"I may be asked to fight in a bloody war," he interrupted. "Reason enough for a man to want a small drink to calm his nerves."

Effie clamped her lips in a tight line.

Harry returned to his chair and everyone sat silently with their thoughts. The clock ticked loudly in the silent room, Anita thumbed the pages of a story book, and Helen crooned a lullaby to her doll in a toy cradle.

Helen looked up to see Harry watching her and she reached over to give the doll a goodnight kiss.

"She's asleep," she said, solemnly.

"Yes, I see," he replied.

She sauntered over and climbed onto his knees as matter-of-factly as she would onto a chair. Her little face was very serious, and she leaned back against his chest. He lifted a hand to smooth the bangs that lay in a straight line across her forehead. He seldom noticed that her hair was the same texture as his, only that it was the rich color of her mother's.

Anita glanced at the two of them snuggled together and quickly looked away.

"Tell me a story, Daddy," Helen requested.

"Not tonight, Shotsy," he replied, calling her by the nickname he had used since she was a tiny baby. For some reason he had never liked the name Helen. Too formal for such an enchanting child. "The grownups are sad tonight because some bad people across the ocean are trying to pull us into a war."

"Is that why you are drinking bad whiskey?"

Alex chuckled. "Out of the mouths of babes," he said, rising to leave. "Harry, I need you at the Hanover Pike farm tomorrow. We must check some fencing brought down by that storm the other night. And come sober, please son."

Harry was doing what he had vowed he would not do. He was drinking again.

He sat alone in the barn—the wild, fugitive whistle of a train passing through town adding to his melancholy. Somewhere a dog barked. The darkened cork, stained from the amber liquid in the squat bottle made its usual welcome, comfortable pop as he removed it, took a long, deep swallow, and felt every nerve and muscle in his body relax under its searing heat.

As the first welcome drink began to warm his stomach he began his now habitual rationalizing: if his oldest daughter didn't treat him like an unwelcome spider; if Effie didn't turn from him in disdain when alcohol occasionally dulled his ardor, if his father would place more trust in him, if he hadn't already lost his driver's license. If . . . if . . . if . . .

He took a long, thoughtful swig from the half-empty bottle. What he really needed was some excitement—a break from this suffocating small town life. Maybe if war came he would join the fracas, cross the ocean, see Europe. He wasn't too old.

President Wilson, a thin-lipped, lantern-jawed scholar, was still pursing peace negotiations with Germany, determined to keep America out of the war in Europe. Teddy Roosevelt called Wilson a coward, too yellow to fight, and privately Harry agreed with his assessment. Roosevelt was his hero, a man's man—prize fighter, western rancher, Rough Rider, elegant ex-President.

He tipped the bottle, letting the liquid fire trickle down his throat. Just recently he had read glowing accounts of the exploits of Black Jack Pershing against Pancho Villa in Mexico. An American warship bombarded a German vessel suspected of unloading munitions for possible anti-American use in the port of VeraCruz and all hell had broken loose.

Harry remembered his grandfather Edward talk longingly of thwarted plans to become a soldier and fight against the Mexicans after the battle of the Alamo. He smiled to himself. Maybe soldiering fever ran in the blood.

Inexplicably, thinking of war excited him. He felt a tightening in his groin, and smiled. All was not dead down there yet!

A small rivulet of whiskey dribbled down his chin. He had tipped the bottle too soon and missed his mouth. He wiped his chin on his shoulder and leaned back on a bale of hay. No one would miss him if he took a little nap.

CHAPTER 24

Effie opened the kitchen screen door to look into the face of the most disreputable bum she had ever seen. It was an ageless face, gaunt with hollow cheeks, dirty and grizzled. His mouth, caved inward indicating a lack of teeth, and his lips were clamped tightly on the long stem of a corn cob pipe. The man's hair was gray at the sides, but a lock of straight brown hair fell almost rakishly over his high forehead. He wore a wide brimmed straw hat, an old canvas jacket buttoned to the chin and a blue bandanna kerchief knotted around his scrawny neck. A hand encased in a worn canvas work glove clutched the bowl of a cold pipe.

"Have you any work, ma'am?" he asked with a nasal twang.

"No, I'm sorry. We've all the help we need just now," Effie said sharply, pushing the screen door shut.

A look of total despair washed over the man's face and she hesitated. "I've some scraps from dinner if you're hungry."

"I ain't et in two . . . three days," he admitted, his Adam's apple bobbing like a cork on a wave.

"Go sit on the porch steps and I'll bring something to you." As he moved away from the door she noticed he walked with a bad limp. Probably a civil war veteran. Lots of them still wandered around the countryside looking for work. Many were southerners, who, having heard of the terrible devastation of their homes and farms, had decided to stay in the north.

She scraped some pot pie, left over from the noon meal, into an old pie tin and laid a large hunk of fresh bread on top. Then, remembering the desperate look on the man's face she added a thick slab of sour cherry pie.

Effie carried the meal out to the porch, then retreated back to the kitchen, making certain she hooked the screen behind her. She didn't like the look of him one bit.

Within minutes she heard voices coming from the porch and looked out to see Harry talking with the old codger.

Surprisingly, Harry was laughing at something that had been said. Trust Harry to make friends with a bum, she thought in annoyance. She busied herself at the sink and almost forgot their presence when she heard the screen door slam and looked up to see Harry take a pail from the pantry.

"His name's Billy Woods and he claims to have a way with horses. And he knows a helluva lot about harness racing. I told him to pick what raspberries are still growing along the fence row and then in the morning he can help Bupp muck out the stables. I'll watch and see how he works around the animals."

Effie wrinkled her brow and tightened her lips. "He looks like a drunk to me. You know we have two young girls here."

"He's just down on his luck, Effie. He was in the war; fought with the Seventh West Virginia Regiment at Gettysburg. His brother was killed there during Picket's Charge and Billy says he couldn't rest until he came back north to find his grave. I'll keep an eye on him and tell him to stay clear of the house."

By fall, Billy Woods had become a fixture on the farm. He worked hard, drank hard, and possessed a genuine love for animals. Billy had the soft hands of a born driver and Harry let him drive the training sulky. Despite Effie's misgivings, Helen adored the scrawny hired hand, finding any excuse to be in the barn when Billy was around; listening to his stories about life in West Virginia and cajoling him to help bandage the myriad injured chickens and cats she found to nurse, and some that weren't injured.

Billy slept in the barn and the only real fault Effie could find with him was that he never took a bath. He had but one set of clothes and occasionally on hot sunny days he would sneak down to the creek at Sell's Station where he would jump in—clothes and all—and then sit on the bank to dry. She hated to think how he would smell when winter came and the creek froze over.

It was nearly nine o'clock when Harry got to the barn one evening in early October. He had gotten into the habit of visiting the barn on Friday evenings where he and Billy would sit for hours discussing the racing possibilities of the newest trotter in training, while they passed a bottle of whiskey back and forth.

Tonight, a cold wind whistled around the corners of the horse barn, showing promise of the winter soon to come, and Harry carried a full pint of apricot brandy in mittened hands. Billy, sprawled in the hay, cast a melancholy look at his approach.

"You look mighty sad tonight," Harry said. "Weather got you down?"

"Na, I'm doin' tole'able well. I was jest a thinkin' on things."

"Well, I brought us a full bottle of brandy. That'll take the chill out of those bones of yours."

Billy just nodded, pulling out his old pipe and clamping it in his mouth. "Don't like October. Lots'a wounded men died in hospitals this time a'year. Guess they didn't wanna face up to a cold winter when they was all busted up and hurtin'."

"You never talk much about the war, Billy. How old was your brother . . . the one that got killed?"

"Joe were seventeen. I were only thirteen. Course, I was jest a Drummer Boy, but I marched right along with our regiment. Joe and me, we'd been together since Shiloh. That was a bad fight . . . lotta men got kilt there . . . but Gettysburg was worse."

Harry pulled the cork from the bottle and handed it over. "Tell me about it."

Billy spat a stringy wad of tobacco juice onto the dirt floor, scratched his whiskers thoughtfully as he gazed at the whiskey, then reached a decision. He took a deep swallow and wiped his toothless mouth with the back of his hand. "We got to Gettysburg on the second day of July an the fightin'd already started. I ain't never heered such a ruckus—it were terr'ble. Cannon roaring and men yellin' and screamin'. That screamin'—that were the worst."

Harry nodded in understanding as he watched Billy Woods's sad, haunted eyes. The way he told it, war didn't sound quite so glamorous.

"Wall," Billy continued, "we got us through that terr'ble day and that night Joe an me, we lay side by side and did a lot a talkin'. We talked of comin' back here oncet the Rebs were licked fer good. I never seed a part o' the country looked purtier, with the orchards hangin' heavy and white mist rising early in the morning off them tender green hills jest like little puffs of smoke from this here pipe o' mine.

Next day, tho,' we was smack in the middle a the worsest fightin' I ever seed. I never seed so many men or horses laid low. Swarms an' swarms of yellin' Rebs come marching across a big field, right at us. I caught a mini-ball just below my knee and went down. Next thing I knowed I was a layin' in a church beggin' em not to cut my leg off. That's how I got separated from Joe. They put me on a train fer Washington, D.C. and it were only later, when they shipped me home to West Virginy, that I heared my brother didn't make it."

Harry passed the bottle. He had no words to answer. He knew that the Seventh West Virginia had been part of Hancock's Second Corp., engaged on the second and third day of the battle at Gettysburg, along the copse of trees historian's now called the "Angle". The Seventh had taken the full brunt of Pickett's Charge; fifteen thousand Southern soldiers marching across open fields, battle flags waving, toward the massed Union forces waiting for them. The miracle was that any of the Seventh West Virginia had survived.

The bottle was almost empty and he was sitting on the barn floor wondering whether or not it was worth the effort of trying to stand up when Billy placed a hand on his arm.

"I 'preciate your kindness ta me, Mr. Rebert," he mumbled drunkenly, a wisp of smoke curling around his head like a chimney.

He began to fumble in his pocket and finally pulled out a faded photograph. "Been wantin' ta show you this."

Harry looked at it for some time before he could bring it into focus. Then he felt a sob catch in his throat and could say nothing. The photograph showed a smiling young man and a handsome boy with curly hair. They were laughing into the camera with arms about each others shoulders, dressed in Union Blue, their forage caps at a rakish angle.

"We look right tole'able, don't you think?" Billy asked, laughing self-consciously.

Harry grinned at him across the top of his whiskey bottle. "Best looking West Virginia recruits I ever laid eyes on."

* * *

For two years President Wilson had kept the United States neutral and out of war. Then, in February 1917 Germany decided to resume unrestricted submarine warfare. Now Harry's friends talked of when, not if, war would come.

February saw not only the escalation of the German conflict, but the miscarriage of Effie's third child. It was a boy.

Harry suspected the pregnancy had been unplanned and wondered about the miscarriage. He felt denied and bitter. Helen, six, and Anita, eleven, were fine daughters, but, damn it all, a man was judged by the number of boys he fathered.

Once recovered from the miscarriage, Effie made it clear she did not want another baby. This time she did not lie to him.

"You are drinking again, when you promised not to. Since you hired Billy Woods you make no attempt to conceal it. He is just a convenient drinking buddy. Besides, you might be drafted if war is declared and I don't want to be left with a newborn to care for alone."

"Don't blame Billy or the war. The truth is you don't love me enough to have my child!" To Harry's dismay tears filled his eyes, but he managed to blink them back. No damn woman would make him cry. In a blur, he threw a full cup of coffee across the room and stormed out of the house.

* * *

April, filled with fresh, budding green, newly plowed fields, and clouds of yellow forsythia, settled upon Adams County with color and birdsong. Harry sat on a fence rail watching two of his new foals romp beside their dams when he saw Bupp sprint across the field waving a newspaper in his hand.

"We're in it," Bupp shouted. "Congress has declared war on Germany."

Harry jumped down and grabbed the paper with its ominous black headline. Over Bupp's excited chatter he read the terse account of America's entrance into the first World War.

"I'm gonna enlist, Mr. Rebert. Deed I am. Soon's we get the spring crops all in. You've got old Billy to help with the horses now and you can always find someone to help with the farming."

"But why, Bupp? This affair in Europe isn't our problem."

"Yeah—well, guess I could do lots worse things than see a little bit of Europe and take part in the biggest scrap this world has ever seen. Besides, girls like soldiers!" He rolled his eyes and slapped his thigh as though delighted with the thought, then looked at Harry curiously. "All the guys in town will be joining up and I sure as shooting don't want to be called a coward."

In disgust, Harry threw the paper to the ground. "Darn if you'll see me running off to fight another man's war and I better never hear anyone call me a coward. Now get back to work! I'm going into the hotel."

But by mid-summer recruiting posters everywhere urged young men to sign up and change the course of history. Hundreds of thousands of citizens responded to the sound of the popular song 'Johnny Get Your Gun' and one by one Harry's friends enlisted, eager to become a part of the great conflict. They joked over farewell drinks, wondering what war was really like, eager to see the show. It became common knowledge that the young warriors already in Europe found relief from battle in cafes and brothels. Thoughts of lusty singing and male comradeship around a blazing campfire, the adoring glances of liberated French damsels, and freedom from family responsibilities began to appeal to Harry.

He arose early one morning, dressed in his best suit, slicked his hair back and without a word to Effie marched off to the nearest recruiting center.

The doctor, a smallish man with a shock of salt and pepper hair and watery eyes behind thick lenses, shook his head gravely. "Not with that leg, I'm afraid. Your only course is the infantry and that knee would never stand up to the intensive marching required. What happened to it, anyway?"

"An accident at the race track many years ago. It doesn't give me any trouble, Doc."

"Maybe not now, but service in the Army is a different story." He picked up his pen, wrote 'rejected' across the application papers, and handed them back.

With dragging footsteps Harry walked into the bright sunlight and the waiting Buick. He turned it toward Hanover and an out-of-the-way tavern he had just heard of. None of his friends would be there to taunt him over his failure. He clutched the steering wheel until his knuckles turned white. He hadn't thought of Jerome in years, but suddenly the old rage boiled up in him, surprising in its intensity. "Jerome is responsible for this rejection. And by God, he'll pay," he muttered through clenched teeth. "Once someone crosses me, they're enemies for life. He'll pay for this—damn if he won't."

* * *

The mares had been placed together at one end of the barn according to their foaling date. Fallacy, Harry's new broodmare purchased from Harper D. Sheppard of the Hanover Shoe Factory, had been bred to Tansy last fall and was expecting her first foal.

Fallacy was two weeks late and Harry and Billy had been watching her closely. A small quantity of milk was visible on the end of each teat, a sign that she would probably foal in the next twelve hours, so Harry decided to sleep in the barn with Billy. If she foaled normally she would not require help from anyone, but if she needed help they would have to call a veterinarian quickly. Harry had an uncomfortable feeling that this might be a difficult first delivery and they could not afford to lose a foal.

They moved Fallacy into a large roomy stall. She was restless, sweating and switching her tail, turning her head back towards her flanks.

"Her knows what's a comin'" Billy said with a chuckle, watching her with a practiced eye. "It'll be tanight, sure. Her udder's full and she's been peeing all over the place."

"Let's get some sleep then, while we can," Harry answered, flopping down on a nearby bale of hay. "We'll hear her when things start to happen."

Several hours later Billy shook him awake. "Fallacy's started to present. Come take a look."

Harry hastily rose from his bed of hay, pulling straw from his tousled hair and brushing his pants. He knelt beside his mare who was laying on her side in the stall, sides heaving. She was blowing and tossing her head, her eyes wide. The thin membrane sack containing the foal was visible, but things were not as they should be. Normally the front feet appear first, heels down, with the head positioned between them. Harry could see only one leg. The other leg must be tucked behind the foal. "We better get Doc Hobart," he said with a concerned frown.

Billy had already removed his old canvas jacket and was pulling off his shirt. "Ain't no time fer that. I seed it done afore. Fallacy is a hurtin'. You gentle her whilst I find that little one's leg." Without hesitation he thrust his skinny arm into the horse's birth canal and within minutes had pulled the leg forward to its normal position.

With blood and mucus dripping from his arm he sat back on his haunches and motioned Harry to remain still. "Let the mare take over now. She knows what ter do her ownself," he whispered. The sack moved forward and within minutes the entire foal had been presented, but for some reason the little foal failed to break free of the membrane surrounding it. Harry swore under his breath. "Help me pull that sack from its face before it drowns," he said anxiously.

Together the two of them broke the placenta and freed the foal's head. Within minutes the umbilical cord separated and the birth process was completed.

Billy wiped his hand on his overalls while Harry squatted beside him in the hay and watched as Fallacy began to clean her infant.

"Looks like a fine little filly," Harry said, slapping Billy on the shoulder. A grin split his face and he added, "now, for God's sake, wash that muck from your arm before I puke. Then I think we need a drink to celebrate this fine event. Damn if I don't feel just like a new father."

Billy's grizzled face looked at him soberly. "You knowed the Doc your Mamma took you to said not one drink, Mr. Harry."

"One won't hurt. Those doctor's don't know what they're talking about when they say I can't stop drinking on my own. I can stop anytime I want to. I need to stay here in the barn until the filly starts to nurse and it's colder than death in here." He walked over to a rough wooden cupboard fastened to the wall and removed a pint of whiskey from behind the liniment bottles.

Two hours, and half a bottle later, Helen burst into the stable and ran straight to Fallacy's stall. The mare stood proudly over her offspring, her big liquid eyes looking anxiously at the intruder as the little reddish-brown filly nursed.

"Oh," breathed Helen, "it's beautiful. Can I touch it?"

At Helen's excited squeal the small head broke away from its mother's teat and looked at her with inquisitive brown eyes. Helen hung on the door of the stall staring in wonder at the little foal.

Harry walked over and picked her up in his arms. "You know,

Shotsy, you are never to go into a stall with a horse," he said, his voice slightly slurred.

"Is it a boy horse or a girl horse?"

"A little girl. A filly just like you."

"What's her name?"

"She doesn't have a name yet." He looked at Helen's enchanted face. God I love this child, he thought, his eyes misting with drunken affection.

"Why don't you pick out a name?"

"Can I? But I'm not sure what would be right." Her face wrinkled in concentration. "She has a white star on her forehead. Maybe we could call her 'Star'."

"Well that's a good name, but it's pretty common. This horse is going to win the Kentucky Futura someday. We need something mighty special, don't you think?"

Helen's blue eyes widened in excitement. "How about 'Miss Margaret'? That's the name of my Sunday School teacher and she's very special."

Then "Miss Margaret" it shall be."

CHAPTER 25

Helen squatted before a pile of dirt that she was carefully spooning into small metal dishes, pretending it was mashed potatoes to serve to her pet kitten. She wished Anita would play with her, but she was busy helping Mamma make tomato juice and through the open kitchen window she could hear Anita complaining about the heat and pesky flies.

She stretched her legs before her and looked down at her legs. A large hole had mysteriously appeared in the knee of her long cotton stockings and one shoestring had become undone. She attempted to tie it, without success, then removed the offending shoes and threw them aside.

Helen jumped up when she saw her grandfather pull his Model-T into the driveway, prepared to run to greet him, but one look at his stormy face told her there was trouble when he stomped past her without a word and entered the kitchen. Despite the fact that she didn't really understand adults she guessed the trouble was her Daddy.

She walked in stocking feet to the screen door and peered into the kitchen. Mamma motioned PaPa to a chair and poured him a cup of the coffee she always had hot on the back of the stove. Anita watched them, a puzzled look on her face.

"Go outside and play with Helen," she heard Mamma order in a stern voice.

"I don't want to play with her. She's got one of the cats dressed up in doll clothes. It won't stay in her stupid baby carriage and when it jumps out she cries. Besides, it's too hot to play."

"Then go into the parlor and dust while I talk to your grandfather. And close the door behind you."

Alex waited for the door to close on Anita's retreating back before he spoke. "I just came from the mill. Mr. Yeager told me Harry is at the bar of the Willard Hotel dead drunk. It's only two o'clock in the afternoon, Effie," he stammered, pulling on his long mustache.

Helen listened, trying to understand what was being said. She understood that Daddy was drunk again, but why was PaPa so upset?

Mamma sank into a chair. "He took the Buick this morning without Bupp. Said he had to take care of some things at the farm on the Hanover Pike."

"You know darn well if he's picked up drunk again, driving without a license, he'll be put in jail. Why don't you keep the keys hidden from him?"

"I'm not his keeper!" Mamma shouted the words, her face screwed up and ugly. Helen's stomach fluttered as Mama continued, "you know his temper when he's drinking. He scares me and he terrifies Anita. He doesn't even look like the same person . . . his eyes turn cold and black and he has the strength of one possessed. I'm . . . I'm frightened of him PaPa. Sometimes I'm afraid he'll kill me when he's drinking."

"I think you exaggerate, Effie. You're his wife, you must control him. Hide the whiskey. Pour it down the sink!"

Helen stopped listening to the angry words coming through the open door and ran back to her dirt pile. She puckered her face in thought, then her lips curved in a smile. "Mamma is mad at Daddy, but we can help him," she said to the kitten sleeping in a tight ball in the bottom of her doll carriage. "I know where he keeps his whiskey."

Quietly she opened the back door and slipped down the inside cellar steps. Halfway down the steps a deep shelf protruded into the stairwell and on the dusty shelf she could see three bottles of the dark whiskey her Daddy liked so well. She stretched her short legs as much as she could, but she couldn't quite reach the bottles.

The top of the cellar wall formed a stone ledge that ran alongside the steps so she retreated to the top step and crawled onto the shallow ledge. Slowly she inched her way along the dirty wall, oblivious to spider webs and mouse droppings, until, on hands and knees, she reached the shelf. With grubby fingers she seized a bottle. Back she went, clutching the bottle tightly until she reached the screen door which she remembered to close quietly before she ran across the backyard to her dirt pile.

In the kitchen Mamma and PaPa still talked loudly about her Daddy. She sat the whiskey carefully in the dirt where she had been playing. It took two more trips until all three bottles were lined up in a neat row.

Helen sat down and smoothed her soiled dress across her lap, studiously examining a knee she had skinned on her travels. With a deep sigh of satisfaction she lifted a bottle, worked the cork out of its neck, and poured the amber liquid onto the ground. She wrinkled her nose at the pungent smell and considered the puddle collecting in the dirt. Carefully she stirred it with her finger. Then she began to construct mud-pies for Daddy's supper.

Effie heard the roar of the Buick as Harry careened into the driveway and she ran to the yard to watch him stagger up the walk. As he rounded the corner of the house he almost stepped on Helen sitting on the ground. She was covered with mud and Effie could smell the whiskey through the open window. Three empty bottles lay beside her.

With a roar of outrage Harry grabbed her arm and yanked her to her feet. He drug the terrified child into the kitchen and ran to his razor strop hanging beside the sink.

Alex jumped to his feet and Effie watched in numbed horror at the sight of Harry's face, distorted with black anger, his eyes crazed, spittle at the corner of his mouth.

Alex tried to grab his arm, but Harry flung him aside. Helen screamed and wet her pants. Anita stood cowering in a corner, as if nailed there, scarcely breathing.

Billy Woods, responding to Helen's screams, came running into the kitchen. It took him only seconds to assess the situation. He grabbed Harry and, without hesitation, gave him a sharp rap to the jaw that sent him sprawling to the floor.

Billy put an arm around Helen and attempted to calm her as Effie sank to a chair with a dull, empty ache. Anita ran to her side, eyes widened in alarm. Alex moved to Harry's side and knelt beside his unconscious body. Tenderly, he lifted his son into his arms and with Billy's help they carried him upstairs to the bedroom.

Effie pulled Helen into her arms, the child's body still trembling, tears running in rivulets down her dirty face.

"I was. . ." Her tiny voice caught on a deep sob. "I was only trying to help Daddy."

Effie felt tears gather in her eyes. Helen was so devoted to Harry. How could she ever say the right words to erase the hurt on the little face?

"I know, sweetheart. And Daddy didn't mean to hurt you. When he drinks that terrible whiskey the devil gets a hold on him and he isn't himself."

"She wet herself," Anita said, pointing with disgust to the puddle on the floor.

"She was frightened and... ."

Effie turned as Alex and Billy reentered the kitchen.

"He'll be alright. He'll sleep till morning," Alex said, his eyes locking with Effie's. "But this has gone on long enough. His mother and I must see about getting him into a alcohol treatment center in Baltimore."

The wise old veteran nodded his shaggy head in ascent. "Your boy, he needs help bad, Mr. Robert. And soon!"

* * *

Harry spent a month at a detoxification center in Baltimore that fall of 1917 while the United States mobilized to build an army of four million men.

Effie did not bring the girls to see him in the hospital and he noted that her own visits were rare. When she did come she sat in the silent room watching him with cold accusation. She threatened to leave him, saying that the children were not safe. And he had to agree. Had to face the fact that he was an alcoholic.

He lay in his hospital bed, face to the wall, frightened of the future, grieving for his lost life, his lost identity.

The doctors worked a small miracle and Harry left the hospital feeling wonderfully young and healthy, full of optimism that he could rebuild his fractured relationship with Effie and the girls.

Bupp had left in the middle of the summer and was already in Europe. Harry followed the war news with avid interest, throwing himself into the war effort by working the farms harder than ever.

"Do Your Bit," "Food Will Win The War," and "Swat the Hun" glared from billboards on every road he traveled. Harry reflected that it definitely was not a good time to be German. Anger towards anyone with German heritage flourished, the German language banned in schools; German-born musicians and scholars publicly insulted; and the New York Times printed a rumor that German spies put poison into bandages in Philadelphia.

"Over There" was a favorite song, "Hanging the Kaiser" became a favorite sport for the cartoonists, and tons of sticky peach stones were collected in public barrels to make gas-mask linings. One such barrel sat on the corner of Queen Street opposite the bank in Littlestown.

Harry chuckled when he saw a picture in the local paper of two hundred women being drummed into the Marine Corps as stenographers and clerks. That would be right up Aunt Belle's alley. He hoped she didn't see the paper.

A frigid blast of cold air entered the kitchen as Billy Woods hurried through the door with an arm full of wood. Helen rushed to close the door and squealed with delight at the sprinkling of snow on the front porch. She ran to Harry, sitting with his feet cocked up on the open slant front desk, reading the paper and smoking a cigarette.

"Daddy, Daddy, will you take us to school in the sleigh if it snows hard tonight?" she cried, looking at him with begging eyes. He laughed and reached over to pull her soft little body close. "It's just a flurry, Shotsy. The Almanac isn't calling for snow so we probably won't have enough to hitch up the sleigh." He ran his hand over her shining chestnut hair, patting her bangs into place, and kissed the top of her head. *God, what a beautiful child she is growing into he thought,* pensively. *She's the one truly bright spot in my life.*

"Go do your homework with Anita, now," he murmured, giving her another squeeze.

His stay in Baltimore had not only worked miracles in his physical well-being but also in his home life. Content now to spend his evenings in the kitchen with Effie and the girls, he read farm journals, poured over his old plans for the horse stables, and he and Effie even made love again.

He looked at her, rocking by the fireplace, reading the Star and Sentinel. The fire cast gleaming lights on her rich hair and her face was soft and peaceful. A lovely woman. She felt his glance and smiled archly at him, running a hand across her waist, carefully smoothing the crisp cotton house dress.

"I see that Funkhouser's Department Store in Gettysburg has just received a shipment of winter dresses with the new pegged skirts. They always have the latest fashions. I wish Littlestown had a modern department store," she said.

"You said yesterday the girls need new coats. Why don't you take the Buick tomorrow and drive over to Gettysburg to do some shopping," Harry said with good humor.

"Maybe I will."

Billy Woods began snoring in the corner beside the fireplace, his eyes closed, his chin resting on his chest. Effie flipped the paper with annoyance. "I don't know why you insist on bringing him into the house."

"It's cold out, Effie. Besides, he goes to the barn to sleep."

Anita sat at the kitchen table, her forehead wrinkled in concentration, struggling with her arithmetic homework. "Mother, I can't figure out this problem," she said, chewing on her pencil. Helen wiggled out of her chair and went to stand by Anita, poking at her paper with curiosity. "You can't help me," Anita said, pushing her away. "I asked Mother."

"I'm not very good with arithmetic," Effie said, turning the paper to the death notices. "Ask your Daddy."

Anita cast a sour glance in his direction. "Last time he came up with all the wrong answers."

"Then you'll just have to figure it out for yourself."

Helen returned to her chair and started scribbling on a tablet with one of her pencils, making screeching noises that set everyone's teeth on edge.

"Stop that, Helen," Effie said, crossly. "Anita can't concentrate."

"What's that funny smell?" Helen asked, wrinkling her nose as she looked in the direction of the fireplace.

Anita sniffed. "It's probably Billy Woods. He hasn't had a bath since summer."

Effie snapped the paper shut and laid it aside.

Harry raised his eyebrow. "It's only some animal dung on the firewood. Come now, Helen, it's past your bedtime and you are keeping Anita from her homework."

"And you don't even know how to do arithmetic yet," Anita said, sarcastically.

His lips twitched in a smile as Shotsy turned and stuck her tongue out at her sister. Good thing Effie hadn't seen that little display.

CHAPTER 26

Harry firmly believed in the theory that a horse never forgot what he learned in the first few weeks of his life, and he began working with the new-born foal immediately by teaching her to lead properly. With Billy's help they rigged a rump rope, a length of clothesline which fit over Miss Margaret's hind quarters beneath her tail. When they led her mother from the stall the young foal naturally wanted to follow and Harry pulled her along using the pressure of the rump rope.

After two weeks of this they turned Fallacy and Miss Margaret out to pasture. Real training wouldn't start until the foal was a yearling, and in the meantime, his other mares were ready to foal.

Harry knew his father resented the time he spent with the horses. Cattle provided their income, not horses, and Papa constantly reminded him of the heavy farm mortgage—a result of the injury to old Mr. Klunk, Harry's hospitalization after the sulky accident, and his more recent confinement in the Baltimore clinic.

He desperately wanted to move the family to the property on the Hanover Pike where the land was gently rolling, more suited to grazing horses. Effie had always dreamed of living in the stately Mansion House and the town school would be much better for Helen and Anita.

He burst into the kitchen one morning, early in May, grabbed Effie by the waist and swung her around in a circle. "Wait until you hear my news," he sang, his face radiant with good cheer. "Mamma talked Papa into letting us move to the house on the Pike."

Effie gaped at him in stunned silence.

"Father is going to move Joe and his wife from the Pike to the tenant house here on this farm, so the Mansion House will be empty in two weeks. We can move anytime before school starts."

"Oh, Harry, I can't believe it. Are you sure?"

"Sure as hell. Mamma convinced him that the girls need to be closer to town and school. 'Course he isn't deeding the property to us, but we can live there rent free and now I'll have room to expand the stables. He gave me permission to start construction for both a broodmare and a stallion barn." Harry's eyes sparkled and he kissed her on the tip of her nose. "Maybe we can even have a breeding arena. Oh, Effie . . . there's no end to my dreams. We'll stop calling that property the Mansion House—from now on it will be called Rebert Stables."

Effie put her arms around him and kissed him full on the lips. The kiss lingered and Harry ran his hand up her back as her lips grew warmer. He shot her a knowing look, his excitement rising, and began to move her toward the parlor. "Can we buy a larger dinning room set," she murmured.

The statement bothered him, but he pushed it aside. "Anything you want, dearest. Now come, we have something far more urgent to tend to."

* * *

One month later, on a flawless April afternoon, a mammoth farm wagon, pulled by two Conestoga horses and filled to overflowing with furniture, rumbled up the gravel driveway of the house on the Hanover Pike and stopped in front of its wrap-around porch. Harry felt a surge of elation as he parked the Buick behind the wagon and gazed upon their new home. The girls tumbled from the back seat shouting with excitement and raced across the lawn while Effie, her eyes glinting with pleasure, gathered her skirts and followed.

The Mansion House sat comfortably back from the Pike, but close enough to be admired by all traveling between Littlestown and Hanover. Stately locust trees, dripping blossoms, shielded the house and the wide comfortable porch of the two-story brick dwelling. The side garden was a riot of tulips, forget-me-nots, bleeding hearts, lilies of the valley and fragrant lilacs and in the pasture behind the barn colts pranced beside mares. The house had always had a tenant so Effie had never been inside, and Harry bounded jauntily up the porch steps to fling open the front door.

Her face flushed with happiness, she looked cheerfully around the foyer, into the parlor and spacious dining room and up the wide oak stairs.

"What a stunning house," she said.

Outside he could hear the joyful shouts of the children as they ran around the yard and he placed an arm around Effie and kissed her warmly, intoxicated with good cheer as he stepped back and gazed into her sparkling eyes.

"It will be our home forever," he promised.

Effie was once more loving and affectionate, and he listened with tolerance to her plans for new carpets and wallpaper and a walnut dining room set. In the fall Helen would be able to attend public school in Littlestown and she had playmates nearby. The Wildisins lived across the road and already Anita had become fast friends with the Wildisin girl. And across the road Christ Church sat serenely atop its small knoll as though keeping a watchful eye on their new home. Life was good!

Effie kept herself busy that summer buying all manner of new furniture while he built a half-mile dirt track next to the barn where he could drive the training sulky.

Hanover Shoe Stables were practically next door to Harry's farm. Harper Sheppard and Clinton Myers, owners of the local shoe company, maintained a sizeable spread where they bred and trained a few standardbreds for races on the Pennsylvania Fair Circuit. Before he started his own building program he decided it might be smart to pay the stables a visit. Maybe he could steal some of their ideas.

After touring the farm with Clinton Myers, and drooling over the sleek racehorses stabled there, Harry returned home deep in thought. Although standardbred racers were still a hobby with the owners, with financial backing from Hanover Shoes they had the potential to become the leading breeding and racing stable in the country. Rebert Stables would surely be small potatoes compared to them. And if he couldn't compete with them he didn't want to play the game. He guessed that was a Rebert trait and he would make no excuses. Perhaps his father was right in urging him to forget horses and concentrate on cattle—a proven business.

Harry parked his phaeton beside the carriage house and walked to the training track. He pulled his flask from his hip pocket, took a deep pull, and leaned his elbows on the fence, looking with pride at what he had already accomplished.

"No! Damned if I'll quit!" he ground out between clenched teeth. "Sheppard and Myers don't have the dreams I do. They're business men, more interested in the shoe business then in horse breeding. Mr. Myers admitted to me that they want nothing more then to breed a few trotters, then send a colt on to the Grand Circuit if one of that caliber comes along."

Harry pounded his fist on the rail, then dug the silver flask from his pocket once more. His plans for his stable were far more extensive.

The sun was hot and the whiskey got to him quickly. Since taking the cure he couldn't tolerate the stuff like he used to. He glanced furtively over his shoulder. Better not let Effie catch him taking a drink—there would be hell to pay.

* * *

Late in October, Anita fell ill from the dreaded influenza sweeping the country, and for days she lingered between life and death. Effie never left her bedside and she pleaded with Harry to protect Helen by keeping her out of the house as much as possible. Little Helen became his shadow, following him everywhere he went on the farm, learning to muck the stables and take the horses on their morning runs. They became inseparable.

Schools closed and every family in Littlestown seemed to have a loved one ill. The newspaper carried headlines telling of the latest casualty figures, worse by far than those killed in the war. The bodiless enemy, spreading westward from Europe, soon affected Americans from coast to coast, and Effie could barely stand to look at the rotogravure in the Sunday paper carrying pictures of flag-draped caskets bearing boys fallen from the flu and not from bullets lining the docks. Unshaven Doctors slept in their clothes; morticians stacked caskets wall to wall; grave diggers worked around the clock.

Anita's fever climbed to 104 and Effie felt a cold fist closing over her heart, certain she was loosing her first born. She swathed her in cold packs, fed her chicken broth, and lifted her on and off the chamber pot as the terrible diarrhea and cramping took its toll.

Then, a week after falling ill Anita's fever broke and Effie woke from a fitful doze to find the child drenched in sweat.

"Harry, Harry. Come quick," Effie called in relief.

He ran into the darkened room. "Is she worse?"

"Still bad, but I think the crisis is over. Her fever is down and she's no longer delirious. Help me lift her so I can change these wet sheets." Effie pushed a strand of damp hair from her cheek and twisted her hands together in an involuntary gesture of relief. "I did all I could."

"You're a marvelous nurse. She would have died without your loving care."

Harry walked slowly to the bedroom window and stared out at the gray, turbulent afternoon. Charcoal clouds were piling up in the west. Geese wheeled noisily over the corn stubble, filling their bellies one more time before starting south. "I believe it's going to snow," he said, cocking his head and giving her a slow smile. "I'll take Shotsy sledding and keep her from bothering you for another day."

Effie looked down at the floor, suppressing a flicker of jealousy at his devotion to Helen. This was only the second time he had been in to see Anita.

* * *

Armistice Day, November 11, 1918, brought delirious celebration to Littlestown. America had been in the war a scant year and a half yet 130,000 American lives had been lost. Still, despite this alarming figure, Harry read that the influenza epidemic had killed 20,000,000 people worldwide, 500,000 people in the United States alone. Thank heavens Anita had recovered, though she was a thin skeleton of her former self.

Littlestown had paid its price in the war just finished. John Ocker was killed in France and buried there, but Bupp returned to the farm, unharmed, as did other members of the military. The barrel of sticky peach pits disappeared from its place in front of the bank and the silk mill converted from making ribbon decorations for the chests of GI's to hatbands and neckties for the citizenry. Life slowly returned to normal. The Kaiser, whom Harry still secretly admired, abdicated, fleeing to Holland and President Wilson began to push for the formation of a League of Nations.

Miss Margaret was a year-and-a-half old when they began to work with her in earnest. First they taught her to stand tied in her stall, a procedure that would be necessary for grooming as well as to apply the harness. Gracefully, she accepted having a bit in her mouth, but slipping the bridle over her head was another matter. Miss Margaret was downright fussy about her ears.

Finally the day came when Harry and Billy were ready to introduce her to the harness. Harry walked toward the filly on her left side, raised his hand slowly and patted her gently on the rump, sliding his hand gently up the halter. "You and I are going to spend a lot of time doing this together," he crooned, "So we might as well get started right."

He held the harness to Miss Margaret's nose and let her smell it, then rubbed it over her hide slowly so she could get accustomed to its feel before he slipped it gently over her head. "Just like making love to a woman," he said, winking at the grinning Billy. "Slow and gentle does it."

Placing the crupper under the horse's tail was more difficult. She became quite fussed at that operation. Harry tried a number of maneuvers before finding one that did not get her all excited. After getting the little filly fully harnessed they let her walk about her stall for a couple of hours getting used to all the equipment. She was upset at first, shaking her head and checking herself, but gradually she quieted and accepted their offering of oats.

"I think she's ready for the training cart," Billy said one beautiful fall morning after he had spent a week walking behind Miss Margaret with the lines in his hands teaching her the basic commands of Stop, Go, Stand, and Turn.

Harry nodded in agreement. He brought the cart into position behind the young horse and very quietly slipped the shafts into the safety girth on the harness. Miss Margaret was wearing blinders so she couldn't see the sulky being maneuvered behind her. Harry got on the cart quickly while Billy, holding a long line attached to her halter, led her forward very slowly. They walked for about an eighth of a mile before Billy removed the lead line and moved off to the side.

Harry let the horse go forward on her own and Miss Margaret started off at a brisk jog. She was taking to this like she really enjoyed it, strong and willing, but with a mind of her own. Harry grinned to himself as they moved around the track. He liked his girls with spirit. He let her run for about a mile and a half before halting her in the middle of the track and unhitching her there.

By mid-November they were following a regular three mile jogging routine, gradually increasing her speed, brushing her up to faster trots, then dropping her back. She was running a mile in about three and a half minutes, seldom making a mistake by breaking out of her natural graceful gait. She was playful, intelligent, full of life and wanted to go fast. Harry had to be careful not to let her get tired or discouraged.

Picking the proper shoe was the most important part of training a trotter. He and Billy finally decided on half-rounds for her front feet. This helped the filly to fold her knees and acquire the proper trotting gait. Miss Margaret was a natural. After getting her toes cut to the right length, and shod with the new shoes, she developed a beautiful rhythmic gait. Since they weren't training her to be a pacer they didn't have to worry about fitting her with hobbles. Harry hated to see a horse hobbled. It was unnatural, not like the elegant, fluid symphony of a trotter's gait.

They worked everyday except Sunday and he felt certain Miss Margaret knew when Sunday rolled around. He would go down to the stable and find her lying down for a good rest, stretched out, snoring away, really enjoying herself.

At the end of five weeks Harry felt she was ready for the serious and final part of her training and development, learning to race on a track with other horses. Up till now Harry had only trained male horses and he soon found out that fillies were entirely different from colts. They were just like women. They got their feelings hurt easily and they tended to get sulky if things didn't go just right. There were days when Miss Margaret didn't seem to feel like pulling him around in a cart and he had to make an extra effort to make her feel she was doing it on her own. It took a lot of patience and understanding and Harry found that Billy had a lot more of that than he did.

Although he tried hard not to make a pet of her, Miss Margaret had a special place in his affections. He loved the smooth flowing lines of her, from the elegant head and neck to the long slender legs and the full, strong chest. Her coat was a golden chestnut that glinted like fire in the sunlight, she was a model of conformation, completely blemish free and he couldn't imagine life without her.

On May 31, 1919, Miss Margaret of Rebert Stables won her maiden race on the half-mile track at Hanover Fairgrounds.

In jubilation, Harry took the family into Hanover to celebrate. He parked the Buick in a garage on Frederick Street and after dropping Effie at the Elite Millinery Parlor on York Street he led Helen and Anita to Smith and Jenkins Drug Store for ice cream treats. The girls sat with legs curled around the wire rungs of the elegant ice cream chairs sipping chocolate sodas and he watched them with quiet pride. They were both so pretty. Anita at fourteen sat straight and prim with grown up dignity, a huge satin bow fixed neatly in her fine brown hair. She had a high forehead, pale blue eyes and gracefully curved brows. Today she was dressed in a straight navy dress adorned with a five inch white sash tied in a large floppy bow below her waist, big puffed sleeves, and a white bib-like collar that encircled her slender neck. A gold locket rested on her flat chest and her slender hands, encased in little white gloves, daintily spooned ice cream into her mouth.

Helen, on the other hand, kept kicking the table legs with restless feet, spilling part of her soda on the little round table. Her pretty face had been warmed by the sun to the color of rich honey, her blue eyes were squeezed shut in laughter, her pug nose wrinkled, and her mouth open wide to receive the ice cream she was shoveling in.

The two girls were as different in looks as they were in nature. Anita always kept him at arm's length, frustrating him with her rejection, while Helen followed him around with such puppy dog affection that she annoyed him at times. He smiled at them now.

"I think we should go across the street to Wentz & Frey's Department Store and buy ourselves something very, very special," he said.

"What Daddy, what?" Helen asked as another puddle of ice cream appeared at the base of her dish.

"Anything you want. We will walk through the store from top to bottom and you can have the one thing you want most. Whatever it is."

"Does it matter what it costs?" Anita asked with interest.

"Nope, whatever strikes your fancy."

An hour later, after much indecision and several trips back to view certain items a second time, the girls made their choices. Helen picked out a rich brown velvet dress with a huge pink satin sash. Anita chose a large teddy bear whose eyes lit up from a hidden battery. Harry wasn't surprised at Helen's choice, but he was at Anita's. He looked at her with interest as she hugged the bear tightly. *Maybe the child needs something fuzzy and soft to hold to herself,* he thought in surprise. Maybe she needed something alive and warm with glowing eyes. She didn't get much of that home. Effie had changed from the caring girl he had married, showing little warmth or affection to either of her daughters. Or for that matter to him.

That reminded him. His wife would surely be wondering what had kept them so long. He took each girl by the hand and they hurried across the street to find Effie standing in front of The Elite, hat box swinging impatiently in her gloved hand.

Helen had insisted on wearing her new dress out of the store and she twirled around in front of her mother to show off her finery.

"What a complete waste of money," Effie grumbled giving Harry a stern look. "That dress can't be washed. It's velvet. And the color certainly isn't good for the child. She gets brown as a little . . . you know what . . . every summer, as it is. I'm always ashamed of her in front of our friends."

"It isn't how Shotsy looks in the dress that's important. It's how she feels," Harry said with a frown.

Undaunted, Helen continued to twist and twirl, admiring her reflection in the large plate glass window of the millinery shop. "And that stuffed animal Anita is holding. That's a toy for a little child not a young lady now in her teens. Honestly, Harry, I don't know what possessed you."

Harry felt the joy drain away. How could a man love such a cold woman? He remembered all the hugs and kisses he had received from his mother when he was growing up. His children got nothing but reprimands and displeasure. What had happened to Effie—to the warmth and passion of their youth? Well, by God, he wouldn't let Effie ruin his day.

"Why don't you finish your shopping," he said, turning a cold eye on his wife, "and I'll drop the girls off at the movie house."

Anita smiled with delight. She loved the silent movies and always begged to go. But Helen frowned, her chubby lips pouting. "Anita always wants to sit through the movie twice and my feet go to sleep. And," she added with displeasure, "I can't read that well yet."

"You only have to sit through it once," he assured her. "I'll pick you both up in one hour. You stay in your seats until I come for you."

But one hour turned into two as he whiled away the evening at the bar of the Capitol Hotel bragging about Miss Margaret's win on the track. After several drinks he forgot his promise to the children.

Effie stalked into the darkened theater, her face flushing with indignation, and claimed the two girls. Bitterly, she paraded Helen and Anita down the deserted street to the empty car waiting in the darkened garage.

"We'll have to wait here. Your father is probably busy at one of the local taverns," she announced, shoving the girls into the car. Helen immediately curled up on the back seat and in minutes fell fast asleep, but Anita sat glumly staring into the night, clutching her teddy bear, absorbing her mother's silent anger.

CHAPTER 27

Belle was sitting on the kitchen porch seeding sour cherries when the dogs began to bark in excitement, announcing the arrival of an automobile.

She looked up and smiled at the speed with which a stream of dust was approaching their house. Only Effie took the rutted, dusty roads that fast, but then her big Buick had isinglass curtains, which she could roll down to protect against the clouds of dust she raised.

Belle met her at the gate as Effie braked with a screech, pulling her dust bonnet off her elaborate pompadour and fanning the dust away. "We certainly need rain," Effie exclaimed, brushing the gray film from her chemise day frock, a fashionable affair that rose to just below the knee. "It was simply too hot to wear that monstrous coat, and now I'm covered with grime."

"If you drove at a reasonable rate of speed, you wouldn't raise such dust," Belle answered absently, curious about the reason for her niece's visit. She picked up the granite dish-pan filled with pitted cherries and emptied the dirty water on the ground. "Come inside and let me put these cherries in the ice box, then I'll make us some lemonade and we can enjoy a nice long talk."

Seated in comfortable, rush-seated rocking chairs near the window of the Rebert's Choice parlor, the two women slowly sipped from their glasses and looked at each other in silence.

Belle had brought her up to date on her family and the impending birth of yet another grandchild. She noticed Effie's unusual silence and to fill the lull in the conversation she launched into what she hoped was an amusing story that might break the tension obvious on Effie's face.

"Last night I finally got the rat that's been in my kitchen. I can't get over the effrontery of his coming in here with a cat in the house, and climbing up on the table and eating apples and pears. I'd love to know how that beast got in here. With the grist mill so close, rats are always a problem. I used to get them with a .22 rifle, but now I just don't bother. He'd been stealing butter. I first suspected kitty, here, and then I figured, no, those tooth marks were not cat marks so I set about trying to catch the wily creature. I've discovered that if you put the trap out three nights in a row with luscious bait on it—cheese with bacon fat and raisins—but not set, he becomes careless like other creatures. Then, on the fourth night, you set it and you've got him. I once caught nineteen mice on one raisin. One after the other. That was some raisin. This was a big wood rat, larger than a Norway rat, brownish with a little white on his belly and long snaggy yellow teeth, like Mr. Samuel Whiskers. I threw him in the fire and cremated him."

Effie gave her a half-smile and then lapsed into silence so lengthy Belle's concern for her niece grew. "Effie! Is something the matter? Are the children alright? Harry? Your parents? You look distraught and you're usually very much in control, you know. Did you really come today, as you said on the porch, just to pay me a visit?"

Still, Effie did not speak. Instead, she placed her empty glass on a small mahogany end table to rise and stand by the window that looked out across the sloping lawn to the creek and grist mill.

"Effie?"

"Oh, Aunt Belle, everything in my life seems to be falling apart," Effie answered, her voice sounding choked. "Harry is drinking again. I'm afraid of his sanity, afraid he'll end up in the sanitorium again. When he drinks he's cruel to me and the girls, especially Anita. And Anita is so frail and thin. She has never completely recovered from her bout with influenza."

"Cruel? Do you mean mentally cruel or physically cruel?"

Effie turned from the window, her lip trembling. "Only mentally so far! Not to Shotsy, but to me and Anita. The whiskey does terrible things to him, Belle, and I'm afraid it might turn physical." As she spoke, anger rose in her voice, her eyes glistened, and she lifted her gaze to the ceiling and back again. She paused, her chin quivering, but the tears did not flow. She took a deep breath, let it out slow, then, after bringing her emotions under control, she began to speak.

Belle listened to Effie's account of Harry's mounting gambling debts, his frequent bouts of drinking which often put him to bed with hallucinations. She heard the story of Helen, and the whiskey mud-pies, which had forced Alex to put his son in the hospital once more. How, wondered Belle, could two such stable and gracious souls like Lillie and Alexander parent such a reckless prodigal. She shook her head in disbelief. "Well, thank God the idiots in Washington have had sense enough to ratify the Prohibition Amendment. Maybe that will put a forcible end to his drinking."

"I hope so. I pray it will."

Belle wrinkled her brow and debated asking her next question. "There's more, isn't there?" she asked gently.

"Harry is so handsome. Handsome and flamboyant. Every time we go to social events the women fawn over him and he eats it up. It makes me sick."

"And in defense you pretend indifference," Bell said, knowingly. "And in turn Harry thinks you don't care. You know, Effie, Harry has always needed a lot of love. Even as a baby he craved attention. A lot of harm was done to Harry by his mother—basically a good person with good intentions—by showering him with too much love and excusing his deceptions."

"You are such good friends with Lillie. Did you . . . did you ever tell her what she was doing?"

Belle moved to stand beside Effie at the window. "You know, my dear, we all tend to idealize those we love and unfortunately when we are forced to see their faults, we hate the one who has forced us to look. I'm afraid I protected our friendship and never spoke my mind to your mother-in-law."

"There is something else, Aunt Belle. He favors Helen and Anita feels it. I'm not sure how to handle that. I don't want the girls to be jealous of one another."

Belle thought for a moment. What could she say? Helen was a beautiful child and Harry had always been attracted to beauty. Anita was . . . well, plain . . . her front teeth protruded slightly, her hair was fine and straight, and her lips were thin and straight, seldom smiling. *But one doesn't say that to a mother*, she thought ruefully. Instead, she smiled in what she hoped was a reassuring way and said, "Most parents, fairly or unfairly, favor one child over another. It often causes friction between husband and wife, because they have different choices. It's something we must guard carefully against. Have you spoken to Harry about it?"

Effie looked guiltily at the floor. "He says I favor Anita."

"So there! You do, you know. I'd just try to work it out between you. Besides, from what you've told me today, you have far more important problems to solve. And I'm afraid I have no magic solution for you, except to feel free to use me as a sounding board—someone to talk to—when the stress gets too much for you to handle alone."

"I'll try to be strong."

"Don't try to trust in your own strength, dear. None of is strong in him or herself. I found that out when Jamie was taken from me. It's the Lord who upholds us. Mother Katie said that to me time and time again."

Effie's expression shifted from somber to skeptical. "If only Harry had inherited some of his grandmother's faith. Is that how you manage to be so self-assured and courageous?"

Belle snorted. "Don't paint me as a saint. I've made many errors in my life. Someone . . . I think it was Mark Twain . . . said "we are like the moon, we all have our dark side, that we never show to anybody."

Effie picked up her bonnet as she moved toward the door. "And me, Aunt Belle? I remember once Harry's mother said I was a spoiled, selfish woman."

Belle took a deep breath. It was time she came right out with it. "Effie, as much as men think they pattern themselves after their fathers, men are really molded by the women in their lives. A child spends all of his formative years at his mother's side, not his father's. Later on it's his wife who takes over, pushing and prodding and maneuvering him. Harry's mother spoiled him and by doing so encouraged his materialistic values. You could have made him strong, but I think you were preoccupied with his wealth and social position. Your need for attention and admiration from the community was as great as Harry's need to love and be loved. I don't know what your sexual relationship is with your husband, nor is it any of my business, but I sense conflict there, too." She could see Effie's face grow pale, but she needed to be totally honest with her. "Harry's drinking seems to be a form of rebellion, from what I don't know. I'm not excusing his abominable behavior, please understand that. But no picture is ever painted in one dimension."

"I certainly didn't expect a lecture when I asked for your advice," Effie said, trying to smile. "I should have known you'd have no real answers for me."

Belle laughed, sadly. "Effie, diplomacy has never been one of my virtues." She stared at Lillie with hard, gray eyes. "When he was young Harry was a very arrogant young man who took his pleasure whenever he wished. He rode his horses too fast, and later he drove too fast. He caroused and he drank." She made a steeple of her fingers. "He gambled, but always paid his debts-or his mother and father did. Anyway you knew all this when you married him, and you made that choice. Because of his mother's obsessive love he has become a man who demands much affection from the women in his life. Perhaps more sexual gratification than you are capable of giving him." She reached over to hug Effie.

Effie returned the hug, then looked into Belle's eyes.

"I . . . I don't mean to be selfish. Would you believe such a thing never crossed my mind?"

"Yes, I believe you. Maybe what Lillie mistakes for selfishness is only the natural result of your always having known exactly what you want. And what you want of Harry."

Effie placed her dust bonnet on her head and tied the stings under her chin. "I'll think about what you've said. I don't think I can change things—Harry is complicated, and he does have a drinking problem—but I fell in love with the wretched man, and I'll just have to try to sort things out."

That night, after putting the girls to bed, Effie went looking for her husband. She found him in their bedroom carefully combing his hair. He was dressed in fresh clothes, a white shirt buttoned at the neck and worn without a necktie, beige sleeveless sweater, brown tweed knickers and brown and black argyle socks.

Effie looked at the man before her, the tall, blue-eyed, handsome man whose face and body were so familiar to her. What had happened to their love? Why did he retreat to the bottle each time he was confronted by a problem? Had he ever really faced the responsibility of raising a family and earning a living like a man should?

Our marriage is in trouble. Deep trouble. The thought assailed her, making her stomach churn. *How can I save our love?*

Do I want to? Impulsively, she moved to his side and put her arms around him.

His eyebrows flew up and he gave her that crooked smile that deepened the cleft in his chin and wrenched her heart.

"What was that for?" he asked.

"You look so grand in that new sweater. It's the one I gave you for Christmas, isn't it?" She gave him a warm, deep kiss.

The look of pleasure that lit up his face made her wince. Belle is right, she thought. He needs a woman's love. He needs more love than I have to give.

He pulled her close. He stank of whiskey and stale tobacco. "I love you, Effie," he said, huskily.

"I love you, too," she said, knowing in her heart it was no longer true, that her love had suffered irreparable damage.

He moved away, glanced into the mirror, and began to smooth his hair once more.

"I don't have to go," his voice was earnest, watching her from half-closed eyes.

"You were going out?" she asked, knowing the answer.

"I've a meeting, at the grange."

Resentment curled in her chest to form a coiled spring in her throat. "You're lying," she snarled, her eyes narrowed in anger and frustration. "The grange only meets once a month." She saw his gaze waver and knew she had wrecked the tenuous bridge that had just been built. She looked at him bleakly.

He began to adjust his tie. "It's a special meeting."

"Then, I think you should go," she said, in a voice of ice.

* * *

Miss Margaret continued to win on the local racing circuit and Harry began to dream of entering her in America's premier harness race, the Kentucky Futurity held at Lexington every fall. But first he had to see how things were handled. He announced his intention to attend the Futurity while at the dinner table.

"You'll do no such thing, Harry Rebert. Racing on that level is completely outside your expertise. Those big time gamblers and operators will eat you alive," Effie said.

"I can hold my own against any of them."

"Well, what about us? The girls have started school. We can't go with you and Alex needs you on the farms."

"Bupp can handle the farming. With me away he won't have any driving to do. It's the perfect time for me to go. Miss Margaret is ready and by next summer I hope to have more foals in training. I need to see what a major race is like."

"You're a dreamer, Harry Rebert. Your Papa will never give you the money to build the kind of racing stable you dream of."

Harry could feel heat flooding his face. Why couldn't Effie love the man he was? Why did she always try to belittle him? It was hard enough to accept that his father didn't trust his business judgement, but he expected some kind of support from his wife.

"I will not spend the rest of my life being bossed around by my parents or my wife. There's a wild, wonderful world outside of Littlestown, Pennsylvania, full of laughter and excitement and I intend to get my share. That race in Kentucky can open all kinds of doors to me."

"Knowing you, you will probably spend all your time in the bar. I doubt you'll even get to see the race. Thank heavens Prohibition will soon become law." Effie looked at him through narrowed eyes. "How many of your racing cronies will be there?"

"Don't you talk to me like that. I'll do as I please, when I please. Furthermore, I don't drink any more than the next man."

Effie sniffed. "Don't you think I see you and that old Billy Woods out in the barn passing the bottle back and forth when you promised the doctor you would never take another drink."

Harry shot to his feet so quickly that his chair fell over backwards and clattered to the floor. Anita cringed in her chair, her eyes wide and fearful as they darted from her mother to her father as if watching a schoolyard fight. Helen sat forlornly, pushing her turnips back and forth on her plate, looking at her father without understanding, yet conscious of the magnitude of this moment. "Daddy. . ."

"Enough," Harry shouted. "I plan to leave for Kentucky on Wednesday. See to it that my clothes are packed."

After checking into a plush hotel in downtown Lexington Harry headed straight for the race track. Crowds of people in a holiday mood milled around the entrance booth and impatiently he pushed himself through the turnstiles. He was uncertain where to go, but he didn't want to appear to be a country bumpkin by asking directions. Seeing a hubbub of activity in the paddock area he hurried in that direction. Owners, trainers, and drivers milled around in great confusion. Harry, of course, had no pass to that privileged area so he had to content himself with peering over the rail. He sucked in his breath, biting his inner lip, savoring every smell of dust, horse flesh, and animal dung. He should be inside, one of the laughing, swearing men, instead of hanging on a fence. Next year, he promised himself.

Reluctantly, he left the paddock and strode toward the clubhouse. All of the wagering windows had long lines of men waiting to place their bets so he climbed the stairs to look out over the track.

Harry stared in amazement at the beauty before him. This was much grander than anything he had ever seen. The broad surface of the dirt track looked as though someone had pulled a giant comb around it. Lush green grass and bright flowers covered the inside of the huge brown oval, and the half-mile track was outlined by a sparkling white rail fence accented at intervals by striped posts. In the distance, beyond the track, Harry could see the busy movement of horses, sulky and drivers in their colorful silks.

"Pretty, isn't it?" asked a middle-aged man lounging near-by studying a racing program.

Harry glanced at him and then turned his eyes back to the track where a tractor was making another sweep, furrowing the surface. "It'll look prettier when the track is filled with horses and sulkies," he answered with a smile.

The man grunted. He looked like a professional gambler—heavy jowled with long strands of black hair carefully arranged over his bald head, dressed in a black pinstripe suit with a heavy brocade vest, a stiff white shirt, and a polka dot bow tie. The man casually extended his wrists from his jacket sleeves revealing flashy gold cuff links. He had the pallor of men who spent a lifetime in dark bars and betting rooms and certainly didn't look like he belonged in one of the expensive clubhouse boxes now beginning to fill with laughing well-dressed men and women.

"Don't recall seeing you around the clubhouse before. This your first time at Lexington?" the man asked, staring directly into Harry's eyes.

"First, but hopefully not my last. I have a promising young filly in my stable that I hope to enter in the races next year." *No harm in spreading it on a little,* he thought.

The man looked at Harry with undisguised interest, his tiny deep set eyes moving slowly from Harry's highly polished soft leather boots to his elegantly tailored broadcloth jacket. "Your stable? And where might that be?"

"Pennsylvania . . . Adams County. I own several farms there and have just started breeding trotters," Harry boasted. It was only a tiny lie.

"Names Tom Martin," the man said, sticking out a pudgy hand. "Welcome to Kentucky. Why don't we go inside to the bar and let me stand you to a drink. It's an hour until the first heat."

Harry hesitated, but he couldn't help noticing the huge glittering rig on the man's right hand. If Tom was a gambler he must be a successful one. Maybe he'd give him a lead on one of the races. And he could use a drink—really use one.

At the bar Tom settled next to an attractive blond whom he greeted warmly. "How you doing, Francie? Haven't seen you around lately."

"I was married for awhile, out of circulation. That's over though." She gave a slight shrug, then added, "you know how it is."

Harry looked at her with interest.

"Meet Francie Brown," Tom said, with a nod in her direction.

"Harry Rebert," he said, giving her a big smile.

Tom turned his attention to the bartender and after ordering drinks for the three of them pulled a heavily marked racing sheet from his pocket and spread it on the bar before him.

"Look at those long odds on Cold Spring in the third," he exclaimed. "She broke stride her last two times out—guess that accounts for it." He tented his fingers on the bar and shook his head. "Johnnie Pitcairn's driving though. In my book he's the best around."

Harry tossed down the last of his whiskey and kept his own racing program in his pocket. He had already picked his bets and decided on another horse in the third. Still . . .

"Who is standing stud at your stable?" Tom suddenly asked.

"Tansy, sired by Bay Hunter. Winner of a dozen blue ribbons at Pennsylvania fairs. Several of his offspring have already raced in the money." Harry raised two fingers to the bartender then, noticing that Francie's glass was also empty, he raised another finger.

Tom kept glancing at his racing sheet while they drank and Harry watched him draw a black circle around Cold Spring in the third. Suddenly Tom heaved himself to his feet. "Think I'll go down to the paddock for a look-see. Want to come along?"

Harry cast a speculative glance at the blond who kept smiling at him. "Na," he answered. "I think I'll have another drink and then wander down to the betting windows before the crowd gets too heavy."

Tom nodded and winked at Francie. As he wandered away Harry slid over beside her. "Care for another?" he asked hopefully. She fixed him with a slow, bold smile as she turned toward him and looked him full in the eyes. She didn't answer for a minute and inwardly he cringed at his nervousness. Years of marriage had dulled what once would have been an easy approach.

"A mint julep, this time," she said, tipping her empty glass toward him. Her voice had a slow Southern drawl and it jarred Harry, making him aware of her difference.

"Do you have a horse entered in the race today?" he asked, searching for conversation.

Her lips curved in self-satisfaction and she fluffed her hair with painted fingernails. "I'm not an owner, more's the pity. I just love the excitement of the race. You know, the pageantry and the color."

"Alone?"

"Don't get any ideas, now. I'm no pickup."

"Of course not. I didn't mean to be forward. I'm a stranger here and just a little lonely."

Her body seemed to relax and she took a small sip of her drink. "I'm not used to sitting at a bar without an escort. My husband and I just divorced. This is the first time I've come alone."

"I'm sorry," he said, trying to appear sympathetic. He cocked his head slightly, causing a thick wave of hair to fall forward on his forehead, smiling into her gray eyes.

They made small talk, bemoaning the new Prohibition Act passed by Congress and due to become law before Christmas. As they talked he gave her sideways glances, observing her heavy blond hair, long slender neck, and heavy wide-spaced breasts. She was wearing a scent, strong and female, that made him think of the hot breeding barn at home.

"Do you live here in Lexington, Francie?"

"No," she answered vaguely. She squirmed slightly on her stool and briefly their legs touched. She gave him a warm, provocative smile. "Have you bet on the first race? They're bringing the horses to the starting line."

Harry frowned. If he left the bar to place a bet she might be gone when he returned. Quickly, he decided what he would do. He'd skip the first two races and triple his bet on the third. He turned his full attention back to Francie.

"I'll pass on the first and second. Don't have a feel for them. Your glass is empty. Why don't we have another; we can watch the race from here."

"Just one more, then. I'm beginning to feel a little woozy." She giggled. "I like talking to you, Harry. You're a real gentleman. I can tell."

He saw the interest in her eyes. The drinks were working on him, too. They ordered another and barely watched the running of the first and second race. Upon closer observation she appeared to be slightly older that he first thought. He noticed her blond hair had a slightly brassy cast to it and there were tiny lines about her mouth. Her body had a ripeness; a maturity that matched her perfume.

Harry gripped his glass with sweaty hands, warm and happy, flushed with drink and desire. He couldn't seem to take his eyes from her ample bosom. He had never cheated on Effie, but he remembered their increasing arguments and her coldness toward him. He'd bet Francie wouldn't be cold. Far from it.

Francie slid off her stool. "I think I need to visit the ladies's washroom, love. And I want to place a small bet on the third race. Can I take your bet?"

Harry wanted to impress this woman. Throwing caution to the wind, he took his money clip from his pants pocket and peeled off three one hundred dollar bills. "Put these on Cold Spring for me, will you honey."

Her eyes widened and she fingered the bills. That had impressed her alright. He already knew how this day was going to end.

"I'll be right back."

He had another drink, watched the second race finish with a winner he had picked and not bet on, then began watching the door anxiously. Francie should be back by now. There must have been quite a crowd at the betting windows.

Francie still hadn't returned when they began leading the horses to the line for the third. He hurried out to the observation platform. The boxes in front of him were filled with elegant people—women in the latest fashions wearing huge picture hats and men in tall top hats, their wealth apparent. He flexed his shoulders and stood tall. Oh, this was grand. This was the life he wanted. He could just picture himself in one of those boxes wearing a fine pin stripe cutaway with Effie sitting beside him like a queen holding a thin parasol and wearing one of those big floppy hats.

He trained his binoculars on the row of horses and sulky at the starting line. Cold Spring was displaying number four and her driver was wearing bright green silks. After being called back twice the drivers were finally given the signal for a good start and they were off.

Uneasily he looked over his shoulders, his eyes searching the room. Still no sign of Francie. She must have run into a friend.

He refocused on the track as the horses came into the far turn, their drivers a blur of color. His glasses picked out the green silks of Cold Spring. She was third on the outside, her gait perfect. The roar of the crowd grew louder. Cold Spring was coming up fast, in second place on the outside. Harry's heart was pounding and he started to yell, caught up in the excitement of the crowd. "Come on Cold Spring! Come on boy!" The green silks swept past the fading front runner and Harry pounded the rail as Cold Spring swept past the finish line.

Slowly his heart returned to normal and he returned to his stool at the bar. Francie still had not returned with his winning ticket. Ice melted in her half-finished drink. He began to feel very uneasy. He spotted Tom talking to several men at the end of the bar and, picking up his drink, wandered over to him.

"I seem to have lost our mutual friend," he joked, smiling only with his mouth. "Have you seen Francie?"

"Not since I left the two of you at the bar. I take it you got acquainted, then?"

"Somewhat. She's some dish. I was hoping to get to know her better." Harry definitely did not want to appear the fool. "Do you know her well?"

"I see her around the tracks, that's all," Tom replied in a slick voice, his eyes darting sideways, his heavy hand tugging at his tie. He seemed anxious to end the conversation and turned back to his friends.

Harry returned to his stool as the appalling realization of his foolishness began to sink in.

He waited another hour, but he knew with a terrible certainty that he waited in vain. Cold Spring had paid six to one. His winning ticket was worth eighteen hundred dollars. Only he didn't have a winning ticket. That little slut—and probably her friend, Tom, who had beat a hasty retreat after talking to him—had a winning ticket. Bitterness rose in his throat like gall.

He swirled the amber liquid in his glass, the fumes almost making him gag. Why did he drink this vile stuff? He knew it clouded his judgement, but somehow it made it easier to cope with the rejection all around him. He had nothing else to draw strength from. As he downed another drink he looked at his reflection in the mirror behind the bar. The face of a fool! A murderous rage, black and frightening like a smoldering cloud, rolled over him and the vision in the mirror swirled and faded.

He picked up the heavy whiskey tumbler and hurled it at the mirror. The bartender ducked from the flying glass splinters and several women screamed. Within minutes a security guard grabbed his arms and yanked him off the stool.

Harry sobbed in frustration as they led him from the Lexington track.

CHAPTER 28

1919-1923

Congress ratified the Volstead Act over President Wilson's veto in mid-October, providing the enforcement teeth needed to enforce the Prohibition Amendment. Almost immediately, after the distillers and liquor distributors went out of business, the bootleggers took over.

This tickled Harry no end. It was fun to find ways to circumvent the hated law, the 18th Amendment, which went into effect early in 1920. For awhile he toyed with the idea of building a still of his own and he laughed aloud at the imagined response that idea would get from his parents. Shame his grandfather, old Jonas Rebert, hadn't stayed in the business.

Harry and his buddies crowded around the bar of a newly opened speakeasy on a snowy afternoon late in February where they could drink the illegal booze among the ribald shouts of already drunk customers.

"Hey, did you hear the latest," a lad barely out of his twenties drawled. "They found an illegal still on the farm of the Texas Senator who wrote the Prohibition law."

Harry laughed. "If you're thirsty you can find liquor anywhere. They're bring it in from Canada, Bermuda, the Bahamas and Mexico. We ougtha go to Chicago, that's the most notorious booze hustling city in the country. I heard they have over a hundred stills per city block."

"I'll bet New York City ain't far behind," Charley Eddington commented.

"Don't really need to go that far. You can get it at the drugstore if you know the right doctor," Harry said.

"And there are at least twenty speakeasies right here in Hanover that I know of," the young man interjected.

Harry swished gin on his tongue and assumed a judicial expression. "You don't know half of them, boy!"

But the stir Prohibition caused was nothing compared to the furor that arose when the seventy-two year old fight for women's suffrage ended with ratification of the 19th Amendment.

Harry drove into the yard of Rebert's Choice on a hot August morning in 1920 and ran into the mill waving the latest edition of the Hanover Sun. Belle was already surrounded by several women, laughing and hugging one another, and he stood watching them, a smile curving his lips. Aunt Belle smiled broadly and waved him over. "Have you ever read such a wonderful tale," she cried, her gray eyes moist with joy.

"Not all of it, really. I just read the headlines and headed over here to tell you in case you hadn't heard."

"Oh, it's wonderful and so fitting that a woman was the power behind the legislator who cast the deciding vote," Belle said.

"What do you mean?"

"As you know only thirty-five of the thirty-six required states voted for ratification, thirteen states resisted. Our women finally drew their battle lines in Tennessee." She smiled archly. "It was called the War of Roses. Suffrage supporters wore yellow roses, opponents red. Anyhow, it was a letter from the mother of the state's youngest legislator, Harry Burn, that made the difference. Mrs. Burn, a well-read, educated widow, was appalled that her illiterate farmhand could vote on matters concerning her land, but she could not, simply because she was a woman and she urged him to be a "good boy" and vote his conscience. He was last to vote and when it came his turn he voted "Aye". Belle slapped her thigh and laughed lustily. "Even though he wore a red rose!"

Harry gave her a hug and headed home. He was happy for her, although he had serious doubts about what women voting would do to the country. Many said that women lacked enough judgement to vote, others feared the decay of the family structure, and Harry remembered an Oregon senator warning that giving women the right to vote would "make every home a hell on earth." *Not*, he thought wryly, *that other factors didn't contribute to the same thing.*

* * *

Harry hadn't seen or heard of Jerome for several years, but he hadn't forgotten him either. He was glancing at a handbill for harness races in Hagerstown, Maryland when he saw a horse named Demon Runner entered in the stakes. His heart leapt. The winner of a stakes race always had the option of buying any of the horses entered. Jerome must be hard up for cash to take that kind of risk. And Demon Runner had to be past his prime on the track. But what a prize he would be at stud.

To Harry's thinking it was only fitting that he get his retribution on a race track. He didn't want to tip his hand to Jerome so he waited until the last minute to enter Miss Margaret under the silks of the Rebert Stables and put his best jockey, Jason Black, up to drive.

The April sun was cloud covered and pale. A cold wind pulled at Harry's clothing and reddened his cheeks as he walked toward the horses and sulky in the gathering area.

He took a deep, satisfying breath. God, how he savored the excitement of the track! The race crowd was brightly dressed, the air alive with their babble and the cries of food vendors hawking their wares.

He found his driver attaching the sulky shafts to Miss Margaret. Jason was tall, well built, with a thatch of hair that gleamed red-gold in the sun, and eyes a deep green. A small scar bisecting his chin, inflicted in an earlier riding accident, served only to add character to his rugged face.

Harry nodded to him and walked to the front of the horse. "How's my baby?" he crooned in a voice soft with love as he rubbed her poll. Miss Margaret nuzzled the sleeves of his jacket, responding to the caress of his hand and voice. "Sorry, but you have to wait till the race is over to get your sugar cube." Her large, wide-spaced eyes looked at him calmly. "And then, only if you win," he reminded her, as the band in front of the stands struck up a lively tune.

Miss Margaret loved the sound of the band and she pricked her ears in its direction and lifted her tail high. Harry chuckled. "Ready to go, are we?" He put a hand on her bridle and Jason climbed atop his perch in the sulky. Slowly they walked to the starting line.

There were seven entrants and Harry's sulky was in the number four position with three horses on either side. Jason sat poised and ready, waiting for the crack of the starter's gun. Harry leaned in close to horse and rider. "Stay clear of Jerome Sinclair's wheels. Keep Miss Margaret on the outside and don't let yourself get boxed in," he warned Jason. "Let someone else set the pace. Just remember, Jerome is a crafty driver . . . crafty and dirty."

Harry gave his horse an affectionate pat on the rump and moved towards the stands. Most of the crowd of fair-goers leaned on the railing, ready to urge on their favorites, and Harry found a space where he had an unobstructed view of the finish line.

The number two horse suddenly bolted forward and there was some delay while the embarrassed driver brought the sulky back into position. Finally, everyone was in position and the starter gun rang out.

Miss Margaret, perhaps distracted by the false start, was immediately boxed in and, as they flashed around the first turn, Jason was well back in the pack.

Harry didn't despair—the start was too fast and several horses would tire. He had made sure of that. Taking no chances, he had bribed a driver to set a lightening fast pace. He smiled with satisfaction as he saw Jerome take the bait and chase the leader.

At the half-way post Jason applied the whip and Miss Margaret began to move forward. Jerome and Demon were leading now and showed no signs of tiring. Had Jason waited too long?

Intently Harry watched the stretch drive through field glasses. Miss Margaret was in second position and gaining. Would she have enough? Jason's cap flew off and his red hair blew in the wind as he pounded the sulky shaft with his whip.

They were only yards from the finish line when Miss Margaret resounded to the whip and moved into the lead, maintaining a gait so smooth and graceful she seemed motionless, only her legs and feet flickering in the sun.

A roar went up from the crowd. Miss Margaret surged across the finish line half a length in front of Demon Runner.

As Jason began to pull her up she stumbled and before Harry's disbelieving eyes his horse fell to the ground. He dashed madly through the crowd, pushing people away as he ran and vaulted over the rail fence onto the track. A crowd had already gathered around the motionless horse and Jason knelt beside her where she lay amid a tangle of broken shafts and harness. Harry reached his beautiful little filly and lifted her head to his lap, running a gentle hand across her velvety poll, the sobs racking his body. Her eyes had rolled up in her head and there was no breath coming from her nostrils.

The track vet examined her briefly then placed a sympathetic hand on Harry's arm. "I'm sorry, Mister. Her heart must have burst. She gave it everything she had."

Harry wiped the bitter tears from his eyes. He had won. But Miss Margaret was dead. He had gotten even—Demon Runner would belong to him—but what a terrible, terrible price he had paid. He shook his head in disbelief. No, that wasn't quite right. His poor innocent filly had paid it for him.

After Miss Margaret's death he couldn't go near the stable. Billy did the best he could, but the work was more than he could handle alone. Papa refused to advance him any more money to hire extra help, demanding that he give up the stables and devote his full attention to cattle and farming. He pleaded with Mamma to intervene on his behalf, but this time she refused. In disgust, he agreed to sell all the stock except Tansy.

On a Saturday morning, late in September, he returned home after spending the better part of the morning talking to young Lawrence Sheppard about buying his broodmares. Lawrence hoped to some day take over the operation of the Hanover Farm Stables despite his father's wish that he enter Hanover Shoes when he finished college. This morning he'd agreed to purchase three of Harry's broodmares for a fair price. The rest Harry would place in the upcoming horse auction at Harrisburg.

He parked the Buick in the driveway and walked over to the stable. He pulled a flask from his pocket and sank down on a bale of hay where he sat for an hour drinking and reminiscing about the many happy hours he had spent with Miss Margaret.

The sun was hot and the whiskey filled his gut with fire.

What he really needed, he decided, was some fun. Something to make him laugh. Maybe he would throw a party. The cattle auction was in late October and with the money that would bring, plus what he got for his string of broodmares, he could throw a real shindig—make everyone sit up and take notice.

Slowly the plan developed in his mind. He'd drive into the Union Hotel and get some ideas from his friends. Giddy with drink and his new-formed plans he lurched into the house and up to his bedroom to dress for an evening on the town. Half an hour later he sauntered into the kitchen to remove his car keys from the peg by the back door. They weren't there.

"Effie," he yelled. "Where are my keys?"

She walked into the kitchen, head high and chin stuck out defiantly. "Your father told me to hide your keys when you are drinking. He said not to let you drive. I've put them away."

Harry could feel his jaw drop as he looked at her in disbelief. "You put my keys away? Well, Missy, you just go get them," he reprimanded with the dignity of the inebriated.

"No, Harry. It's not safe for you to drive."

"I'm not drunk. I'm going into town and no simpering woman is going to stop me."

Effie's eyes bored into his. They were cold and full of disdain. "You've been drinking all day, Harry. You are in no condition to drive and Bupp isn't here to take you. Go back upstairs and go to bed. You can go to town tomorrow."

"Don't treat me like a little boy. I've had enough of that from my mother. Now give me the damn keys!"

"No." She looked toward the table where Helen and Anita were watching the exchange with worried eyes. She grabbed him by the arm. "Please Harry. You're frightening the girls. If I didn't love you I wouldn't care what you did to yourself."

"Love! Love! You call the way you treat me love! The only thing you love is this house and its precious possessions. They matter more than anything else. You've never loved me. You love what I stand for. What I can buy. Things—that's what you love—not people. Now you're trying to turn my daughters against me. Anita never shows me any affection, she defends everything you do."

Black anger suffused Harry. He wanted to strike out, to hit something. He jerked his arm free from Effie's clutching hands, gave her a mighty push and stormed out the door.

The next morning Effie moved his clothes into the spare room. He no longer cared—in ways it was easier. Secretly, she was worried about his uncontrollable anger when he was drinking. He must be a totally different person. It was as though some dark evil person he didn't know inhabited his body at those times and took advantage of his drunkenness to emerge. Maybe Mamma was right and whiskey was the devil appearing in liquid form.

He came and went as he pleased and on those occasions when they were required to present themselves as a family he was proud to escort Effie and the girls. Effie was still a handsome woman, always stylishly dressed, and Helen was growing into a real beauty. She worried him sometimes with an overactive interest in boys. She had always preferred male companionship and, whereas Anita frequently had girlfriends at the house, Helen seldom did. She still wanted to go everywhere with him, trailing him about the farm like a devoted puppy. Anita, on the other hand, avoided him and spent all of her time in the house dusting the damn furniture and shining the silver. He was restless and unhappy and although he occasionally sought sexual gratification from Effie he found himself impotent with her. He acknowledged that whiskey ruled his life. His drinking had led him into a tangled web with no beginning and no end. But he also had to acknowledge that he really didn't want to change.

As the summer of '24 moved toward another fall he began to think again about his thwarted party plans. Cattle prices were high and they had a good herd ready for market. The weather had been good and the crops were abundant. Why not rent a hall and an orchestra in York or Baltimore and celebrate the election of 1924? Cal Coolidge, who had succeeded to the presidency last year when Harding died in office, was sure to be re-elected. Prohibition was a joke. He could get all the booze he wanted.

The more he thought about an election party the more excited he got. It would be the talk of Littlestown. He and his friends met at a local speakeasy and talked all night planning every detail; music, bathtub gin, and as many call girls as they could muster.

The dance was booked for November 7th at the German Club in Baltimore, Maryland. On October 27th Harry attended the final cattle auction of the season and stuffed the money into a money clip in his pocket. He should pay Mr. Hemp at the Lancaster Stockyard for the scrubs furnished in the spring, but he liked the feel of the big wad of bills bulging in his pants pocket. Besides, it wouldn't hurt to have a little extra cash in case the party ran more than he expected. He'd pay Hemp after the party. Effie treated him with cold indifference and, as he anticipated, had no interest in attending the party, so, with undisguised relief, he left for Baltimore alone.

That evening Harry stood quietly on the sidelines surveying the crowd. As expected, Coolidge had been re-elected and all the

Republican politicians from Adams County were on hand to celebrate. From the size of the crowd it looked as though half of Littlestown was here also. Banners were draped everywhere and balloons floated high above the dance floor. The dance floor was packed with gyrating bodies as girls in flapper dresses moved to the upbeat tempo of 'Yes We Have No Bananas.'

Women crowded around the bar, many of them with cigarettes dangling from their fingers, their legs crossed, their short skirts revealing shapely legs and rolled stockings. Booze flowed freely as everyone seemed bent on breaking the law and the Ten Commandments.

I love it, he thought. This was life as it should be.

A thin young girl moved close to him and coyly ran her fingers across the cleft in his chin. "Why, Henny," she whispered, "are you all alone?"

"Not anymore," he said, slipping a practiced arm around her slim waist and leading her to the dance floor.

As the night wore on the party got nosier and the crowd drunker. Harry danced every dance with the young girl, their bodies swaying in unison, her breath warm on his cheek. He found himself responding to her gyrating body. By God, he bet he wouldn't be impotent with this one!

He woke slowly the next morning, aware of an agonizing headache, and with a vague sense of foreboding. The girl was gone, her cheap perfume lingering in the stale air. Ignoring the waves of nausea that surged over him he made his way to a small wooden chair beside the bed where his pants and jacket were neatly hung. With mounting dread he searched the pockets of his trousers.

They were empty.

CHAPTER 29

Harry was in deep trouble. He hadn't paid the stockyard and the money from the auction was to have lasted through the winter. He couldn't go to the bank for a loan, all the properties were in his parent's name. Effie's father wouldn't help him—George Riffle hated him and lost no opportunity to remind Effie of her mistake in marrying him. He had always been able to tap either his mother or father for funds, but he knew they were out of patience with him. He had exhausted the largess of all his friends and after his escapade in Lexington even Grandmother Sophia had thrown up her hands in despair and told him never to ask for money again.

But he had no choice. He'd have to go to Mamma and beg for help one more time. This was the last time, he vowed, sick with self-loathing.

Mamma took one look at his face and burst into tears.
"What is it this time, Harry?"
Harry shifted his feet. The parlor smelled of old wallpaper, lavender, and beeswax; the only sound the gentle ticking of the mantle clock. A lamp had been lit and a fire burned in the rough-stone fireplace. It looked cheerful and inviting and as Harry settled his narrow rump in the low, rush-seated chair by the fireplace, he had a sense of homecoming. He'd always thought of White Hall as home, he realized with surprise. It was the one constant in a life he had chosen to fill with change. He ran his fingers through his hair and cleared his throat. "I'm in trouble with the stockyard, Mamma. I had the money owed Mr. Hemp with me when I went to the election party in Baltimore. Some dame rolled me. Took every cent I had."

"All of it?" she gasped. "All the money from the fall auction?"

"All of it." He felt tears stinging his eyelids as he watched the color drain from her sweet face. She was only sixty-seven, but she looked much older. And her pain would only get worse. He hadn't told her everything.

"I'm afraid there's more," he stammered. "I've taken a few fliers in the stock market and lost pretty heavily." His blue eyes stared at the floor. He couldn't stand to see the look in his mother's eyes; the disbelief and denial and anger.

"I know . . . I know you've helped me before and I swore I wouldn't ask again, only.. . ." Harry's voice dropped to a whisper, saddening the room, that room filled with memories in which chrysanthemums and the last of the geraniums stood in clay pots among family photographs, where Grandmother Katie's spinning wheel stood in the corner, and the family bible lay open on a marble top table. Who would ever guess that a family possessing so much could have such trouble?

"Harry, we've mortgaged everything for you. The bankers won't lend us anymore. They said the last time we had borrowed more than the farms are worth. If your Papa hadn't been on the Board we wouldn't have gotten the last loan."

"I didn't realize everything was so heavily mortgaged," Harry stammered.

"You had to be aware of it. First there were payments to that man you crippled years ago, then your treatments for your drinking at those expensive detoxification clinics. Then you had to be bailed out of jail in Lexington and the damages to the clubhouse paid for. Plus all the minor scraps we've bailed you out of over the years. There isn't any more. You've destroyed everything. Everything your family worked so hard to build." A huge shudder shook her tiny body and in a voice so charged with emotion he hardly recognized it she added, "and you've almost destroyed us."

Harry couldn't stand to look at the anguish on her beloved face. His gaze fastened on the window where lace curtains moved softly in the gentle breeze. Behind Mamma he saw the embroidered motto that had always hung above the mantle. "Whiskey Is Sorrow" it read.

She saw him looking at it. "Your great-grandfather began the family fortune by distilling whiskey, but he knew enough not to use it himself. You, Harry, have lost it all by over-indulging, by not realizing that for some it can be the devil's brew."

"You must hate me," he mumbled.

"No, son, I love you. I've always loved you. We love people in spite of what they are, not because of what they are. I'm aware that it's been a possessive love, so much so that I've forced myself to keep an emotional distance over these last few years so as not to smother you. But I don't love you blindly. I see signs of dissipation in your face that was once so handsome, tiny wrinkles around your blue eyes, puffiness in your once strong jaw. I see your faults, Harry, but it isn't up to me to pass judgement on you. Only God can do that." She sat looking at her curled-up fingers, studying them intently while she spoke, as though she had never seen them before. When she spoke again her voice was so soft he had to strain to listen. "God's love is unconditional . . . and so is a mother's."

Harry sighed. "Mamma, why does everything in my life go wrong. I don't want to hurt people, don't try to create trouble. I'm not a bad person. I'm just always in some sort of predicament. Don't other people get themselves in a fix?"

"Life is full of predicaments that test our characters. It's how we handle them that counts. And no one can handle them through a bottle, son."

I'm only trying to keep pace with today's society, a voice in his head cried out. How could he explain to this loving woman that things in America had changed. He was no different than his friends. Everyone drank and laughed at Prohibition and poked fun at the government for thinking they could legislate men's lives.

But those excuses couldn't help him now. She wasn't going to give him the money—couldn't give him the money. Dear God, what was he going to do? He felt sick inside, sick and frightened as though someone had opened a door and let in a blast of winter. Tears swam in his eyes, Mamma's face a blur.

She rose slowly from her chair and came to his side, placing her hand gently on his shoulder, pressing her lips in his hair. He turned into her arms and buried his face on her chest and held on for dear life.

"It's partly my fault," she murmured. "I'm the one who gave you so much as a child you had nothing to strive for. We'll work things out, Harry."

"No mother, this is my problem. You and Papa have done enough."

"Will Effie stick by you?"

"I don't know. I wouldn't blame her if she didn't."

He rose and walked toward the door. He had disappointed everyone that mattered to him—Mamma, Papa, Effie, and his children. Betrayed their love—and the reality of his failure hurt more than he could ever have imagined.

This was it then. He would have to work his way out of this predicament himself. God only knew how.

He smiled ruefully. Maybe he should have thought of God sooner.

* * *

The day of the auction dawned cool and clear.

Smaller pieces of his farm went first; pitchforks, shovels, odd pieces of lumber, Harry's tools. Then the larger pieces of machinery. By noon the livestock was gone; that was the hardest part.

Harry stood away from the crowd, his slender back pushed tight against a maple tree, as they led Tansy by a halter rope in a tight circle before the bidders. Age had marked him. His temples showed shallow hollows and his bones were beginning to show in the way of old horses when their flesh seems to shrink in on itself. But the big, dark bay was still superb, strength and intelligence showing in every line. Harry closed his eyes. Tansy was well past his prime and the bidding was low. Not worth much to anyone but Harry. And who could place a value on the years of love and companionship shared by horse and owner. He was tempted to call out—to save this one shred of his life. Instead, he clenched his hands in his pockets and remained silent. He couldn't take a horse where he was going—to work in the Lancaster stockyards to pay off his debt.

He opened his eyes to find Helen at his side. Silently, she slipped her hand into his and leaned against his side.

"I know how you must feel, Daddy. We're all sorry to see Tansy go."

"You and Anita and Mamma are losing as much today as I am." His voice was tight, caught in his throat.

"No, those are only things. Tansy is part of our family." She squeezed his hand and looked at him with a hint of a smile on her pretty face. "But I guess we can't take a horse to the city can we?"

"Hardly." He found himself smiling back. "And we do have a whole big adventure ahead of us don't we?"

"Oh, yes. I'll bet I'll go to a big high school in Lancaster where they will have dances and everything. Did you know there is a college in Lancaster, Daddy? I'll bet there will be hordes of handsome boys walking past our house everyday."

Harry laughed and reached out to tousle her hair. When he looked at the crowd of people still milling around the auctioneer, Tansy was gone. Best he didn't know who the new owner was.

Against the bright orange sunset a skein of Canada geese flew over the farm. They swooped down over the slate roof of the Mansion House and landed in the corn field, the sight bringing a tentative smile to his face. Their autumn flight was a family excursion, not unlike his own. The geese must fly south in order to find food, but the flight is instinctive, made for its own sake, because it has become a fever in their bones.

Harry straightened his shoulders. The flight of the geese was not a flight of failure, it was a restless desire of the spirit, put there by God. Who knew what new pastures lay just ahead—for him and for the geese.

* * *

Moving day came with surprising speed. Effie and the girls spent the morning rolling glasses and plates in old newspapers and packing them carefully in chicken crates. By noon their clothing and linens were packed, carpets had been rolled up, and what furniture they had left loaded into a rented truck.

Now that the actual day was upon them Helen and Anita realized what moving really meant. Helen jiggled with excitement, speculating about Lancaster, Franklin and Marshall College, and the beckoning new world full of excitement, new experiences, and college boys. Anita had been quieter. Effie realized that Anita, being five years older, felt the pain and uncertainty that relinquishing the homeplace brought.

Tears coursed down Effie's face as the family piled into the Buick and she refused to look back as Harry pulled out of the driveway onto the Hanover Pike and turned east toward Lancaster. Harry's knuckles were white on the steering wheel and a cigarette dangled from his tight mouth. Helen thankfully had stopped her prattle and Anita's fingers laboriously creased a pleat in her skirt, over and over again.

They drove in silence for three hours until the outskirts of Lancaster came into view. The entrance to the city, the first large city the girls had ever seen, was an introduction to another world and Helen gazed through the windshield, her cheeks flushed and her eyes sparkling.

The Buick moved along streets lined with stately elm trees and Harry circled the magnificent campus of Franklin and Marshall College, its giant oaks shading brick buildings clustered around a green common.

"Oh, Anita, look at all those handsome boys," Helen exclaimed.

Anita glared at her. "That's all you ever think about—boys, boys, boys."

"Well, that's more fun than thinking about polishing the silver and dusting the furniture."

"If you'd do your share I wouldn't have to do so much."

"You're just an old prude!"

"You girls stop bickering," Harry retorted, directing a stern look at Shotsy, but unable to keep a quirk from his lips. "Look, Effie, here is Wheatland, President James Buchanan's home." He drove slowly past the dignified mansion, then turned toward downtown Lancaster. They drove past the Fulton Opera House sitting on the corner of King and Prince then through Penn Square, past the Courthouse with its gleaming golden dome, the beautiful old Lutheran Church with its fine spire and the many old red-brick houses with graceful doorways.

Harry continued to acquaint them with their new city. "Notice the street names—King, Queen, Prince, and Duke—they surely speak of a royalist past. Did you know that in the early days of the Republic, Lancaster was America's largest inland city?"

"Really, Daddy? You sure know a lot," Helen said.

Effie stopped twisting her handkerchief to lean forward and gaze keenly at the handsome department stores lining King Street.

"Where are we going to have lunch?" she asked, caustically.

"I think it should be someplace special . . . special to mark the Reberts arrival in Lancaster . . . someplace we'll all use to remember this momentous day. I hear the Hound and Hare on Walnut Street is nice. Why don't we go there."

Effie's lips curled with disgust. How dare he make a game of this? Of leaving their home and everything precious to her. Silently, she vowed she would never forgive him.

"Yes, Daddy," Helen said, her face radiant with good cheer. "It must be very special . . . with a name like that."

After a quiet luncheon they again piled into the Buick. As they pulled away from the curb streetcars rattled by, people hurried across the busy street dodging dozens of automobiles, draymen shouted to plodding horses, and horns beeped.

"I'm going to love it here . . . just love it," Helen said, nodding her head up and down.

Effie gave her a scorching look. "You'd love anyplace your father picked."

Harry had rented a house on Duke Street, large enough to accommodate several roomers, and only a short distance from the stockyards. Anita enrolled in Proust's Business School, the tuition a gift from her Grandmother Schwartz, and Helen worked after school watching the children of a wealthy family on Lemon Street.

Effie interviewed prospective boarders with dogged determination and Harry went to work for Mr. Hemp at the Lancaster Stockyard to pay off his debt. They had to have an income to survive and no other course of action was open to him.

From the first moment he entered the stockyard he hated it. Hated the crude, raw elemental odor from the fifteen thousand hogs, cattle, and sheep which were slaughtered everyday. The smell permeated everything, not from the meat itself, but from tons of blood, bones, and hooves which were cooked into fertilizer and glue.

Harry had always thought he wanted the excitement of life in the city. But soberly realistic in the hustle and bustle of the thriving city he felt an overwhelming loneliness. Now, with Christmas approaching, he trudged through the sloppy streets on his way to a local speakeasy gripped with uneasiness. His eyes scanned the sky. It was a wet moon, good for the seeds waiting to spring forth from newly turned earth on the farm. He smiled ruefully. In Lancaster his life was no longer dependent on the weather. Weather didn't count in the scheme of city life except for the inconveniences it caused.

* * *

Effie dreaded the advent of Christmas that year of 1924. Memories of the house on the Hanover Pike assailed her daily. Harry insisted they put up a large tree and invite the boarders to bring a guest and partake in a Christmas festivity, but despite her best efforts it was a bleak affair.

She sat in the corner of a green serpentine-back sofa, her daughters beside her, and watched the gaiety swirling around her, like leaves before an autumn gale, unable to penetrate her private island of isolation. Strangers, these people, no one she really cared about.

Harry was watching her from half-closed eyes. He leaned down to hand her a glass of sherry, a wave of hair, gray at the temples but still thick and wavy, falling across his forehead. He gave her a tilted smile that deepened the cleft in his chin. God help her, she still felt a rush of heat whenever he looked at her that way. Despite the decline of their finances he still dressed with a casual elegance. Today, he wore a mountain green wool suit, the coat opened to reveal a vest with gold buttons, his white shirt, linen of the finest quality adorned with gold cufflinks, blinked in the reflected lamp light.

Tears misted her eyes. She looked away from him, across the unfamiliar parlor at the inferior tree adorned with store bought ornaments. How different this was from Christmases at the Mansion House; how very special they had been. Friends and neighbors flocked to see their glorious tree which soared to the ceiling in the large front parlor, surrounded by a large "yard" complete with a farm house furnished with doll furniture, a barn with cows that mooed and horses that nodded their heads, cotton draped mountains and mirror lakes reflecting hand painted geese and white ducks. She always served her special fruit cake prepared months in advance and kept moist with rum soaked linen cloths. Harry kidded her about getting their guests drunk on her fruit cake and mincemeat pie, also prepared with a generous tot of rum.

Her face twisted in anguish. Nothing but memories now. Everything of value in her life was gone—all gone.

Harry removed the rug and sprinkled soap powder on the wooden floor so couples could dance. He could be a generous host, warm and charming when sober. If only he would stay that way. Unfortunately, he was one of those ill-fated people who underwent a complete change of personality when inebriated. She watched him now, laughing with Helen, dancing the rambunctious Charleston.

Music pulsed from the victrola and couples swayed to the strains of "Tea for Two." Harry laid a warm hand against Effie's cheek and with beseeching eyes pulled her to her feet and led her to the dancing area. Despite herself, she felt her heart lurch. That sherry must really be working, she thought wryly. He touched her hip, and a jolt of electricity shot through her. She looked into his blue eyes and saw that he knew exactly what she felt. Then her mouth tightened and the smile faded from her lips. He was an expert at making women tremble at his touch. She saw his eyes flicker in reaction to her change of expression and he gave a deep sigh before leading her back to the couch.

* * *

Harry jammed his hands into the pockets of his overcoat as he walked home in the gloom of a cold, gray day in March. The wind swirling from the east carried the foul odor of the stockyards and the sky was the color of wet cement. His right hand curled around the silver flask of bootleg gin. It was almost empty. He'd been swigging on it since morning. He had to quit. Bootleg swill was unhealthy, dangerous, and disgusting. He tipped it to his mouth.

Life in Lancaster was anything but an exciting adventure. The job at the stockyards was intolerable; he hated Effie's tearful reminders of what she had lost, hated turning their home into a boardinghouse with strange men sharing his bathroom and his table. And Helen and Anita bickered constantly. In an attempt to provoke parental punishment, Anita tattled every time Helen so much as looked at a boy. And Helen refused to be the prim, proper young lady her sister was, criticizing Anita's lack of style and her serious demeanor.

Harry turned the corner of Duke Street, leaning against the wind, and his thoughts returned to his beloved Shotsy. He worried about her. She was growing into a beautiful girl with her mother's high cheekbones and his thick chestnut hair. Boys were drawn to her like moths to a flame and she had always gravitated toward masculine rather than feminine companionship. He'd have to ask Effie if she had told Helen the personal things she needed to know.

He mounted the steps of their boardinghouse, stomped into the kitchen, and threw his overcoat onto a chair. Effie turned from the pot of stew bubbling on the stove and wrinkled her nose.

"Get that coat out of the kitchen. Hang it in the pantry off the porch. It's wet and it smells like cow dung."

Harry picked it up and started for the door then stopped with a frown and flung it back on the chair. *He was trying wasn't he? But, damn Effie, she gave his anger justification at every turn. Her precious kitchen was more important than his feelings.*

She looked at him in disgust. "And you smell of gin," she added.

"I need it to get through these interminable days."

"You can't hide in a bottle, Harry."

He felt a muscle jerk in his jaw. His eyes squinted, and he set his mouth grimly. "Yes, I drink, and you want to know why? I drink because I have to compete with your superior airs . . . airs that are degrading to me."

"Don't try to make me the villain in this sorry state of affairs, Harry Rebert. It's your carousing and gambling that have brought the entire family to financial ruin. Why do you treat me like you do? It's as though you hate women."

"I haven't much respect for them. Except for my mother, every woman I ever met is out for what she can get. Even Aunt Belle made a play for Papa when she needed someone to run the damn grist mill."

Effie's eyes widened in anger. "And, me?"

"Especially you. You want THINGS! All I ever wanted from you was love and laughter. But love was never enough for you."

"A family can't live on love. That's infantile, that's the ranting of a small child."

"And you treat me like a child, castigating me with your mockery and cold disdain. Why can't you love me like my mother does?"

"Your mother! She gave you everything you ever wanted . . . her type of love is obsessive, it has made you the weakling you are today."

Fury, black as Satan, coiled in his gut. He started toward her and she cried out in fear. Her fear served only to inflame his mounting anger and a surprising flood of sexual arousal. He pushed Effie against the table and began to fumble with his pants. Effie stood petrified, mesmerized as a rabbit by a snake.

Suddenly the kitchen door flew open and Anita ran sobbing to her mother's side, followed by a white faced Helen. Anita pushed him aside with surprising strength and put her skinny arms around her mother.

"Leave her alone," she screamed, her eyes flaming with hatred.

Shotsy took his hand and tugged gently. "Come, Daddy."

Anita turned her vitriol gaze on Helen. "And don't take his side, you little sneak."

Helen looked uncertainly at her father, then at her mother, then at her sister. Her face grew red and she clenched her fists. "Don't you.. . ."

Effie shook Anita's hand from her waist and strode toward Harry, her arm outstretched, her finger pointing at him. "Leave! Get out of this house. Now!"

Harry took his valise from the wardrobe and began to fill it with shirts and underwear. He had become an animal in his own home—out of control—almost raping his wife. He had to leave before he seriously hurt someone.

As he pulled open a dresser drawer he looked at himself in the mirror and pulled out a comb. At forty-three, he still had a full head of hair. It was his one remaining vanity; he always combed it before he retired and first thing in the morning and anytime he passed a mirror. But tonight the comb would not work its soothing miracle. His eyes, dark orbs of pain, mocked him. He saw his life slipping through his fingers like sand through the hourglass. He loathed himself, loathed what he had become, loathed what he was doing to his family. He didn't know if he could change, didn't know if he wanted to.

It was best if he left . . . left to fight his personal demons himself. Daily, Helen and Anita grew more alienated from each other as they chose sides between him and Effie. And his wife . . . dear God, he had loved her once and look what he had done tonight. True, she had goaded him till he lost control, but that did not excuse his actions. If he loved his family the greatest gift he still had to give was to leave them.

He emptied the drawer and secured the straps of the valise. There was a train for New York in an hour. He would be on it.

CHAPTER 30

New York City, 1925

Harry emerged from Pennsylvania Station, purchased an evening Herald and a pack of Camels from a newsstand and strolled up 33rd Street to Madison Avenue where he entered an all-night lunch room.

Munching on a thick corned beef sandwich and coffee, he scanned the want adds for likely rooms, circling several addresses, then leaned back and sipping on his well-laced coffee, looked through the fly-speckled plate glass window. Across the street, a lighted sign above the door of a brooding sandstone building proclaimed the Murray Hill Hotel.

He spent the night at the Murray and the next morning, full of optimism, set out in search of a boardinghouse. A romantic readiness for the throbbing life of the big city possessed him and he bounded down the stairs of an uptown subway station eager to begin his new life.

The long station platform teemed with noisy commuters and incredible noise as the train, with a roar and a screech, soared out of the black tunnel and came to a halt. Doors flew open and a mass of people poured out as an equal number of combatants attempted to enter. Harry pressed in before the doors could close and the subway entered the cavernous passage on its way to the bowels of the city.

He left the subway at 140th Street and walked two blocks east to Amsterdam Avenue, the first address on his list. It was a narrow brownstone, sandwiched between a ten story hotel and a Jewish delicatessen, on a tiny spit of real estate not yet devoured by hungry developers.

The landlady, dubious and dingy, led him up the stairs to inspect the eligible accommodations. The room was unprosperous and bare; a strip of threadbare carpet, a scarred dresser topped by a cloudy mirror, a single bed, and a disjointed chair its only furnishings. She pointed to the corner where a frail, rickety wash stand held a basin and a weblike towel. "These are your lavatory arrangements—bath is at end of the hall—but mind it is usually busy so don't linger when you use it. Most boardinghouses fill up for the winter and the only reason I have this room is because Mr. Gilbert went to be with the Lord."

Slightly taken aback, Harry did some quick thinking. He'd better take it, the rent was right and the location good. Why waste precious time and money running around the city if rooms were indeed scarce.

Negotiations dispatched, the landlady relinquished a key and left him to unpack.

He went to the window, raised the green shade as far as it would go, and leaned on the soot covered sill looking out at his new world. The sky was leaden, the streets littered and slushy. Neon flickered over an all-night restaurant—EAT Open 24 hours—making shadows on the dirty snow.

With a sigh, Harry turned from the window and took off his coat. He laid it carefully on the sagging bed covered by a stained bedspread. Stained, he thought, momentarily depressed, just like everything in his life had been stained or marred by stupid choices or mistakes.

Unbidden, bodiless faces floated on the black canvas of his mind: Effie, her eyes narrowed in anger; Shotsy, her young face filled with love and admiration as he danced her around the room on Duke Street; his mother bending over her beloved flowers to place thick stems of peonies in a wicker basket.

Like a child awakened from a nap, Harry was startled out of his reverie by a tap on his door.

A stout woman in her mid-fifties, wearing a red scarf over peppery-gray blond hair, with a pair of wire spectacles perched on her nose, handed him a bath towel and a washcloth. She spoke in a voice that suggested Nordic origins. "I'll be in every Friday to clean your room. Leave your dirty linens on the bureau. Follow me, I'll show you the bath."

The woman led him down a hallway, dim with faded wallpaper and a low watt bulb, and gave a curt nod toward the proper door before shuffling off.

Harry was about to try the knob when the door opened and a female emerged, a copy of Town Tattler clutched in fingers weighed down with numerous rings of gaudy proportions. Black, bobbed hair framed a long face powdered milky white. Her eyebrows had been plucked clean and drawn on, one slightly higher than the other, giving her a slightly startled look.

"Well . . . well," she drawled in a coarse voice. "What have we here? A new boarder?"

"Harry Rebert," he said, extending his hand.

She looked him flush in the eye. "Sophie Price," she said, her hand lingering in his. "Your accent isn't New York. Are you new to town?"

"Arrived last night."

"Then you must give me a chance to introduce you to all the joys the city has to offer." She gave a hitch to her short skirt and Harry looked down at long legs with black stockings rolled below her knee. A good-time gal if he ever saw one—intrigue oozed from her pores. He felt a quiver in his groin. If he read those eyes correctly there would be joy of a nature he had not hoped to find so soon.

"Where might a fellow buy some hootch?" he asked, tapping his hip flask.

"There's a "blind pig" behind the bakery store, two doors down. Same side of the street."

"Blind pig?"

Sophie laughed. "A New Yorker term for a speakeasy. Blind pigs are false fronts—innocent appearing establishments like tobacco stores, barbershops, even funeral parlors. The speak is in back of the bakery, behind a peephole door. Just identify yourself by saying, "Sophie sent me." Later you might want to get a membership card."

"I'll check it out. Why don't you go with me this first time?"

"Give me a few minutes to freshen my lipstick." She smiled, a dreamy expression in her eyes, as though anticipating something more than a casual trip to a speakeasy.

The next morning, after leaving Sophie in a drunken sleep, he staggered up the dark hall to his room and lay down heavily with his bottle and his writing tablet to guiltily compose a letter to his family and tell them of his whereabouts. After he'd finished that one he wrote to his parents. Then he took both letters and tore them to shreds. He slept with bits of the paper clutched in his hand and his shoes on and in the middle of the morning he awoke to vomit in the toilet at the end of the hall.

It was several weeks before Harry found a job in the garment district delivering racks of men's suits to downtown department stores.

The city seethed and roared, the clangor of streetcars mingling with swearing taxi drivers, shouting draymen and the hoarse bellowing of newsboys. He felt transformed by the city's rage and passion, thrilled to the constant sway of men and women and machines on the jammed streets, savored the smell of the street vendors hot chestnuts, and listened with delight to the hurdy-gurdy hand organs. In the evenings he walked home, peering into shop windows, sometimes feeling the dregs of loneliness despite the racy, adventurous feel of the city. He loved to wander over to the theater district, where he stood and watched the never ending stream of people pouring out of taxicabs, sweeping into brightly lit theater lobbies. Tall, statuesque women with a flair for furs and flowered hats; flappers with short skirts, heavy makeup and bobbed hair; and slick men with brilliantine hair brushed back in a pompadour and dressed in long, shaggy coats made of raccoon pelts.

Harry had indeed read the message in Sophia's eyes correctly and he soon settled into a comfortable relationship with her.

A year passed, Christmas was over—New Years Eve just ahead. Harry and Sophie were smoking, naked in bed, on a steamy August night listening to Fred Waring and his Pennsylvanians on Sophie's radio when the orchestra swung into the strains of "Left All Alone Again Blues." A wave of homesickness swept over him and he rolled away from Sophie and viciously stubbed out his cigarette. The room stank of cheap perfume, tobacco, and sex.

She looked at him from hooded lids. "I often wonder about your wife and kids. Do you ever miss them?"

"Yeah," he answered honestly. "I do. Especially Shotsy. I keep wondering what she looks like now . . . whether she has a boyfriend and if so what kind of a boy he is. And how Anita is making out in business school."

Sophia worked a long fingernail over the cleft in his chin. "And your wife . . . ?"

Harry didn't answer immediately. His love for Effie had turned bitter, but he still remembered the good times, the days of their youth. Now, in his mind's eye he saw her oval face, her arrogant nose, her full sensuous mouth. He could still hear her deep husky laugh, sadly quiet in the years before he left her.

"Effie is a very intelligent woman . . . intelligent and very, very independent. I'm sure she is managing just fine without me. Better than if I had stayed."

He raised himself on his elbow and lit another cigarette from the one in Sophie's hand. He lay back, took a deep breath and exhaled. The smoke rose in a perfect circle. *All of us revolve in a circle*, he thought with startling clarity. Politics, love, life itself. Damn, he was being philosophical tonight.

"And you, Sophia? Were you ever married? You never said."

"Once."

"How long were you. . ."

"A year."

Harry touched her hand. There'd been pain in her reply, something to tell him that she, too, had demons. He let the moment pass and did not say anything more.

He rose and went into the bathroom to relieve himself, and paused in front of the fractured mirror long enough to run tobacco-stained fingers through his hair. His hair was still thick, worn dramatically in the "slick" look currently in vogue. His eyes were still blue, although puffy bags were now in evidence. His skin showed tiny lines and his throat was beginning to sag. Soberly he looked at the man he had become: a jumble of self-doubt, fear, and difficult pride. He had grown into the man he was from the inside out and he was no longer proud of what he saw. What he did see was his life slipping through his fingers.

Turning away from the mirror, he once more lay down beside Sophia. She moved against him. "Henny, sweetie, I've made you sad." Her hand moved to his groin. "Let me make things right again."

With a sigh he pulled her close. In the morning he'd tell her of the decision he'd just made. As soon as the holidays were over and he could arrange for some time off he was going to Lancaster to see his family.

* * *

"Lindy, Lindy, up in the sky—
Fair or windy, he's flying high—
Peerless, fearless, knows every cloud,
The kind of son makes a mother feel proud. . . .

Harry picked out the tune of the hero-worshiping ballad about Lindberg, then swung into the livelier "Yes, We Have No Bananas" and "Barney Google, With His Goo Goo Googly Eyes." The New

Year's Eve crowd, in the smoke filled speakeasy, sang lustily as Harry played on the battered piano at the end of the bar.

It was a wonderful time to be an American—especially wonderful if one were privileged to live in a city pulsing with life like New York. Here people sang crazy songs, drank bathtub gin and danced the Charleston. There were as many women at the bar as men, smoking cigarettes in long holders, their skirts riding high on slender hips, their brightly painted lips curled in laughter.

Harry squinted to see through the smoke. Throngs of talking, laughing, people kept up a noisy chatter and dancing feet had the bar ringing with an ocean of sound. He raised his bottle of gin and guzzled directly from the bottle. He was gloriously drunk and uproariously happy. Wasn't he?

This was the age of flappers, gun molls, tin lizzies, and jazz. The consumer culture predominated everyday life and Harry and his new cronies, spurred by advertising and new forms of credit eagerly bought radios, phonographs, and clothes. They gathered nightly in the local speakeasy smoking and drinking and womanizing and whereas they had once expressed their individuality in their work and family, now they sought identification with popular heros like Charles Lindberg, Jack Dempsey, Babe Ruth and even Al Capone.

Harry, like most New Yorkers, flouted the prohibition law and morality by patronizing speaks, swearing in public, and wearing outlandish clothes. This past year he had reveled in every moment of his new found freedom, but now as he looked around the smoke filled room he felt the gaiety was forced, the women straining to flout convention, the men laughing to cover their uncertainty about their change in status.

As he swung into a slow waltz, Harry felt a peculiar detachment from the crowd. What were any of them doing here, drinking, smoking, swearing, in a run down speakeasy in the dark hours of the night; what were they so feverishly happy about?

Suddenly the stink of tobacco smoke and stale beer filled him with loathing. Viciously, he stubbed his cigarette into an overflowing ashtray and swung into a lively rendition of "Happy Days Are Here Again." New Years Eve was no time for melancholy.

As midnight approached and the crowd began the countdown to 1928 a dark haired girl, a stranger to him, sidled over and draped her skinny arms around his neck. Dark circles were embedded under her eyes and red lines radiated out from her dark brown irises like the spokes on a wheel. As the crowd bellowed "Happy New Year," she pressed herself tight against him and kissed him with open mouth.

Harry groaned. God, he needed a woman! That's why he had felt lonely in this crowded barroom. He pushed her against a table and had she not stopped him he would have taken her there, in the crowded speak, before the oblivious, drunken mob.

"I've a room, nearby," she whispered.

* * *

The next evening Harry walked the deserted street toward his boarding house, his experience in the speakeasy a bitter taste in his mouth. He was damn unhappy and he didn't know why.

The moon was full, the black sky brilliant with a million stars. He lifted his face and stood for a moment drinking in the small limited expanse visible between Manhattan's towering buildings, but it was the sky of his youth he remembered, the great sweep of the Milky Way, the brilliance of the North Star, the unbelievable expanse of the heavens.

The incredible silence of the starlit night was broken by voices raised in song. Light pooled onto the sidewalk from a nearby doorway, open to catch the evening breeze, and Harry moved closer to the opening to catch the familiar strains of NEARER MY GOD TO THEE.

A placard taped to the window of a storefront mission, formerly home to Abraham's Delicatessen, announced:

CHRISTIAN ALLIANCE ASSEMBLY OF FAITH
Patrick McKay, world renowned Evangelist
8:30 Pm. New Year's Day
NEW BEGINNINGS

Harry moved closer to peer in the fly specked window of the mission. The singing voices released a flood of memories: memories of his mother humming as she worked among her flowers, of Effie, regal and tall in the choir loft at Redeemers, and of his two girls in the Youth Choir at Christ Church. The song ended and he started to move away when his attention was caught by the arresting figure of the black clad evangelist mounting a makeshift platform.

Why not hear what the man had to say? It would be a pleasant diversion, a laugh probably.

Harry slipped inside, slouching against the door frame and sipped from his hip flask.

The evangelist began to speak. "A JOYFUL NEW BEGINNING is the title of my sermon today."

"Well, I could certainly use that," Harry murmured to himself. The evangelist's rich voice carried to every corner of the mission as he began to speak.

"The beginning of a new year is always a period of renewal and refreshment and a time of hope. No matter how bad things were the previous year there's something about the beginning of a new year that gives us hope. You know, some of us have had great problems in our lives, and many disappointments, and many of you have been touched by the death of a loved one, or a financial loss, or a decline in health. For some of you it wasn't a very good year."

You got that right, Harry thought ruefully.

The evangelist gazed earnestly at the congregation. "And so when we come to the beginning of 1928 in many ways it's good to say: well 1927 is past, it's history, it's gone, and now lying out in front of us is a fresh clean calendar, and we don't really know what's going to be written on it, but a calendar that we hope is full of promise. It's a time of new beginnings, of expectations. A new beginning in our lives."

Harry leaned forward and stared at the evangelist. A shock of white hair crowned his stern face; his side-whiskers were black and luxurious. He was clad all in black and wore a broad brimmed black hat.

The room was silent, the people immersed in the message of hope being offered them. Harry quietly sat down on a folding chair in the last row and slipped his flask into his hip pocket.

The evangelist continued. "Could you use a joyful new beginning in your life? Could you use a fresh start as you begin 1928? Well, the good news is that it is possible in God. Because God is the giver of fresh starts. And he desires for each of us to have joy and to be filled with hope. And that is why we've gathered here this evening. To have our faith renewed, to have our faith strengthened. And our part in this is to desire it . . . to want it . . . and to do what's necessary on our part to receive, from God, that new beginning.

In Jeremiah, Chapter 31: 7-14, God gave Israel a joyful new beginning. And that text of scripture is a very moving text because it was written during a time of national decline in Israel and also in Judah." The preacher went on to tell of Jeremiah's prophesy that all of Israel would fall captive to the Babylonians if they did not turn from their idol worship, turn from their immorality, and repent. But they didn't repent, and God disciplined them for their rebelliousness and they were conquered and placed into slavery for 70 years."

Harry squirmed in his seat. Was God, in fact, punishing him for his rebelliousness by not allowing him the pleasure he thought would be his in this great city? For the bitter taste of defeat in his mouth? He shook his head and forced his attention back to the words washing the crowded room.

" . . . and after they had been enslaved they were released and returned to the promised land and there was much joy, much celebration, much crying because they were so glad to be released from their oppression. And they did have a joyful new beginning.

Friends, we too can have new beginnings. God's new beginning to Israel was based purely on his GRACE to them, not to anything they had done to receive this redemption. Let me read Verse 11 again. "For the Lord will ransom Jacob and redeem them from the hand of those stronger than they." The Babylonians were certainly stronger than the Israelites and they were completely dependent upon outside intervention to be released from their captivity. So the Lord would do it. He would ransom them. He would redeem them. And God did. He intervened for Israel—and friends He will intervene for you.

When we redeem someone we buy them back. We ransom them, and give them their freedom again. And so God redeemed and ransomed the Israel nation and gave them back something that they really didn't earn, really didn't deserve because of their waywardness and their sinfulness. He gave them back the promised land. He gave them back their lives with a joyful new beginning."

Harry's hands began to tremble and he tugged at the flask in his pocket. A desperate need for self-control flooded his face and neck with heat and he pulled his empty hands to his sides and clenched his fists.

The compassionate gaze of the evangelist seemed to seek and find Harry and he continued quietly. "As we begin this new year we can look into our own lives and realize how much we need God's grace too. How much we need redemption; how much we need to be ransomed. How much we need to be released from that which has kept us in bondage. It's a pure act of grace. The grace of God that has been expressed to us in Jesus Christ. That God so loved the world that he sent his son. He sent his son into the world to give his life. As what? A ransom. To redeem us from the slavery of sin and the tyrannical rule of the devil. The scriptures are very clear that we have been bought at a price. And that price is the blood of Jesus Christ.

New beginnings are an act of God's grace. It's a gift. God gives us a gift of the new beginning. A new start. I am reminded of the scripture in 2nd Corinthians, 5:17 that says "if any man is in Christ he is a new creation. The old is gone the new is come." And we are redeemed and set free and a new beginning is possible. A new birth even is possible, because of God's grace and God's gift to us of Christ Jesus.

An observation I made out of this passage is that Israel's new beginning was accompanied with humility. As the people were released from captivity they were so full of joy that they began to weep. But the weeping was a result of humility. Because they recognized that it was truly a gift from God—something that they had not earned. And I believe it was accompanied with a spirit of repentance. Repentance! Because they recognized that it was their evil deeds and their evil ways that had placed them where they were . . . and repentance is a major step on a pathway to a new beginning. We won't have new beginnings in our lives without looking into our own hearts and asking; what is it that I have done, or have not done, that's preventing me from having the kind of joy in my life that God wants me to have? If the joy of the Lord is lacking in your lives, if you feel enslaved to the forces of evil, search your heart and see what you have done. Only when you repent, turn control of your life over to Jesus, will you find peace and a new beginning."

Aha, thought Harry. There's the catch. Ministers . . . ministers and mothers . . . always want you to repent. Repent? What for? Memories of last night flowed through his mind like ricocheting bullets. Heaven help him he didn't even know the name of the black-haired girl he had spent the night with.

He'd better get out of here now, before he succumbed to the entries of the evangelist beseeching those present not to harbor an inner anger towards God because they didn't understand why adversity had to be part of their lives. And about the joy that could be theirs if they only realized that joy accompanies the knowledge that God forgives them and promises to take care of them. "It's a joy," the minister stated in his quiet voice, "to know, as we are here together at the beginning of this new year, that the best is yet to come in our lives as Christians. This life has much joy, but it also has much sorrow, tears and weeping, yet the great hope we have in the Resurrection of Jesus, the great hope we have for the future is that the best is yet to come.

God continues to be with us. He said He'd always be with us. He'd never leave us or forsake us. With a love like that who or what can stand against us? Tribulation, trial, suffering, death? If God's for us, we are more than conquerors to Him that loved us.

God does not want us to lead discouraged, backward looking, defeated lives We can move ahead, we can move on. We can have a new beginning.

I don't know what each of you might have lost . . . perhaps your ability to care for your family, your health, your dignity. Many losses. But one thing you can't lose. One thing you can't lose! That's your faith. They can't take that away . . . and deep down inside I believe your faith is telling you that you belong to God. And you do matter!"

The minister had all of Harry's attention now, and a tear crept down his cheek. Nothing had filled the void left by the loss of his family. Materialism hadn't satisfied, sex hadn't satisfied, booze hadn't satisfied. He was still searching—searching—searching. Oh God, his soul ached with the searching.

Reverend McKay's rich voice vibrated with emotion. "Receive God's grace. Just open your life up and receive it. It's a gift. You can receive it by doing what you need to do to put yourself in a position to receive it. If there are things you need to repent of—repent. Ask His forgiveness and then receive his grace. Recognize his marvelous gift and receive it."

The evangelist closed his bible and extended his arms.

Turn in your hymnals to page 320, "Come As You Are".

The audience began to sing and Harry began to perspire. Because, he realized, he'd never been willing to offer control to anything other than the bottle, not God, not his wife, not anyone.

Maybe that was why he'd never found love. All his life he'd been looking in the wrong direction. He remembered his mother's voice saying *"Destiny is not a matter of chance, Harry,—its a matter of choice."*

A quietness invaded his soul. It wasn't just the song the worshipers were singing. It was the anguish of all sinners breaking out in a cry across time, sung over and over again, by different throats, by different cultures, yet always the same cry. Now, finally, Harry heard the answer to it, the quiet answer.

Almost in a whisper the congregation reached the chorus:

> "Come just as you are. O come just as you
> are. Turn from your sin, let the Savior come in,
> And come just as you are . . . "

Harry rose from his seat. He smiled that familiar tilted smile, cocked his head, and again there was a light in those blue eyes of his. He slowly buttoned his loose-fitting coat. He placed his silver flask in a trash can and, with steps faltering at first, then stronger, then eager, walked forward.

THE END